We The People

FREEDOM LOST

Other Books by The Author

Coffee Table Philosophy
A Book of Photos and Thoughts
First edition Copyright © 2011 Sorenson Studios
Second edition Copyright © 2020 Sorenson Studios
ISBN: 978-0-9856781-1-1

Fundamentals of Life
Know Yourself, Be Yourself
Copyright © 2020 Sorenson Studios
Paperback ISBN: 978-0-9856781-2-8
Hardcover ISBN: 978-0-9856781-3-5
eBook ISBN: 978-0-9856781-5-9

A Logical Approach To Data Management
3 Questions
Copyright © 2021 Sorenson Studios
Paperback ISBN: 978-0-9856781-6-6
Hardcover ISBN: 978-0-9856781-8-0
eBook ISBN: 978-0-9856781-9-7

My Grandma Is A Hippie
Copyright © 2021 Sorenson Studios
Paperback ISBN: 979-8-9852335-0-6
Hardcover ISBN: 978-0-9856781-7-3
Special Edition ISBN: 979-8-9852335-4-4

Such A Life
Copyright © 2022 Sorenson Studios
Autobiography - Not publicly available

We The People

Freedom Lost

Rick Sorenson

We The People: Freedom Lost

Published by Sorenson Studios

Paperback ISBN: 979-8-9852335-1-3
Hardcover ISBN: 979-8-9852335-2-0
eBook ISBN: 979-8-9852335-3-7

Library of Congress Control Number: 2023903565

Acknowledgment

I want to acknowledge the people that still have respect and honor as well as the integrity and fortitude to represent those qualities in their everyday life. To those that truly serve the country and mankind, thank you. They do not expect or even desire any personal reward or glory for their actions. They are the people that allow me to hang on to hope.

Table of Contents

Preface

When I started writing the preface for this book I didn't know if the book would be fiction or non-fiction, much less what it would be about. I had a few topics that I wanted to cover and it seemed they were all related to some matter of human behavior. Before I started writing the first chapter I knew that this book would be my first novel. I still had no idea of a story and just let my mind ramble with only the outline of a few human behaviors and idiosyncrasies. The working title of the book was "Ramble On" which is indicative of the lack of direction with which it started.

It is a work of fiction and like most works of fiction has some inspiration in reality. It seems that in the past few years I have taken much more of an interest in politics. This was not by design or with any forethought. It is likely that my life-long interest in human behavior drove me in that direction.

The behavior of people in politics, the reaction of people to the people in politics, and the use of politics for nothing related to the politics came to the forefront for me in a way that I could not ignore.

People's behaviors, in general, seem to have become less and less appealing. There is so much self-interest, greed, and even evil that seems to be spreading and it often shows itself quite blatantly in politics. Some would say that I only think that because I am getting older and previous generations have said the same thing about the changes happening in their time, and yet we are still here. I really believe this is different. I would not dispute that the raw human behaviors have not changed much, but both the visibility and impact have become far more pervasive.

When I finished the book, it sat for a couple of months while I was trying to find the right title for this book that had just evolved from my own personal series of rambles. As I was paging through a set of pictures, I ran across a picture of the Constitution. *We the people* has always been a powerful phrase with deep meaning for me. The implications of the phrase are such that the power lies with the *people*, but who are these people to whom it applies? That never used to be a question for me and I find it disturbing that it is a question now. The world is most certainly not the same as when those words were written and some would say that makes the words outdated and irrelevant. Some would even go so far as to say that the people that wrote it were evil.

"We The People" combined with "freedom" creates a message that for me is a good summation of this country and a culture with which I have associated. I have concerns that the meaning is lost on an increasing number of people. The further we get from freedom, the harder it is to recognize the loss. There are people that believe that freedom is easy or that freedom is free. Freedom means to some that they get free stuff or that there are no rules and they can do whatever they want. Oh, how far we are from freedom if that is the case. Freedom does not guarantee results. Freedom allows for both good and bad choices and the resulting consequences. Guaranteed results are the antithesis of freedom. Freedom *must* include the freedom to fail.

While this book evolved into a story with a political setting, it is not really about politics; it is a reflection of human behavior, human emotions, and society. Politics is just a mechanism that provides a window into examples of human behavior. And with that mindset, this story begins.

Chapter 1
Just Another Day
Early Day 1

It's not like I woke this morning with a revelation that the world needed to hear my very important message. It was more like a "normal" morning where the dog was eagerly waiting for his morning old-age medicine, a healthy breakfast, and a well-deserved romp in the back yard for a little relief. It was no different than any other morning until the toaster started on fire and the smoke alarm started screaming FIRE, FIRE. Yes, the alarm system yells FIRE, and then the phone rings wanting to confirm a passphrase while my house is supposedly burning. If I can't remember the passphrase and fast, the fire department will be dispatched in about 60 seconds. This is no time for my mind to ramble through the various hundreds of passwords that I have used. This is a time for succinct action to recall that alarm-halting set of magic words. I yell, "say yippee", as if yelling would increase the likelihood that it was correct.

Surprisingly it was correct and the person on the phone thanked me so the panic should be over and the dog should be able to come out from under the bed. The alarm not only yells FIRE, but there is also a high-pitched screech every 2 seconds that forces everyone to look for some way to cover their ears. It is painful and nerve twisting for me so I imagine that it is extra painful for the dog. As I hung up the phone I realized that my assumption of the panic being over was wrong. Nothing had changed with the level of anxiety shadowing the entire house or the volume of screeching whaling so loud that the neighbors were gathering in their yards across the street. The only thing that changed was the box on the wall was now asking me for the passcode. "What!?"

It is not like I do this every day and someone apparently decided that it was a good idea to have an additional security feature that required a different passcode, one that is only used in dire emergency situations. Would you not think that the person calling you on the phone could shut down the control panel after verifying the passphrase so you didn't have to deal with a second emergency? They *are* monitoring the panel after all.

Who was it that sat in a design session for a complex security system and made this wonderful decision? It doesn't matter who, but it does matter that people do stupid things that can completely undermine the purpose of what they are supposedly trying to do. In this case that is assuming that their purpose was to make the system convenient and functional for the people that paid thousands of dollars for it. I know *I* didn't buy the system to add to my stress life.

Okay, I am just upset and trying to shut this thing up. I have no fire. I just have burnt toast. The fire flashed and stopped and nobody is in danger. I am not in danger from fire, but the mental anxiety, the pain in the ears, the risk of the dog peeing under the bed, and the potential cost of having the fire department dispatched when there is no emergency, are all real.

How did this situation turn into thoughts of how and why things are happening? It did because *everything* does. Every situation seems to raise questions of cause and effect as well as the desire to understand *why* someone did or would do something. These situations result in information that is taken into a large vault in my head with other information that is sorted, analyzed, and reported on (back to myself) in an ever-growing bank of events, rambles, and temporary conclusions that are then used again on the next event. How utterly intense, boring, and completely nerdy that must sound to most people. It is my life and I not only accept it, I thoroughly enjoy it and consider it a gift. It is certainly not a burden and it leads to completely new worlds of realization that I otherwise would have never discovered.

The mind is near the top of the list of one of the 86,432 wonders of the world. Of course that is not real number, but to declare that there are only 7 is ludicrous. Okay, I rambled for a brief moment, so back to the *perceived* FIRE. While all of this blaring is going on and I am searching my memory banks for the answer to the question, I just blurted out "121689". The box flashed and said, "Thank you. Fire department dispatch cancelled."

Is it over yet? Could this be more difficult? What could I do to make it better other than replacing my security system? I don't write the passcode down because that would defeat the security of the system (even though I can't say that I understand or agree with the design), but fortunately the rambling anticipation of such a stressful event led to the selection of a passphrase that would likely be used even without really remembering it. For me it was almost as good as making the passphrase "I don't remember."

And such is my life. A series of rambles tied together in a complex matrix that overlaps in innumerable ways that eventually lands on repeatable patterns that identify conclusions that become not only my perceptions, but also my beliefs in some cases. In some cases they result in very reliable predictions of the result of actions and in some cases they result in a passion to influence others. That passion to influence occasionally results in rants. Tying the evolution of rambles to rants is not always a process flow that can be put to paper. The mind is a wonder. It is capable of wondrous associations and processing. I am not foolish enough to believe that the conclusions are always correct or that my mind might not have been influenced by some other force with an unscrupulous intent.

Maybe all of this sounds like just an elaborate way to describe the fact that I think. So what! Everybody thinks, don't they? Of course everybody thinks, but does everybody assess the constant correlation between the events and behaviors?

The screeching has stopped. The dog is quiet. The whole house is quiet. The smoke seems to be slowly dissipating and

I am momentarily left with my thoughts, but it is not a long moment; the phone rings.

Chapter 2
Rambles vs. Rants
Later Day 1

I answer the phone with the most benign hello I could muster. I consider the various ways that a simple hello can be expressed. When I first picked up the phone this time to answer, I was wondering who was calling and actually thought about answering with a questioning tone, you know that tone that implies "who is calling?" I decided, while the phone was in my hand, to just flatten it out and simply state "hello", as though I just want to say, "I answered the phone" and nothing more. I know that I have answered the phone at other times with a bit of an attitude that might sound more like "What the hell do *you* want?" There are many variations that fall between "I'm excited that you called" and "This better be good you bothersome twit."

Now, *there* was an unintended ramble on communication by intonation. What a crazy thing to ramble about. Because this type of thought process is my nature, most rambles are unintended. That is a good entry point to explaining rambles and the difference between rambles and rants.

A number of small rambles have occurred already today. A ramble can be very short or quite long. It is all driven by opportunity, opportunity for the freedom to allow the thought process to roam. There are generally two categories of dictionary definitions of ramble, one for walking and one for talking. My use of the word is the walking version, but applied to thinking. The walking definitions use descriptions like *wander with no specific destination*. The talking definitions take on a negative connotation by adding that the speech *goes on and on and never makes a point*. That is not the case with my use of ramble. Rambles definitely wander, but it is part of the ramble journey to *find* a purpose. There is *not* a predefined purpose or path. It is truly about the journey and it is very much about capturing information and making associations along the way. The only predefined purpose is to discover whatever I can.

That definition, in itself, may make me somewhat of a freak to many. I know that it does to some because they have told me so and *I don't care*. The lack of a destination is so often seen as a lack of motivation. Oh, so not so. I know that I am a *very* motivated person. Lack of a destination for some things (or even most things) does not mean that there are no goals. The purpose of an undefined journey is to discover. I could argue that those that do not do that either have a perception that they have nothing to learn, maybe because they think that they have it all figured out, or they really don't care to learn anything new. Either of these situations can lead to all sorts of behaviors that *always* have negative impacts.

My defense of the benefits of rambles seems to border on a rant. It probably is. How can I be anything other than a lunatic if I use both sides of this argument? Since some may think that, I should explain further. Rambles and rants are not opposing viewpoints; they are, for some topics, a different point in time of the evolution of a thought regarding the same topic. It is not only that, it is a change of purpose, discovery versus sharing what has been discovered. Rambling is inward and ranting is outward. That does not mean that everything outward is a rant, some things are just conversations. I have lived a life of rambling for a very long time but what people see are the rants, the opinionated and strong viewpoints on a particular subject. This may give people the idea that I am in the category that I previously described as being a know-it-all and that I feel that I have nothing to learn. The truth is that I believe that I know very little in the realm of possible knowledge, and I have more to learn than I ever possibly can.

A piece of extremely burnt toast that emitted clouds of smoke certainly set off a series of rambles. It also provided examples of human behavior to store for future use. In addition, it could have resulted in a rant or two if I was of the mindset to do so. I walked out the front door, after the screeching stopped, and found that the neighbors that had gathered across the street were still there for the most part. Some were starting to wander away, but this social gathering would likely not have happened without the stimulus of my toaster.

I had already opened windows and doors in the back of the house to try to clear the pungent burnt toast smoke, but opening the front door created a crosswind that sent a billow of smoke escorting me out the door. It must have looked like the house truly was on fire and yet the alarm had stopped and there were no fire trucks lighting up the neighborhood. The dog of course made his escape from the house along with me as if to finally be free of the terror that had been caused in his life.

I stepped away from the cloud of smoke and into the front yard so I could see better and stop coughing. Fortunately the dog is well behaved and pretty much stays in his yard, but the combination of escaping the traumatic experience and the nearly irresistible lure of people that might pet him stretched the limits of his self-control. He started creeping toward the street but refrained with a simple "come." It is amazing how much restraint and loyalty an animal has that is thought to be so much 'lower' than humans. There are so many aspects of a dog's behavior that are admirable and that many humans would benefit from emulating (including myself).

The dog's behavior was not my focus at this point however. I thought about yelling out to the neighbors, "There's nothing to look at here. You can all go home", but I didn't. I also didn't let the more abrasive "What the f#%k are you looking at?" emit from my mouth. It's not like they were there to help. It's not like they were concerned because nobody said a word. They seemed to be drawn to the possibility of disaster or at least some form of entertainment. Why would it be that they gather together and talk amongst themselves and yet say nothing to me? In rambling and observing human behavior it is important to not get caught up in paranoia that would lead to a distorted perspective of information.

This pondering on the cause and looking for the *why* is one type of ramble. Delving into why is a reasonable and almost essential behavior, but it is not one that presents itself as fact. These potential causes build up over time and can lead to possibilities, probabilities, and even beliefs based on an overwhelming consistency of patterns. I do not take these lightly but they are rarely facts.

I know what part of the neighbors' activity was a fact. After the alarms went off and smoke was coming from the open windows, neighbors gathered across the street. Note I did not say that they gathered *because* of the smoke and alarm but rather that they did gather. I am leaving that open for now. Maybe they had a preplanned neighborhood gathering that I was not invited to and the time coincidentally coincided with the toaster event in my house. Wait, why was I not invited to this gathering? Rambles are good, but that rabbit hole is one I choose not to pursue at this time since its whole basis is something that was highly improbable. Not being invited to something that probably didn't exist seems a bit 'off the ledge', but it did trigger the thought of why they were doing what they were actually doing. If I wasn't coming down from this perception of fire experience and trying to calm my dog, I might have spent the energy and walked across the street and asked them what they were up to. Regardless of what I can imagine, the fact is that neighbors gathered across the street gawking at my house, didn't say a word to me, and didn't offer to help.

I know that I am considerably older than all of the people on this block. They all have kids about the same age, or younger, than my grandchildren, and I did not have kids when I was real young. There is occasionally a wave at a neighbor as they drive or walk by, but that is the current extent of my contact with the neighbors. I don't mention these things to complain or to imply that they are bad people. I simply recognize a very clear pattern of interaction (or lack thereof) with the neighbors. Oh my, how far have I gone from the topic of rambles vs. rants? I have actually not gone very far.

This ramble is a reasonable example of some thoughts that flew by during this time. It is not an in-depth analysis; they are just thoughts. They are thoughts that could have gone negative and could have reached premature conclusions. Instead they just added to a bank of information and started overlaying previous experiences, not only with the neighbors but also with people in general. This ramble did not go very far or last very long (probably a minute at most), but it will likely prove useful in the future. I know that I will not expect my neighbors to come and help when they see potential trouble. It doesn't mean that they won't, but I have zero expectation of that. When you add this event to other interactions with the neighbors and a pattern not only develops, the conclusion increases in its probability.

There were two different neighbors that hit my mailbox and did not come to tell me that they did it. I happened to see one directly and caught the other one on a security camera. In the case of the neighbors, I know that they are not my friends, I know that I do not trust them, and I know that I would not count on them to step up in an emergency. I have not concluded how they feel about me or why they do what they do, but I have concluded how I feel about those things and will use that information going forward.

This very little example hits some key points of a ramble. I really don't know where it is going when it starts. It is a freeform process that could go anywhere and the current moment and emotions can drive what direction and what boundaries I might apply. A major point of a ramble is that it is for *my* benefit. I don't want you to think that this example of a ramble is the only type. It might be triggered by something that happened in my life, or something on TV, something I read in a book, an emotion, or just about anything. All triggers create additional thoughts that ramble through whatever path they take. The nature of rambles is that they are generally just thoughts and are very seldom written down. Writing thoughts tends to distort the thoughts to some degree because I don't think that anybody can type as fast as they think. I certainly can't.

From all of these various rambles, there eventually comes a conclusion. From some conclusions come beliefs. Some beliefs, the ones that I am passionate about, become rants. Rants are those beliefs that must be expressed to others. It is likely that I believe that it is possible to improve on the results of my conclusion by sharing it with others. Okay, a rant is not just sharing; it is passionately expressing my opinion on a subject for which I have both a strong belief and a strong commitment.

There are some common perceptions of rants, which include the skinny, longhaired, dirty man standing on the sidewalk with a very large sign above his head stating, "The end of the world is near!" He is yelling that we all are doomed. He may or may not be offering a course of action, but regardless he is largely dismissed as a lunatic because he is ranting on a subject that nobody cares to consider, much less believe.

Another common image of someone ranting would be an old man going on and on about the loud music that isn't really music. This one could just as well be complaints of the cost of hamburger today, or the lack of respect that youngsters have. "Those lazy kids have it so easy! When I was a kid…" and on and on. Once again there is a high probability of dismissal because it's just a bunch of complaints from an old man. I'm not sure which one is easier to reject, the man because he is old and nobody of notoriety, or what he is saying that seems so petty and completely unrelatable to others. Certainly the combination of the two is a killer.

These two examples are not the same as the rants to which I refer. At least I tell myself that they are not the latter. I know I am not standing on a street corner with a sign, but I do know that I am what most would consider old. Being old sounds like a reasonable ramble with which I am familiar, so I'll hang on to that one for future use. I often do that when I run across a subject at a time where my focus is on something else. It's not like I keep a notebook or any sort of written record of these potential future rambles. They are just tucked away in my head for future retrieval. I don't have a formal process for this and I suspect that I forget many of them, but the world is full of potential rambles. I suspect that many of these topics that are tucked away just act as an extra push to address the topic when it comes up again. The best rambles are ones that present themselves many times over, but I was trying to explain rants so back to that.

My rants, and I have many, are not topics that are petty or that lack proof such as the end of the world. It may be that the world is ending and the person with the sign (as well as others) believe it to be so, but *proving* some beliefs is impossible. This is similar to proving or disproving the existence of God. It does not mean that they are not real beliefs or that the beliefs are wrong, it just means that facts will not prove either argument. That is OK and that is a legitimate rant, it is just not mine. That does not mean that I don't have beliefs that cannot be proven, it just means that I try not to turn them into rants.

I was walking down the sidewalk the other day and it was a particularly foul day. It was hot and sticky and the events of the day had been frustrating to say the least. I imagined myself stopping at the hardware store there on Main Street and buying the supplies to make a sign. I would then find a stump to stand on and just start dishing out the rants to anybody within shouting distance. Fortunately I have a fair amount of self-control and stopped short of the purchase. That was a pure feeling of the need to vent. I certainly need to vent now and again, as we likely all do. It helps to have someone available that you know will listen (even if it is your dog).

It would seem that ranting is and will be one of the topics that I ramble about. As I have mentioned some rambles do turn into rants when the evidence and importance are in alignment. Just because rants can come from rambles it doesn't mean that they have to. Some will come from a single event, but even with a single event there is likely previous observations that have given this single event more credence and importance.

Lies are one of those things that can trigger both rambles and rants for me. I sat down to watch a little TV and the news was on. My feelings about the news have changed over the last couple decades. Keeping up with what is going on is important to me, but it has become increasingly difficult to find out what is really going on. So I sit down to watch a little TV and off I go into a ramble just thinking about the act of watching TV. I used to believe, whether it was true or not, that newspeople were journalists and after the truth rather than propaganda facilitators that forced you to question everything that they say. You *better* question everything that is said! And there goes the rant.

I saw this high-level government administration person on the news saying something that was clearly a lie. OK, to be factual, it was not true but I will give them the benefit of the doubt and not call it a lie for now. Did this person know that they were lying or were they just misinformed (or stupid)? This person was in a position of authority that not only had access to the data, but also had authority over the organization that created it. The actual data was completely opposite of the statement that was just made. This is a point when I either yell "liar" or "stupid" at the TV. This does not take a lot of previous rambles to build this case; it was just evident in the moment and their words contradicted their own data. This one instance would also not likely be a rant for me and there really wasn't anything to ponder and create a ramble out of this one statement. However, the previous 50 similar statements not only present fodder for a ramble, but a full-blown rant.

What does one do when they discover this information that seems so evident and yet millions and millions of people cannot or will not see it? I rant for one thing. I am not going to get my sign and stump and hit the sidewalk (yet), but I will consistently convey my opinion to others, especially those that seem to be adamantly opposed to seeing reality. There just was not enough of an audience for me in my circle of friends so I contemplated what might be the modern-day sidewalk rant; blogs. I started writing blogs but not actually making them available on the internet. They were flowing from my irate mind and more and more came about every day so I thought, I should write a book of rants. I got so far as contemplating titles and looked for existing books and to my surprise the few titles that I considered already existed.

I started buying rant books and discovered a lot of similarities to mine. They were certainly not positioned the way that I would have done it, but there were many of the same topics. None of these were best sellers, but I found them both interesting and somewhat humorous. I am pretty sure that they were not intended to be humorous, but I find that I probably see humor in some pretty sad and serious things as a mechanism to tolerate the catastrophic behaviors that sometimes surround us. That book of my rants has not been written yet, but I still continue to write them in the form of unpublished blogs. Based on my definition of a rant being outward, is an unpublished blog or book a rant? They haven't actually been shared but they meet all of the other qualifications and they are *intended* to be shared, so I guess I will tweak my definition. I better recap where I am so far:

- rambles are really just thoughts and observations for internal use
- some rambles lead to rants
- not all rambles result in rants
- not all rants start with rambles but are often supported by them

- rambles can go *anywhere*
- rambles are for yourself and are seldom written
- rants are *beliefs* until they are expressed outwardly and passionately
- some rants are only to complain but others are for the expressed purpose of trying to help those that do not yet see

I was still thinking through the list and there was a pounding at my front door. This was not knocking; it was more like something exploding against my door. And then again, and again! Had the neighbors finally come to help? This was not a friendly announcement of their presence and then I realized that someone was yelling, "We have a warrant!" What the hell is going on? Did I fall asleep and dream all of these rants and rambles? Am I still sleeping and this dream is turning into a nightmare? If it's a dream, it's way too real. Just then the door blew open. I mean it blew open. It came clear off its hinges and landed 10 feet from its previous standing position. A wave of armed dark figures came charging through the doorway behind it. There was no conversation, no questions, not even an attempt at intimidation; it was total action and I was on the floor with knees in my back, guns to my head, and my hands being bound. WTF? This just can't be real and if it is, what the hell is it?

Did I get caught up in a ramble or did a rant set off this crazy situation? One thing about really good rambles is that they can be very creative and go down some unexpected paths. Rants on the other hand are quite real and can set off all sorts of reactions in others that could be irrational and extreme. It's not that the rants are irrational and extreme, it is that the reality of the topics can often trigger responses from people that are either afraid of that reality or choose for some reason to suppress it.

I already knew that rambles were inward and rants were outward (or intended to be), but this situation brought a further understanding of the difference. Rambles, while in search of reality, may use some elaborate and fantastical mechanisms to find that reality. It is freeform and without structure other than the self-imposed guardrails which are sometimes very wide. Rants on the other hand live in the real world with real actions and real consequences. I find myself in a position debating the reality of this situation because it is just so crazy. If it is real, did I do something to trigger this? What could it have been? I have been writing blogs but not publishing or making them public. I have not been standing on a stump on the sidewalk with a sign. Wait a minute. I have not been blasting to the masses, but I have let some of my rants be known via emails and social media responses to ludicrous posts. I do not post my rants but I do reply to some posts that might expose my beliefs. That sounds too paranoid doesn't it? As if anybody would watch *my* emails or my social media replies. Of course they could and the technology certainly exists to do that and more, but did they? And if they did, was that the cause of this?

While I am trying to discern reality from fantasy the action continues. I am thoroughly subdued (physically anyway) and now the 'conversation' begins. "Where are your firearms?" This seemed to come almost simultaneously from several people and one looked at the others as if to say, "Shut up!" It was at least now clear who was in charge. I have to admit that I didn't really think any of these people were actually 'in charge', but one person was the lead in the room and I should probably focus there for now. I also noted that they didn't ask *if* I had firearms, but rather where they were. They were either making an assumption or they had information that I had not shared. Wait, of course I shared it. Why do you think you have to register guns?

I tried to offer some sort of response (of course not the one that they would want), but it is difficult when your face is planted against the floor. That was the first thing that needed to be addressed so I said, "I can't talk with my face plugged into the floor." To which I received a, "What?" I took that as my queue to continue with some inaudible mumbles that might convey my position better than the English language. Sure enough, in moments I was sitting upright and answered the insistent "What did you say?" with, "Who wants to know?" And back down on the floor I went. It seemed a reasonable question, but these were clearly not reasonable people and I was not in a reasonable position to exercise any authority.

My assumption was that these were people with some level of government authority and direction but I honestly didn't know. There had been no declaration of who they were and they had not offered anything since taking over my house. I wonder where my dog is. I am yanked up by the back of my shirt and this supposed leader actually growls, "You want to try this again?" For the first time my eyes were able to focus on some of the people. Prior to this moment they were just big dark figures that invaded my house. They were all dressed the same and they were for the most part equipped the same. I am assuming their vests were bulletproof. Most of them had what some like to call assault weapons pointed at me. They also had handguns and other accessories surrounding their waists. This was true except for the head assailant and a couple that were focused on tearing my house apart.

At the risk of being thrown to the floor again I asked, "Who are you?" As those words came out of my mouth I remembered that they said they had a warrant before entering. That statement certainly did not identify them because what would you expect someone to say who was planning to blast into your house and take you down? Maybe they would be honest and say, "We are here to destroy your house and abuse you." Enough of this contemplation and rambling on something for which I was awaiting an answer. The answer that I got was, "We are the ones asking the questions." And I was back down on the floor.

This time I'm not sure that I was forced to the floor. I was tired and I just wanted to lie down. Was I tired because it had been a really tough day? Did they drug me? Even in this almost unconscious state I find myself wondering if the neighbors are outside across the street. Maybe they're making bets on why this is going on in my house or maybe they already know why? Am I paranoid? As I'm going further and further down I have to wonder again if this is even real. My head tells me it is, but I am pretty fuzzy right now. And as I turn my head to lie down I see two people walking out the door and on their back is clearly FBI.

I am really tired and it's dark. I think this is good night.

Chapter 3
Age and Understanding
Morning Day 2

I think that I might be waking up with my eyes closed rambling on the impact of my age. Why does age come to mind in this drowsy state? Maybe I'm thinking about it because my birthday is next week and it's one of those decade milestones. Maybe it's because I really did spend time restrained on the floor last night and my bones and muscles are aching with that old age pain. Now that I weigh that, I'm not really sure that it is even morning, but it feels like it because of what seems like daylight coming through my eyelids.

Why do you have to get so old before you understand? On the surface that seems like a fair question. First off, I am older than I imagined I would ever be when I was younger, and yet I hope to live longer. Many people are older than me; do they understand more? Maybe. Do some people that are younger understand more than me? Maybe. As I ramble through this, I have to wonder if this is even a valid question.

First off, understand what? I mean understand more of what life is about and what is important. To say that I understand more now than I did when I was 20 is a very true statement. Is that true for everyone? It is likely true for anyone more than 10 years past 20. What I cannot do is make the comparison across people. Clearly not everyone learns and understands at the same rate, and since people are exposed to different experiences they have different opportunities that trigger or even force growth.

I have tried to share my life experiences with others in hope that it might accelerate their rate of understanding. I wonder if that is even possible. I hope that it is. Reading about something happening to someone else is absolutely not equivalent to experiencing it for yourself. So is it required that we go through life until enough crap happens to us to make a light bulb go off? For some it may be a light bulb and for others it may be like a very slow sunrise bringing light to a new day.

However it happens, it doesn't just happen once and then you know everything. There are incremental steps that happen along the way telling you, "You really didn't get it until now." Then some get far enough down the path of learning to comprehend that the idea of completely *understanding* is ludicrous. You know more than you did, and you have acquired some very important and potentially life-changing information along the way, but repeatedly the thought of "I get it now" seems to be a lie. This may happen over and over until you finally get the message that what you do know is an infinitesimally small part of what there is to be known. In other words, you don't know squat, but at least now you know *that*. That's a pretty big deal considering that I don't even know if the events of last night were real.

If I know 10 times more than I previously did, does it matter if I still know less than 1 percent of what is to be known? For me, I would say of course! I always want to know more, but not everybody is driven in that same way because people are different. Some people may think that learning is not only a process that happens over time, but also that there is one path to learning or that there is one end-point in the learning. That is the nature of most structured education programs.

At the end of the learning is there one ultimate truth? If it were possible to know everything, and if we *all* knew everything, would we all know the same thing? No human has reached that point where there is nothing left to learn and under that belief, the question of knowing everything must be rhetorical.

I could hypothesize that there is one set of correct answers at the end, but I certainly could not prove it. I can, with far more certainty, state that the path to get there, regardless of the "endpoint", is very different for everybody. Even if people have a very similar experience, what (if anything) they learn from it can be *far* different. To that point, I can then conclude that what you learn ultimately changes everything that you learn from then on. Each learning experience is then more impactful and profound based on the volume and depth of previous learnings. Maybe this is getting closer to the original thought of why you have to get old before you understand or maybe it's just that we feel closer to death and it's time to pay attention to what's important.

Along this unique path that each of us walks, there can be what seems to be epiphanies (the light bulb going off). These can happen at any point along the path and seems to have little bearing on age. I don't see this as a contradiction of the increasing learning by age; I see it as an intersection of two types of opportunities to understand. They can complement each other. It is also possible that an epiphany might destroy some earlier 'knowledge', but that is to be expected. We all learn incorrect things along the way. That is maybe why it is so hard for others to get any benefit from the experiences of others; they have not yet learned the wrong things.

If I tell you about my events of last night, does it create a learning experience for you? Regardless of your age, it would be unlikely. I can share what I know, but even that needs clarity. I can share what I *experienced*, but I have little evidence even for myself at this point that it was real. Without that most basic information I have nothing to learn from it. I know that my age has brought me to a more mature state with far more information (some of which came from rambles) to use in the processing of further information. I know that I know far more than I did, but I haven't figured out yet how that it is helping me deal with my current situation. Maybe that's because I'm not really sure what my current situation is.

I shook my head to try to change from my ramble about age to focusing on distinguishing reality from anything else that it might be. I started waking up some time ago I think, but I have yet to open my eyes. My body feels aches and pains but I'm not sure if that is related to last night or just another one of those things that simply comes along with age. I find that waking from sleep is not the same as I get older. It seems to be especially true after a nap and I never ever used to take naps. Now if I nap, waking up seems to take at least an hour even if the nap was only a ½ hour. The first few minutes are the worst; being in that state where I am not sure where I am, what time it is, or if there is something I am missing. Sometimes I am so far removed from feeling a good grip on reality that I'm not sure if I am supposed to have arms and legs or flippers. It is a very unnerving feeling and it doesn't seem to matter if my eyes are open or closed, I still can't focus to bring me to reality. This is the state that I am trying to escape right now. It's odd that even in this state that rambles can be so lucid (I think).

This state of altered reality coupled with the events of last night is making me feel far from wise. I feel that I have zero idea what to expect when the day around me finally comes into focus. It is a feeling of vulnerability. Understanding things such as reality is usually not nearly as bad as the fear of it. Taking things head on with confidence is one of the things that came to me over time. Caring less about what others think of me came along with it. That feeling, by the way, is very freeing. More than I can express.

I am certainly not worried about what people think at this moment. My focus for this very small segment of time is not what is in store for me (which it maybe should be), but rather about what has happened and why. If it didn't really happen, why do I believe that it did, and if it did happen, why? This makes the determination of which *why* to focus on front and center for my immediate future. I need some real evidence to determine if it actually happened.

My eyes need to open but it seems that they won't. Maybe I just don't want them to. Maybe the potential reality is better dealt with by keeping my eyes closed. I see a glimmer of light. I smell coffee, but I don't drink coffee anymore. OK, they're open I think. I seem to be on my bed. I see a very familiar picture on the wall across the room above my dresser. It's a picture of a … well, I'm not really sure what it is but my kids gave it to me on one of those decade declaring birthdays. That was more than 20 years ago now. Sitting on the dresser are pictures of my kids from happier times. If those were happier times but I am wiser now, is there some negative correlation between wisdom and unhappiness? Maybe it's between knowledge and unhappiness. The more you know, the more despair seems to invade your world. That can't be it! That would seem like such a hopeless situation, but it would potentially explain why so many choose to remain unaware of reality. Do I want to make that choice? I believe it's too late for that.

As things continue to evolve, the room comes more into focus. I feel more confident that I know who I am and that I am in my bedroom. I have more of a confirmation that it is morning because of the angle of the light coming through the window I would guess it to be about 7:00 AM. My very heavy head flops to the side and the clock confirms that I was close. It is 6:49. I wouldn't be so precise but that is one of the results of digital clocks. A regular clock with hands would have been 10 to 7. The clock on my nightstand is joined by various tokens of the past. There is a rock from a camping trip to the North Shore, a very small and heavy Statue of Liberty, two small dishes made by my kids, a couple of guitar picks, and an array of small pictures of kids and my dog. There is an open door to the bathroom, a door to the closet that is closed for some reason and a bed for the dog on the floor. The bed is there for him but he usually manages to sleep on my bed.

I walk into the bathroom for my morning routine. A shower is always a good way to wake up. I'm not talking cold shower wake up. That's too much of a jolt. A nice long almost hot shower is just what I need. This is so good and so far-removed from my picture of events from last night that I am starting to conclude that it all must have been a bad dream, just a very *bad* dream. I know that I have always tried to be fair and honest. I worked a variety of jobs in my life, but none of them entailed criminal activities or were of a nature that should result in the FBI invading my house. It *had* to be a bad dream.

My rambles took me places that were bizarre sometimes in the search for that which is not only possible, but also probable. This didn't seem to fall in that category of probable. My rambles also took me to some conclusions that had not yet turned to rants but were of a political nature. Discussions around these beliefs that I had formed seemed to solicit agitated responses from a number of people. This agitation is the closest thing that I can think of that might solicit a response that would have an unfavorable impact on me, but certainly not one that would entail the FBI. I am up and taking a shower as if it is a pretty typical day and there is no evidence of any type of disturbance, but I am still upstairs and all of that took place downstairs. I really can't believe that I am still considering it a possibility that it was real. That is just absurd and yet something feels *off*.

Along with the knowledge and wisdom that I believe have been enhanced by my age and experience has come a trust in myself. That trust in myself is also something that I believe has been formed by my many experiences and the ensuing rambles. My ability to anticipate impacts and outcomes has grown with the same observations of patterns that repeat with almost supernatural accuracy. As little as I know about life and the available knowledge of the world, there are patterns that show themselves at a rudimentary level. I have learned not to be gullible, but I have also learned not to dismiss the almost unbelievable options until proven otherwise. For me the achievement of 'proven otherwise' is no small task, so being true to my nature, earned wisdom, and trust in myself, I still need to keep the option open that all of this was real regardless of how improbable it seems.

If the FBI was in my house, how is it that I am in my bedroom and they just disappeared? Well, they didn't disappear from my bedroom. They were never in my bedroom that I saw anyway. I ran out of the bathroom to go to my closet so I can get dressed and I trip over the dog bed. I open the closet door and it's empty. What?! Why would anyone take my clothes? I look back at the bed, which is now made and there were clothes laid out. There was a striped shirt, black pants, black socks, and some ugly traditional white underwear, the likes of which I haven't worn since I was a boy and my mommy was buying my underwear. At the end of the bed was a pair of black lace-up winged tips. I haven't worn lace-up shoes for over a decade and dress shoes for even longer. This *has to* still be some bizarre dream. I have had some bizarre dreams but I don't recall thinking they were bizarre until *after* I woke up.

It seems as though the dream insists that I wear these clothes. I could just go downstairs naked. It's not like nobody ever walks around naked in their own house, but I have no idea what I will encounter. Did someone lay out those clothes while I was in the shower or was I just still so out of it that I didn't notice? There could be people downstairs even though I have heard no sounds. There could be people waiting for me and I may need to try to escape out the front door. I would *not* want to be naked for that. I get dressed.

In my younger years, I am pretty sure that I would have just dashed headstrong down the stairs with no fear and no consideration of the potential consequences. Considering consequences and potential outcomes does not make one weak; it makes for better decisions. I may not know the outcome, but I know that I don't know the outcome and that makes caution a wise consideration. There are times when it may seem that I choose to throw caution to the wind, but even those choices are couched in not only experience and wisdom, but in priorities.

There are some decisions that are based on priorities and all of the various considerations are irrelevant due to the priority that is placed at risk. I know that beforehand and it takes all other considerations off the table. Running into a burning building to save a child would be one of those scenarios. The life of a child is a priority over the risk of the building falling, another fire truck coming around the corner, or any other thought that would just take time away from taking action. This is *not* one of those situations.

I am still in a very strange state of mind and want to find my way out of it. I want answers to what happened to my closet, why are there clothes that are not mine, and most of all the reality vs. dream question of both now and last night. This was a time of discovery and taking in my surroundings, not a time for rushing toward something of unknown origin or intent. I take a deep breath and head toward the bedroom door.

On a normal morning I would usually swing the door open and head down the stairs in almost a single movement. This is *not* a usual morning. I turned the knob on the door and was somewhat relieved to find that it wasn't locked even though the bedroom door doesn't have a lock on it. I peeked out still expecting really odd things to keep coming at me. I could see the stairway and the hallway that overlooked the main level and at first glance everything seemed to be in order. Yep, it's all in order as I walk down the stairs in someone else's clothes. The living room furniture seems to be all in place. If the event was real, there would certainly be a mess, wouldn't there?

I can see into the kitchen and that seems to be OK. I walk over to my desk and now there is a difference; a big difference. My computer is gone! Oh, there is a computer there but it's not mine. Someone did a very poor job of replacing it. They couldn't seriously be trying to fool me with this and think I wouldn't notice. My computer is a laptop with a mango logo and this one is an old desktop with a door logo. This is not even a reasonable attempt to deceive unless whoever did it is stupid, thinks I am stupid, or believes me to not use my computer or be the least bit observant. The other option is that they didn't care if I knew, but if that was it why even replace it?

If this is so obvious, what else will I find out of place if I look closer? It sure seems like I am asking a lot of questions of myself. I guess I always do that as part of a ramble as it's a good way to help the process, but this is different. I also know that my initial scan was very likely incorrect. It could have been that my scan was so fast and just looking for things like broken or missing furniture or it could have been influenced by wishful thinking. Regardless, I need to look closer. The major disruption besides interrogation was the door blowing open, but the front door was in place. I walked to the front door and could easily see that the doorframe had been ripped apart and the door hinges were screwed back in place with much bigger screws. Again, clearly nobody was trying to hide the fact of the disruption. I put my hands to my head in complete confusion and that is when I noticed the abrasions on my wrists.

If this was the FBI that broke into my house and restrained me, why am I not in custody? I never did see a warrant that I recall and certainly was never read my rights. It appears as though rights were not a consideration. There was so much that was off from what I would have thought to be protocol for any law enforcement agency; if it wasn't the FBI, who was it? Maybe protocol doesn't matter? I need to keep looking.

So far I have a missing computer, a front door that was so crudely put back in place, and don't forget the empty closet. Those things in addition to the abrasions on my wrists would seem to support the events of last night being real. But now a new twist, why such shoddy cover-ups? On top of that, why am I wearing someone else's clothes? Since the computer is missing, maybe other electronics would be an important place to check. My phone! Where's my phone? I have a button to push on my watch to find my phone. Where's my watch? At least they didn't put a cheap watch on my wrist to replace it. Still no phone! My phone appears to be missing. I have a pretty "smart house" so the app to tell the house things to do maybe has a playback. "Anita, was anyone here last night?" Anita responds with a simple "yes." "Anita, playback all requests from last night." I have never tried this, but I know that many people are concerned about what these devices listen to, so maybe it is also stored. Anita says, "I'm sorry, I cannot do that right now." I wonder if "right now" were carefully chosen words.

Computer, phone, watch, and what else? I have a lot of smart devices that do things but it's unlikely they capture anything. Wait, I have a security system with cameras and it records events. Crap, I access the videos on my phone. This is all too much. My computer, watch, phone, clothes, and who knows what else is missing. Where's my dog? Why didn't I notice before this? Where's my dog? I have to get out of here!

Chapter 4
Cranky Old People
Mid Morning Day 2

I run out the door and immediately turn right at the sidewalk like I knew where I was going. The only thing that I knew was that I needed to get out of my house and that my dog was missing. After I got two blocks from my house the run gave way to a walk. I haven't been able to run two blocks in a long time so that was either pure adrenaline or more evidence that this whole thing is not real. I start to yell "Reggie" and now I am drawing attention. People are looking at me with maybe a bit of both concern and trepidation. I can even hear some young punk say, "Lose your dog you cranky old bastard?"

In general, old people are not cranky; they just don't care what you think. That does not equate to being mean or having a lack of compassion. It simply means that they have realized that what you think of them has very little, if any, impact on them so they will do and say what is true to what they actually believe. There is not time nor importance given to putting soft language around a thought. There is usually a more direct way of stating something, so why waste time. I had more important things on my mind right now, so I let my honest comment to the little twit slide.

Does this projected perception of crankiness really have to do with the realization that there is little time left? It may not be little time, as in minutes or days, but rather the realization of an inevitable end becomes more and more real the older you get. Young people may think that they know what I am referring to, but they don't. There again, there are exceptions. Some young person that has a terminal illness might experience a much more rapid mental aging and understanding of priorities than others. That is even more evidence that there are so many unique paths in our lives. Even though the young person feeling closer to the end may have a rapid increase in understanding, I believe that they are not likely to be seen in the same way as the *cranky old people*. I would conclude that the impression of being cranky and not caring what others think does not just come from the realization that there is little time.

It is more likely that crankiness grew beyond understanding priorities and not caring what others think, to include being tired of trying to do what inevitably doesn't matter. A young person has not had all the failures or all of the learning the "wrong things". They have likely not had the volume of losses of family and friends. They have not seen all of the changes in the world that they could not control. They have not wasted as much time and energy on things that didn't matter. That cranky attitude is *earned* over time. This perceived crankiness does not come from just frustration and it is not defeat; it is a just realization of reality.

If you know a cranky old person, you likely know that they are not entirely how they are perceived. When I say know a cranky old person, I don't mean know of one, I mean really *know* one. I speak of this from experience because I know that many perceive me as being a cranky old person and yet I know that the few people that really know me don't really believe that. I know that I actually do care far less about what people think of me and yet I find myself using the term of a cranky old person rather than what I would have previously stated to be a cranky old man. After all, I am a man and perceived to be cranky.

Did I, this cranky old man, just use a politically correct term? This seems to me to be like salesperson or congressperson rather than salesman or congressman. It is even like humankind vs. mankind. I always thought of mankind as being non-gender specific. Was I wrong to think that? Maybe I would have a different perspective if I was a woman, but I would like to think not. I honestly never thought that mankind or salesmen did not include women. If a woman calls herself an actor, is she wrong because she should be an actress? Of course not. Actor is not gender specific just like mankind is not, but actress is gender specific.

It seems that maybe those that say they want to be inclusive are doing the most to separate. Sure there were, and still are, sexist people that think otherwise but it is not because of words. Even further evidence of it being about words is the push to eliminate gender completely from the language. I can tell that my ramble is drifting into another subject but to some degree that is what rambling is about. I will likely come back to 'words' and political correctness at some other time, but I want to come back to my rambling for a bit on being cranky and old if I can.

I was thinking about a cranky person not really being how they are perceived. This is likely to pertain to any label that can be put on any person. People generally do not get to know people before they judge them and put them in a category with a label. Quite often that label is demeaning. How about putting a different perspective (spin) on the attributes that make a person seem to be cranky? They get to the point. They are passionate. They understand their priorities. They will defend their beliefs and their inner circle of people without hesitation. They like to have fun but their idea of fun may be different than yours, and they don't like to waste time. They mind their own business and wish you would mind yours. Of course these are generalizations, but so is calling someone cranky.

I am not going to try to defend all of the cranky old people in the world because it is likely that *some* of them are just jerks. The same is true of all labels. Even while my mind is flowing through these thoughts, I know that I have continued to yell for Reggie and walk. I am not even sure how far I have walked but there has been no sign of Reggie. It is really rare for him to not be near me. He is my trusted and loyal buddy that I am quite sure doesn't think I am cranky. I do know him well enough however to know that he is always so excited to meet new people that he might stray for a little while for a little new-person attention. I'm not offended by that because he's just a people 'person' and loves to play and meet new people. He's not cranky at all but he too is old. He doesn't know it, like many old people, but nonetheless he is pretty old.

Just then a car drives by on this quiet street and slows way down. I was walking almost as fast as they were driving. It was a shiny black car with very dark windows. I couldn't see anybody or anything inside of the car but I could feel them looking. This had to stop! I either need to wake up or have some sort of explanation. Explanation it is. I step over to the car with every intention of beating on the window and yell, "What the hell do you want and who the hell are you?" As I got within inches of the car they sped up and drove away. I'm going to at least get a license plate number. It even crossed my mind that they might just remove the license plate for that very reason. I ended up with only a partial plate but not because it was removed or blocked; I was distracted by the top of the plate saying U.S. GOVERNMENT and the bottom saying FOR OFFICIAL USE ONLY. As the car got further away I squinted to see the plate number and all I got was W 6. That was it and where I come from a plate number starting with W is referred to as a whiskey plate and are given to those that have had prior DUIs. Do you think they actually issue whiskey plates to government cars?

Even though they are about a block away I yell, "Where is my dog!?" It wasn't a rhetorical question but I didn't expect an answer. If Reggie has been gone since last night he would have come back home, found a safe place to be, or a scenario that I don't want to consider a possibility at this point. Of course I know that it is possible, but it was getting no more time allocated in my thoughts. Maybe thinking positive, despite the perception of crankiness, is one of the attributes that comes with old age? Nope! It might present itself that way at the moment but it is much deeper and darker than that. It is not that I think only the positive is possible or even probable, it is that I know that spending time thinking the worst feels very bad, causes depression and lack of action, and has absolutely no benefit. I miss my most loyal and trusted friend; that is depressing enough.

Considering the logical alternatives to his location, walking the streets and yelling is not likely the most constructive effort that I can put forward. I need to head home and make a plan; home, that location of bizarre and somewhat terrifying events. I really have no place else to go. Reggie is my best friend. It's not like I have zero friends, but I have very few. Don't take that as though I scared them all away by being cranky, I just have a very high standard for people that I allow myself to call friends. I will not start on that rant right now, but I could. Even in the middle of all this the thought of my kids having 450 'friends' on social media when they have met less than ¼ of them says enough for now. My work has transitioned to work-at-home self-employed activities since I retired from corporate life and that makes Reggie all the more prevalent in in my life. With the possibility that he might have gone home, it's time for me to go home.

As I am thinking about the next steps while walking home in someone else's clothes, I remember that I find myself without a phone or a computer and how much of an issue that is going to be. Even this cranky old man has become very dependent on technology and I get quite irritated when it doesn't work. Right now, I don't even have it. My first step is still to find Reggie and then I drift back to the phone and the thought that I have not talked to anyone. I have not called a single person or even called the police. I guess they weren't my priorities and something tells me that the police are not likely to be of any help, but I have to call them. Phone first. No Reggie first, then phone.

I am now within a couple blocks of my house and I start yelling again, "Reggie! Come on buddy!" I call him buddy a lot (for obvious reasons). I am now walking up my front walk and there is still no sign of him. I was just about to go in the front door and heard something that sounded like it came from the side of the house. That made me think that, in all of the searching I did through the house, I never checked the garage. I wonder now if I even still have a car. I need my car, if for nothing else, to go get a new phone. I walked to the side of the house and saw nothing. I wasn't sure I wanted to just open the garage door without any indication of what was inside. My mind started flooding with things that I had so foolishly missed in the search for missing items. Some of the obvious items were guns. They had even asked where my guns were. It might not be a bad idea to go get a gun before opening the garage. Enough of this! I banged on the garage door, which may have been foolish but I think if they were out to kill me it would have been over by now and I was tired of getting nowhere. A very vicious sounding bark came from the other side of the garage door. Oh my god, it's Reggie! "Reggie, hey buddy."

I punched in the numbers on the keypad to open the garage and there was a very happy Reggie, along with a very happy me. His butt was wagging so hard that he fell down. He has a cropped tail so you don't really see a tail wag but rather an entire butt wag. He is old and his hips are bad and not very stable at times, so he was wagging so hard that his legs collapsed. He didn't seem to mind and was right back up in a second. That vicious bark comes out of this dog whenever anybody is outside of our house, but as soon as the door is open, it is pet me, play with me, be my friend. "Reggie, my old buddy. I'm so sorry you were locked out of the house in the garage all night." He is never locked out and would have likely pawed at the door but I apparently couldn't hear it. I was upstairs in bed, and now I realize that I have no idea how I got there or what happened between the last thing I remember on the floor downstairs and morning. But I have my pal back and for now that makes this cranky old man very happy. Very, very happy!

Chapter 5
What If I Woke Up?
Late Morning Day 2

We head into the house to get Reggie some breakfast with a stop along the way in the yard for a little relief. Relief for Reggie not me; I'm not that old or disconnected yet. In fact, I feel like I am quite acute and astute with a very stable mind, that is up until the events of today and last night, which made me question almost everything. Now that I have my pal back as a bit of a grounding mechanism, I may be able to think with a slightly different orientation. And this ramble begins…

As you know, all rambles don't start in the same way and this one has been building through some pretty bizarre and traumatic events. It is going to start pretty deep at the foundation of all of this, reality. What if this is all a dream, or a nightmare if you prefer to distinguish between them? Personally, I believe that there is a dream state and things that happen in dreams by the definition of a dream do not happen in the physical world. I say physical world rather than real world because often the dream state pushes the boundaries of reality. Those things can be good, bad, weird, or a combination of those and other reflective emotions. If you had a dream that was both good and bad, would you say that you had a dream, then a nightmare, then back to a dream, and then..? Probably not, so it is OK in my mind to just all be referred to as dreams.

Maybe the difference is that I am talking about a dream state rather than the concept of "I have a dream". I want something and I dream of it or aspire to it. I get that concept but this is certainly not that. I woke up this morning wondering if the events of last night were real or if I dreamt it. What if I woke up again now and wondered if me waking up this morning was real or just part of the dream?

If I cannot be sure of my waking this morning and my memories upon waking, why would I be sure of any waking. What if I woke up wondering if my entire life was a dream? To take it even further, what if I discovered that my entire life *was* a dream? How would I know that the *discovery* was not part of a dream? Oh what a loop of unawareness I would be in. It seems a valid question, but one without possible final resolution.

If I stayed in that loop of no resolution, it would not only have no resolution, but it would be a total waste of time. Worse yet, I would go completely nuts debating or anticipating the *real* wakeup call. Given that wondering if my entire life is not real inevitably ends poorly, I *should* choose to dismiss that as an option. After all, I wouldn't have had kids, I wouldn't be a grandpa, I wouldn't have written books or been a musician, I wouldn't have saved two kids' lives, I wouldn't have consulted with fortune 50 companies, and the list goes on of things I would have never really been or done.

I can't even seem to end the confusion and mystery of the last 24 hours; how could I solve a mystery of something far bigger? These bizarre and extreme thoughts are sometimes part of a ramble and it doesn't make them seem any less crazy. However, it is only through the extremes and the unimaginable that new discoveries are made. Unimaginable things do happen for both good and otherwise. Maybe that is why many of the great inventors and artists were believed to have gone crazy. Maybe it was because of their ability and willingness to think crazy things that they were great. Even more have been seen as eccentric, which in many circles is pretty close to, if not equivalent to, crazy. Maybe *they* got caught up in rambles too.

So, why not an entire life being a dream? It is not like I think that I fell asleep and slept long enough to dream an entire lifetime of events, but what about someone *making* it happen? What about someone "injecting" memories into someone so they were certain that those memories were theirs? What about someone lying on a table or in a container of some sort hooked up to all sorts of things believing that they are actually living out a life? What about just a very wild imagination that has distorted the past? There are so many possibilities other than the mundane living of a real life, except living a real life is *not* mundane. Why are there so many movie and book themes about just such things? So many things seen in movies have later come to pass and yet other things (as far as we know) are simply there for entertainment and the shock or horror factor.

Still, the ludicrous ideas and rambles are the fodder for great discoveries. I believe that almost anything is possible. Who could have imagined entering space even less than 100 years ago? Who could have imagined that a derivative of mold could save many lives? Who would have thought that a machine would be referred to as "smart"? The world of inventions is full of insanely crazy ideas. And such is the world of rambles. Has the cranky old person turned into the crazy old person? It is much more likely that the world of possibilities seen by the perceived cranky old people has given them hope and belief in the seemingly impossible. When you believe in the impossible, your concern for superficial and inconsequential pleasantries takes a bit of a backseat. "Get to the point so that the impossible is more possible."

Now that I have rambled down the winding road in this world of impossible possibilities, I will make a choice for the moment with the understanding that life can change at any moment. Do I believe that my entire life is and has been a dream? No, I don't. Just because I consider the impossible possible does not mean that I believe that everything that is seemingly impossible has happened. The purpose of rambling is freedom, opportunity, exploration, *openness* to the possibilities, and predominantly discovery of patterns that provide for probabilities. Probabilities are a layer on top of the possible and I have not yet found patterns that increase the probability of a lifelong dream. I will therefore move forward with the probability that my life is real. On the outside chance that I am incorrect, for now it will still be my perceived reality. And just like possession being nine tenths of the law, perception is nine tenths of reality. That is why people's perceptions are far more impactful than reality or facts.

My perception that my entire life is not a dream does not necessarily eliminate a shorter-term dream. That would be entirely possible for last night, but my dream would have had to carry through with dreaming that I woke up this morning, found things missing, found my dog, and am currently still wearing someone else's clothes. I remember that I have had at least one dream where I woke up in a dream, but not ever do I recall giving it this level of analysis in the dream and physically feeling this duration of time pass. That, coupled with a meaningless pinch of my arm that hurt, is putting me in a place where my house was actually raided by the FBI last night. Talk about things that would seem highly improbable, but the evidence is mounting. No, I take that back. There is evidence that I was restrained by the markings on my wrists and that property has been taken and in some cases crudely replaced. There is also the fact that Reggie was in the garage and that someone left me these clothes to wear.

Was it the FBI? Why would the FBI do that, but then again why would anyone? If I believe these events then I probably should also trust my eyes that I saw FBI on the backs of some vests. So it was either the FBI or someone pretending to be the FBI. Even when I draw conclusions I am always open to new information that would disprove it or raise question. Further confirmation is always good, so further examination of my house is in order. "Come on Reggie."

Chapter 6
Adjusting to Differences
Later Morning Day 2

Reggie seemed hesitant to walk into the house as though he sensed something was off. The difference in his behavior is obvious because he is usually barreling through the doorway and running to pick up some toy. Then again, he had just been locked in the garage all night so things *are* off. He knows when things are different and seems to know in advance of things happening. I have wondered how he knows those things, but it is very likely that he recognizes patterns that have just become so engrained in my activity that I don't give them a second thought. For example, when my kid or grandkids are coming over, he will lay by the front door staring out the window for an hour or two before they arrive. It's not like I told him that the kids are coming. Maybe I pick up certain things or change my clothes or some combination of things that I am unaware of that he picks up on.

There are some things that are more obvious for certain predictions of events. He loves to go for walks and he certainly knows the word "walk" and it makes his ears perk up, but he seems to realize that the word is used at times when he is not going for a walk. However, the second I get a plastic poop bag from the closet he is prancing, panting, and spinning circles. The circles have gotten a little less controlled in his old age and the walks have gotten shorter but the heart and emotion are still there. The one thing that has not changed is the verified trigger to know what is going to happen next. This prediction is not magic or engaging some power of seeing the future, but rather the recognition of patterns as well as behavior repetition. It is not only dogs that learn and adapt to repetition.

When we do not control those changes it can result in us unknowingly adapting to change. Much of that change is change that we would not have chosen. In other words, we have been manipulated. It happens a great deal and for so many it would seem to go unnoticed. Even if it is noticed, widespread repetition and acceptance by others often causes it to become engrained in our lives anyway. Those that resist are often labeled with any number of ridiculing names such as trouble-maker, agitator, rebel, conspirator, stupid, or even traitor.

This type of manipulation shows up in many areas of life and it seems that the older people are, the more they notice the change. Many will not say anything more than grumbling under their breath, but those of us with more of that grumpy attitude might be more inclined to say something. I have never been a fan of being manipulated and it's hard for me to imagine people that are OK with it, but that is the power of acceptance via repeated behavior.

A few may remember when a gas station was called a service station for a reason. They provided service. They pumped the gas, checked the oil, and washed the windows. There was a not-so-gradual ease out of that. Some service stations started offering full-service pumps along with the serve-yourself pumps. The serve-yourself pumps were a couple cents cheaper per gallon. I am not sure how the usage of each service worked out, but it wasn't long before it got harder and harder to find full-service gas stations and in a very short while there were none to be found. People accepted that they had to pay the full price for the not so full service (actually no service at all).

A similar thing happened with checkouts in stores. Self-checkout, what a great concept to pay full price to do what the store used to pay someone to do for you. Grocery stores used to not only check you out and bag your groceries, they would take them to your car and load them for you. I still have an issue with self-checkout. They just keep pushing for acceptance. They put more and more self-checkout stations in and fewer and fewer people working at the regular checkouts so the lines intentionally get so long that you just want to do it yourself so you can get the hell out of there. Then when they do run the checkout for you, most still expect you to bag your own groceries. Many reading this could not imagine that someone would actually take your groceries to your car for you. Most are at the point now where paying more for less is not only accepted but expected. Some may even be upset by referring to gas stations rather than fueling stations (many of which do not have gas), but that is for another time.

These are the easy ones, but look at a broader subject of "service" in general. People used to come to your house and it was expected, even doctors did. You could call a customer service person that would help you and stay with you until you were satisfied. On the rare occasion that you can talk to a person now, they are usually in another country and reading a script that they don't understand and has nothing to do with why you are calling. Most companies have stopped customer service agents altogether and have replaced them with email that gets a universal answer to all questions or a chat bot that is more frustrating and no more helpful. The reason that you need to talk to someone in the first place is that the quality of products has gone in the toilet. They metaphorically went from metal, to fiberglass, to thin plastic, to cardboard, to paper. And once again not only do people accept it, they expect it. It's just the way it is. A few of us still expect better quality, some actual service, and are willing to take the time to complain. This didn't just happen, this was a planned manipulation of behavior.

These are examples that have been well accepted, but compared to others they are quite obvious. One that is not as obvious is the definition of words. You would think that words have meaning. I have heard that phrase quite a lot in my life and I have even used it because it *should* be true. But when I started researching terms for books that I was writing I found some interesting, and for me disturbing, information. First there are copyright laws that prevent dictionaries from using the exact same definition. How about that; laws written to protect the written word require that the meaning cannot be consistent. That is not the acceptance example because you could just pick one dictionary, but what the dictionary companies are doing I find ludicrous and very frustrating. They change definitions of words based on societal use of a word. That means that if society starts using a word in a completely unintended and sometimes contradictory way, they will change the definition to align with the abuse of the word. Words no longer have meaning, which is required as a grounding point for conversation, communication, and understanding. They are simply symbols that float freely with the wind and thus undermine the ability for grounding and communication. Words become pliable balls of clay that can be used to manipulate and create plausible deniability as well as a mechanism for blaming others for not understanding.

There are manipulations that are far more covert and far more invasive in their results. Taking a step into a small example of that, there is the general concept of quality education. The education system has failed so many, so rather than step up the quality of education the standards are lowered to give the appearance that more kids are passing and that therefore means that the quality has improved. The intended message on this is that we are supposed to believe that because the standards were lowered we have a better-educated society, but quite the opposite is the reality of the manipulation.

These types of more covert manipulations are the ones that bother me the most. They are also the ones that make some believe me to be, or accuse me of being, a conspiracy theorist.

In another form of accepted behavior, people have accepted giving away their personal information, including financial, medical, social, and their complete identity. Nobody reads privacy policies (well I do). The emergence of high technology and mass data storage has made the collection of massive amounts of data possible. How many people give their social security number for identification? So many ask for it and few question it. The websites that you visit and the apps that you use on your phone all track much more information than you realize and they do things with it that you would likely not want them to, and yet you have agreed to *all of it*. The plain print in their policies states that by continuing to use their site you agree to all conditions of their policy that you have not read. Most never read or question and just give it away. People could be agreeing to give them access to their bank account (and they kind of are). What are people doing with all of that data? Two things for sure are being done; they are making money from your data and your data is allowing you to be manipulated in so many ways.

The *even more* disturbing manipulation is what the government is doing to not just your way of life but to your life itself. What the government is doing has been the topic of many of my rambles. I just realized that I am talking to myself as though I am talking to someone else. I think I just crossed the line into a rant, but I am not talking to anyone other than myself. It must be a practice rant. It is certainly a topic for which I have both a belief and a passion. How did I get here?

I got here by Reggie sensing that something was different going into the house and he did not just accept it; he changed his behavior. I am not accepting it either and I am going to take another look around with Reggie and see what we can find. The first and obvious thing that I did see is that the front door was clearly blown off its hinges and screwed back on with screws so big that it destroyed any esthetic value of the doorframe. The door was dented and cracked anyway and will have to be replaced. Who is paying for all of this stuff? The hardwood floor in the foyer heading into the living room had a couple good gouges in it presumably from the front door sliding across it. My computer was still missing and stupidly replaced with what might as well have been a Commodore 64.

The house gave no appearance of being completely turned upside down as you would expect by watching TV shows and movies where the cops and anyone looking for something literally turn everything upside down and dump everything on the floor. This was not the case. They clearly seemed to have some predetermined objective, but what? Even in the living room where I was thrown to the floor, there was no furniture out of place. It was like they moved things back into place.

The kitchen all seemed to be in place with no drawers emptied. I went upstairs and into my room and the bathroom looked pretty normal and the closet was still empty. I proceeded into the two other rooms upstairs, one that I use as a studio for my creative activities and one as a spare bedroom. I was horrified, which after the events of last night and missing Reggie this morning, says a lot. I have two computers in my studio, one for music and one for book formatting and photography. They were both gone with no attempt to replace them. They were gone along with the 4 external hard drives attached to them. It's one thing to be missing my office computer that is used for mostly email, short communications, and notes, but to lose my creative work that is in progress is devastating. I, of course, had my work backed up to an external hard drive which is now gone. Those backups are to protect against a hard drive failure, not an FBI raid.

Fortunately I was very paranoid about the potential loss from fire, so much of it is backed up to the cloud (I hope). I have not restored from there and I occasionally get a notice that the backup to the cloud failed, but they are not frequent and I have validated that there is data in the cloud. If I give my mind a little time to settle down, there should be a reasonable hope that I will eventually get my creative data back. Maybe it is not reasonable, but it is a hope. So the focus seems to be electronics so far because my computers, phone, and even my watch are gone. Okay, it wasn't all electronics; they took my clothes.

The guest room seemed to be left alone and the guest bathroom as well. I had not yet been to the basement, which was primarily an entertainment area with a pool table, bar, foosball, large screen projection TV, and a very large collection of vinyl records. There was of course the stereo system and turntable to go with the records. All seemed to be OK. The only spaces left are the workshop and the utility area. I have a small shop for woodworking, picture framing, and other building activities. The tools seem to be in place and a framing project is still laid out on the bench. The utility room looks to be another story. In addition to the furnace, water heater, and water softener, this is the place where all of the cabling enters the house. The cable modem for the internet connection and the router for Wi-Fi in the house are both gone. Again, there was no attempt to cover-up. Wires are hanging where the devices used to be.

OK, so it's electronics and clothes. It's bizarre enough that the FBI would enter, show no warrant, restrain me, and take my stuff, but the clothes and the very poor replacement of my office computer are beyond me right now. My current situation is not something that I will just adapt to. I need some resolution. I need to get a phone so I can start to function and make some contacts but first, one more quick pass through the house. How could I have forgotten?! The security system!

They surely must be on the security system. I caught my neighbor hitting my mailbox that way so let's have a look. I always look at footage on my phone but that's gone. Maybe there is a way from the console, the console that yells when the fire alarm goes off. I was almost surprised to see it still on the wall, after all it is electronic. I have never looked at footage on the console, but you would think that I could. I can tell if the cameras are operational and reset them and everything else, but apparently you need the app on the phone to see the footage. Not a surprise I guess with this company. I had the issue with other functions that I wanted to use that didn't work without the app.

I can see live camera footage on the console but no recorded footage. Looking through the live cameras I noticed that something was wrong. I have an inside camera but decided that with all of the alarms and the 5 outside cameras, I didn't want or need the camera turned on inside the house recording every movement I make in front of the camera. That would be more like an anti-security feature. I bought that camera when I got the system without giving it full thought of the ramifications.

I had disabled the inside camera but now it was live. It had been disconnected for more than 4 years and someone reconnected it. I had left it in place but unplugged it, so reconnecting it was just a matter of plugging it in. It did give me reason to ponder more. They had clearly *not* missed the security system but did they think they were clumsy and accidentally unplugged it, or did they connect it to use for their own purposes? That would seem a bit odd considering everything else they did. If they wanted to watch and listen to my activity in the house, they would likely plant their own devices. Crap! This on top of everything else; my house is probably bugged. Their devices would be so small that I would likely never find them. I need help and I need more information. And I need a phone.

Chapter 7

Retirement

Early Afternoon Day 2

I go to the garage and start my car. I am almost surprised that it started and it didn't blow up. I know I have covered this before; if they wanted me dead I would be. They want something else. I pull out of the driveway and head for the phone store. I look over and see Reggie looking out the front window. I feel bad but it has gotten really hard for him to get in and out of my SUV and you never know how long it will take at a phone store to get a new phone. It always seems to take half of a day for some reason.

Through this whole mess I at least have the luxury of not being tied to a corporate job. I am free to do what I want and when most of the time unless I am taking some very short-term consulting gig. Many people think of retirement as being the end of someone's life. Partly for that reason I don't like using the term. I told people when I 'retired' from my corporate life that I was changing jobs. I still got retirement cards and a cake but I have not been idle. I have not been traveling the world (not that I could afford it) and I don't spend my days fishing or wondering what to do with my life. I am busy.

I need to be productive and fortunately I have many ways to do that. I see retirement as a time to do all of the things that I want to do that might have been either too financially risky or known to pay little or nothing. I haven't given up on making money and I am definitely not opposed to it, but I can allow it to be secondary now. I had a family and responsibilities so I was previously not afforded that luxury. Some make out that way and are able to do just what they want while still sustaining an adequate income during their life prior to retirement. In that case they are not likely to retire until the mental or physical capabilities fail. That was not the case for me.

I liked many of my jobs and I made the best of them while persevering in my personal integrity. Money was important but I was not a suck-up. Boy, was I not a suck-up. I made decent money and many people were amazed that I still had a job with the way that I behaved at work. Many appreciated it but most did not have either the integrity or pure guts to stand up to some of the BS that floods corporate life. I don't see that I was a jerk or a detriment to the company, but I was probably a detriment to some of the leaders in some of the companies. I didn't play games and I told the truth rather than putting the spin on the information that would make the leaders or myself look better. I really pissed off some people in fact. I got out at a point when I was making the most money, but it was getting too hard to find any value at all in what I was doing. I may not have always been doing what I would really like, but I still needed to find value in it.

The current point about my so-called retirement is that I have the freedom of flexible time management to try to chase this situation down, starting with getting a phone. I pull up to the store in this little strip mall and even though the sign on the door says they open at 10:00, they appear to be closed. It is 10:25 according to the clock in the dry cleaner's window and the clock in my car has 10:28. Most of the other stores in this little strip of stores also appear to be closed, but they appear to be closed permanently, as in out of business. The liquor store is shut down along with the sub shop, the hardware store, and the ladies' clothing store. In fact the only store that appears to be currently active is the IPS store. Apparently getting packages out of town still has some value.

I was just about to pull away and head for another town when I saw a light turn on inside the phone store. I decided to go give the door a pull and of course it was locked. I saw movement in the back so I knocked on the door. Then I knocked again. I can be patient when there is reason to be, but I saw no reason at this point and me not getting a phone was more than just a little inconvenience. Finally someone was walking toward the door. I'm trying to keep an open mind, but I didn't have a good feeling about this person that I was dependent upon for aiding me with my need.

I was greeted with, "Okay, okay, you don't have to be so rude!" No apology, not even a passing "sorry". I would normally be inclined to explain that he was the one that was rude and that I was the customer, but my immediate need drove me past that for the moment. I decided not to go into the explanation of the FBI and take the easiest path that came to mind. I told him that I lost my phone and wanted to buy another one. He started to explain the features of finding a lost phone and my initial reaction was to just reject any conversation and just get the new phone and then curiosity hit me. I wonder where my phone would show up? They seemed to have been kind of stupid in some things so maybe this would lead me right to my phone and the people that took it so I said, "Let's give it a try."

My initial impression of this kid may have been wrong, but then again it was too soon to tell. He started by looking up the IMEI, which is the unique ID of my phone. This was a more accurate way of identifying a phone rather than the phone number, which can be changed. As he was looking though my account and jumping through pages he was muttering "hmm" over and over and finally a "WTF! I have never seen this." With the events of the last 24 hours, I guess this shouldn't be a surprise that more was going on but what was it? I just said, "Please tell me what is going on." He started repeating in an increasing volume and clarity, "They locked me out. They locked me out!" He seemed more than just surprised; he seemed pissed off.

"Did the phone company lock you out of the system or out of my account?" He said, "The phone company didn't lock me out of either one of those. I don't *think* the phone company locked me out of anything, but somebody either locked me out of your phone or somehow hid your phone." He kept explaining in detail how the ID and all locating components had been manipulated or removed. This was not just a matter of turning the phone off. The information about the phone in all locations, including those outside of the phone system, had been removed, locked, or altered. He went on with, "You didn't just lose your phone; somebody hacked the history of your phone and not just anybody can do that."

Now he sounded challenged rather than pissed off. I asked him to explain how he knew what he seemed to have concluded. He explained all of the databases that he had searched after not receiving any response from my phone in multiple ways that he had tried. He told me that he had heard of such things happening, but only if someone had complete access to *everything*. The odd thing was that the record of my phone still existed in the phone company's system. He had been keeping local records on a server in the store of all the customers originating from here and that's what he was looking at. He usually refreshed it once a week and that would be tomorrow. This was not standard practice, it was something that he did because he could and after all he was the manager.

This kid was the manager? He was obviously a geek with a lot of technical knowledge about phones, but also a bit of a rebel that was willing to color outside of the lines just because he could. I decided to take a chance and explain the happenings of last night. This really got his interest and he eagerly asked, "What can I do to help?" And then added, "Those bastards!"

I said, "First I need a phone." He was off to grab a phone but to activate it he had to connect to the main system. When he tried to replace my phone, he was blocked. He tried to add a phone to my account and was blocked. It seems someone had locked my account for any activity from the carrier. It was also confirmed that according to the main system the IMEI of my missing phone was different than what he had stored locally and it had been marked as being turned in and the account closed. It didn't look like a normal closed account to him, but who would have expected less. The account was marked with a DO NOT REINSTATE BY ORDER OF THE FEDERAL GOVERNMENT. He had never seen this and I have never heard of such a thing. Property being taken, being restrained, and now being denied access to a phone, all with no arrest and no warrant.

I realized I didn't even know the kid's name and he had already provided some valuable assistance. We exchanged names and normally would have exchanged contact information but… I asked Zack what options I had to deal with this and we discussed a few possibilities. One thing that seemed unlikely was retrieval of any of my information that was stored in the cloud because my account had been locked and the cloud storage was tied to my account.

There was a possibility that the cloud storage that I used across my electronic devices could be intact, but that is something that I will have to look into later when I get around to replacing my computer(s). For now there was nothing preventing him from setting up a new account under another name and a different address. This would normally require an ID with that name and address, but since there was no scanning of an ID, he could enter anything that he wanted. It was clear that I could not have done this without happening across Zack, the late opening store manager rebel.

I started to get hit with an internal flood of concerns triggered by this phone account experience. If they have done this, what else have they done? What other accounts could they have locked me out of? Are they maybe just watching accounts and how many accounts do I have that they could watch? My mind flashed back to potential surveillance devices in my house.

Then it went to the even bigger question, why? I discussed all of this with Zack, which is very much against my nature. I do not give trust without some level of confidence. On the other hand I consider myself pretty good at reading people, but I have been wrong before. If he was working with *them* I was not giving him any information that they already didn't know. I hadn't told him any other accounts or contacts. I had also not revealed my plans for next steps. I needed a little time to trust him further, but he could be very useful and seemed very willing to help. After talking over some concerns he suggested that I hold off on setting up another account and just go buy a burner phone or two. A phone where the minutes are prepaid and there is not a registered and billable account associated with it. He also suggested, which I had already considered, that I pay with cash for the phones. He had suggested a few places where I could get them and he did add the cash aspect; those were both steps in the right direction.

I wasn't ready to ask him yet but I wondered if he might have access to bug sweeping technology. I need to start with a couple phones and see where I get with the police and contacting the FBI. Those are my next steps. I needed to report what I would certainly consider a crime and maybe the local police were at least informed of the FBI being in the vicinity. I said goodbye to Zack and told him I would check in with him later.

As I was walking out the door, he stopped me with a very polite, "Excuse me. Would you be interested in attending a meeting of some like-minded people that are not fans of the type of thing that happened to you?" This caught me off guard and it seemed he was willing to trust me more than I was willing to trust him. It did cross my mind that this could be part of some undercover plan to trap me into something, but I had to check it out. I said, "What do you mean?" to see if I could get a little more insight so I wasn't going in totally blind. He said, "There is a small group of us that just get together and share stories of government agencies that are abusing their power. We get together about once a month and it just happens that our meeting is tonight in the basement of St. Augustine's." I had to check this out so I told him that I would try to make it. "Hope to see you there. We meet at 8:00. Good luck with the phone." And I was off to phone shop again.

My first stop before getting a phone was the bank. If I was going to be spending cash, I obviously needed to have some. I have withdrawn what might be considered larger amounts of cash before and they always treat me like a criminal. "Do you need this much? What are you using it for? The manager needs to approve this." And here comes the manager to eye you up and down. That was the way when I banked at one of the larger chain banks. It was for that reason, combined with a few others, that I switched banks. I actually switched to a different larger bank and realized they seemed to be all pretty much the same.

I now bank at a local credit union in addition to a big bank and have found the experience and the people much more pleasant. It takes a while to switch everything over so I still use the big bank in the transition. The people that work at the credit union are actually from here and they even remember my name. It doesn't take a lot of effort to please me and it takes no effort to piss me off. I don't just accept poor service and poor treatment, but I was still banking at a big bank (for now). I withdrew $5,000 with the normal evil-eyed process and was on my way.

It hit me that I was withdrawing cash in order to live this 'secret life'. Living off the grid (sort of) and hiding from someone with no understanding of why. That is really against my nature. I am a pretty private person, as in not sharing things with people that are really none of their business. Personal items are personal. Nobody needs to know my issues unless they are involved. It is so different for so many on social media today.

On one hand I am a private person and yet I am not accustomed to putting on a front or hiding things because I truly don't care what people think of me. Those are not conflicting; not telling people everything is not the same as hiding things. I knew that it was prudent to "be careful" with what activity and information I was making available to those that might be interested until I knew more of what was going on. It still didn't feel right because I know in my heart and soul that I have done nothing wrong. What does someone think that I did? I'm a "retired" old man for God's sake.

I am thinking in a way that I have never thought before. My latest corporate and consulting career being related to data privacy didn't hurt, but this went beyond that. Applying some basic logic and caution seems to be all that I can do right now. Even before I pick up my first phone, I start thinking through how I will use it. Its purpose is to not allow someone to track my calls and location. In order to know this prepaid phone is mine, I or the person that I was talking to would have to give up information that would identify me. That means that if I make a call that gives up that information, I have to get rid of the phone.

I stop at a gas station to get gas thinking that I would pay cash but there is nothing about this gas station or its location that provides any new or useful information and it's probably better to show some normal activity. I walked inside the station and noticed that they had prepaid phones. Hmmm. I decided not to buy one, even with cash, at the same place I got gas and used a card. Too cautious? It's not a big deal if it is. I'm just being safe, and again in my head it rings, safe from what?

I live in a relatively small town but there are a couple of larger towns within 10-15 miles. I drove to one of those towns and stopped at a couple gas stations before finding another that sold phones. I got one with 30 minutes loaded. This would be the one that I would use once or twice where I might be identified and toss. I went to a big chain store and bought one with a couple hundred minutes. Now I am thinking that there is going to be activity that someone watching would expect to see and actually should be associated with my name if possible. They had blocked the reinstatement of the account, but that doesn't mean that they would block the creation of a new one especially with a different carrier. Maybe they just wanted to make sure I didn't have access to anything on my account.

I went to another phone store and figured I would try to get a new phone with no mention of my previous service or what happened. I'm sure they all share data but I would soon find out if I could get a new account. I did and two hours later I walked out of the phone store with my third phone purchase of the day. Was this overboard? It was the freakin' FBI. It was a government agency and I have to assume that not much is overboard until I know otherwise. I had spent most of my 'free day' so far chasing phones, but I felt progress had been made.

I know that I needed to call the police or it could look suspicious in waiting so long. I made the call to the police from my latest phone. They said that they would send a detective over. I was only 5 minutes from home now so I am pretty sure they won't beat me there. I got home and marked my prepaid phones with "long" and "short". I know what it means and what to use them for.

The detective arrived about a half hour later and of course Reggie greeted him at the door. I went through the whole story of last night from the door blasting, through restraint, and this morning up to the point of discovering what was missing. After I finished he started to recap what he had captured and asked if they took my firearms. Of course I had forgotten to look for the obvious. I had told him that they asked where my firearms were but that is where it ended. I don't remember answering that question but I also didn't look for my guns this morning. I have a gun safe downstairs with three handguns and a shotgun and a small safe in my bedroom closet with a handgun.

He went with me to the bedroom closet and it hit me as I walked in, my clothes weren't the only things missing. The gun safe was gone. It was a small one and the purpose was not to protect it from theft, but rather a safe place for storage when my grandkids came over. The safe was gone along with a briefcase that I previously used far more often than I have recently, file boxes of papers, and miscellaneous stuff that had built up over the years. The papers in the boxes were old tax returns, a couple of manuscripts, and work-related papers. Everything that was in the closet was gone! It was empty. I guess the trauma of the occasion made me miss more than I thought.

We headed to the basement and the gun safe was there. It probably weighed over 400 pounds and was bolted into the cement floor. That should mean my guns are still there, but I opened it anyway and I was wrong. All of the guns and all of the ammunition are gone. All of the guns and a couple thousand rounds of ammunition are all gone. To some that might seem like a lot of ammunition but with four different caliber guns and fairly frequent trips to the range, it really was not. It was empty! What else? One more thing that I had forgotten, I had a fireproof bag in that safe with $20,000. Everything was gone! After everything so far I guess I wasn't surprised since they specifically asked about the guns. And I can't believe that I forgot about the money. Now I am certain that I was more flustered than I realized.

Do I tell the detective about the money? Why not, I wasn't keeping it there because it was illegal and keeping cash in your house is certainly not illegal. I had it for unexpected emergencies and with the world and the country in the state that they are, 20 grand actually seems like a small amount for emergencies. Emergencies like a cyber-attack on the financial system or something that could shut down access to my funds. I told him about the cash and he asked why I was keeping so much cash. I wanted to tell him it was none of his freaking business and that

I was the one that had property stolen. It seems that everybody thinks they have a right to know about your cash. Maybe he moonlights as a bank manager.

People that think that the financial or other key infrastructure systems cannot be hacked are quite foolish. Of course they can and they could be hacked on a mass scale. I am not saying that it will happen, but it is certainly possible. Think about what technology dependencies are in all of our lives and in the country's existence. If someone wants to attack the country, it will not likely be in the conventional way. I know that talk like that makes some people think that I am a bit loony, but I do know more than most about data and technology vulnerabilities. I don't spend a lot of time trying to explain that to people and I certainly wasn't going to do it with this cop. I just told him it was for emergencies with no other commentary.

He must have asked me a dozen times about seeing FBI on the vests but I know what I saw. I didn't tell him that the federal government had locked my phone account as additional evidence that it truly was the FBI. He said that he wasn't involved in any FBI action but the report would be filed and, "We'll get back to you." I held little to no hope of actually hearing anything from the local police; this was way above them, but the report had been filed. After he was out the door and I heard him pulling away, I grabbed some paper and wrote down his name and badge number. DETECTIVE DOUGHTRY, badge 341. I was going to document everything I could remember going forward. I also took the time to write down everything that I could remember from last night and today while it was still fresh. It's not that

I would forget but having a dated and documented record may come in handy. All of this writing, I need a computer.

I wonder if that piece of junk they left me to replace my laptop actually works? I went over and turned it on and it made some noises for what seemed like 5 minutes but I waited. Slowly the screen started to come in focus. What displayed on the screen was not a standard desktop or any OS logo. It was just big letters that said "RETIRE."

Chapter 8
Why Me?

Late Afternoon Day 2

Retire. What the hell does that mean? Well I know what it means, but why is someone telling me to retire? I feel a major ramble coming but for now I need to keep it at just another clue. I have a lot to do. That message on the screen is all there is. The keyboard doesn't work and there is no mouse so the entire purpose of the cheap replacement computer would seem to be to just send this one-word message. They could have written it on a piece of paper.

I just realized that the detective didn't take any fingerprints from anywhere. I assume that to mean that he had reason to believe that it actually was the FBI or that he simply had no intention of helping me. That gives me even more reason to believe that I will not hear from him again. The local police will not be likely to interfere with whatever the FBI is doing. Even if they are not 'in on it' they will cooperate or turn away.

Why is this happening to me? What did I do? What do they want? Many people would say, "What did I do to deserve this?" I try to never say that because I generally believe that *deserve* has little to do with anything. People overuse the word for things such as saying that they deserve a new car or a bigger house or on and on. They don't. The types of things that I might agree that people deserve are the types of things that all people deserve because they are people, not because of who they are or what they have done. The negative of that is also true. "Why did this happen to me?" "What did I do to deserve this?" I see that as just a lazy way to look at things and a way to get stuck in a rut, feel sorry for yourself, or blame someone else. It is just a fact that bad things happen to good people and also that good things happen to bad people. I also understand that the people that believe 'everything happens for a reason' may not appreciate my perspective.

Why me? Why not me? What a way to spend your life. I have certainly had enough things in my life where that could have been a question, but I don't recall that it ever was. Why did I get so sick that I had to leave college in my third year? Why did I get in a horrible car accident? Why did I get cancer in my twenties and three more cases of cancer later in life? Why, why, why? Even one of the most devastating discoveries of cancer in my twenties and being told I may only have 6 months to live did not result in that question. The question was, what do I do with 6 months?

Obviously 6 months was long ago and I could ask the positive side of that, "Why me?" I would be more inclined to do that, but for me it is much more about recognition and *appreciation* for the extension of my life. That experience is one of the major contributors to who I am. It changed my life. Of all the bad things that happen to others and the good that happens to most (if they recognize it), it is hard to understand the whining of the *Why Me Crowd*. I do not understand asking the question that implies blame. Someone must have caused bad things to happen to people, but if something good happens they must have deserved it. Give me a break!

In my current situation some might think I am saying, "Why Me", but my question is "What do they want with me" or "What do they think I am doing or did?" This is not something that happened randomly (I don't think). I can't imagine that the FBI just randomly hits houses or has a weekly lottery where people's names are drawn for fun, but maybe they do. Somebody in or above the FBI thinks that I did or am doing something, and I take the RETIRE message to mean that they want me to stop. Stop what? As far as I know, I am not doing anything that anyone wouldn't do. I also have to admit that I am probably wrong about that. Someone perceives that I am doing something, and whether it is real or not, it is *their* reality so I need to deal with that unknown reality.

Why me is not a question I am asking myself, but it is a question that I need to ask someone else. I found the number for the local FBI field office and called them. This was one of those calls that it did no harm for them to know about a new phone. I also had to assume that from this call forward that all calls from this phone would be monitored. It was ringing.

"Federal Bureau of Investigation field office. How can I direct your call?" It sure seemed like a real person answering the phone. That is unusual these days; one of those expectations that have been set in the last few years. I said that I would like to talk to someone who might be able to tell me anything about the FBI entering my house last night. After getting my name, phone, and address, he said "Just one minute." I was put on hold with dead silence, which I guess for the FBI is better than an elevator music version of "Don't Worry, Be Sappy."

The silence was broken with, "Hello, Mr. Thompson, this is special agent Smith. How can I help you?" Really, special agent *Smith*? This has to be a joke, but then again, I don't get the impression that the FBI is full of jokesters (smart asses maybe but not jokesters). I gave special agent Smith the short story of last night fully expecting that he already knew the details and then asked what he could tell me about it. He gave me nothing more than I would expect such as, "I show no record of any arrests or warrants executed for you or anyone at your address."

People treating me like I am stupid is just a more irritating trigger, but I tried (a little) to suppress it. "I know there were no arrests and no warrants executed because neither happened. That is not what I asked you." He jumped right in and said, "It sounds like you have an attitude issue." At this point with most companies on the phone I would start tying into them with a line of facts and their failure to meet the most basic service expectation. I would start making proposals of what my next actions might be such as online reviews, BBB, other pertinent agencies, news media, and possibly legal action. I didn't pull the trigger on that with the FBI. I still had no idea why I was in this mess or who was instigating it.

I certainly couldn't trust what was coming from this person but I had to ask again, "What can you tell me about what happened? Am I being investigated or targeted for some reason?" I got a very smug, "I already answered your question." Of course he had not, and obviously he was not going to. I had to reiterate that I had no idea why it would have happened and said, "If someone thinks that I did or am doing something, it would be nice to know what someone thinks I have done, because I have no idea." I wanted to throw in what I knew about the Federal Government lock on my phone account but this was not the right time, place, or person for that. To this he replied, "Is there anything else I can do for you?" What an ass! This was clearly getting nowhere and asking to talk to the special agent in charge was premature as well. There is always tomorrow and I had at least made the initial call.

What a pain this whole thing is and it seems pretty clear to me that this is just the beginning. I have no idea why I have been selected for this or by whom. It is still not worthy of a poor, poor, pitiful me 'why me' moment. It was a dig in and find out why me moment. I am fortunate to be in the retired state that I am and not have to go to work daily. Most of my business is done via the internet, either through my website or email but my phone is tied to a number of accounts and used for two-factor authentication so now I am going to have to change all of that.

The FBI now has my new phone number (at least the one that I want them to know about) and I have to do more to make sure that stays straight. Because of tracking capabilities that having a phone provides I think I should even figure out when I should even be carrying my phone. What else do I need to be concerned about carrying around with me that could make me traceable? It's not like I am a criminal and need to disappear. It is that there may be things along the way that I don't want them to know that I am doing or places that I am going. The rest needs to be as ordinary as possible.

I am going to need a computer for my email, website management, banking and more. I can do some of it from my phone but it is a pain for some things. The studio work is likely going to take a backseat for a while. I don't like that idea, but this is a priority right now and that ticks me off. My studio work is important to me and they messed with that. I will still try to at least find out what data is in the cloud and what is lost. I can use a library computer for some things that I want to do some research on like bug detection and FBI practices, but I need to make sure that I do nothing on that same library computer that could tie to me like logging into an account of any kind. That would be able to tie all activity in that computer session to me. My technical and data management background is helpful, but I know that there are things that I am not thinking about.

It's 6 o'clock and I am pretty sure I haven't eaten anything today and I am feeling a bit nauseous. I better get something for both Reggie and I to eat. It has been one crazy and very full day and I'd like to take a little time to just sit and hang out with my dog. Then I remember there is that meeting that Zack invited me to tonight at 8:00. I wonder what this group is about. I am thinking, or maybe just hoping, that they will have some info that could help me.

Chapter 9
Oh My God

Evening Day 2

I sat around with Reggie for a while and headed out about 7:45. I felt a bit guilty about leaving Reggie again. When I was working full-time out of the house he was used to it but I have been out of that life for a couple of years now and have mostly been home. It has been a traumatic day for me and I imagine for him as well. I wish I could bring him with but I figured this meeting shouldn't be very long, although I really had no idea what to expect.

I pulled into the church parking lot and immediately started reminiscing and rambling on the topic of God and religion. Now that is a long ramble that I have had many times over. It is the type of ramble that seems to reach conclusion and yet keeps returning and has never turned to a rant. This triggers so many paths of rambles that I cannot possibly go down right now, but they do include a few things that I consider to be either fact or belief. That statement alone includes the understanding that there is a significant difference between fact and belief. Most people believe that their beliefs are fact but they are not. God and religion are prime examples of that. That is why it is called faith. I have faith (belief) in something that not only has not been proven, it *cannot* be proven with the facts available today. Some take the idea that it cannot be proven as proof that it is not true; that is purely moronic. A very simple logical deduction would conclude that just because something is not proven does not mean that it cannot be true. The same is true for proving that God does not exist. Some people believe that God does not exist but they cannot prove it. It is a belief regardless of which side you are on and there is nothing wrong with beliefs.

This then leads to the ramble of *science*, which I am going to stay away from for the moment. The concept of science is theory that perceives some evidence, but in the vast majority of cases lacks proof. This concept has been proven over and over by the number of scientific "facts" that have changed over time. I have to stop for now; this abuse of science *is* one of my rants.

Believing in God (or not) and the concept of formal religion are two different things. Religion is too much of a reflection of man for me. It has often taken on attributes of greed, control, judgment, piety, and miscellaneous hypocritical activity. I was raised in a strong Lutheran family that went to church every week, read from a devotion book before every meal, and participated in seemingly almost every church activity. I was fully into that as a child and went to Sunday School after church every Sunday, participated in summer Bible Camp, went on trips with Luther League, was confirmed with a small confirmation class, and in my later teens taught Sunday School classes and played my guitar in church and other church events. It was pretty well embedded in me and I believed in the concept of giving, honesty, honor, respect, and loving and I still do, but something changed on the religion front.

Around the time of confirmation class I started to think about the literal words of the Bible and the conflicts that I could see with the literal words. The pastor, or anyone I asked, tried to just brush it away as me being a kid and saying that I didn't understand. It was them that were not listening to my questions. Later some would explain that it was different people writing the Bible so some inconsistencies in details might be expected, which then meant that it should not be taken as word for word literal but they would not say that. I had already had my IQ tested by this time and I knew that I was not lacking in the ability to comprehend. My IQ was about 170 and it is not something that I advertised but I did realize that many people were intimidated by me even though they did not know my IQ. I would ask questions that put people in a corner and logic and truth seems to intimidate people. They didn't like either one of those things.

While still in the confirmation class, one assignment was to bring in a song (as in a record) to be discussed. We were supposed to discuss how it might be related to the confirmation class and our religion. I brought in a Beatles' song (I'm not positive but I think it was *A Day In The Life*) and the pastor immediately rejected it as the devil's work. This was before hearing even 2 seconds of the song. It never came out of the sleeve and it was the devil's work. I doubt that was because he knew the song, but he sure knew of the band. That was it and no discussion. I tried to push back and that irritated him and it was over. I was young and as much as that irritated me and raised more question about the church, or at least this person, I graduated with the rest of confirmation class.

I stayed with it until about my senior year of high school. My hair was starting to get longer, but it was not nearly as long as it is now. At this time I was regularly teaching Sunday school. My class was 5 and 6 year olds as I recall. A few weeks into the Sunday school year the pastor informed me that they no longer 'needed' me to teach. I asked if anyone had complained or if I was doing anything wrong. I pushed on it and he finally told me that it was because of my hair and what a bad example it sets. I said, "Have you looked at a picture of Jesus lately?" That was it. I didn't go back.

So here I am in a church parking lot. It's not like I haven't been in a church since then, but it certainly made my mind wander for a while. I still do believe in a higher power. I believe in the content of the Ten Commandments and the golden rule, and I understand that many "religious" people do not live that way. I don't believe in a show for others, I believe that it matters how we live.

I look up from my rambling and I see Zack standing outside of the church. I was glad to see him so I wouldn't have to figure out which door to use and where they were. He waved me over and said, "Glad to see you made it. How has your day been?" I told him it had been a long day and I had done a lot resulting in little new information. He asked if I had a phone on me and if so would I please turn it off. I had left my "real" phone at home and brought one of the prepaid phones so I verified that it was off, and it was. He said, "We'll talk about a few other precautions but let's go in and meet the group."

We walked in the side door that led down about 8 steps. At the bottom of the steps was a hallway with doors on each side and what looked like a dining hall at the end. We entered the second door on the right that had a sign on the door that said Bible Study. This was clearly not a Bible study group and I made some comment to that effect. He said, "Actually more than half of the group attends this church and goes to Bible study, but you are correct that this is not a Bible study group."

I walked into the room and the chairs were set up in a circle as I would expect to see for a group therapy session. Someone said, "Should we get started?" Everyone started to take a seat and Zack and I sat down. That same person that I was assuming to be the leader said, "Zack has invited someone to our group tonight. Let's go around the room and introduce ourselves." At this point I usually lower my expectations of remembering because until something else happens worth remembering, I probably will not remember names. It might seem cold, but I honestly think that I choose not to even try. Names are somewhat irrelevant and wasted space in my head until there is some reason to remember them, and at this point I had no idea if there was going to be a reason. I certainly remembered Zack almost right off because there was good reason to. I never tell people to not bother telling me their name because I don't care, but it would save some initial time. Everyone introduced themselves and when it came to my turn I did my duty in the pleasantry department and gave them my name along with a comment that I had no idea what the group was really about. I hoped that I hadn't thrown Zack under the bus for not telling me more. I counted 10 people in the room including Zack and myself, and they were all men except for one.

Most times I wouldn't even notice such superficial things, but this was a group of people that someone thought would be of interest to me because of my experience last night. It was not an all-male group and it was not an all-white group. About half of the group (well a little more than half of the group I think) was not white. There was also quite an age range in the group. It was a pretty eclectic group that apparently had something in common. That is not a surprise in itself, in fact it is a relief, but I want to know more about what they all have in common.

John, whose name I now remember because he is the one that has seemed to be the leader said, "Let's do the initial checks and then give our guest an introduction to what we are about." What the heck were initial checks? I soon found out. Everyone took out their phones and verified that they were off. Every phone was off without exception. Everyone also verified that their phone was off before they left home. Then the wallets or anything containing credit cards or IDs came out. I was asked to bring mine out as well and I was becoming more and more concerned about this group and what type of radical ideas might be behind this group. I was handed a bag to put my wallet in and wondered if I was making a donation. I was not. I was told it was temporary and I could hang onto the bag.

John then made a statement that, "We do these things not as protection but as a reminder of the diligence that we must regularly keep in mind." I wasn't sure what that meant. He continued, "For our guest I will summarize the common factor and purpose of this group. We are a group of people that believe in the rights recognized by and provided by the laws and Constitution of the state and country in which we live. We believe that the government, in a growing number of cases, is violating those rights and that we need to be aware of these in order to help protect ourselves and preserve our rights. We meet to share experiences, approaches, and information in order to better achieve that end. We are *not* a radical group. We are not attempting to overthrow the government. We mostly wish to be left alone, but that is not what is happening."

He continued, "We all have our own personal reasons for being here; some of us have experienced the violation of these rights, others have a general interest in helping to preserve these rights. Many of us have a technical background, which is extremely helpful since much, but not all, of the violation is technology based. Some of it is change in policy and we are represented in that area as well. We have not advertised or recruited for this group. We have grown simply through natural grassroots encounters such as Zack inviting you. Do you have any questions?"

The first thing that hit me after that very interesting summary was, "How do you know that you are not inviting someone that would be disruptive to your purpose?" Saying that made it sound like protecting an underground movement so I added, "And why all of the secrecy if this is about protecting rights?" As soon as I said that I knew the answer because of what I had been through, but I let it ride to get another perspective.

"Those are two reasonable questions and if you don't mind I will answer the second one first." I said, "of course" and he continued with, "The answer is in the question. It is not about secrecy of the group, it is about protecting our individual rights. We understand that you have experienced something in the last day that may give you reason to be concerned about your rights being violated. Our group exists to benefit us as individuals, not as a group. The information that we share and the fact that we meet are not secrets but they can be used to infer, manipulate, and twist reality that is then used against individuals in the group regardless of this group's purpose or intent. It is just part of the caution and awareness that we need to understand and execute in our daily lives." That was far more of an answer than I expected and it at least made me want to know more as I found myself living with caution today without understanding why, and I offered, "Thank you for that explanation."

John continued, "And now the first question, how do we know that we are not inviting someone that might not be aligned with the group and could be disruptive or even someone intentionally misrepresenting themselves? The honest answer is that we don't, but we do know more than a simple referral and gut feeling from a member. The government has more access than we have, but simple research that is available to the public provides some basic information which is just the tip of the iceberg that the government has access to. We know:

- You your birthday is April 1
- You are 69 years old
- You were born in Wisconsin
- Your mother and father were Albert and Greta

- You went to Thomas Jefferson High School
- You were diagnosed with cancer in your 20s and a few times since then
- You have been married and divorced twice
- Your first wife was Lisa and the second was JoAnn
- You have a fairly cordial relationship with your first wife
- You have two children and two grandchildren
- You are closer with one child than the other right now and you adore your grandchildren
- You have worked in many careers that I won't bother listing but I could
- A couple of those careers would indicate that you might have both interest in and benefit for members of this group
- You have had a few traffic violations but no arrests
- You live at 1462 West Sparrow Lane
- Prior to that you lived at 1110 Hilltop Ave.
- I know the bank that holds one of your credit cards
- I know that you resisted social media because of the risks that you are aware of but you joined one 2 years ago when you retired for the purpose of business promotion
- You had lunch with your friend Sandy last Tuesday at Pete's Café and dinner and drinks with Frank last Friday night.
- You are not afraid to stand up for what you believe in or to call people out for lying

- And the FBI did a number on you and your house last night

I could go on and on but I think you get the picture that we don't blindly let people come to a meeting."

I was impressed that they took the time to research and not surprised that they were able to access all of this information and more and I told them so. "I appreciate the fact that you took the time to find out more about me but that was nothing that is all that surprising." John replied, "The only purpose in sharing that was to answer your question, not to set off an alarm or intimidate you. The scary part of your information is what the government has access to. Even with all of the additional information that they have access to it is not so much about what they have access to, but what they do with it. There is a lot for us to discuss, when and if you are interested, but for now I would like to move on with our meeting if nobody minds." Everybody agreed and I was certainly in no position to object. I am sure that I will learn a lot more just by listening.

I found as the meeting went along that there was some structure and rules to the discussion. The first set of discussions was about triggers, actions, and experiences. This consisted of examples of government overreach or what someone believes triggers them. First-hand experience was preferred but second-hand was accepted. Anything beyond that, such as something that you read on-line or in a 'news' article, was not presented unless you directly saw or talked to the person that was involved first-hand. The idea was to stick to actual information and not get caught up in rumors, distorted information, or plain false information. There was plenty to talk about without getting caught up in that.

The second half of the sharing was about new technology updates and self-protection steps. This also had the no third-hand info rule. Occasionally someone would bring something up that was borderline and call it out with an explanation of the source for group's approval.

With my background in the areas of data security, management, and privacy, this would have been very interesting to me before, but the government 'overreach' aspect added another level and twist to the subject and to my interest. It's one thing to protect your data but the things that are going on are way beyond that. As John had mentioned, it is not just the massive volumes of data that they can access about you, but what they do with it. It may be beyond what they do with it, but also how they distort, manipulate, and 'add' to it.

This was a lot to take in, but suffice it to say I was not alone in the type of experience that I had. They were not the exact same set of events, but there were people being targeted with no arrests and no warrants. Someone lost their job because of false information passed to their employer. People were getting threatening phone calls from people that believed things that they had heard about them. My experience was awful but so far it was private; there were some that had very public smear campaigns leveled at them. I had so many questions but I just sat and listened.

The segment dedicated to technology and protection methods was very informative. I found out that this segment added to an ongoing list of items. I was just thinking that I really wanted to get my hands on that list when John said, "We will get you the full list." What an eye-opening evening this has been. The meeting adjourned and I stayed to talk to a couple of the members. The introductions were first name only and no other information, but I found out that the group had an attorney, a doctor, a councilman, a few IT people, a plumber, and pretty wide variety of professions, income levels, and general demographics. The common element was their passion for freedom and their individual rights.

John told me that I could keep the bag that my wallet was in and I realized that nobody had ever explained what that was about. John told me, "There are potentially a number of cards in your wallet that could contain an RFID chip. These chips can be read from up to 30 feet away. The primary examples are drivers' licenses and credit cards. Not all have them but some do. The bag is an RFID blocker. Most in the group either have ensured that all of their cards are not RFID chipped or carry them in a RFID blocking wallet. That exercise with turning our phones off, that can be tracked even when you are not using it, and the wallet checks are just reminders for us to always be mindful of our protection. You will find these and a lot more on the list that I gave you." We walked out of the Bible study room together and as we stepped outside into the warm night, the massive amount of information that I just heard hit me along with my good fortune of meeting these people. As I pull out of the parking lot thinking about what had transpired in just the last day I hear myself say, "Oh my God!"

I drove home to Reggie for what I hoped would be a peaceful and restful night.

Chapter 10
Social Media
Morning Day 3

It was a surprisingly restful night. I came home, let Reggie out, and hit it. When my head hit the bed, I was out. I am sure that by the end of the day I was running on adrenalin and was completely exhausted, both physically and emotionally. I woke with Reggie still on the bed and he is usually up before I am and waiting for breakfast. He was probably exhausted as well. It was a new day and it was time to start planning out the day's activities, but first it's wake-up time. Even before retiring I have had a traditional one-hour wake-up time and I missed it yesterday. I am surprised that yesterday was as productive as it was because missing my wake-up time usually throws the whole day off.

The routine consists of a bathroom stop, washing up to get the night sleep off (shower would come later), putting some clothes on (which still aren't mine), and going downstairs for

Reggie's breakfast and cruise around the yard. He always seemed to take about the same twelve minutes; a minute and a half to take care of business and the rest of the time to check out the yard. He had his ritual path that he took around the edge of the yard and then a couple trips through the middle intently sniffing all the way. I figure that he can probably tell most of what had happened in his yard since his last visit just by sniffing.

The next step is to get myself breakfast, which is seldom more than a couple pieces of toast that I have to share with Reggie. I always give him the two top corners of the crust. I guess we both have our rituals. I then sit for most of the remainder of the hour and just gather my thoughts and catch-up on some news (both real and imagined). Today my thought gathering and news catching would vary from the traditional.

I would usually grab my laptop as part of the routine but I didn't have one. This morning the documents that I got last night would be my morning news for the day. I was anxious to dig into it. It was about 10 pages of two-sided material. There was a cover page followed by various sections. The heading was Considerations for Personal Protection. The overview read: It is always good to protect your privacy and your identity. These considerations are not for the purpose of protecting illegal activity but for protecting undesired and unapproved use of your information and information about you.

The first section is titled GENERAL INTERNET USAGE. I skimmed through it and took mental note of a few items:

- When connecting to the internet from your personal computer or phone, use a VPN to obfuscate your IP address. This is not foolproof but your IP address is one of the more common ways of linking all of your activity on the internet.

- Configure your firewall to block all possible inbound traffic that is not a response to your request. Use whitelists rather than blacklists. (Declare what is allowed rather than what is not allowed).

- When using a public computer, *never* enter any personally identifiable information and never login to *any* accounts of any type.

- Do not use sites that do not support encryption (https vs. http).

- Keep your malware and spyware detection current on all devices.

- Change your passwords a minimum of twice per year and never use the same password for different accounts.

- Enable two-factor authentication when supported.

- Assume that every action on the internet is captured, stored, and shared. This includes what you search for, what pages you look at and for how long, what you buy or even think about buying, and *everything*.

- Every possible piece of information about your computer and anything attached to your network is captured.

- Read the policies of every page/site visited. Most sites state that they can do pretty much anything they want with your information. Do not use them and yes, this will greatly limit your internet usage.

- Research and consider the potential pros and cons of using Tor.
- Clear browsing/cache/cookie history frequently on your computer and when finished with a public computer.
- Regardless of the site that you are visiting, it is highly likely that the physical servers, data storage, and networks, are owned and operated by one of the two major technology infrastructure companies. Most people do not see them as infrastructure companies; they are better known for their primary business, which is data collection and usage. As such, they have a vested interest in your information.

This is not all of the items on the list, but just a few that stood out while skimming. I knew most of these (not that I always practiced them) but there are a couple of new ideas. Like many, I believe that for some things I really didn't care because I wasn't doing anything wrong. My perception has now unfortunately changed. I saw that my passwords, account information, and identifying information were the most critical and it is from an identity and security management perspective. Then I thought there was another category of data that people have no right to and shouldn't have, but that data now takes on another meaning and level of concern that hadn't really hit me before.

The next section is titled SOCIAL MEDIA. There are obvious risks with all social media platforms. This reminded me of one of my unpublished blogs that I had written titled "Antisocial Media." The commentary on social media in that blog was not so much about the security aspect (although it was mentioned), but rather about how the concept of social media promotes antisocial behavior. The term 'friend' is abused and distorts the meaning and value of friends and it opens the floodgates to verbal abuse and potshots at people for which there are no consequences. It fails to recognize the value of face-to-face communication. I am not going to try to restate the entire blog, but it does make me wonder if I will see that blog and many others ever again. It was on my laptop and I don't know yet if I can access and recover that data from the cloud.

Social media in this case I suspect is all about exposure and risk. The brackets under the social media heading gave a clear indication of that, it said "(Don't Do It!)". I guess they could have just stopped there, but it went on with quite a bit more explanation. The points include:

- Assume that anything that you post is visible to the world and lasts forever regardless of your settings or deletions. You have no control of what the platforms or the people that see your information do with it. You don't know where they saved it, how many times, and who they shared it with. It's gone and the world has it.

- Simply having an account is an exposure even if you do nothing with it. Other people can reference you through some association to their activity or comments. They can reference you without an account but it is not an automatic link to your account. They can also hack your account whether you use it or not and pretend to be you.

- Do not link accounts regardless of types of account. Do not link from one social media account to another or a social media account to a non-social media account. This is highly promoted as 'making your life easier.'

Most of the rest of the things continued to be pretty basic and obvious recommendations about the type of data not to post. People are so crazy with their check-ins and locations as well as who they are with. They might as well put a sign on their house saying "I'm not home, come and take some stuff."

The document continued with phones, credit cards, cars, security cameras, facial recognition, email, driver's license and other IDs, and a number of other categories. The rest of the document held pretty consistently with the first part. I knew most of the things but got a few good new thoughts; mostly I got a new perspective that brought a sense of even more importance. For most of them, I probably thought like many others, I have nothing to hide. I need to protect theft of my identity and my sensitive data but what I search for and what things I buy did not really concern me until now. It annoyed me that the information was captured and shared, but I saw it as an invasion of privacy rather than a threat.

It was never outright stated in this document that the threat was the government. This is the United States where individuals have rights that are protected by the Constitution and not some dictatorship or communist country, right? After my experience, I'm not so sure of that. I do however know that my views have changed. If someone saw the list of avoiding tracking considerations, they would likely believe that it was to support criminal activity. Who would go to such lengths to avoid detection other than those engaged in criminal activities?

Now I am considering the idea that avoiding tracking in itself provides incriminating evidence for those who would choose to believe it. It seems similar to the older cop shows where they ask the person "If you didn't do anything wrong, why did you run away?" It still was not illegal or criminal, but here I am back to thinking about perceptions. I don't care what people think, right? No I don't, but I do care when someone violates my rights and has the power to take action that impacts my life. And now my ramble leads me to the concept that I am hiding, and hiding does have some sort of negative perception. It is not really my nature to hide when someone treats me in a way that is inappropriate, or when someone lies. I have more than once faced companies that I have done business with and bosses within companies that I worked for knowing that my actions could and did have consequences on my livelihood. This is different.

Even if it was the government, I have challenged things like fees for permits, traffic tickets, and written many letters to congressmen. This is still different. This arm of the government and others like the DOJ, the NSA, and even the IRS have power that is in another category from the administrative pushback that I had been involved with. It was evident that this situation would not be resolved by an 'administrative pushback' when my house was raided and the official position is "there is no evidence of arrests or warrants for you or your address."

As this ramble continues I look down at the last page of the document and see the closing statement, "It is not about individual pieces of data, its threat is when it is combined with other data, analyzed, manipulated, and twisted beyond any recognizable truth." The statement that *it is not about that someone has access to the data, it is what they do with it*, is becoming more meaningful. Still the government was not mentioned, but why would it be in a written document? All of this is bringing so many questions to light. I want to be able to talk to the group right now, but I am still in my morning wake-up time. I have crossed over my typical timeframe of an hour, but I am learning more by the minute, and my rambles from prior to the FBI event are starting to overlap into some patterns. They are not fully formed, but I can tell that something is coming together.

I am *not* running and hiding. I am looking for information. I have no idea who or what to fight, much less how. I know I saw FBI but I have no idea if others were involved or who they might be. Even more importantly, I still have absolutely no idea why. I have so much to do and I need to get started with my day. I have no computer to make notes and even if I did, I probably wouldn't use it to write this stuff down. It's time for good old-fashioned pen and paper. I start with a simple list for today. I just finished writing "clothes" and the doorbell rings. What now?

The doorbell rang? The doorbell is connected to my security system and it doesn't work without it. That means the security system is working. I have not yet tried to install the security app and connect to my system and the footage that might have been recorded, but I could use the console for current camera views. There is a kid at the front door and he is pulling a wagon and carrying a sheet of paper. He rang the doorbell again and is standing there rocking back and forth like he has to pee. I think he is a neighborhood kid so I went to the door.

Many times I will admit that I just don't answer the door when there are kids obviously selling something. I know that presents itself as a cranky old man, if not a mean old man to the neighborhood, but that is not it at all. It's not like I don't have a heart or don't care about kids, it's the whole process of fundraisers related to school and clubs. They are a scam and I would, and do, support kids but not the scammers behind them. There are the fundraising companies that make a haul but the part that bothers me the most are the schools and clubs. They act like they are doing the kids a favor by sending them out door-to-door to sell overpriced goods. They sell a $10 pizza for $20 and of that the kid gets a dollar toward their event cost. This is not hard math. If people would go buy the pizza for $10 and just give $5 to the kid they would save $5 and the kid would get 5 times as much money. Add to that the concept that the people that buy the pizza probably didn't really want it in the first place. In addition, you have no idea how many times this pizza has been thawed and refrozen or left out too long in this mass distribution process by kids and school or club personnel that know nothing about handling food.

I have offered to just give kids money without buying the product because I don't want to support the scam and I don't need pizzas, candles, or coupons for products that I don't use. Most of them are so confused that they just say, "I can't do that." I give them credit for their attempt at honesty by not doing something that they haven't been told how to do, but it is further evidence that it is not about helping the kids or donations would always be an option. Where does all that other money go and why do these groups shame kids that don't participate or sell a lot? It's pretty clear to me. And when the 2-week effort pans out in $16 of credit toward the event for the kid, who pays the balance of this overpriced trip for the choir or sport team to go to Florida to play or perform? Of course, the parents pay. And parents pay it because they want their children to have everything. I know I did. I think that simple doorbell ring turned into a ramble with a known conclusion (I guess it was an inward facing rant that's not supposed to exist).

I open the door and the kid says, "Would you like to buy some coupons for local stores?" I take a look at the coupon book to show some interest and of course they are for places like Betty's Dress Shop, Jewelry Is Me, We Can Do It women's fitness club, and Mary's Nails. That's all of the things that I use all of the time. Where are the men's clothing and computer store coupons when I could use them? He appeared to be about 10 or 12 years old and he had not even said what he was raising money for, who he was, or if he lived in the neighborhood. I care about the second two, but I asked all three. I found out his name is Cody and he lives about 6 houses away. As I am talking to Cody I noticed a couple of neighbors across the street standing in the yard again. It seems that regardless of what is going on at my house, it is of interest.

I ask Cody if he would like me to buy a coupon book for $20 or just give him $10 that he could stick in his pocket. History would indicate that he would take buying a coupon book but he said, "Will you tell anyone that you gave me $10?" I told him that I wouldn't tell anyone, but I wouldn't lie if his parents asked me. That was good enough for him and he took the $10. I asked him if he had seen any activity at my house a couple nights ago. He looked down and kind of sheepishly said, "Yeah I guess, but my dad said that I shouldn't talk to you about it." He paused and then continued, "Umm, he actually said that I should stay away from you. He said it looked like you were finally getting what was coming to you." Wow, from this kid was some real insight into the sentiment of at least one neighbor. One neighbor that I had never met and who knows nothing about me other than what he imagined or chose to believe, and he felt strongly enough about it to share it with his children.

I wanted to tell Cody to tell his dad oh so many things, but that would be very inappropriate and that message is something better delivered in person. I said, "You know what Cody, I'll take one of those coupon books too. Thank you for being such a nice kid and good luck with your sales." He gave me a quiet, "Thank you" and walked away down the driveway stopping to turn and look back with a big smile on his face. He waved and headed to the next house. There were still people standing across the street.

I went back into the house to finish my list for the day. Clothes was the only thing on it so far and it had to be the first as strange as that might seem. Wearing clothes that aren't mine got a little lost on me yesterday, but I need to start being me again in more ways than one, so I finished the list:

- Clothes
- Modem and router
- Visit Zack
- Install home security app and connect to service

- Set up secure home network
- Connect to cloud to look for backups

Chapter 11

Wants vs. Needs

Late Morning Day 3

My lists are typically not sequential. In other words, it usually doesn't matter what order they are done other than the obvious ones such as you have to acquire something before you can install it. I know myself and life well enough to know that on-the-fly adaptation is required. It's too hard to predict all of the influencing factors and their impact on the sequence. The order needs to be flexible in order to be efficient and effective. The list is the initial idea of things to accomplish. Even what is on the list can change with the addition or removal of items. It is usually adding rather than removing unless something has happened that makes that item impossible. In this case clothes were definitely first.

Was putting clothes first giving priority to comfort over need or want over need? The line between need and want is a very complex one except for the most rudimentary items. If people want to live, they need food and water. Are they the only allowable needs and everything else is *want*? With the right qualifiers almost anything can be turned into a need. The *if* that precedes the need is critical. I could cut this ramble short by simplifying the conclusion that *everything* is a want because it is appropriate to state the *if* as a want. Even living is a want (if I want to live). Not everybody wants all of the same things.

Why am I even going down this need/want ramble? I'm pretty sure it's because I am talking myself through the justification for putting clothes before anything else on my list. I don't have to justify it to myself but in the effort to make sure I am doing the right thing I sometimes take off on a little side trip, and that's what rambles are. Considering everything that has transpired over the last couple days you might think that *something* would be more critical than clothes. In my head I thought that I 'need' clothes. That thought immediately jumped to people saying that they need something so that others will provide it. That application of the word is what triggered my ramble.

It is clear that the intended outcome of the use of the word is important to me. You would think that would start with the conditional "if" as the qualifier, but that only works if people are honest. You are not likely to find too many statements of need qualified by, "If I want to get free stuff."

This is a very slippery slope. Consider a simplistic and superfluous example of your kid saying that he or she needs a $250 pair of jeans. You might be tempted to just say no or maybe ask why. Asking why in this case is the same as defining the *if*. You might get to, "If I want to be cool" or "If I want to dress like my friends do." You might also get, "If I want to meet the dress code requirements of the new job that I am starting on Monday." You might question the requirements of the job, but if it is true, that answer is quite different than the first two. The first two become a situation where the want justifies the need and if *any* want justifies the need then we are sliding down that unrecoverable slope where there is no difference between want and need. In some ways, I think society is very close to that.

So far there are two important factors involved in the *need* assessment:

1. What is the IF?
2. Is anyone else involved (expected to provide)?

The IF qualifier is purely subjective unless it is framed by something that sets the boundaries for rights (such as the Constitution). Destruction of such framing of rights creates chaos and ridiculous demands for needs. And such is the nature of a good ramble, from buying clothes to chaos and destruction.

Even after that journey, I seem to have come *almost* full circle to the difference between need and want being subjective *unless* there is a framework that defines *rights*. Without that, many will insist that their want is a right and we have seen that from people for a very long time. For me that equates to other words such as greedy, entitled, lazy, and a list of other unappealing attributes.

Regarding the second condition of anyone else involved, there is one caveat regarding that as well. For the most part I believe that what people choose as their wants and needs within themselves is irrelevant to anyone else and is certainly none of their business. There is one exception that I can think of, but I guess it still breaks the line of involving someone else. Those caught up in that situation might not recognize it. If you are defining your personal needs and the needs that involve others are put aside, you have just involved them. You are not asking them for something, you are taking it from them. Examples of that would be not paying your bills because you 'needed' another pair of shoes or not going to a birthday party that you promised to go to because you 'needed' to go to a football game.

The 'need' in my head about clothes does not take anything from anyone else that I can think of. I can still pay my bills. That would make my trigger of buying clothes nobody else's business and it becomes irrelevant whether it is want or need. Now I really am back where I started. That happens with rambles many times. My trigger for justifying the purchase of clothes first was purely internal and was just a good quality check. It might even be better stated as defining my priorities rather than needs. That would have made this easier from the start and would have likely avoided this ramble. Well, next time.

So back to my internal justification, why clothes? Because the ones that I am wearing are not mine, I don't have the time with all else going on right now to wash clothes every day, and the shoes are giving me blisters. My clothes were stolen! By wearing the clothes provided to me I feel like I am being manipulated by someone and that feeling bothers me a great deal. I will think better and act more like myself if I am dressed as I normally would. I need to be myself and not what someone else wants (and that goes deeper than clothes). I don't need a full wardrobe, but I need some clothes in order to be *me*.

After all of that rambling, I just pulled into the only got-it-all big box store in town. I don't usually buy my clothes here but they do have clothes. I went in with an open mind of not needing a precise style, just something that physically fit, was comfortable, and didn't stand out too much. I grabbed a 6-pack of underwear (not sure if that was a priority or just what happened). I found a pair of comfortable shoes, 2 pairs of pants, 3 darker colored t-shirts, and a couple button shirts. I didn't bother with socks because I haven't worn them since I retired and if the need comes up I have the pair left for me along with the slightly too tight dress shoes.

And just like that, clothes shopping was done. Well, it was done except for paying for it. I flashed through the precautions list in my head and decided that using my credit card was not an issue. Someone who took my clothes would expect me to buy more, and this location was not far from my house so I was not giving up anything of import. I remembered as I was getting close to the checkout that this store also sold computers, but I passed on that for now for a number of reasons.

I took a quick dash home to change clothes and get my plan for the day a little more organized. I had rushed through the list pretty fast just to get out the door and get going. I wanted to just stay home and hang out with my pal. He was happy to see me and offered no judgment and no game playing. Well, maybe once in a while he would pretend that he needed to go outside just to get a little attention. That was okay with me. I could even tell when he was faking it and it was still okay. I played along. I was not playing now. Somebody was messing with me and my primary feelings were shifting from fear, to confusion, to an impassioned mission.

I looked at my list while sitting in my own chair in my own clothes and it was clear that as much as I wanted to talk to Zack and others in the group I needed to get access to my recorded security footage as well as checking my cloud backups. Before I did anything on the internet I need to get a VPN installed. I would need to connect without a VPN in order to download it. Then it hit me that I had enabled two-factor authentication on a number of accounts, which for some would mean texting or calling my phone, which I no longer had. The list was getting longer for things that I wanted to talk to Zack about. I had thought that my questions were more about strategy, but now it seemed like it would be a good idea to bounce the short-term technology issues off of someone. How was I going to talk to Zack without adding exposure to our connection?

All of the things that I could think of seemed like pretty cornball cloak and dagger ideas that could have some flaws. If I was spotted trying to pull off an obvious 'sneaky' contact, it would be worse than just walking into the store. There are many reasons that I would go back into the store, such as checking to see if the status of my phone or account had changed. I thought it was better to be open about this, but then it seemed like I had been saying that for too many things. "It's innocent. They would expect me to be doing these things." Would they really expect that I would go back into this store after I had gone to another store for a new phone? Maybe that was a stretch. I am definitely starting to second-guess myself and bouncing this off someone else seems more critical. Was I going overboard with this? I wasn't a criminal, I wasn't a terrorist, I wasn't trying to overthrow the government, and yet the FBI raided my house. I am just an ordinary guy. I have no power or authority. It seems more and more unbelievable with the passage of time, but I have to take it seriously.

I thought about calling the store with a prepaid phone, but what if there is a tap or even simply business recording of messages. Why didn't I ask how to contact anyone in the group? Maybe they would have told me if it mattered. We all met together at a church and talked in the parking lot. Okay, that is enough. I need to ease up a bit, but not too much. I made a list of questions for Zack on a piece of paper and another one with one question on it, and off I go again to the phone store.

The store was clearly open this time and fortunately there was no sign of anyone else being in the store. I walked in and saw Zack behind the counter. I said, "I just stopped in to see if the status of my account has changed." He said, "Let me check" and as he was looking I slid one piece of paper over to him on the counter. It simply said, "Is it ok for us to talk openly here?" He said, "No change to your account. I still can't access or reinstate it." I thought that probably meant that it was not okay to talk and then he started laughing. "I appreciate you asking but yes it is okay. We do have cameras at the front door but there are no listening or recording devices inside the store. I sweep it regularly." I was relieved that I hadn't really blown it and said, "I was concerned about even coming in here. I have a whole list of questions but what I would really like to do, is sit down for a while with you or someone from the group now that all of this has had a little time to settle in." Zack said that he understood but "We should not talk for a long time here. I can try to answer a few questions and then set up some time to meet."

Fortunately, I had made this list in the order of importance in anticipation of not having much time. The first was about getting VPN on my phone without leaving a trail that I had gotten a VPN. He said, "Give me your phone." He plugged my phone into his and said, "Keep talking." Okay, I kept going, "Can I get my old phone number on my new phone with a different carrier?" The answer was not what I wanted to hear, "You can ask your new carrier but I suspect not since your account is locked. Your number is probably locked as well to prevent it from transfer." He reached across the counter and handed my phone back to me and pointed at the VPN that he had installed.

I looked at the rest of the list and it seemed like it would take an hour so I had to find out how to continue. "How can I safely contact you?" He said, "Give me your prepaid number and I will use mine to call you. Don't save my name with the number that I call you from. I will call you later and set up a time to meet." I was all in with Zack at this point, which is very fast for me to trust someone. He and the entire group could be part of the *whole thing* (whatever the whole thing is) and just playing me to find out something. I don't have something to find out so I am going with cautious trust at this point and I gave Zack one of my prepaid phone numbers. The most urgent questions have been answered and I figured that I should be getting going. I turned toward the front of the store and saw a black car out in front. It wasn't parked but it was moving very slowly. It looked like the car that had gone by so slow when I was looking for Reggie, but then again there are a lot of black cars. I ran to the door to see if

I could identify the car. It pulled away pretty fast and yes; it was another (or the same) government plate.

Zack looked a little surprised and a bit disturbed. He said, "This has never happened before. We really do need to talk." I assured him that I wanted to talk as soon as it could be arranged. He was willing to meet with me before, but now he seemed to have a heightened desire to do so. I realized that the camera on the door would have captured me running toward the door, but it was just a passing thought. There are far more important things to be addressed.

The more things that happen like this, the shorter my patience grows and the temptation to blast forward, with little more information than I had to begin with, increases. I had to try to resist that, but I was being pushed. Maybe that is what they are doing, pushing to see what I will do? I needed to stay on my path for now and get a better assessment of the status of my situation. I said goodbye to Zack and said "Thank you." He gave me the kind of nod that meant "I will see you soon." It's interesting how simple gestures and looks can say so much. I walked across the parking lot and got in my car with a sigh of relief. I'm not sure what I was relieved about, but at this point maybe it was just that I survived this part of my day.

I started this day wondering if my day was planned around reacquiring comforts of my own clothes, phones, computers, and those things that are not basic food and water and the things that arguably some do not have. I had eliminated the distinction between need and want for my own use, but it was building to so much more. I was now driven to find answers and these things are just the means to enable that drive. I turned my phone off, slipped my wallet into the bag that I still had from the meeting, sat back in the comfort of my car, and drove to another town about 30 miles away. I took county roads, partially for the distraction and partially to avoid the cameras that are on state and interstate highways. License plate tracking is one of those real things mentioned in the document. And now I really did feel like a fugitive. I know who I am and I still have no clue what is really happening. This seems like a movie about someone else's life. I pulled into a small park that would give me a place for calm and a reassessment of my status. I walked to a picnic table under a very weathered pavilion and pulled out my two lists and a pen.

If I *want* to find out what is going on, protect myself, and try to live in a country that aligns with the country that I have known, there are things that I *need*. That fits my constraints of using need and I am good with *needing* those things.

Chapter 12

Constant Reassessment

Afternoon Day 3

I am just staring at the lists and reprocessing the recent events. Constant reassessment is not a paranoid behavior. It is also not a position of weakness or indecision. It is an acknowledgement that I do not have all of the information that might exist and that I don't know everything. Continuing to reassess is the most open approach to life. It is a willingness to continually learn. It helps, along with the rambles, to find patterns that are useful going forward. Sometimes a reassessment validates a position, sometimes it adds to the questions, sometimes it identifies new patterns, and sometimes it changes a previous conclusion. Unless we are open to change and learning there will never be progress and falsehoods will prevail.

It seems that happens more and more and it seems a little bit ironic that a person that is thought to be old and stuck in their ways is one that is open to learning. So many people seem eager to believe anything, and I believe that is because it is *easy*. Looking for easy only makes us susceptible to manipulation. "I'll do that for you" has so much power and so many fail to recognize that they just lost the ability to do or decide for themselves. "I'll pay for that" overshadows the recognition that you are now dependent and promotes the idea that you don't need to *earn* anything. Constant reassessment is the only way, in my mind, to maintain any form of control and grasp on reality. That applies to the recent events, my list for the day, my trust in Zack, and my entire life.

My two lists consist of my actions for today in no particular order and my list of questions for Zack or the group. I am scanning back and forth between the lists looking for anything from one list that might change something on the other. Nothing is evident at this point but that could change. The more urgent list may be the one for today and it is also the shortest list so that is first. I look it over:

- √ Clothes
- Modem and router
- √ Visit Zack
- Install home security app and connect to service
- Set up secure home network
- Connect to cloud to look for backups

Clothes done and visit Zack done, but under Zack was a long list. One of those was critical to the execution of other things on this list and that was the VPN on my phone, which is now done. Checking to see if there is any home security footage would seem to be the most important next step. I want to preserve the footage of the FBI if it is there. Why would it not be? There are 2 or three cameras that should have captured something. There is no reason to wait is there? I had turned my phone off and if I turn it on and download the app I would clearly be traceable. As much as I want to do it now, I should wait until I get back home or close to it. Almost everything else occurs at home except for picking up hardware. I need to get the hardware and head home. The other list needs to wait because checking for the security footage is a pretty big deal.

I set out for the big box electronics store that I knew to be in this town and tried to take as many side roads as I could but I could only do so much of that. I just needed to be extra careful with traffic violations. I made it to the store and paid cash for the hardware. No rewards card, no credit card, no extended warranty, just sell me the hardware. And I was off.

I took pretty much the same roads home and it seemed that everywhere I looked I saw black cars. I didn't however see any government plates on them, but I looked. That made me reassess the idea of both cars that I had encountered. I will admit that those encounters added a level of urgency and concern. Applying very little logic in a more calm state it *had to* be for that purpose. It is not like they were trying to be secretive about the cars following me. Government agencies like the FBI certainly have access to unmarked cars with regular plates for covert operations. They chose not to do that. They went slow and of course I could see the plates. Just like the message on the computer and the clothes. They were head games. They had to be. Nobody was arresting me or even threatening to arrest me. This was a pattern. They were terrorizing me. Drawing that conclusion made me want to mess with them, but not yet. I had more to discover, but somehow I felt a *little bit* better.

That didn't last long. I drove in the driveway and noticed something on the front door. I clicked the garage door opener, drove in, and closed the door behind me. I went inside through the garage to a very welcoming buddy. Reggie was always glad to see me and that felt good, but now to check out the front door. I opened the door and grabbed the paper that had been stuck there with a tack. It said "YOU DON'T BELONG IN OUR NICE NEIGHBORHOOD". Now, isn't that nice? It's such a nice neighborhood. Time to get to work and let that childish crap go.

I turned my phone on and pulled my wallet out of the bag. I made sure that the VPN was active and went to the app store to download the security app for my system. That all went fine and the app was installed. Fortunately I remembered the password but I seemed to be screwed on the two-factor authentication. They must hit this in other circumstances when someone changes their contact for authentication, so I called them. The number was on the console. I explained that my phone and computer had been stolen and that I had a new phone number for the two-factor auth and couldn't get into the app. They asked for *both* of the system passwords, the answer to the security question, and had me push some buttons on the console. I guess I passed because they asked for my new number for the authentication but also to update their contact information if there was an alarm. This person was actually helpful. I frequently write reviews and send complaints for bad service and when someone stands out on the positive side I do as well, so I asked for her name and thanked her for her help.

I was able to login and now was the moment of truth. The video clips show time and date and I needed two days ago at about 8:00 PM. There was nothing older than 1:00 AM the next morning. Damn it! I called the security company again. I was not lucky enough to get the same person. I explained that I really need to find that timeframe and wanted to know if they can recover it. "Sir, we don't control what our customers do with their data and if you deleted it, it is gone." Definitely not the same person. I tried again, "I did not delete it. Can you tell me who did?" Again the condescending response, "Sir, if you delete it, it is gone. We do not delete videos unless you exceeded your storage limit, which you clearly did not. I verified that you deleted the videos for all cameras at 12:53 AM yesterday morning from the app on your phone." I should have figured as much and explaining to this person what happened would obviously not help. Also explaining that data that is 'deleted' on most systems is not actually deleted would likely be a waste of time. This company may be good at house security but they seem to have little concept of data security. Obviously if someone takes your phone, they can delete any evidence of that from your cameras. Great!

Even though I assumed it to be a waste of time I had to try, "Is there any way to recover the files that have been deleted? This is an emergency because my house was robbed." I heard the same tone only a little louder, "There is no way to recover what has been deleted and maybe you should have been more careful about deleting files." OK enough, "I would like to speak to your supervisor." Sometimes you get a person that just refuses to let you talk to their supervisor. That behavior is not just this company; I have encountered it in many places. It's not like that request is my first go-to solution, but it seems more frequently that the ability for a customer service person to have basic listening and comprehension skills is rare. This phone call took way too much time and it ended with nothing accomplished except confirmation from two levels of supervisors that the files could not (or would not) be recovered. There goes my evidence that the FBI actually raided my house.

I scanned through the files that were recorded after 1:00 AM yesterday and found something interesting. The same black car, whose license plate I now had, went past my house slowly at least 4 times in the last 24 hours. I saw nobody come to the house from the car. There was, however, a neighbor caught on camera pinning a note to my front door. They either didn't care if they were caught or they are just stupid. At this point I am thinking the latter. I saved the black car and note hanger videos to my phone. Knowing what time the FBI videos were deleted at least saved me the process of beating myself up for not getting to the files sooner. They were gone before I woke up the next day. Another conclusion formed out of this discovery and that is that I must have been drugged to not remember how I got to my room, have any recollection of anyone clearing out my closet, and sleeping through the night. I never sleep through the night.

That took care of everything on the today list except for setting up the home network and connecting to the cloud backup to see what was there. The home network was not urgent right now since I didn't have a computer yet and I didn't mind cellular for data at home on my phone. It was still via VPN and the location of my phone was just my house and not a big deal, but I needed to connect to the cloud for backups. I had only done that via one of my computers and I don't know if it's possible on a phone. I'm putting that on hold for today. I want to review the list for Zack and company. I am still hopeful that I will be able to meet with someone tonight and I want to be ready. That list might also add something to today's list after what has happened so far (reassessment).

I did a quick look down that list and then started thinking of things to add. The current list is:

- √ OK to come in store?
- √ How to get VPN without internet exposure?
- How to contact them?
- Share details about the FBI events, cars, and messages.
- What would you suggest for next steps?
- Should I get a lawyer?
- What do you think they want in general and with me specifically?
- Who do you think is behind this?
- What would be the drawback to going public (news media)?
- Do you have a recommendation for a particular encrypted email solution, and do you trust it enough to talk about this stuff?
- How many that you know have had similar experiences as me?
- Does anybody have any plans of how to address this either individually or as a group?

- If we are not doing anything illegal, what can they possibly do?

This will likely take a long time to get through all of this unless the answer for all or most of it is, "I don't know." It is also possible that I will add more before I talk with him. In the meantime, I will have a little me-and-my-pal time and turn on the TV. The TV, I hadn't even really noticed it was still here. There is nothing that would be stored on the TV so I guess that would be of no interest. The news came on and the first words that I hear are, "Terrorists continue to subvert the government. If you see something, say something." And I turned the TV off. It seems it is always the same thing. Maybe time would be better spent with more reassessment or just playing with my loyal friend.

Chapter 13

300 Channels Better Than 3?

Late Afternoon Day 3

I grabbed a brush and started brushing Reggie. He likes that and he hasn't had much attention lately. I was kind of staring at the black TV screen and started thinking that I just turned the TV off instantly even though I must have about 300 channels. Even with 300 channels, it seems like there is nothing to watch. There is a set of reruns, the same words across all news channels, and the same stupid advertisements that take up about 70% of the programming.

When I was a kid, we had 3 channels and occasionally a 4th after 7:00 PM if the weather was just right. The stations signed off the air at midnight and yet it seemed like there was so much more to watch, less advertising, and all of the stations were not the same. Of course I was a kid, but I really don't think that is it, at least it's not only that.

Oh, and the cost! It is absolutely crazy what the 300 channels cost. I have thought so many times of dropping it and just having internet and an antenna, but then one thing hits me. I even got as far as buying an antenna and I was amazed at how many channels there were and many of them had some of the old TV programming from when I was a kid (with more commercials of course). With all of these 300 channels, there is *one* channel that I get something out of occasionally. It's not a coincidence that you can't just get that channel and it does not come in the 60-channel package, or the 125-channel package or the 200-channel package. It only comes in the 300-channel package. Seems like they might have held out for the 500-channel package, but here I am with 300 channels all for the desire to have *one* channel.

A phone rang and even though it was on vibrate it made me jump a bit. I have never heard this phone ring and I just wasn't expecting it to ring. It must be Zack. Of course it's Zack; he's the only one that has this number. I quickly stepped outside, because I still wasn't sure if anyone was listening or watching inside the house, and simply said, "yes?" That reminds me that I didn't ask Zack about sweeping the house.

Zack said, "Can you meet at 6:30 at Three Tree Park in New Riverton?" That was the park that I was just at this afternoon, so of course I replied, "I'll be there." And he said, "I'm bringing Sharon along if that's okay." It took me a while to remember who Sharon might be, but even though I am horrible with names, I did remember Sharon from the meeting. That was probably because she was the only woman there. By this point I bet Zack was wondering why I was taking so long to answer so

I hurried and said, "Of course, that's just fine. It just took me a minute to place the name." That was the end of the conversation and with quick goodbyes we hung up.

I had an hour before I had to leave and as good as it felt to just sit, I felt like important time was slipping away. I bought the network hardware, but I'm not sure why it didn't hit me until now, I will need a computer to configure the router. That stuff is going to sit in the box for now. The phone ringing did remind me of one thing that I need to do. I need to call my kids and give them my new phone number. It wouldn't be good if they called me and got a message that the phone was out of service. There is no way that I will tell them what happened. I will just say that I lost my phone and decided to switch carriers and phone numbers.

I could also throw my new clothes in the washer. I am wearing new clothes that haven't been washed now and I don't usually do that. It's better than wearing someone else's clothes and I'm going to wash those as well.

I called daughter number one and she didn't answer, very possibly because she didn't recognize the number. I left a short message, "Hi pumpkin, it's your papa. I have a new number with my new phone so change my contact info. I had a mishap with my old phone and decided to switch carriers and keeping the old number was just too much of an issue for some reason." The call to my second daughter went pretty much the same way.

Here I sit with Reggie, clothes are in the washer, called the kids, have a list ready for the park, and no, 300 channels are not better than 3.

Chapter 14

White Lies

Evening Day 3

I'm sitting here almost drifting off and wondering if I lied to my kids. As I think back on it I believe that it was carefully worded so that it would not be a lie. It is true that something happened to my phone (a mishap) and that I decided to change carriers (after I was blocked from keeping the same one) and that keeping the same number was too much of an issue (because the Federal Government locked it down). It was definitely spin. It was maybe a lie of omission if there is such a thing. My parents would have said that not telling the whole truth is a lie. It was not a white lie as some like to call some category of lies to make themselves feel better, it was one of those black lies, but nobody calls them black lies.

I think that some people believe that white lies are 'minor' lies that have no negative consequences. How can they know what the consequences will be? I know I have told lies that might fall in that category. Maybe they include things that you don't know but hope to be true along with the things that we know are not true but see it as harmless to believe in fantasy. Telling children about Santa Claus is clearly a lie, albeit a very common lie. It would likely be difficult to explain to other parents and kids why you were not going along with the lie. Besides, it is really fun and gives children something fun to believe in for a while. The idea that someone is watching for good and bad behavior is not a bad concept either. It is true that if parents (at least some) could watch over their children like Santa Claus, they would.

Put Santa aside for a moment in this ramble and go back to the lie of omission. I don't like to lie and I do believe that it is wrong, however I saw no reason to tell my kids about the FBI and involve them in this in any way. I was protecting them. This sounds too close to the end justifies the means, and I don't like how that feels. Lies should be black and white shouldn't they? Either it's a lie or it's not. That is probably what I want because it is starting to feel like want vs. need, where there are likely required to be qualifiers and *then* who decides?

In the case of lies, the qualifier might be less likely to be the condition of purpose, but rather the consequences. It may not be the consequences to the liar but rather the person(s) being lied to. As I go through this, I'm not sure I believe that either. Maybe I need to start at both ends of the spectrum of lies and work toward the middle and I think my lie of omission is not on either end. It's interesting that while I want lies to be black and white, I start by presuming that there is a spectrum of lies. Santa Claus seems to be at one end simply because so many understand it and it's fun for children. It is so much fun that children pass it on from generation to generation. One could argue that the outcome is happy children that learn that it is okay to believe in something.

If I look for the other end, I am not sure I can find it. There are blatant lies such as saying that the front door is closed when you can look at it and see that it is wide open. If that is all there is to it, who is harmed other than the liar because they have lost integrity and trust. I watched one granddaughter hit her sister and I asked her why she hit her sister and her response was, "I didn't hit her." I was not dreaming. I saw it 30 seconds ago sitting four feet away. Neither one of these are about the impact to the person being lied to. I am back to it being about the motivation for the lie. If the lie about the door being closed was related to the liar being responsible for closing the door then that might be similar to the hitting example. The lie was intended to protect the liar.

If I added, Fred must have opened the door, then it becomes blame. Many lies are self-protection and many are self-inflation (making the liar look or sound better than reality). Others are about hurting someone else, such as blaming someone for something or simply stating negative comments about someone (that are not true) in order to change someone's perception of them. It seems so far that the degree of lies maybe has to do with the intended purpose.

Lies and perception have a great deal to do with each other because neither is dependent on the truth or even evidence. That does not answer the question about whether there are actually white lies and if so, can they be defined? Does it matter? Is a lie a lie?

There is at least one type of lie that is not in these two categories and that would include the first "door is closed" example. It was clearly a lie, but for what purpose? Some people just lie. They are pathological liars. They do exist. All of these variants of this ramble and I have not gotten any further on my initial trigger of whether I was lying to my children by omitting some things. Not everybody needs to know everything, right? Organizations of any kind could not work effectively if everybody needed to know everything. That is why people have different roles and one of my roles as a parent is to protect my children. It seems like that is just rationalization and it really was a lie, but a justifiable one that was made only to protect them. They might still think it was kind of snaky.

I looked down at the floor and saw a very large snake slithering past my feet. I jumped and startled awake. I had fallen asleep somewhere through this ramble and the snake appeared in my dream, but I did look down again just to make sure. I am not one for analyzing dreams, but this one seemed overly obvious. Sometimes rambles turn into dreams and the ramble can continue through the dream. That does not make the dream any more or less relevant so it really doesn't matter when I fell asleep. It does however matter what time it is now. I need to leave in about 15 minutes. I got Reggie his supper, which he eats extremely fast, and then let him outside for his backyard stroll.

It's 5:45 and I have 45 minutes to make it to the park. I hadn't thought of this before but I started to wonder if 'they' were watching my house and if they would follow me. I took pretty much the same path that I had earlier and of course my wallet is in the bag and the phone was off. Actually both phones are off. I brought my new regular phone and the prepaid that I had used with Zack. I kept looking in my rearview mirror for any signs of being followed and I didn't see anything but that's no guarantee.

I pulled into the parking lot right on time and I could see what I assumed to be them, sitting at a picnic table. It was not the one under the pavilion. It was a small park but it was mealtime and there was a family using the pavilion and the park grill. The park had a fairly long windy entrance and I sat in my car for a couple of minutes waiting to see if another car would pull in. It didn't so I walked over to Zack and Sharon and sat down. "I want to thank you for meeting me. I really appreciate it. There is so much going on, I need to talk to someone that might understand. But first I have to ask if you think there is a chance that they would be following me. I looked for any signs and didn't see anything but I don't want to add risk to others." They said that they weren't worried about this conversation and then they said they were glad to do it. Sharon asked, "Would you mind recapping for me what has been going on?" That was my plan anyway so it was a good lead-in. Zack knew some of it, but even he didn't really know the whole story.

I started with what is now only about 48 hours ago. I shared the way the door was breached, the way I was thrown down and restrained, and the questions they asked. I covered the next morning and my discoveries of what was missing, including the clothes laid out for me, and the message on the replacement computer. They seemed genuinely surprised at the situation with my clothes. I covered what I had done regarding replacement of missing property, my visit to the police, my call to the FBI, my behaviors with getting cash, when I used cash and when I used my credit card, and pretty much everything I had done. I almost forgot to tell them about the two incidents with the black car and the federal government plates.

When I stopped they almost simultaneously said, "Wow." Sharon added, "That's a lot for 48 hours, even for the government. And no encounters prior to two nights ago?" I wondered if maybe they had second thoughts regarding not being worried about me be followed, but I didn't ask and just said, "No, nothing that I noticed. It just seemed to start with a bang, literally."

I jumped right in before they could ask more, "Before I get to my long list of questions I have to ask if you know of others that have experienced anything like this and do you know what the hell is going on?" There was actually a bit of a smile from both of them before Zack said, "Well the clothes and the crappy computer are things that I haven't heard, but the rest is in a category of things that have been happening more than the vast majority of the country would believe. We think we know quite a bit of *what* is going on, it is the *why* that is difficult to prove. *Prove* is a loaded word because it implies that there is someone to prove it to that might care." Well, that was a loaded answer that probably added 5 more questions to my list. I said, "I would love to just sit and have a conversation, but I have so many questions that I want to make sure that I ask. Do you mind if I just use my list and ask you questions?" I'm going to use the list but I also have to improvise a little, so my first question is, "Should

I be scared? What can they do to me?" Again, I got a bit of a smile indicating that I was not the only person to ask this type of question.

Zack started with, "We can't tell you whether to be scared or not. As for what they can do, I think you have seen a pretty good indication that they can do most anything they choose to. While what they have done to you is bad, imagine if they did something like locked *all* of your funds or took your house. There seems to be no rules or accountability for them. Actually there probably is accountability to someone or some group that is directing them on what to do or at least what *types* of things to do, but there seems to be no accountability that is in our favor." Sharon added, "Most of us have decided to be careful, but *not* afraid. Being afraid would change who we are and most of us are not willing to do that. I believe that us being afraid is part of what they want and I am not going to give them that." I could relate to that response but I wanted to understand a little more.

Two questions come to mind that relate to a couple of items on my list. As much as I have rejected the question, looking at it in a different light I asked, "Why me? What is it that I did that triggered this and what do they want?" Again the smiles but this time they explained. "We are certainly not laughing at you and this is serious business, but you have hit three of the most prominent and important questions right off the bat. People do not understand why they would be targeted because they are not criminals. They have not robbed a bank and most don't even have traffic tickets. We are law-abiding citizens; one would argue more law-abiding than those targeting us. Most people are actually afraid to know *why them*. For this we can probably help, but we will need to know more about you in order to confirm the pattern." They are talking about patterns. I like them.

Zack continued, "We would like to ask a few questions before explaining our beliefs." The fact that he used the term "beliefs" set off a little bit of concern. It was just a word that indicated that they believed something as all do, but the word belief has a religious-type connotation for some. I need to know more so I agreed, "Ask away."

This time Sharon was asking, "Would you consider that you have fairly strong opinions on political matters? Do you ever talk about political matters or matters of the government on social media or in email? Have you ever had any of your comments blocked or flagged on social media? Have you communicated your opinions in other forms? Do you search the internet for government published information? Do you search for news stories? Have you ever attended political rallies, stores, booths at fairs, or donated to a political cause? Do you write to congressmen at the state or federal level? Do you post negative reviews about anything (not just political or government related)?" Wow. This almost sounded like interrogation questions, but it didn't feel that way. There was an obvious pattern that I was pretty sure would be verified soon. The simple answer to all of the questions was yes. Sharon paused for a moment and then continued, "I am interested in a bit more detail for curiosity's sake, but your answers checked all of the boxes. Just one more question; do your political views differ from the current administration?" I almost wanted to say "duh", but I kept it to "they sure do."

Zack jumped in with "Suspicion confirmed. Everyone in the group and every example that we have of other targets are all of the mindset of dissenting opinions from the current administration." With all of the things that I had seen and heard via the 'underground news', general conversations (that could be rumors), and now my recent personal experiences, that seemed plausible. However most of the examples making the 'news' were about famous or at least highly visible people. In one way that would seem to make them more likely to be a target because of their status and in another way you would think it would make it harder for them to be targeted, and yet they have been in some unbelievable ways. I let out a very audible sigh, leaned back, and said, "Damn."

Where do I begin? I guess this is not a complete surprise, but hearing it out loud from someone else is different. It seemed like minutes were passing in silence like they both understood that I needed a little time to process this. I sure did. I started with, "I think it is my turn for some questions now." They both nodded. "I think it is possible that a number of my questions have been answered already but let me ask, and I may even take a shot at answering them myself. Let me know if I am off, okay?" Again, nods.

I looked at the list, took my pen out and checked off:

√ Share details about the FBI events, cars, and messages.

√ Who do you think is behind this?

√ How many that you know of have had similar experiences as me?

√ If we are not doing anything illegal, what can they possibly do?

Next:

- Should I get a lawyer?
- What would be the drawback to going public (news media)?

"I am going to group two questions together. The first relates to getting a lawyer and the second is about going to the news media. I believe that the answer would be that it might not be a bad idea, but I am not going to find a lawyer or a news channel to take my story or case. The lawyers that might take it are already working on high profile cases and being paid very well. News media is not going to run my story because they seldom (if ever) run anything like this even if it's related to high-profile cases. We are just the little people and those options may not be dead for us, but they are old and weak. The underground media might not be afraid to run the story, but with the high-profile stories and the quantity of non-high profile ones would just have me buried as an insignificant blip. I would likely not be of any special interest other than a number to add to the list of casualties. How did I do?"

Zack jumped in on this one, "You are very close but I will add a little more for clarification. We actually have a lawyer in the group that would likely be willing to take the case, however he has taken two cases to court and they were thrown out. So finding a lawyer is not impossible, but achieving anything does seem highly unlikely. The justice system has changed. As far as going public, the standard news media is not going to care about your story, in fact they might be more likely to turn your attempt to share your story against you and call you a conspiracy theorist. You are right about the underground news media and the volume of low priority cases. There is one other method that you didn't mention and that is social media. Again, the standard social media reviewers will likely shut you down with a claim of false accusations. You would very likely be banned from the platforms as well, not just your story. There are still the groups on Tor and you will find a lot of sympathetic ears there but it is not the sympathetic ears that will have impact." I took it all in and summarized, "So you are saying I'm screwed?"

Sharon looked a little sad and said, "I wouldn't have put it quite like that, but in the context that you are asking, I would say so." Without thinking about jumping to another question I said, "So what am I supposed to do now? Does anybody have any plans to fight this individually or as a group?" And just like that I had covered two more questions:

√   What would you suggest for next steps?

√   Does anybody have any plans of how to address this either individually or as a group?

It was Zack's turn I guess, "There are groups out there that are attempting to do things but they are primarily focused on trying to dispense truth and education and that is an uphill battle to say the least. The government forces are so engrained in all facets of life that that they block pretty much all attempts. They are in places that you probably have not thought of yet and their methods can be harsh. Those methods work and many times they are not harsh in a way that is obvious. People get rewarded for doing their bidding. People are manipulated to see things in a way that supports the government's purpose. This manipulation is so powerful that even when someone sees something that is obviously a lie. It is 'excused' because of who it is or whom it supports.

"This did not happen overnight. This has been evolving for decades and has become so engrained in society that a turn in the other direction could take decades as well. The efforts to turn the direction are met with very powerful roadblocks that do things in the name of 'protecting society.' It is because of these types of things that we are not a group that is trying to fight the machine. We are more of a survivalist group. We are cautious, we apply technologies in a way that helps us keep a low profile, and we share information with each other."

I really had a hard time believing what I was hearing. I understand the power of the government and how pervasive the problem is, at least I think I do, but this sounded like hiding. "Zack, Sharon, I appreciate your honesty and what you are sharing, but I am confused." Zack said, "I know. It is a lot to take in." My response was quick, "That's not it. I am confused by you and your statement that you choose not to be scared and let these things that you have described change your lives. It seems like that is exactly what it has done, and what you are doing is hiding."

Zack started to say something but I said, "Please let me finish. I know that the government is powerful and their arms reach everywhere. I am not saying that I know what to do to fight it, but damn it, this is wrong in so many ways. Up until two days ago, I still believed that I had rights and that laws meant something and I still believed that I lived in the United States of America. I know things are at risk and I saw things happen that are warnings and even appalling, but it seems like someone flipped a switch. I refuse to accept that I have lost my freedom of speech or maybe even my freedom of opinion. I am not even a person, if all I do is what I am told." There was a bit of a pause and Zack said, "And *that* is why you are a target." This time we all smiled.

Zach said, "I think it would be a really good idea for you to meet with John. He can provide you a bit more insight into tactics. He has been in a lot of roles in his life that have given him a different perspective on the activities. Before moving on to that, are there any remaining questions?" I check the list quick and said, "Just a couple of housekeeping items like, how do I contact you going forward (assuming it is okay)? Can you recommend a particular fully encrypted email? And is there any reason that I shouldn't replace my computer(s)?" Sharon said, "I'll take these. You have Zack's prepaid number and here is mine. You can call me anytime." She handed me a piece of paper that said "girl" and a phone number. She continued, "The list that we gave you regarding practices and technologies has an up-to-date technology recommendation list in the back. I use the first one in the encrypted email technology list. Getting a replacement computer is fine, but I would strongly recommend that you keep everything on it and everything backed up outside of it encrypted. Even that doesn't mean that they won't still find a way to access what you are doing but it makes it harder. That is one of the reasons that Tor is listed as a consideration but not a recommendation, because the government is known to have created viruses on Tor. For that reason as well, please use one of the recommended virus protection packages that are less likely to have cooperated with the government to allow government viruses.

"I could go on and on, but there is a lot of info in that document. When it comes down to them accessing your data for their purposes, they will do *anything* including create data that is magically *your* data. Yes, no surprise. They will falsify evidence and they will lie. And why will they lie? They will lie because they are protecting the safety of the people."

She was clearly stating that is what they would say, but they were protecting themselves and their own power and control. I asked, "Do you have a guess of what they want from me?" Zack said, "That seems pretty clear from the message on your replacement computer, RETIRE. They want you to stop. Stop doing what you are doing and that likely includes anything that disagrees with them, questions them, or makes them look bad in any form. But be advised, their desire for you to stop can quickly turn to revenge and a desire to just crush you." What I thought sounded bad a few minutes ago has somehow become worse. This is going to take a while to process and I told them that. I also said that I would like to meet with John as well. I must have thanked them twenty times for meeting with me and for all of the insight. Somehow hugs seemed in order. This was not a business meeting; it went deeper than that.

We left the picnic table together but left the park a few minutes apart. It was just one of those things that seemed appropriate, but there is no indication that it actually did any good. It seems that not much will actually solve any problem other than doing whatever 'they' want. Even then there is no guarantee because if they want you they will make shit up and they will lie. There are no white lies here because they will say that everything that they do is for the benefit of society and that lie becomes the justification for the 'honorable' intent of the white lie. *There are no white lies.*

Chapter 15

Artificial Intelligence

Late Night Day 3

On my drive home my head is just spinning and I realize that I am not checking for anyone following me because right now it doesn't seem to matter. I don't even really remember driving as I am pulling in my driveway. I park in the garage and just sit, let my head fall back, and close my eyes. This has been an exhausting day, especially tonight. What the hell has happened to my country and even to anything logical, moral, or rational? Where did the laws of the land and rights go? It seems pretty clear based on tonight that they are gone. I wonder seriously (only for a moment) what other country I could live in. Right now this seems like a place I don't want to live. I lift my head slowly and walk inside.

Of course Reggie is happy to see me and I sit down and talk to him for a while. He's a good listener. I am not sure why I turned the TV on, but I did. Maybe I'm looking for a little normalcy. As soon as I thought that, I realized it was a stupid thought, there is nothing normal about TV (at least not by *my* definition of normal). There was a documentary about artificial intelligence on. I probably felt more like watching cartoons than a documentary, but I was too lazy to look through the channels so I left it. As tired as I was the TV started to attract my attention. I heard words like "predict" and "prevent", and then I heard "we can start to know what people are thinking."

All of this, of course, was being presented in a positive light. By knowing what people are thinking and predicting their actions we may be able to start to get a grip on some of the violence that has been running rampant. Murders, rapes, and mass shootings have been escalating for a long time to a point where the places that people go and what they do have dramatically changed. There are places that used to be very popular attractions, but the amount of people willing to go there has dropped by 70%. Most of those businesses no longer exist and yet leaders in those areas will say everything is under control and it is safe. Their own data shows otherwise. Just another lie, but here comes someone with an approach to curb violence. That will get some support.

Now I start paying more attention. Knowing what I do about how data can be used it was easy for me to see where this was going. They talked about the massive amounts of data available from various sources and how the access to all of that data was to everybody's best interest. By assessing certain types of patterns and behaviors, conclusions could be drawn on the probability for someone to take particular actions. They were framing this in the context of preventing murders, but of course the same technology could be applied to finding the probability of *any* action or behavior, such as disagreeing with the government. Of course they talked of probability as though it was fact and as though it was proof. That idea of proof is just another concept that has been or will be lost in the name of protecting people.

They were listing all sorts of sources of data that I would not have thought of or would have thought to be off limits without a warrant or at least some just cause. Here again, it seems more and more evident that the just cause is that it is being done for the betterment of all people and to make society better. They were not just talking about obvious sources such as internet searches, social media, purchases and location data. They included banking information, private emails, texts, and something called behavior recognition. This is similar to facial recognition but goes beyond that. People have unique behaviors in their movements, speech patterns, the clothes they wear, the time they get up and go to bed and the food they eat. Imagine being able to identify a person by behavior patterns or being able to predict future behaviors by current behaviors. Someone is buying a gun and their behavior patterns before and while buying a gun can predict their likelihood of committing a crime with that gun. When you combine that with all of the other information about that person, the accuracy is increased dramatically. They could stop crimes before they happened.

They went on and on about what a great achievement it would be and the sources of data were just matter-of-fact and the other potential uses were never mentioned except for one. Imagine how it could be used to make your life easier. Something could predict your every want and desire. The shopping could be done before you even thought of doing it. You would never run out of things or find yourself saying, "I wish I would have thought of getting xyz." In other words, it knows what you are going to think before you do. They went on to explain how close the technology was to this being a reality and what aspects are already in place.

It is crazy how much is in place and you know that they are not divulging everything. This seems to be how it has progressed. Nobody has said, "We are going to watch your every move and evaluate you to determine if you are a threat to us." Of course they didn't say that and they wouldn't. They wrap it up in a slow moving message of, "We are helping you and we are protecting." They were essentially saying it's a good thing that you don't have to even think anymore, we will tell you what you are going to think. How is it that this is not terrifying to most and that most do not understand what they would be giving up?

Artificial intelligence they say. All this really means is that someone has written a program to do things faster than they can. It is still their logic, still their will, and still used for their predetermined objectives. When you add that to the increased processing power and the access to massive amounts of data, the power and invasion into personal space is undeniable. And yet, nobody seems to be complaining about the invasion, about the unauthorized access to personal data, or the conclusions that are used as though they are facts when they are no more than computed assertions. This ramble has quickly turned to an internal rant because the insanity of it is overwhelming.

I see the reason not to feed the machine information about anything that can be avoided, but the reality still exists that if driven to do so, false 'evidence' seems to be no issue. I have no idea what, if anything, they have made up about me or if they used any type of AI to get to me being a threat. As I go over the discussions and discoveries of the last couple days I can see that if they are threatened by those that simply disagree with them, I have provided them with plenty. And now they have my unpublished blogs and the first few chapters of my new book. My new book has a working title of "The Inherent Corruption of Government." It is actually not about this government but about how the structure, purpose, and power of government inherently leads to corruption, regardless of which government. I'm sure that they wouldn't recognize that nuance and see the book's title itself as a threat. They wouldn't have likely known about that book prior to taking my computer, but they have it now.

The unpublished blogs that they now have include Anti-Social Media, Misinformation, A New World Order, Separation of Church And State, The Myth of Science, and Conspiracies Are Real. Like the Corrupt Government book, the conspiracy blog is not about a particular conspiracy, but rather about describing the definition, behaviors, and reality related to conspiracies. There are quite a few more and yes I do pretty consistently disagree with the government. I did write a lot, but much of it had not gone public. It is unlikely that they had them before unless they had hacked my network or my external backup storage. That makes it unlikely that those things are what triggered me being a target. If you are allowed to combine all data in any way that you want (which they seem to be) there is plenty more that can be added. I have certainly commented on a few ridiculous social media posts and have written other books that *are* published. These books are not political but there are obvious personal philosophies contained in the books that reflect perspectives that are contrary to some of the administration's positions.

I understood that they were contrary to some of the current rhetoric, but I never mentioned any current politics or disagreements with any politicians. I probably used some key words that triggered something like *freedom, privacy, rights, racism, equity, chaos,* etc. I encouraged people to think rather than telling them what they should think and there is probably nothing more threatening than that.

There is no artificial intelligence required for those triggers but if you added my behaviors such as searches related to definitions of words, government statutes, government provided statistics, as well as calling and emailing senators, they would have even more. Sharon's questions came flashing back to me. Now add every possible piece of information such as what I ate, most of what I said, what I looked at, how my body movements change, when I went to the bathroom, when my heart rate changed, and a system large enough to store and process all of that information and you have a plausible story that you can not only predict what I will do, but what I am thinking and why. I can almost guarantee it would be wrong, but plausible.

It is plausible because it seems that people will believe anything and proof means nothing, even when there is exculpatory evidence. The conclusion bias will cherry-pick the information that leads to a forgone conclusion. This happens a lot today but add the perceived validation of a computer and who is going to feel that they can argue with that? The power of intimidation. This is not fantasy. This data is collected today on so many people and it is done with little to no resistance because of the pretense under which it is collected. "We are here to help. We will make your life easier."

People have a hard time with this concept and believe it to be centuries away, if at all. It is mostly in place today. A toy seller can track how many times (when and where) you looked at a particular type of toy, how many kids you have that fit the profile, your propensity to buy based on sale prices, your preferred stores, your income, where you live, all related holidays and birthdays, know when you pull into a parking lot at a store that carries the product to send you a notice of a 1 hour sale on that item, and when you get to the aisle with the product to send an additional 10% off for the next 10 minutes. If someone selling toys can do that (and more) what can a government do with all of its money and power? How much would a government be willing to do for control of a country as compared to the sale of a toy? People understand that they get sale notifications at very convenient times and that after looking at something it seems to come up more in many ways, but isn't that just convenience and isn't that helping? Why do people have such a hard time transferring the capability of control and manipulation to other objectives?

Okay, I know I went off here for a bit, but this whole situation brings things to greater light than I have known and understood for some time. Like others, it is hard for me to believe that it is really happening and to the degree that was thought to be very unlikely (if not impossible) in this country. I look back at the TV and they are still praising the advancement, and the convenience and safety that furthering AI will bring to everyone.

I look at the time and only about 15 minutes has passed. It was time for bed so I let Reggie out. I went outside with him and sat down on one of the wicker chairs. I leaned back and took a deep breath. It was not out of exhaustion. It felt as if I was taking a breath of freedom. It was like taking a deep breath before diving underwater.

Chapter 16
The Other Media
Morning Day 4

I woke this morning feeling surprisingly refreshed and ready for more. What more could there be? Something told me there would be a lot more and I also knew that I *needed* more because I couldn't just accept this. It hit me before I got in the shower that I had left my laundry in the washer yesterday, so I ran downstairs to wash them again on a quick cycle. I gave Reggie his breakfast and put some bread in the toaster for me. I grabbed my toast and went outside with Reggie again. He would normally run outside for his morning relief but I was outside and I had food. It was a nice morning and sitting outside with Reggie made this feel a little more normal. Of course, that feeling is what I wanted so it was likely a temporary illusion that I created rather than any form of reality.

While Reggie was looping the back yard I ran inside and grabbed my lists from yesterday, a pad of paper, and a pen.

My conversation last night had gotten all of those questions answered in some form and gave me a path to finish the other list. I added the two remaining items of setting up the home network and getting a computer to my new list. The two old lists will be shredded. I am still bothered by the feeling of hiding and I need to find a way resolve that, but for now the steps of protecting information about me seems appropriate.

I decide that I need to withdraw some more cash from the bank. I will likely take a larger amount out in case they decide to freeze my assets. I am definitely stepping this up a notch. I was going to get a safe deposit box or more secure home safe, but I should probably try to figure out how not to register it to my name. I need to add a more secure safe. They seemed to have no issue breaking into my current safe. I also need a supply of flash drives (some smaller and some big). I had something in mind for the flash drives. So far my list looks like this:

- Withdraw cash
- Computer
- Flash drives
- External hard drive
- Malware/virus/web scan
- Set up network
- Set up VPN
- Install virus protection
- Set up encrypted email
- Set up full encryption on computer and backups
- Check for cloud backup
- Research safe deposit box
- Research more secure safe

- Maybe talk with John

It seems like it is going to be mostly a technical day. I make sure Reggie is set, but I shouldn't be gone that long. Wallet in the bag (I need a better solution), phones off, and hit the road. The bank is the first stop. I knew I would be in for another eyeballing and drilling by the bank manager, but that's too freakin' bad. It's my money. I probably had a bit of an attitude walking in and said I would like $15,000 cash from this account and put my card on the counter. "I'm going to have to get the manager." Here comes the manager again and says, "So $15,000 in cash. What kind of plans do you have for this much cash?" I said, "I figured I'd go to the roof of the building next door and throw it over the edge so you might want to get out in the street with a net." He didn't find it funny and offered a scowl with, "Really sir, what's the real story." He asked so I told him, "The real story is that I'm sick of pompous ass bank managers asking me questions that are none of their f%#king business. Now please get me my cash unless you would prefer that I close *all* of my accounts." He said, "We can mail you the money in three days." Now I was getting really pissed off. I said, "I just got cash yesterday and it didn't have to be mailed." He was such a jerk and snottily said, "We have a $10,000 dollar per day limit." I took a deep breath to help restrain what I wanted to do and say, but just settled for, "You could have and should have just told me that instead of being such an ass. Give me the $10,000 and send me the rest of the total of all of my accounts in the mail in three days. What do I need to sign to close the accounts?" It shouldn't have been, but it was a surprise that he said, "We can't do that. We don't have someone here to close accounts. You have to call the main number." They counted out my money and I huffed, "My, isn't that convenient. You can wave around the power of the bank manager, but you really don't have any authority at all."

I know people that work in banks and other workers in other places are very limited on what they can and cannot do and that is not their fault, but it is their issue when they pretend to be more than what they are. I always try to tell people that I am dealing with that I am not upset with them personally when I am frustrated by the nonsense that I know is company protocol. This was not one of those cases. There are cases, and this *was* one of them, where they are just being an ass, and that *is* on them.

I drove off to the most reasonable place to find a computer and other peripherals. As I am wandering around the store rounding up the small items and looking at computers, I was debating whether to spend cash or use my card while I still can. I certainly should preserve my cash to use when appropriate. If I used my card, I would be identified with the sale, and the serial number of the computer would be associated with me. The serial number might be able to get them to the MAC address, which in the right circumstances could identify me. I decided to pay cash for the computer and buy the other items elsewhere. There was another store almost across the parking lot where I could get the rest and use my credit card. My shopping is done for the day, I think, so I'm heading home.

I got home and realized that between yesterday and today, I am carrying a lot of cash. My gun safe has been breached and my other safe stolen so where can I put part of it, under the mattress? Just kidding, but it did cross my mind. Bury it in the back yard? That actually might not be that bad, and then oh my God, I remembered that I had gotten too comfortable and forgot that there could be monitoring devices in the house listening and watching. In all of the questions that I asked and had answered, that one slipped by again. That is why I make lists and this was probably assumed to be under "talk to Zack". My mistake. I couldn't hide money or a number of other things until the house was swept. For the time being, I'll just carry the money.

I went to the basement where my cable comes in and started setting up the modem and got the router out of the box. My prepaid phone rang and it was Zack. He said, "John is wondering if you can by chance meet now in the same place?" I said, "Sure but it will take me about 40 minutes to get there." We were on and I headed off again after throwing my clothes in the dryer and doing the leave-the-house rituals. I grabbed my laptop and other things to bring with as well just in case.

In no time I was sitting at a familiar picnic table with John. He wasted no time, "Zach and Sharon said that they told you that you should meet with me but didn't tell you why." That was right and I told him so and he continued. "You seem to have both an attitude and an aptitude about you that they felt would likely align with my way of thinking. You also seem to be of the mindset that you cannot just sit back and do what you are told." I was adamantly nodding. "Then you should first understand more of how pervasive the control is. There was a discussion in the group and the document refers to social media a lot from a protection standpoint, but it does not address the other type of media and the information flowing in the other direction. The information that people provide to social media is important but the information disseminated from social media and the other media outlets is a significant factor in the control of the country."

This did not surprise me, but I had a feeling that there was more to come. John kept going, "If you listen to, or read, or watch any form of news media you will hear the exact same words across all of them. *Exactly the same.* This happens regularly. Even one instance would be an unbelievable coincidence across that many channels, but this happens almost daily and it happens especially when the administration wants to get a message across. When all media sources are in sync, it is easy to make a lie the truth. There is nobody to dispute the information. In order to make that work, it cannot only be about what is said, but also about what is suppressed. It is total control of the messaging. There is a word for that."

I told him that I had noticed that, but he wasn't done. "If the government controls the other media, it should be expected that the same is true for social media and now we are stepping into big tech companies. The social media companies are in far more than the social media business. They are about collecting information about people, massive amounts of data. They collect data from all sources possible including other companies and the government itself, but most of all they store it and analyze it. They create profiles of people. What better situation for control than the manipulation of all media outlets and the big tech companies with the money, technology, and resources to create and assess a full library of people? Is it sounding more and more hopeless as I go on?" I nodded and he said, "I'm not done yet.

"They need massive amounts of people to support and defend them regardless of facts. They suppress groups with large amounts of people that may believe in God-given rights and morality such as churches and religion in general. They increase the volume of people that are dependent on the government by giving them more and more and destroying the concept of self-dependence. They create hatred for those that disagree with them. Their platform becomes one of hatred for those that oppose them and one of increased dependency. They enlist (pay for) the support of large volumes of working people through unions. One significant union in that mix is the educator's union, which brings them the influence of the minds of the future. This didn't happen overnight."

I have a feeling that he could keep going for a long time so I interrupted. "This is all quite interesting and disturbing and yet not surprising. I have noticed and suspected as much for some time; I was just not sure that it truly was this organized. What is a surprise to me is that someone like me fits into this and that federal officials would somehow see me as a target. It also seemed like Zack and Sharon had some particular idea why I should talk to you." He smiled. What is it with these smiling people in the middle of this insanity? He said, "You do get to the point and you do seem to have a grip of where things are. You also seem not willing to accept it and do what you are told. Let me get to it. I am glad that you have been able to see all of this, but what I had not gotten to was the enforcement agencies' growing involvement. Judges, military, FBI, NSA,

DOJ, IRS, Attorney's General and even some police have all become part of the operations of the administration. With that level of control and resources, any disturbance in the order can become a target. Those type of targets are sweeping wider and deeper; that includes you."

Now we were deeper than I thought we would get and this does explain a few things, but I really don't know this guy. As with any source, I need to see some evidence for myself, and that would seemingly be hard to come by considering the assertion of such pervasive control. I have a few things to ask about all of this. "You are right about me not being willing to just accept this and just comply with direction. Is there any source of information where some of these things can be validated?" Jon said, "That is a very good question and I would expect nothing less.

"There used to be a news channel that would challenge the administration and investigate things that looked like they were going the wrong way. That channel no longer exists, at least not in the very public form that it did previously. The leaders of that network, as you may remember, were prosecuted for treason. The fact that they could even be charged with treason is part of the evidence. If you look at what is publicly available regarding the charges and evidence, they refer to treason against the administration, not the country. That is made quite clear and that actually was the case, and yet it sailed through. The evidence presented would have never held up in any previous court, but this became a mission to crush the enemy. It is all there in the court documents. It is bold and blatant because the premise is that very few will look and even fewer will challenge or dare to say anything. Targeting people like you just minimizes that risk.

Most of the things that I have stated and the evidence to support their approach are actually in government documents. They are never held accountable for their lies."

This is a good example but as I'm sure he would agree that it is evidence, not proof. That does not mean that I don't believe it, but this is getting deep enough that I need to be cautious. Everything I hear just keeps getting worse, but I have to ask, "So what can anybody do other than hide, which I am not a fan of?" John again grinned and said, "And that is why we are talking. You want to do more than hide. I will tell you that you are not alone even though it seems that all of the power is on the other side. There are others of us that want to do more to save our country. We are not mounting a coup, we are not trying to overthrow the government; we truly believe that truth is more powerful than lies. So many times lies seem to prevail over the truth, but this is a long-game. They used a long-game plan to get here and it will take a long-game plan to get out. In the meantime we are not hiding (as in giving up), we are being cautious on our long-game path. Their strategy is lies, deception, and misdirection and ours is to simply use their own information to slowly turn the tide. We cannot lean on the non-existent *news* media to bite the hand that feeds them."

Chapter 17
Hiding?
Afternoon Day 4

John's last comments especially seemed very intriguing and I wanted to know more. He explained to me that he wanted to make sure I had at least some of the background and state of affairs before talking about strategy and another group of people. He told me that he believes that most people run from what seems to be such overwhelming odds. I am still here; in fact it made me even more interested. The other thing is that I 'need' to know more about this strategy. I want to know what it is, who is involved, and what my participation would look like before I assess if it is right for me.

John seemed to be getting a bit nervous. After all we had been talking for about an hour and this is the same place that I had met with Zack and Sharon yesterday. He explained, "The group that you met with meets pretty much in the open and most people in that group are not aware of any other group. You are the fastest anyone has been given the opportunity to participate in another group. We know even more about you now than we did when you came to the other group and we know you have a particular mindset. This other group meets more frequently and there are quite a few more conditions of attendance. The meeting space is highly protected and secure.

"A few basics that you must understand and agree to are that the meeting time and date will never be shared in the same communication. Nobody is allowed to the meeting that has not been Faraday protected from home to meeting location. Communication with anyone in the group is only in person at the secure site or via a burner phone with full encryption. We do not write down codes, names, objectives, strategies, or anything that would expose the group (a good memory is critical). Our group has a geographic scope and we never attempt to expand beyond that scope. Even with all of the safeguards, we must limit the exposure. Of course there is a larger initiative, but the communication to and from that larger and higher-level initiative is only made from one person and nobody in the group, other than *that* person, knows who it is. I will tell you it is not me. The higher level group does not give orders, they provide us with ideas and we provide them with newly discovered risks and successes in our area.

"This will be the last time we meet like this. You can continue with the other group in the same fashion, but do not speak of this meeting." He told me the specific phone encryption service to use and his code and told me to call him on a fresh burner phone this afternoon between three and five. I had to ask one more urgent item, "The FBI was in my house and took all sorts of things as you know, but I am concerned that they may have bugged the place." He nodded acknowledging a valid concern and said, "I'll send someone over." That was it. No idea who or when.

He left and I just sat for a while. I felt more stunned with every meeting. I know that I am a reasonably intelligent person, that I stand up for what I believe, and that I have written some books and unpublished blogs, but I am still just an ordinary guy. I am a dad, a grandpa, and a retired cranky old man. I was never a politician, a wealthy businessman with influence, an attorney, a doctor, or held any position in or out of government that I felt was in any way powerful or influential. And yet, here I am seemingly about to enter some secret society that is fighting for truth and the rights that used to be a given in this country. Things seem almost futile with the total control that the government appears to have and now this. Yes, this. Is this actually hope or something else? There seem to be more people that believe it is not okay to just submit.

This idea of the truth being more powerful sounded like a good thing to say and I believe it in theory, but knowing the power and manipulation that exists, it seems like maybe too little, too late. They have power, they have authority, they have control of so much, but mostly they have no morals and the end justifies the means. They manipulate through lies and intimidation. How do you win when your opponent cheats? This is not the first time I find myself asking this question and it is one that I will ask the new group. I addressed this in one of my unpublished blogs and it has already come up in the Inherent Corruption of Government book that I started.

One example that I used was elections. How do good people that tell the truth win? The reason for asking this is that I believe it is part of the reason that we find ourselves where we are. Consider the situation where one person is saying that they are going to fix a problem (regardless of what it is and regardless of their lack of authority to do it) and the other person is truthfully saying that they recognize that there is an issue and the role that they are running for does not have the authority to fix it, but they will support others in fixing it; who will be the most popular? One is telling the truth and the other is telling bold-faced lies, and the liar will likely win. People like promises even if they are lies for some reason. They want to believe that they will be taken care of or they don't care to understand that one is lying. This seems strange to me but I think I understand that it is real. Candidates that promise free stuff never mention that somebody pays for it and that you will pay in the end either through taxes, inflation, or loss of freedom. Many people choose free regardless of the ultimate cost. Is it their greed, lack of interest, laziness, or pure gullibility? I don't think it matters why at this point, but it is a pattern. The liars and cheaters win, so how does an honest and truthful person win? Maybe they don't. It's not obvious anyway.

The answer can't be to cheat as well can it? When your opponent tells a lie, tell a bigger one? That doesn't really fit with the issue that I have with the liars, but even if I could justify it, they have been at it so long that the message matters less and less. It has become personal. The opposition attacks people rather than policy and purpose. Promoting and nurturing hate makes it even harder for the person that is hated to tell the less desirable truth. The more I ramble through this and think about any writing that I have done, there is no silver bullet that I have found. The old phrase that stated "cheaters never win" seems to be very wrong in this regard. Cheaters almost always win (in politics).

There is a principle conflict that also gets in the way. When the current government is about control and we are about freedom, they are obviously in direct conflict. Those that want freedom should understand that their own principles hamper their ability to organize a cohesive effort. How do you maintain unity amongst a group of people that want freedom and support individual choices in order to beat the 'controlling side' when your message is "leave me alone"?

Beyond that, *freedom is work*. I have come to wonder if the majority of people have just become lazy and easy is more important than freedom. Most don't associate those as a trade off, but they are. How do you convince the masses to want work over easy? Lies make everything easy if they are never challenged. I keep getting deeper into the realm of wondering how anyone can possibly win against that.

I came out of my ramble daze and drove home. The thought of how to win against cheaters is still haunting me. I am all for not submitting, but I am also all for being productive. The drive seemed to fly by in about 2 minutes. I turned the corner to my house and saw a cable van pull in my driveway. I pulled in beside him, got out of my car, and walked over to the van. He said simply, "John sent me." We walked into the garage and he waved me to stop. He punched in something on a device, set it down on the floor, and then proceeded into the house. I just watched from the doorway. He proceeded to methodically pass through the house high and low and went upstairs and downstairs. He came back and said, "You're clean."

As he was inside scanning the house I had two thoughts that it seemed I should have had before and it gave me a bit of a chill that I hadn't thought of them. The FBI leaving the clothes has always been a rather obscure event and I hadn't thought that it might be as basic as them putting listening or tracking devices in the clothes. The other thought was what about putting tracking on my car? I asked him about it and told him where the clothes and shoes were and he assured me that he would have found it if it was there. He said, "As for your car, pull it in the garage and I will check it quick." It didn't take long and he cleared my car as well.

I opened the garage door and he stated, "There was nothing anywhere here. That includes audio, video, and tracking devices. I am on my lunch break so I have to run. If you talk to the cable company for anything, please don't mention that I was here." And he was gone. It seems they didn't see me as the type of threat that justified bugging or tracking. I could read a lot into that but I'm going to leave it at that for now.

I had 3-4 hours remaining before making the call to John, so it was time to get to work on the rest of my list with the added phone encryption service. The phone encryption service was the first thing I set up to be used with the phone I had not yet used. It didn't take long. I think I am set but I checked myself to make sure that I remembered John's access code without writing it down.

I headed downstairs with the rest of my gear to set up the home network. I had set up a few in my day so most of it was a familiar task, but still not something I did every day. After a call to the cable company, the modem was working with the computer plugged in directly. They needed to register the modem because I don't use theirs like most others do. I don't like getting ripped off on monthly charges and I like to own and control what is running my network internet connection. Next the router, the encryption, the firewall, my computer encryption, and VPN, and I was set for a test drive. There were a few bumps along the way because of the extra security, but most of it seems to be ready to go and the first thing on the list is checking my cloud backups.

I had admittedly gotten lazy about changing my passwords and the backup password had been the same for about 2 years with every login since then being an automated login. That is the nature of backups, they have to work from the device they are backing up without someone having to login. Am I going to remember my password? All of my passwords are at least 12 characters long, but there is a method to my madness that would give me an indication rather than an answer. I tried once, twice, and three times and I was locked out. There was no option to reset the password after a lockout on this system. I simply got a message to try again in 24 hours. I would have to wait.

The next step was to set up full end-to-end encryption email. I would keep my old services and accounts but would not use them for anything that I didn't want the public and the government to see. I should have checked my old email first because there were a couple of interesting messages. I had just changed my email password in the last week so it was fresh in mind. One new message was from the cloud backup service saying that an unexpected access attempt was made from an IP address that they provided and because of these attempts, I would have to reset my password. I couldn't do it now for 24 hours; stupid.

There were about 100 more emails and 5 more were from accounts that had unusual login attempts tried. I saw no evidence that anybody had identified my password madness. It seems as though they really don't care if they leave evidence that they tried to get into my accounts and from what IP address. They would be so stupid or arrogant if these were real IP addresses, but I took note of all of them anyway. At first I found it interesting what accounts where flagged with these attempts and that email was not one of them. Of course, they weren't interested in taking over my email and my computer already had my existing emails. My bank accounts and any financial accounts were safer because I didn't even save my username (which isn't my email) for those accounts. They would likely have to use 'official' means to access those accounts, but I still wanted to have more cash on hand.

I still have some more things to get done but it is after 3:00 so I call John. Even though this is thoroughly encrypted communication he says, "Yep." Then paused and added, "10:00." Another pause and he asked for my encrypted email address. I told him and he hung up. About 2 minutes later I heard an email come in on the encrypted email and all it said was "tonight." I got it that there was a meeting at 10:00 PM tonight, but I had no idea where. Did he forget that I didn't know? I had to give him more credit than that and assume that he would let me know, but I really don't like making assumptions.

I had some time so I started checking my list. Only these items remained:

- Set up full encryption on computer and backups
- Check for cloud backup
- Research safe deposit box
- Research more secure safe

The first two were partially done. I had to wait until tomorrow for checking on the cloud backups and encryption is set on the computer, but I haven't set up any backups yet. The research items can be worked on. I started with researching safe deposit boxes and it didn't take me long to decide it wasn't a good idea. It would have to be in my name unless I brought someone else into this and I wasn't about to do that. It would also be susceptible to the same freeze that the government could potentially put on my assets. I did enough research on safes to know that the minimum I could probably spend would be $2,000 and many were much more than that. It had to be not easily drillable, heat resistant, able to be attached into a cement floor, and a very good combination and keyed lock together. The one for 2K was quite small but would likely work for what I needed.

I potentially needed a place for cash and for computer backups. I'm not sure what else I would put in there at this point. Putting things in various places around the house might have to work for now. It would be like an Easter egg hunt. Then there is always burying money in the back yard. That is actually not a bad idea because I have a lot of landscaped area with mulch that would be easy to dig and cover with mulch without leaving any sign of disruption. If I used plastic rather than metal, it would be even harder to find. That would probably work for some backup cash but not daily use. I still need a secure easy-to-access place.

Chapter 18
How Can You Win?
Evening Day 4

My dedicated encrypted phone rang and when I answered someone said, "Knock twice and take 5 steps back" and hung up. I figured that it must have been John, but it didn't really sound like him. A minute later the phone rang again and someone said, "432 Holbrook, Nortonville, backdoor." That was it. John sure was not kidding about a good memory being required. I estimated the drive time to be about a half hour and it was now 9:15. I let Reggie out and started my pre-travel routine with the Faraday bag and the devices off. I double-checked all door locks, made sure that the security system was set to go, and added the steps to clear the cache, cookies, and browsing history from my computer.

I am not in the habit of looking out the front door before going into the garage, but for some reason I did and I saw a black car parked in the street and one of the neighbors was standing there talking to someone in the car. I couldn't leave to this secret meeting with a suspicious car outside. I can't see the plates but I'm not going to take a chance. This could be nothing but I had to know. I was just getting ready to go out the front door with Reggie for a pretend walk so I could see the plates, but before I opened the door, the car pulled away and the neighbor walked back to their house. I couldn't clearly see the plates but they didn't appear to be the same design as a government plate. I went as fast as I could to the garage and left in a calm manner keeping an eye out for any cars going in my same direction. I saw nothing. It was a pretty quiet neighborhood at this time of night.

The first turn that I took would have taken me the opposite direction that I needed to go to Nortonville, but I went down that road for about a mile and then did a U-turn. Still nothing so I headed for Nortonville. I hadn't thought of this because everything had been so rushed, but I was not real familiar with the streets in Nortonville and I couldn't use my GPS. Fortunately it wasn't a real big town and with the address I had to assume it was not far off from the center of town. I was making good time, but not speeding, so I pulled off the road onto a county road for just a minute to see if there was any car activity around me. There was nothing that was obvious to me so I continued to the center of Nortonville, found 4th Street, and picked a direction. I would not say that I am generally a lucky person, but this time worked out well. Holbrook was only about 3 blocks off from the main street. This was a pretty typical small town for the area with at least one bar on every block covering 3-4 blocks from the center of town, a number of closed stores, a few second-hand stores, insurance companies, and few specialty eateries.

I found the building, I think, because there were no numbers on the building but the buildings on each side indicated that this would be the one. On the window was painted Nortonville Ice Cream Emporium and there was a closed sign hanging on the door. It didn't appear to be permanently closed but it *was* nearly 10:00 in a small town after all. I drove around the building and there was an alley. It was quite narrow at the beginning; it would make for quite an ambush location. As I got a few more buildings into the alley it opened to a number of small parking areas. I spotted the address on the back of the building. A sign hung above the door that said POTTERY CLASSES *By Appointment Only.*

I parked, went to the door, knocked, and stepped 5 paces back as instructed. It seemed like a very long time and I was beginning to wonder if I had done something wrong when the door opened slowly. I heard a voice from behind the door say, "Come in" and when I got to the door the same voice said, "Password?" I don't remember being given a password and I am sure I was making noises wondering what to say. I figured I better just tell them that I didn't know. John stepped out from behind the door and said, "Just kidding." Now John did not seem like a joking type person but I guess I really didn't know him. He said, "This is serious business but everybody has to smile and have a little fun once in a while. Come on in and meet the group."

I walked down a partial flight of stairs and there was a large room that was set up for pottery. I saw two big kilns in the corner and potter's wheels along the wall. In the middle of the room was a number of large tables and seated around them were what I guessed to be almost twenty people. This was a far bigger group than I expected. Keeping secrets across so many people must be difficult. John said, "We are not going to bother with introductions because you have enough to remember without flooding your head with all of these names. They will come in time. I looked around the room to see if I saw any familiar faces and there were. I saw John of course, the cable guy, and Sharon. I did not see Zack. A thin well-dressed man stood up and said, "Welcome. Thank you for coming." He was clearly talking to me and continued, "I know you are going to have a lot of questions, but it is better if we start off explaining the group, our rules, our process, and our purpose. That will likely answer many of your questions.

"Let's start with some rules:
- We don't write anything down regarding this group or operations related to this group.
- All communication within the group for group business is via agreed upon encryption methods, except in this room.
- Communication amongst individual members (outside of encryption) is acceptable as long as it is legitimate non-group business.
- We operate in complete blackout between home and this location.
- There is zero communication allowed in or out of this meeting place.
- You do not bring anybody to this meeting."

All of those things seemed quite logical and should be easy to remember. The thin man continued, "The processes might seem a little more complex, but you will get them:

- Everybody in the group has a role and we all do not need to know the details of each other's role

- We do not have a regular meeting schedule. This is our meeting place for now and the frequency is as needed. Time and date are distributed in separate communications, as you know.

- There is a higher-level leadership and coordination group above this group, but the point of contact in this group is not known to anyone other than that person. That may seem a bit overboard, but it is pure protection. Everyone in this group may get direct personal messages from the coordination group. This type of communication is purely for protection of our effort.

- We do not take orders. We are provided suggestions.

- We do not break laws.

- Our meetings are in this place until there is risk of exposure. This place is protected by some of the highest tech available. We are honored to have some quite high-level technical people in this group.

- More processes will become clear as we move on. I don't want to overwhelm you with too much.

"We are going to talk about what we do, why we do it, and how we do it next, but any questions so far?"

I said that I would wait because most of my questions are probably about how. A different person now stood up and said, "That's good because that is the meat of why we meet, but it is good to stay grounded in why we are here. Since you have made it this far, you probably have a very good idea, but I will state it clearly and concisely; we believe in the rights of the people of this country as described in the Constitution and we believe that those rights are being violated by the current government. We are committed to turning this country and its people away from the totalitarian government that has this country in the state that it is in. We believe that we can achieve this with the truth. People are being lied to and are willing to accept the lies. We need to help them see the pain that the lies cause rather than the pleasure that the lies promise. This is who we are and what we aim to achieve, to recover our country and our rights." This guy sounded like a motivational speaker or a preacher and maybe he was, but his tone was very calm and the excitement was raised by the words rather than by the tone and loudness of his voice or the waving of arms. This is what truth is about but this is a group that fits the term "preaching to the choir". We already accept the words.

He continued, "And now for the *how*, the how is a long road and we know that. We are *not* arming a military takeover and we are not forcing people to believe what we believe. Our opponents use hate and fear as their primary tools and that is not for us. Those tools are powerful and hard to overcome, but using them defeats the message of the truth. We are however not a totally passive group that just sits and waits to be hit again. We will protect ourselves, but we will do it in a planful way. And in times of immediate danger, we will defend ourselves and our family as provided for in the Constitution.

"We will use some of our opponents' strategies in that we recognize that most people are swayed by emotion rather than logic, by pleasure rather than fact, and by free rather than cost. Those are not the things that defeat us; those are the things that will let us win. We have two methods in our approach; they are misdirection to our opponent and positive emotion with truth to the people."

I was interested but without a little more meat it still sounds a little like a pipe dream that will never win. I was bursting to say something so I asked, "Can I ask a question?" He nodded and I kept going, "How can we possibly win this when they are so powerful and cheat and lie all of the time?" The response was quick, "There are more of us than you probably realize. I don't mean in a formal organization, but people that are sick of one thing or another and are starting to recognize that freedom has been lost. The short answer to your question is that we turn their efforts back on them. They lie, we tell the truth and expose the lie, but more than that we offer the results that spur emotion. We emphasize the value of safety in our streets, the look in your children's eyes, and we expose the real cost of *free*. We do not do this through coercion and lies; we do it by being part of the people in all facets of life. Bad is still bad regardless of the government and sad and happy are real emotions that can be addressed. We offer potential solutions rather than simple hatred. Small successes will lead to a groundswell. We bring about a way of thought that starts to permeate into all professions and all areas of the country. That does not happen fast and in order to do that we need to protect our effort. They will lie about us and we cannot stop that, but we can make it harder. We can make it harder by not giving them fodder for their lies, but rather giving them the opposite. We give them the perception of what they say that they want us to be. This is the misdirection that they use on the people and we will use it on them. That is why we don't go totally dark. We become, if anything, more visible in the 'acceptable' things that we do. We make unencrypted phone calls and meet with people and have parties and all the things that a happy member of society does. We do not misdirect the people; we *redirect* the people to the truth. We do this, not to hide or accept, but to win. That is how we win when others cheat."

That was getting closer to what I was looking for, but it still had a bit of fairytale feel to it. That is possibly related to my cranky old man state of mind. I see no need to pull punches and be anything other than blunt. Then again, that feeling was born in a country where free speech actually existed. I don't have any idea of an alternative and it seems at least plausible, but I'm not sure how I will hold up to this under-the-radar mentality. I let them know how I was feeling about it and they said they appreciated the honesty. A number of people said that they initially felt the same until they got further in; there was also an admission that a couple of people had dropped out for similar reasons.

Details or examples of actions would maybe help, but I imagine the details will become evident over time. A person, this time a woman, spoke, "The details of these actions are individual to our skills, aptitude, and our passions. Now that you have an overview, let me introduce you to the group. Don't worry about the names for now, but you may find that our occupations provide a little insight into our roles in the group. We are from various locations around our group's area that covers four counties. John, who you know, is a professor at the state university and like you has had many careers in his life. He is also our initial screener/greeter for the group. Sharon, who you also know, is a computer programmer and cyber security designer. Carl is the cable guy, but is a general electronic device specialist. Tim is ex-military intelligence. Jennifer is a senior director and at one of the local fortune 50 companies. Will is a minister. Sam is a waste management truck driver. Gabe works in manufacturing at Homer Industries and is a union rep. Hank is the mayor of Brayton. Charles is a pilot, Bob is a retiree and greeter at a big box store, Melanie is a doctor, and Sam is a corporate attorney. We have Mary that is a city hall clerk, and Tom is an ironworker and sculptor. Kelly is a reporter at Channel 7 News and I am Terri, a kindergarten teacher and member of the educator's union. There are a couple of people that are not here. We ask that you try to attend when notified but people have lives that they must maintain and sometimes it is not possible without drawing unnecessary attention. As you can see, we are a diverse group and have varied talents as well as varied interests, but we also have a common desire to recover our rights. I know this has been a lot, but after all of this what questions do you have?"

Yep, my head was spinning a bit but I took it all in and the intentional diversity was obvious. The 'movement', if you will, had to be growing outside of this group or it would defeat the purpose of the group. All of these thoughts and more went through my head while the introductions were proceeding, so I was ready for the question.

I began, "This group represents an impressive cross-section of local society that I assume presents opportunities for both influence as well as keeping a pulse on different factions of society. I assume this is by design and I also assume that people are not selected for this group primarily for the diversity, but rather because of their common desire and passion and then filtered by the diversity to maintain the right balance in the group for size and efficiency. That makes sense for the make-up of this group, but the objectives are not about this group. The promotion of the growth of the *movement*, or whatever you may refer to it as, outside of this small group has to be extremely important. So question 1 is, how is that growth managed and maintained? Question 2 is, how do I fit into this diverse and efficient model?"

Terri said, "I have to answer your second question first. Your summary and questions are the type of observation and deductions that add value to the group. You have an ability to rapidly see patterns and form reasonable conclusions regarding those patterns. The patterns of behavior of the government and the people in our area are key to our success. You also have a very diverse background including a very important understanding of data management and accurate analysis. We know that your propensity is to speak out and not hold back so some of this approach might seem difficult at first, but we also know that you can see the big picture and should be able to fairly rapidly see the benefits of your participation in our approach."

Terri continued, "We would suggest a couple things for you. Your city has two open at-large city council positions and the window for declaring candidacy closes in one week. We suggest that you run. These are non-partisan positions and there is expected to be very low participation of candidates. Even if you don't win it gives you a perfect reason to get out and meet people, starting with your neighborhood. Second, we suggest that you join the local chapter of MENSA (we know you qualify). This is more opportunity to meet people and have discussions in a hopefully more logical construct (but no guarantees). That is for starters and now for the first question."

She took a deep breath and started again, "Trying to keep track of the growth and approach outside of this group is recognized as a challenge, but the activity is not completely invisible to us. There are other groups such as the one you originally attended. We have temporary involvement with some of those, and some are created on their own. Nobody in those groups, other than the members of this group, can know any operational information about this group including its members. We track general swings of interests and influences but since this is under the radar, we do not have any communication or coordination with the masses. We have a small group working on just that issue and we would like you to join that group. We would then run any potential proposal past the higher-level group before executing. We do have a method to submit ideas to the next level without knowing anything about that level, its members, or this group's primary contact."

Okay, that was not the answer I was hoping for, especially when you combine lack of communication, lack of tracking, and the fact that it seems to be a very long-range plan. I had to say something about it. "This seems to be a major gap in your plan. With the structure and plan that you have for this group, how can it be that you have no way to track or communicate with the people that you are trying to educate and influence? Honestly, this seems like a lot of good and well-intended people without a complete plan. I don't mean to insult the effort that has likely gone into getting things this far, but I don't see how this can get to the masses of people that it will take to turn things around."

I could tell that I had offended some people but in my true form, I didn't care. I don't have time to waste. There was silence so I thought I better say more. "I know this is a long-game but even a long-game requires a fully executable plan. Excuse me if I am off base with my comments. I am more than willing to admit if I am wrong and I am also willing to participate in the group to see what we can come up with. I know that we just met and that there is no way that I can have the full picture of everything that you are doing, so I am just offering you my first impression based on what you have told me and what I have observed. I understand that I cannot be this blunt with the general public in trying to turn things, but I need to know that it's okay to be blunt in this group. If it's not, I should probably wish you well and just move on." I think this was maybe even more disarming than my first comment. Again, there was silence.

John broke the silence with, " The purpose of this meeting was for us to meet you and you to meet us. It seems that we have provided each other additional information. It is required that we now meet as a group to discuss what has been said. With that, your portion of this meeting is adjourned and I would ask that you just remember to stay bagged until you are home. We will be in touch." It felt like a "Don't call us, we'll call you" dismissal. I'm not sure it was, but it did feel like it. I said, "Thank you. It was good to meet you all and regardless of what is happening here, I wish you well. It is a just cause." And with that I turned and walked up the stairs. I believe I heard a few faint thank-yous and goodbyes, but nobody was speaking for the group.

I was in the alley once again and the day was getting close to an end with a feeling of surrealism. I had a lot to think about on the way home. I assumed that they were talking about whether I was appropriate for the group and if not, what actions they would take to protect themselves. I assumed that they would move the meeting place. In addition to my inherent cranky old man perspective that allows me to not care what people think of me, I reminded myself that I didn't ask for this. They asked me to this meeting. It's not like I was applying for a job that I really wanted. On the other hand, I believe in what they are trying to do, maybe just not completely the way that they are doing it. I believe in staying open to new ideas and some of what they suggested makes sense.

I realize that I have just been sitting in my car in the alley and haven't started driving yet. I'm not sure if I did that subconsciously thinking that they would come out before I left, but it is time to get going. I am just about to the end of the alley and a car pulls in. It's a cop car. Shit! The car parked and I am feeling a little bit panicked. I think it is more about not wanting to expose the group than concern for anything I have done. The officer gets out of the car and is shining a flashlight on me. I can tell by the uniform that it is a county sheriff. He comes next to my window and I roll it down. "What are you doing in this alley at this time of night?" The best lies are somewhat based on truth and if someone was watching me, they would know where I went so I said, "I was just trying out a pottery class." I heard his radio "squawk" twice and then silence. He pointed in the direction that I had come from and said, "Would you mind backing up to a parking spot so we aren't blocking the alley?" I found this quite odd because I have never seen police care about what road they are blocking when making a stop and this was an alley late at night. Something was going on and red flags were up all over the place, but I had no idea what to do other than to go along.

I backed into a parking stall and he parked next to me rather than in front of me. He got out of his car again, but this time with no light. He came to the window and instructed me to "Get out of the car." It occurred to me that he has not asked me for my identification. The idea that he would ask me to get out of the car without knowing who I was or checking warrants seemed unlikely, which means he probably already knows who I am. What could I do to protect the group? That was all I could think. He looks at me and with a wave says, "Go on in the pottery shop." I assume the door is locked and I won't be able to get in so no harm. I walk to the door with him right behind me as if trying to use me as a shield. It was then that I realized what a large man he was. I knocked and waited. As expected, nothing. I was waiting for the other shoe to drop and it did. He said, "Knock again." He paused and then continued, "And take 5 steps back." What the hell? Had he been watching? He stood next to me as the door opened and I heard a voice from behind the door, "Come on in. I see you've met Deputy Sheriff Mike."

John stood up and said, "Welcome back. This is Mike, one of the members that was working tonight. Come in." As we walked he explained more, "This was not set up for no reason; we did need to discuss your membership, especially after your statements. We want you to be a member of this group; it was unanimous (which it must be) and your statements made it even more evident that you can likely add great value. You were close to right with your assessment, so we will set you up with the small team."

I found out that there truly was no radio wave communication out of the building, but they had a single hardwired button that sends a number of interrupts to Mike depending on the decision. Obviously two was for yes. I also found out that the back door, the entire alley, and the front of the building had heavy camera coverage so they would not let anybody in that they didn't know. There was really nothing special about 5 steps back except a better view for the cameras and the fact that someone knew to do it.

Terri explained more about making recommendations and suggestions to the next level up. "There are some people, primarily anyone that wants to, that have the ability to make direct suggestions. The coordinating group requires that anybody wishing to make recommendations directly set up a phone that allows that group to wipe your phone anytime they want. That same phone is also used for an additional authentication method. You would be sent a code to that phone that was good for 20 seconds and then it would change. You are also given a fob that plugs into your computer which is encrypted and communicating via VPN to the central virtual server array that is widely distributed, moved frequently, and never uses any major hosting facilities for the servers." So, some things are written down but it seems only into this system and only under these special conditions, and I have no idea what happens to it after it is submitted.

Terri said that I should stick around for a minute or two and meet with the small team to discuss the logistics of meeting. The team is Tim, Sam, Carl, and Sharon. I said hi to the team and made a request. "I am retired from my full-time position and my other activities are very flexible. This is the most important activity that I have going on right now so I can meet pretty much anytime. If you don't mind I would like to start with understanding what you have going on or have been working on in this regard. I know it's late so I expect that people need to get going, but I would like to ask one quick question." They all said, "sure." "Do you have the ability to store data in some form of a database in a very secure method that you would trust?" Sharon answered with, "Possibly." The way that I asked that question would mean that the answer was really no. I wanted to keep asking questions, but they would come. Sharon walked over to a wall and looked at a sheet hanging on the wall. It was a schedule for the pottery shop. She said, "Does tomorrow night at 9:00 work for everyone?" Head nods all around. That was it for the night and we all headed for the door. Terri was still there and said, "I'll take care of shutting down and locking up. Good night all."

This time pulling out of the alley had no surprises, thank God. I'm still not sure I know or believe how you win when others cheat, but it has been another very long day. I am home in no time and feeling exhausted. I let Reggie out for a bit and hit it.

Chapter 19
Friends, Family, and Neighbors
Morning Day 5

It seems like I just laid down and it is morning and I don't usually sleep through the night. I can't say that I feel refreshed, but there is too much going on in my head to try to sleep any more.

It is time for the morning routine with Reggie, and I am appreciating that routine more every day. It seems one of the few constants in my life these days. It also makes me feel worse about leaving Reggie as much as I have been. I took an extra long time sitting outside with him. It is a great fresh morning. It reminds me of days of camping with my kids and fixing breakfast over a campfire. I'm going to call my kids today.

It didn't take long for the events of last night to come to the forefront. Without rehashing everything, it seems that their desired short-term assignments for me seemed to fit a pattern of making me a 'people person.' I have never considered myself a people person and even less so the older I get. I have always been somewhat shy and yet able to perform in front of thousands and give speeches to very large crowds. I guess it's the one-on-one chitchat, especially with people that I don't know that has always been outside of my comfort zone, and that seems to be where they are suggesting I go. Maybe they really don't know me very well.

After a little consideration, I think I am going to file for a city council position and get out and meet people. The chance of being elected even with the support of the group would be minimal and probably close to zero without, but I will likely learn along the way and I can't sit and do nothing.

I am not going to follow the recommendation to join MENSA at this point because the intelligent people that I know and respect do not belong to MENSA. I know people in MENSA and they are, pretty much without exception, an arrogant self-righteous group of people. My exposure to MENSA members is limited but I will pass on that one for now.

I give in to the beckoning of the day and go inside to start the research for the city council process. It is actually quite easy. Fill out a single one-page form, have it notarized, and take it to city hall with $5.00. That is it. I should be a registered candidate by noon. I will need to decide if I am going to do any campaigning other than door-to-door meeting people such as yard signs, flyers, and ads. There was a cut-off of reporting campaign funds of over $750 and I can't imagine that I would spend anything close to that. I need something to leave at doors if people weren't home and I should have a website and email for contact and information. The website and email will be easy; I have set up dozens over the years for various endeavors. It also doesn't need any special security because this was very public activity and there will be no money changing hands. That thought makes me wonder if the other side will do something to smear me if they see me running for office. I'm not sure it matters unless they think that me running for community office has something to do with what they wanted me to stop. I can't spend all of my time trying to understand how they might think or I will do nothing else. It is a reasonable concern, but the primary point of running is to get out and connect with friends, family, and neighbors. Winning would only be a bonus and certainly not an expectation.

I was thinking through the process of ringing the neighbors' doorbells, what I would say, and what I would leave if nobody answered. I suspect that in my direct neighborhood there would be quite a number of people that would not answer the door. Oh yea, my studio computer is gone. It had all of the professional software required to make up some good-looking flyers. I will have to find an online solution and print some with my printer before getting a larger quantity with a local print shop. It dawned on me that I hadn't noticed one way or another whether my printer in my creative space was gone. I did a quick run to the room and it is there. It sits somewhat behind the door when it's open so I hadn't even noticed. Good, one less thing that I have to replace. I can see this whole campaigning thing running away and I need to hold back a little because I tend to be all-in when I decide to do something. That is both good and bad at times. I have a lot to do by noon.

I got the form filled out and I'm not going to go back to my bank for the notary. I really am going to drop that bank but I will still need some banking services so I need to start using the local credit union where I opened an account. It also gives me an opportunity to start testing the city council discussion. I will talk to the branch manager and the banker, and that is everyone working there. That is good with me; it is a nice small start. We talk briefly about the city and my run for city council. I ask them if they have any concerns regarding matters of the city. It is a good introduction to framing up my conversation. I say goodbye to Diane and Barry and I'm off to city hall. That filing took about 10 minutes because I had to wait in line for 8 minutes for the clerk. There was one person ahead of me and they were not filing for candidacy, they were disputing their water bill. It is a small city hall. I am now a registered candidate and it is only 10:30. Off to make flyers.

I get online at home and remember that some of my design software is subscription software so as long as I remembered the password, I will be able to use it. I remembered and no two-factor auth for this. It's a good time to call my kids while the program is downloading. It was a good catch-up conversation that did not include anything that I have been subjected to in the last few days except for the city council candidacy. Surprising to me, they were not surprised. I guess they have come to expect the unexpected with me. I have tried to instill in them that they can do anything and it doesn't have to be what others expect. It was good just to talk for a while.

The download isn't quite finished yet so I decided to call a couple of friends that live in town. I will call others that don't live in town, but I am being selfish and starting with those that can vote for me. It was again more practice. I didn't make the call all about me running and I of course said nothing of the past few days. I sent a couple more texts just to check-in with a few others and the download was finished.

The structure of a flyer didn't take long. I had to write up my bio, which also didn't take long, as I had written many for various reasons. I need to add an email address, so I quickly register a domain name and set up my mail. The website will come later. These are just temporary flyers that can be updated. I wrote up some fairly generic objectives and concerns making sure to use key phrases like "serve the community", "public safety", "transparency", and "listening to the people." I won't mention, "keep the damn government out of your personal life" or "respect your privacy and rights." I hit print for 40 copies to use for my neighborhood excursion.

While I do believe in being who I am, I made use of a couple pieces of the clothes that had been left for me. I kept my own shoes and underwear but made use of the pants and shirt (no jacket). There is maybe a little bit of irony as I head out to campaign in the clothes left by the FBI. I take a casual walk to the end of the block, watching along the way to see if I can see anyone watching me. I still have the anticipation of rejection or no-answers by most. The nosey, staring, note-leaving neighbors are not exactly what I perceive to be friendly natives. For all I know, one or more of them, are responsible for sending the FBI my way. But if this government direction is going to change, it has to be supported by the 'people'. The people: friends, family, and neighbors (that I will try to assume are people).

Chapter 20
Asshole or Stupid
Afternoon Day 5

As I head out the door my mind floats to a phrase that has been in play for me for a very long time, "Asshole or stupid." It is actually on my list of books to write. This ramble was certainly triggered by the thought of knocking on my neighbors' doors and the way that they have acted toward me, but the phrase is so relevant to all of life including the government. This phrase offends some people and the nicer way of saying it might be, "They believe they are more important than you or they don't know any better." That really doesn't work for me because it is not enough to the point and it allows for all sorts of ways to worm out of being accountable for their actions. Some could say that, "under these circumstances they *were* more important" or that, "they didn't know because nobody told them" making it someone else's fault. BS. It is more likely that if they truly didn't know, it was because they didn't listen or didn't care.

Clearly there are not just two categories of people. The two categories refer to the reason that people do bad, stupid, inappropriate, rude, wrong, illegal, etc. things. Some of those words are subjective, but even if you limit it to the obvious ones all people will land there at some point because anybody can make a mistake. It is not mistakes that I refer to, some people *live* in those spaces. These repeated behaviors tell a lot about people and what you should expect of them.

An example that always comes to mind is merging lanes. The right lane ends and it seems that so many people either believe that the right lane that is ending has the right of way or they don't care (asshole or stupid). Somebody did tell them. It was on a test to get their license, but people will still not even turn their head to the left to check for traffic to merge and will run someone off the road if they don't give them the right of way. Merging is not the point, but it is often a trigger for this ramble that is another one of those rambles that is very, very close to a rant. By the time I get to the book, it likely will be.

This concept is also relevant to the people that are willing to believe the lies told by the government. They are either not thinking or they see something in it for them. Not thinking is the major kind of stupid that I am referring to and letting greed overshadow the impact to others is a kind of asshole. When people at high levels in government lie, I generally do not believe that it is because they don't know that there is proof to the contrary, and if they don't know they shouldn't be in that office. Either way, the actions have the same impact, but I like to know what characteristics I am working with.

Stupid certainly has a negative connotation but it is not an attack on a person's mental capacity. In my mind I have already clarified that stupid does not mean those that do not have the capacity to understand. That *would be* offensive but the vast majority of stupid people and people doing stupid things are stupid by choice and very much have the mental capacity. That is the stupid people to which I refer. In their mind they did not make a decision to be stupid, but they *did* make a choice. They either chose to not care to learn, to be lazy, to let someone else make their decision (which I might say is lazy), but regardless of why, they chose not to make any effort to understand and I guess that is all lazy. Regardless of why they have the ability but not the desire to understand, educating the stupid is far more possible than educating the assholes that operate on pure emotional arrogance and disregard for others. They believe that they already know everything, so who is going to teach them anything or change their emotional state of mind? It certainly wouldn't be someone that they disagree with. They may not be a total lost cause, but they are not the place to start.

I might get some indication of these people with just a simple conversation. I would not be asking obvious questions but behavior tends to show itself without digging for it in many cases. As I am thinking about these classifications and how they apply to my candidacy and the small group meeting tonight, I started forming ideas of data collection. I know that I want to keep track of the streets and houses that I have covered, but I might as well keep track of more if I have the opportunity.

Okay, here I am at the end of the block, 1402 West Sparrow Lane. "Ding Dong." I have a feeling nobody is going to answer.

They did. "Hi, I'm Carey Thompson. I live just down the street and I am out meeting people today to let you know that I am running for city council." The door was still open. "I would like to leave you a brochure and ask if you have any questions for me or concerns about the operations of ...." And the door was closed. No comment, no question, just a door closed in my face. Maybe I should appreciate that there was no yelling or name-calling. This one was easy to code: 1402 West Sparrow Lane,h,a,nb,nm,nc. This stood for the people at 1402 West Sparrow Lane were home, they were assholes, didn't take a brochure, provided no email, and made no comments. This was my starting point but it would likely get tweaked a little along the way. What a great start.

I know that I can't judge this effort or even this neighborhood by just one house, but it does make me wonder. I am not wondering if the whole neighborhood are assholes, I am wondering if my approach is wrong and if I have rushed into this without the appropriate planning. I'll try one more house. As I rang the doorbell, I realize whose house this is. It is Cody's house, and it is Cody that came to the door. He smiled and said, "You want more pizza?" It was very cute and he clearly does not hate me, but his dad is a different story. I looked up and saw his dad standing behind him.

I introduced myself and started with, "I am running for city council and..." That was it. Cody's dad jumped in and said, "I could care less what you are running for, but I know what you better run from. You and your kind don't belong here and you better..." It was my turn to interrupt and I said, "So does that mean that you don't want a brochure?" It was hard not to laugh but I didn't and I knew there was more coming. "I don't want no damn brochure and my kid don't want your damn money, and we don't want you around here. Now get!" I said, "Thank you very much for your consideration and I am counting on your vote." I started walking away and turned around and said, "By the way, I got your note." He yelled, "You're damn right you did" and slammed the door. Cody was still outside. I wave to Cody and he put his head down but waved back. I think he was embarrassed by his dad; such a nice neighbor and such a nice dad. My responses might have been a little bit sarcastic but they were very toned down for me. I gave this house 1410 West Sparrow Lane,h,aa,nb,nm, left note on my door. The "aa" is for double asshole but it also makes me realize that there needs to be an option in my future book for *both* an asshole and stupid. I understand these are subjective classifications and may not work globally, but they work for me for now. Of course there would be other codes to cover nice people, but it is looking like I won't be needing those anytime soon. I really don't think the whole neighborhood will be this hostile, but then again I feel like I need to be better prepared.

I remembered that there was a mayor in the group and thought that would be a perfect person to ask for some advice. I will ask the group tonight about contacting him. I have plenty of time before the election, but I'm sure that time will go fast. It is a pretty small town, but not *that* small. I guess I'll head home and figure out my next steps. At least I have confirmation of who left the note. He could also be the person that 'flagged' me with the government. That is another route that the government's pervasive control has taken. They encourage and enable not only hatred but provide a mechanism to turn in your friends, family, and neighbors. My how the definitions and expectations of friends, family, and neighbors have changed.

It used to be that the concept of asshole or stupid would not apply to friends and less frequently to family. It might apply to neighbors but not to the degree that it seems to today. I know that people think me to be a cranky old man, and focusing so much on asshole and stupid would seem to support that notion. But my purpose is understanding people rather than condemning people and when so many fit in those two categories it becomes less complex.

I have not forgotten that *not everybody* is either an asshole or stupid. I know there are people that are not either and are generally good caring people that occasionally make mistakes. It's just that they seem to be getting fewer and fewer. The more I recognize that, the more my friends seem to be getting fewer. Family by blood or marriage are who they are, and they do contain some in the *A or S* category. Neighbors are similar in that if they physically live near you; they are neighbors but they may not be *neighborly*. That word used to have some meaning, but I'm not sure it does for many anymore.

The division and hatred that has been promoted has certainly increased the number that fall in the A or S category, but there has always been those that were there based on greed, laziness, or a complete lack of honor and respect. I have dozens, if not hundreds, of examples of *A* and *S* flowing through my head. I know that I often use example scenarios as a way to test my ramble theories. Rambles are usually just floating freeform but sometimes they are searching for resolution in patterns.

When people knowingly lie they are quite clearly in the *A* category. When people don't tell the truth but think that they are, they are either in the *S* category or they have not been allowed the access to evidence to the contrary. An example that frequently comes up in discussions about 'science' is reasonable to try against this; that is the idea that the world was flat. In the earliest days people could see a horizon that looked like the end of the earth. During that time there was little evidence one way or the other. There were people with different theories, but many sided with flat. There was clearly a lack of evidence so *A* or *S* didn't really apply unless somebody was using that debate as a mechanism for some other motive. That motive then became the lie.

The evidence of the earth not being flat mounted over time and with the available evidence came the ability to identify the purpose of a lie, as well as identify the people that were stuck in their belief of flatness and refused to see what was available to them. Prior to the overwhelming evidence, people would take sides for various reasons, just as with any subject matter. The behaviors are likely very similar across any topic as they seem to be about human behavior rather than subject matter. Some chose to just go with what was easy, some chose to believe their trusted source regardless of which side or evidence, some chose to go with what their friends did so that they would fit in, and a few actually assessed the evidence for themselves.

Through that time more and more people accepted that the world was not flat. I can't say whether this growth took place because of logic or something more akin to mob mentality. Today, with an abundance of evidence that the world is not flat, there are some that will still profess that it is. Are they kidding or just trying to be contrary? It seems as though I am back to the start of determining that A or S really has nothing to do with the belief or the subject matter, but rather the motivation or lack thereof. If the evidence is before you, you have a choice and why you make the choice that you do is really the important factor.

I walked down this example scenario thinking it might help and I am not sure that it did. Maybe it helped solidify some things, but not what I was looking for. As there was more and more evidence against the flat-world theory, the motivation to continue professing to others that it was flat took on some ulterior motive. It was no longer about belief; it was about something else. Money, power, ego, or (here it comes) stupidity replaced evidence. Money, power, and ego are all in the category of A when used as the sole basis for a decision.

The people continuing to actually believe the lies despite the overwhelming evidence to the contrary pretty consistently fall into the S category. Those that have no access to evidence are excluded, but as time went on the vast majority had access. As with all things, they may choose to be lazy and not look, that is stupid. They may blindly trust what a person is saying regardless of evidence; that is stupid. They may just want to follow their friends and neighbors and that is stupid. It is a *choice* to not think for yourself, and that is stupid. These harsh statements and back and forth with myself is exactly why this is a ramble and not a rant or a book (yet). More rambling is required, but with each ramble and each example more information is collected for the next one.

I do believe that the leaders that lie are assholes the vast majority of the time. The likelihood that it is stupidity and they don't know that they are lying *should be* an extreme rarity, because that would mean that they didn't have access to information for which they are responsible (or maybe that they didn't understand it). Stupid people in leadership positions? Oh, that is a whole other ramble because as much as stupid people should not be leaders, way too often they are. That would seem to potentially contradict my assumption that most leaders' falsehoods are lies. For that reason, I believe that it is time better spent to look at the underlying benefit of the lie rather than how they possibly made it to a level of leadership being so stupid. And as I say that, I already have a caveat. It depends on the level of leadership, there are 'lower-level leaders' that made it there simply by agreeing with everything the highest level leaders say. They are just patsies in search of power and control but are nothing more than pseudo-leaders that are driven by the perception of power. The corporate and government world is loaded with them. Occasionally they wake up, realize what they are, and get out. They may also realize it and just change from *S* to *A*. Most stay in their pretend world of power and wreak real havoc on real people by being a power-hungry asshole whose only excuse is that they are stupid enough to believe that their power is real and worth anything at all.

If I could conclude from this ramble that the people that are stupid outnumber the people that are assholes, then there is hope. I still believe that the stupid can learn and the assholes will not, but neither is easy. The appropriate motivation to care or *think* needs to be presented. In the end, I believe that the classifications of asshole or stupid will be useful to me regardless of how some may find it insensitive if they knew about it. The classifications consider the motivation of people, and what motivates people is important if you want to have any influence. This quite lengthy ramble may seem a waste to some, but to me it was an important exploration of some fundamental human behaviors.

Chapter 21
Everybody Needs a Plan
Later Afternoon Day 5

I got home and am sitting at the table starting to make lists. I need a list for the meeting tonight consisting mostly of questions. The answers to questions will be critical to evaluating the viability of potential plans that are forming in my head. I will not write down any plans. The other list will be of a plan for the rest of the day. The day is flying by but it seems that I accomplished a fair amount so far. I always count rambles as accomplishments even if they don't result in conclusions. They add value even if it is not immediate. Thinking is always useful and it is critical to finding patterns; patterns should be the basis for plans and plans are critical to success.

When I refer to success, I mean success of your goals not success as might be defined by society or even your friends, family, and neighbors. If we are going to succeed, the patterns and subsequent plan is critical. Because of so many uncontrollable factors, the plan also needs to be flexible. Some might think that a flexible plan is no plan at all, but a flexible plan is the most resilient plan. It can bend but not break.

I would normally start with a list for the day but since one of the most important things on the list for today would be to create a list for tonight, I might as well do tonight's list and leave it off the today list. Here goes:

- What so far
- Secure DB and availability
- Metadata
- Outbound comms
- Site
- Social Media
- Mayor
- Comm to leaders

That should be cryptic enough if anybody were to find it, but it means a lot to me. And now for the rest of today, which doesn't have that much time left:

- Start city council website
- Verify verification
- Safe
- Cloud
- Backups

The list is not long but the day is short and I may not get all of this done. I was thinking that I would start with the safe and order it online because it didn't initially seem like something I should have to hide. I had second thoughts on that because getting a safe should not imply anything other than wanting security against robbery or fire, but when it was the FBI that took things, it likely implies that I have something to hide. It shouldn't imply that because people used to have a simple and basic right to privacy, but when it comes to the current government it is a very different story. I need to find a place to get a safe not too far away and pay cash. That will not be today.

I started on the campaign website because I can put a website together pretty fast with the tools available today. I used the information that I had in the brochure for starters and added a couple of forms. One form is for contacting me and one is for signing up for updates. I at least have a landing point with something for anybody that might end up there.

It is more than 24 hours since I was locked out, so it is time to try the cloud backup login again. I should have written down the three that I tried so I didn't try them again, but I think I remember. It is amazing how much I do remember with all of the rambles floating around in my head. For example, I have 3 bank cards and I know all three of their 16-digit numbers along with expiration dates and security codes. This memory is definitely an asset for what is going on right now, not that it isn't any other time. I remember going to the doctor once and I had forgotten my wallet for the co-pay. I asked if I could just give them the card numbers and they looked at me like I was from Mars. I had just gotten a new card the week before that I wanted to use and I gave them the numbers and it went through. The point is that you would think that I could remember passwords, but I probably have close to 100 passwords and none of them are the same. That might even be possible with my 'formula', but then there so many reasons that I have had to change many of them over the years and some do not allow reuse of previous passwords. It starts to get pretty deep in possibilities, even with a formula.

The first attempt was a fail. Then I have a feeling that I know what it is. Sometimes I get that feeling that I just know. Sometimes it's because something connected and I remembered, and other times it is just because of a 'feeling'. It was like that the first time I had surgery to have a tumor removed. I was told there was only a 5% chance that it was cancer because of my age and the type of cancer that it would be. I *knew* before they told me that it was cancer. That wasn't a fear, it was *knowing*. The password worked and I am in.

This is a good hurdle to have crossed but I have never really done anything with these backups (shame on me for not testing) other than occasionally looking to see if backups were completed. I could see that something was there and that was a great start, but there was no way for me to know just by looking if everything was there. It shows dates of backups but some days there is nothing to backup and some days backups fail for various reasons like connectivity issues, so judging by dates didn't really mean anything. Even if it did, unless I can restore the data, it means nothing. That's one more thing on my list that will be delayed beyond today to complete. That's okay. I am going to assume that they accessed everything that was there from my computers anyway, so it really is a matter of whether I can restore about 20 years of creative work for myself.

I fix something to eat, give Reggie his supper, change my clothes, and go outside for a while. Going outside with Reggie is not a chore but something to relish. It is bigger than a routine that carries a feeling of normalcy. Reggie is my pal and being outside in the back yard still has a feeling of connecting with something bigger. The yard sits at the edge of a wooded area with plenty of birds and other creatures that are willing to taunt Reggie. The air feels different if I remember to slow down and take notice. It is a very much-needed respite at times but it is often a very short respite.

I take a look at my today list and the only thing left that I hadn't addressed is backups. I have nothing to back up yet and my plan is to just use flash drives. I will save all of my work to a flash drive rather than the local drive and once a week (or more) I will copy the contents of one drive to another one giving me two instances of backups that will not be attached to the computer. The question is, where to put them. That is the same question of where to put some cash. I will be getting a safe for some things but regardless of the safe, not everything can go in one place. In this case it is not just making sure that I am able to keep a copy, but also reduce the risk of anyone else getting a copy. I knew at that point that I would never store anything that would expose the group but I will store things that could be used against me.

I am getting quite anxious for the meeting tonight and hoping that it will be productive. I start having thoughts again about whether I would be able to change my behavior for the benefit of the long game. I completely understand long-range plans; in fact I believe that you can't have effective short-term plans unless you know the long-range plans that they fit into. Actually, the short-term plans that fit in the long-range plan are all part of the same plan.

In my thoughts about how I knew that I had cancer the first time was embedded the primary reason that I am so driven to do all that I can today. I was given a prognosis that was a very short life expectancy, which for me forced the concept of living each day as if it is your last. Many people have not seen a sign to that effect, but eventually most will understand what it really means and how real it is. It is sometimes hard to keep up that pace, but it has stuck with me for a very long time. Along with pushing hard each day comes the lesson of never giving up hope. I cannot stop my drive and a number of times since the first time, cancer has reappeared along with other events that make me continually grateful with a reignited drive to make use of *today*.

My drive was reignited once again just two days before the FBI charged in. Did they know that I had once again been given a very unfavorable prognosis? I don't think it matters if they knew and I am quite certain that it would not have changed their plans one way or another because the motivation driving that was not about people, but rather about power. I do not give up hope, but I need to know that I am doing all that I can in the short-term because that may be all I have. I do understand that even if I don't live to see the long-range results, my short-term activities can impact it. I need to make sure I am doing that.

My health status is probably not something that the group knows and I wonder if they would consider it a risk rather than a benefit if they did know. They may think that it might impair my judgment. And if I don't tell them, am I lying to them? I think I already know that answer from previous rambles, but in some sense it doesn't matter. Not everybody tells everybody everything and it never even occurred to me until now. I am not hiding or telling partial truths to manipulate their perspective, and nobody has talked about their personal health or their personal life such as family. That does not mean that everything that is not known is a lie. I may be good. If anybody in the group asks, I won't lie. That applies to all aspects of my life. It's all part of a plan, even if it's not exactly my original plan.

Chapter 22
All Part of the Plan
Evening Day 5

Those things that are unexpected are precisely why a plan needs to be flexible in order to keep with the same general objective and purpose. Plan B is somewhat of a misnomer in that it is really part of the same plan that includes the flexibility of a different path to the same objective. Anticipation of problems and unforeseen roadblocks is not paranoia or pessimism, but rather part of careful planning.

I think I may have actually dozed a little sitting outside, but fortunately I woke up in plenty of time to get off to my meeting. I pull into the alley at 8:45. I am 15 minutes early and I have not thought about it before, but I wonder who has the ability to get in without the knock and 5 steps back process. It doesn't really matter; I am just curious about almost everything, but my questions tonight will not be simply to satisfy my curiosity. They are about making a plan. I waited 5 more minutes, went to the door and knocked, and took 5 steps back. The door opened and I am ready to dig in.

This size group is very close to perfect. There are varied skillsets and backgrounds and not so many people that collaboration becomes complex. This is planning, not executing after all. Everybody is here (I guess I didn't need to wait in the car) and we all sat at one of the tables after Tim checked all of the systems and made sure the door was locked. I know the first question on my list without looking but decide to add something before that question. I start with, "I'd like to thank you all for letting me be part of this group. How long has this group been meeting?" Tim offered, "About three months and we have had three meetings." It hit me then that I didn't know how long any of the groups had been meeting and that might tell a story about the organization if it took a long time to form this group, but I need to keep that out of scope for now. I just want to have an idea of how much would be reasonable to expect that they have accomplished so far. I figured it might not be that much but it is a good lead in to the first question on my list. "Would you mind filling me in on what you have so far?" Tim looked at Sam and said, "You want to take this one?"

Sam started explaining the legal risks and the ramifications that had been assessed when trying to recruit more people. "Wait a minute" I said, "Recruit more people? Recruit more people for what? Maybe I should start with asking the objectives of this group and how it fits into the overall objective." Sam answered, "Recruit more people that believe what we believe." I was almost dumfounded by this and had to comment. "Is there really that much of a disconnect somewhere? Either a disconnect between the larger group and this one or between what I thought this whole group was about and what it really is about." There was that reality vs. perception question again.

All I got was, "What do you mean?" I really hadn't planned on this but then again, this type of assessment is what I do and maybe why I am here. I began, "I believe that the overall objective is to preserve, or get back the rights of the people that have been taken away by the current government. Would you agree?" I got head nods. "And the method is not via a military takeover of the government but by educating the people so that they can hopefully see what is and has happened. Agreed?" This time I got head nods and a couple of yeps. "Well, taking that to what I thought would be the obvious purpose of providing information to the people is so that they will vote out the current administration and all that goes with it. Regardless of all of the challenges that there are with that, without forcefully taking over the government, is there another play?" Sam said, "That sounds like a bigger initiative than what this group is." WTF? I can't believe I am hearing this and I thought this was the perfect group, but I had really not talked to anyone much, if at all, other than Sharon. I think this group and the bigger group wanted to do the right thing but I don't think they had any form of a real plan. They had emotions and a desire to do something to make it better. They had defined a list of things they would and would not do, but it seems that it doesn't tie together into a plan.

I started thinking that I would take a shot at setting a path, at least for this meeting. "Do you mind if I wind this back a little so that there might be some definable objectives and problems that we can try to solve?" I didn't wait for an answer. "If you accept that one of the primary objectives of the larger group is to get people to vote by offering them the truth, it gives us a goal. We are not out trying to recruit people into this group, correct?" And again I didn't wait for an answer. "We accept that people may spin up their own groups and own initiatives, but that is not something that we can directly support. If this group is to devise a plan to support the objective of getting people the truth in order to influence their vote, it would seem that we have two initial problems to solve. How do we identify and keep track of the people and how do we communicate with them? If we focus on that we should have a reasonably scoped problem to solve."

I continued to make sure I was being clear, "We would not focus on how to identify the truths to share or how to message them to make them more palatable. That has maybe been solved or would be by another group. If not, maybe this group could start to address that after solving the first two problems. Knowing what to say does no good if you have no idea who to say it to or how to get it to them. Please tell me if I have misstated something or missed something. I know that I am new to this group so I would expect that there is something I have missed."

Carl was the first to say something, "How are we supposed to keep track of the identified people if we are not allowed to write anything down?" I was quick on this one, "Well that is the problem isn't it? I think that was the essence of the question that I asked and was told that this group was assigned to devise a plan for that. Before discussing that solve, is there any disagreement with the objectives?" I got a very weak "no." "Well then, is there agreement with the objectives?" If this was the only thing accomplished in this meeting, it would be successful, but very disappointing. I wasn't getting resounding answers of yes or no, which to me was proof that I needed to be here. "Let me make a proposal then. How about if you accept those objectives for the purpose of this meeting? We then take these objectives back to the larger group for verification." I did get agreement with that and it's good because I think I might need to walk out if all they are going to talk about is 'recruiting.'

I have been thinking about approaches since I found out about this group. It was not a specific ramble most of the time but one of those background rambles. You know, the rambles that run like background applications on a computer. You are not actively using them but they are doing their job when appropriate and when processing time allows. Rambles are definitely multitasking processes.

I start with my thoughts first by addressing Sharon, "I asked if there was some form of a database that could be used that would be trusted and secure. I got an answer of possibly. Could you explain that please?" She said, "I meant that I could imagine that there would be the possibility of creating one. There are, after all, all sorts of encryption methods available, but we don't have one built because of the other layers of protection that would be required. We haven't explored it further because we are not authorized to write things down." I need to try to cut this short or we would go nowhere. "Let's consider two approaches and split the effort:

1. There is a central communication process for submitting ideas that has multiple layers of protection and has been seemingly approved and used at the

highest level. That must have storage behind it. Sam and Tim, how about if you try to find out if those sets of technologies can be used for our purposes (either the same solution or a replica)?

2. As a plan B, Carl and Sharon please put together a plan of technologies and design that would be required to secure the database, the application, and the connections against all conceivable risks.

3. I will put together a list of proposed data that could be used in either approach that would provide us the basic information and the least exposure if found.

"The bottom line is that we need a place to store the information related to people and we need a way to access it. It does not have to be accessed by a lot of people, which should help with part of the protection solution. We should be able to come up with these options within a week. This is part one of two. Is this acceptable and clear enough?" Sam said, "It sounds good to me." Others nodded. This was not a very talkative group. I keep hoping that there is more to this group than what it seems so far. They seem to be completely rudderless.

I continued, "Part two is the communication with the people. This could be communication to specific people or to the world, but focus on a method specific to a list. The communication needs to not be traceable back to us. It can be any form. Be creative. Include phone, text, email, letters, TV, radio, social media, websites, or any method that you can think of. In addition to hiding the source, consider misdirection in the solution as well. Expect that someone will discover some of the communications and it might be interesting to give them someplace else to look. I don't have specific ideas on how to split this up so I would suggest that we think about this individually and get back together to discuss what options and ideas we have in the next few days.

"I know the timelines that I am proposing are more aggressive than how you have been operating so far, but there is a major election in 4 months. It is probably too late to have a big impact on it, but we only have a window of opportunity every two years for country-wide impact so we need to push. Again, I would urge you to be creative. Some solutions are likely to be pure technology based and others may be in the approach or the messaging rather than the technical solution. Remember, the purpose is not to necessarily hide the message, but to hide anything that would expose anything about our operations or us. These are the two objectives that I see this group needing to propose solutions for. Keep in mind as well that these two solutions may benefit from the ability to merge the two solutions such as sending a specific message to people of a particular profile. We will take the proposal or options back to the larger group before executing anything."

I took a breather thinking that someone might want to jump in with something but I'm not going to let the silence hang too long. I was about to start talking again and a light started flashing on the wall and the computer screen showed a car pulling in the alley. We all stayed silent and watched the screen. The car stopped and then backed out of the alley. The camera was clear enough to know that it was not a government plate but was it anything to be concerned about? Tim said,

"That happens sometimes and we can't check on every license plate that comes into the alley as being suspicious. We have not noticed any repeat cars with the same pattern." I had comments about that but I let it go.

After that interlude I continued, "Are we all okay with this approach? I know that this may seem like I have come in and just tried to take over. I am not trying to take over anything. I am trying to help and this is how I help." Tim jumped in and said, "I would like to suggest that Carl and I trade places on the teams. I know that Carl has done some work with setting up the connections and access to the existing system and I may have some help from contacts that I have regarding technology designs. I would not need to divulge anything to my contacts to get some information. They are all used to need-to-know concepts." Everybody was in agreement.

I wanted to close the concept of an apparent takeover with one comment; "I believe that I may have disrupted whatever your plans were for this meeting so I will step back if someone wants to move your previous plans forward." Sam said, "With where we are now, I believe anything that we would have discussed is quite irrelevant." He then added, "And I like where we are going." There was a mumble, mumble, nod, and smiles in response to that and I said, "Can someone set up the next meeting regarding communications for 4-5 days out?" Sam said that he would. And that was it, "Alright then. We have a plan."

We were walking out and I remember to ask how to get in touch with the mayor in the group. Sharon suggested that I contact John and he could put me in touch with Hank. One plan in place and now I need a campaigning plan. Somehow this plan feels bigger than campaigning but I'm sure there are lessons to be learned that will benefit both and they are both parts of a much bigger plan (I hope).

There was no run-in with officer Mike on the way out of the alley and once again my head is spinning with all that had transpired this evening. I don't want to say that they were clueless because they are clearly some intelligent people, but it sure seems like they were floundering in their small-group special assignment. It really can't be as bad as it seems, can it? If it is, is it that bad in the larger group or worse yet, is it that way at the level above? There must be some bigger plan that is just not visible. But if it's not visible, it's not much of plan. This is a national problem that I understand needs grassroots support but a national problem needs a national plan.

Ideas are already forming in my ramble on the way home. There are so many what-ifs, so many possibilities. It is a good ramble that may contribute to solutions when we meet in a few days. I am really tired and more planning now would likely not be beneficial, so I let Reggie out and went to bed.

Chapter 23

Give Peace a Chance

Morning Day 6

I woke in the morning with a renewed feeling of urgency. Today's list is already starting to form in my head as I go rapidly through the morning routine. My normal wake-up time might have been shortened a little bit. I needed to contact John, hopefully talk to Hank, start a list of data to collect and how to code it, create cryptic notes on communication options, update the city council website, check city council email (had to get in the habit of doing that at least twice per day even though I expect little activity), find a place to get a safe, make a list for a Hank discussion, and find storage locations around the house. The written list looks like this:

- Mayor
- CC updates
- Safe
- Lists (com opts, attrib, CC?)

- Temp store

I would know what they mean and it is time to start the first one. I called John on the secure phone connection and he gave me Hank's secure connection. I called Hank and no answer. It was maybe a bad time to call a mayor just kicking off the day. I'll try again in about an hour.

I got online and found a store with the type of safe that I was looking for about 45 minutes away. I want to try Hank one more time before leaving and having no connectivity. I decided to wander around the house and see if anything hits me for hiding spots. I walk into the kitchen and it seems like all I can see are the cliché places like the freezer and the cookie jar. It needs to be a little more challenging. If I had a little more time a false bottom in a drawer might not be bad.

I'm looking up and down and see the sliding patio doors. There is a doorstop that slides into the doorframe. It is vinyl and semi hollow. I had discovered this during a thorough spring-cleaning session of doors and windows. The hollow portion is just big enough to slide a flash drive in. Perfect. I have two sliding doors but if they found one they would find the other. I walk into the living room and see my stereo cabinet. I have a receiver, power regulator, DVD player, and a couple of game consoles. One of the game consoles is hooked up but doesn't work. I thought stashing money inside a game console might be good but then if my house was robbed by thugs and not the government, they might take the game console. I wandered some more and seemed to find a reason not to use every place I found. I would have to continue this later, but I found one good spot.

I called Hank and got him this time. I ask if he would have some time to share his thoughts on best approaches for campaigning. He said that he would be glad to but didn't know how much help he would be. He said that he was busy today, but he could meet tomorrow morning at his office. Hank is a realtor and has his own business. Being a mayor in a small town is not a full-time job, pretty similar to the city council position I was running for. We also agreed that this was an open conversation and that I should call his regular phone to talk about an interview so that there would be a record of it. I call right back on my registered phone and we are set. Now I am free to go look at safes.

I load the Faraday bag in the usual manner, and off I go. I had to double-check that I had the right place because it was just a little hole-in-the-wall shop with a small sign hanging in the window. It didn't take me too long to pick out a safe but there was a problem that I hadn't really thought through. There was no way that I could get it into my house myself and get it installed. I also didn't want a truck with a big safe sign on it pulling up to my house. The safe that I picked is just 8" x 10" inside, but weighs over 500 pounds. I asked if they could load it in my truck today and then come later in a vehicle that doesn't have safe signage on it. They said that was no problem and it is not all that unique of a request. I pulled in my garage with the safe in the back of my truck.

I sat for a moment thinking how fortunate I was. I could wallow in the crap that is happening but *everything is relative.*

I am not the only person that bad things have happened to and some have had far worse things happen. I have been very fortunate in meeting the people that I have in just a few days and buying a safe is not something that everybody would be able to do. I am not what I would consider rich. I am living on social security, but I did manage to save a little money in the last few years. It was supposed to last longer than it has so far but these were times that I had to make some quick decisions about spending money and the safe was one of them. It's good that I had a little money, but it won't last long. It is a shame what has happened to the elderly on social security. Between the economy and inflation of the past decade or more, it has been devastating to many.

Social security is just another lie of the government. There has been an ongoing scare about social security running out and people being left to fend for themselves in their old age. The government now tells the story of how they not only saved social security but also how they have steadily increased the social security payment. One of the lies that is a lie of omission is that for every 5% they increase social security, they increase Medicare premium by 20-30%. They don't say this but anybody that looks can clearly see it. They also don't tell you that the only way they are covering any of it is by printing more money, which decreases the value of what we do have left even more. All in plain sight and yet they are praised for saving and increasing social security. The end result is that more elderly have been forced into a dependency on other government programs; more dependence on the government by more people. I am still okay for now, but many are not.

Today is flying by and the people will be here to install the safe in about an hour. I still have three lists to make. The one I need the soonest is also probably the easiest so I'll start with mayor questions:

- What do you think it is that got you elected?
- What do you believe is the most effective place to spend time and money?
- What approach did you take with door-to-door campaigning if you did it?
- Did you use a website, brochures, cards, yard signs, social media, and anything else?
- What has been your biggest challenge, both before and after election?
- Please offer me anything that you can for suggestions in my campaign

I know this list was worded as a questionnaire, which is not the way my lists typically are. This was more of a conversation outline that was intended to be able to be completely understood if found.

The next list would be the start of attributes to collect. This would be the first list to go in my computer since I have a plan and a place for a flash drive. I would still not be too obvious and even misleading by associating it with the city council run. Nothing on this list can provide any information to expose the group or its operations. The data itself would need to identify a person in various ways because we cannot count on people providing all data points. I can be consistent with the address for campaigning, but I don't know the various ways that information might be collected for the group. So I start my file named citycouncilpolling:

- First Name
- Last Name
- Street Address
- City
- State
- Zip
- Email
- Phone
- Text ok? (Y/N)
- Subscribed
- Support profile (1-10)
- School age children
- Income profile
- Ethnicity
- Source
- Personal contact (Y/N)
- Future attributes

The storage design needs to be expandable but this is a starting point. It might seem like some of the attributes are pushing the limit of appropriateness, but I know how they fit and I will explain to the group.

As I finish up the first draft of this and make sure it is only saved to my flash drive, I am feeling a bit overwhelmed by the enormity of the effort. We are essentially taking on the power-hungry and controlling government of the United States. I am flashing back to one of my initial questions of, "How do you win when your opponent cheats?" The answer was essentially *the truth* and not using their same strategy of lies. We need to bring people together with the truth. This sounds very much like airport tambourine people chanting "Give peace a chance." I have the desire for peace and I believe in the truth, but giving peace a chance has the connotation of being passive. I believe it is that passiveness, along with apathy, that assisted getting us into the position that we are in. Passive peace clearly is not a defense against an aggressive hate machine. They have proven that they will do anything to satisfy their insatiable thirst for power. Insatiable is key. They will *never* stop and they will start feeding on their own, in fact they already have.

Okay, we can launch this effort without violence, but that does not mean being passive. If anything, we need to be even more aggressive. We will use the truth but it has to be more than the truth because the truth is available now to all that want it. It is not giving them the truth that is our biggest challenge; it is making them want it. Okay, we can't *make* them want it but we can offer incentives and encouragement.

We also need to use some of their tactics that play to human behavior. They are really good at that and we need to be better. The truth is stronger than lies when seen in the light of day, but how do we get people into the light. I have a feeling that someone listening to my thoughts would think this to be conspiratorial and manipulative. When people have been manipulated into trusting those that would harm them and believing lies to be the truth, something has to change. Is it manipulative? Sure. There is a big *but* that goes with that. It is not manipulating with lies and deception, it is providing factual information that emphasizes the benefits of the truth. It is possible that some may even hang on to their hatred and refocus it in the other direction. That is not the intended outcome, but hating lies seems a bit more logical than hating the truth.

Almost everything in life is manipulation. People want to help you feel better so they say something in a particular way to increase the probability of that. All advertising is manipulation. Manipulation does not mean that it is a lie and we cannot let that connotation hold us back. I really do not like salesmen because their purpose is to manipulate people to buy something. It is irrelevant to them whether someone needs it or not and for most whether it is lies that gets them to buy. We would just be providing a spec sheet that compares products with the truth about all of them. Our challenge is to get them to read the sheet and trust the source. Is that manipulation? Give peace a chance; sure. But in order for peace to have a chance, people will need to have their already manipulated behavior of supporting hatred and lies altered. This ramble will likely play directly into a strategy for the communication list.

Chapter 24
Big City Life
Afternoon Day 6

The doorbell rings. The safe guys are right on time and as promised there was no sign of them being here to install a safe. I let them in and showed them where I wanted the safe in the basement and they went to work. They estimated two hours to complete. I don't need to watch them so I start my next list. The communication ideas list is about bringing thoughts to the group so that everybody would be able to participate and add to the initial thoughts or find the flaws in the ideas. There is so much power in small groups that work together. It usually creates solutions that are far more robust and resilient than a single person's thoughts. That takes leaving ego and arrogance behind, which is yet another good ramble.

This list is going to take a bit more time and thought but I want to get started. My first thoughts are around a few requirements. The source of the communication must be hidden or deflected. Misrepresenting the source of the communication is ok if not preferred. That does not mean misrepresenting the *source* of the data; that would not be okay. It would be ideal if it appeared as though the communication came from the government. It would be even better if it actually *did* come from the government. There is so much that the government does that is not 'smart' so getting them to communicate something that they think is to their benefit (but isn't) should be possible. Using the government against itself is one of the primary themes. The data that provides the truth will mostly come from the government anyway so why not push it further and use the government as the means of communication in some cases?

Some of the data about people will likely come from the same sources that the government uses against the people. Large data stores are often eager to share their data if they see something in it for them, and that includes the government itself. We would actually be 'partnering' with the government and its cohorts. This could also include the communication methods and technologies such as the news media and social media. There are many ways of disguising actual intent.

Everything so far falls into two general categories. I am not going to write all of this down, but I need to capture the short version of its intent.

- Use the opponents and their partners' resources where possible.
- Hide or misrepresent the source of the comm.

These are directional thoughts that *should* bring some very interesting discussions. Another way of stating the two categories would be to say that we would either hide the source and be very clear in the message or hide the intent of the message and be clear about the source. Hiding the source is technology based and hiding the intent of the message is content based. Using both approaches would be best. I am guessing the group is only thinking technology based because of what I had said, so maybe a short list on ideas for technology solutions. Hiding the source could consist of a distributed randomized ring of servers in many locations (ideally around the world), randomized IP spoofing, registration layers and redirects, routing redirects, and of course all of the highest levels of encryption and access controls.

As I am creating this list I think there might be one variant that is between the two categories. If you think about what has happened and how the domestic opponents of the government have been blocked from the news and social media but the foreign enemies have not, is that an opportunity? Of course that scenario in itself is a major red flag deserving of an answer as to why it is allowed, but it may be a situation created by them that can be used against them. Foreign enemies can apparently say anything they want (maybe because they are not really the enemies of our government) so why not use them as a source to disseminate information? It is at least another discussion trigger.

Someone came up from the basement and asked me to come down. The safe looked like it should have been sitting up on a table rather than the floor, but it was going nowhere. It was fastened into the cement floor so that the only way of removing it would be with a jackhammer. The combination was in a sealed envelope and there was also a physical key that had to be used together with the combination, not instead of. I can't guarantee that the government couldn't eventually get into it but it would sure slow them down and no normal house thief would have a chance. I tried the combination and key before they left and we were set. I went and got half of the cash that I had left and put it in the safe. One flash drive would still stay in the hiding place that I had found and the weekly copy would go in the safe. Speaking of that, I have made enough notes on my computer for now so I made sure that it was all saved to the flash drive and nowhere else, went through my computer clearing and shutdown process, put the drive in its place, and took a big sigh of relief.

As I watched them pull away I saw a military vehicle drive by. This was very unusual for this neighborhood, but the times are changing and people have gotten used to things that would have caused an uprising not that long ago. It *seems* not that long ago, but I know that the change has been over many years and very consistent so I have to wonder if even I have not really noticed some of the change. Military trucks in my quiet neighborhood did not go unnoticed. I didn't see it stop anywhere so I went and got Reggie and me something to eat and we went to the back yard. It was time for a little relaxation. For me relaxation usually turned into a ramble. Maybe many would not see that as relaxing at all, but I guess I really don't know that. I have never really talked to people about rambling.

I took note of the military truck that passed through the neighborhood but while the neighborhood would all come out to watch activities at my house, nobody seemed to notice the military. Does that mean that they think I am more interesting, or more of a threat? It's not like we're in a big city. It just hit me what that thought meant. It seems that the concept of military patrolling the streets of big cities has been accepted for some time. It seems only a short while ago that it wasn't true, but the policies that encouraged crime and the subsequent fear led to just that result. Even the most violent and costly crimes went unpunished and the police were punished instead.

It became hard to find people that were willing to work in that once noble profession of being a cop. It seemed the only consequences were for those trying to enforce the law rather than the ones breaking it. People got tired of it and there was an attempt to change the policies, but it had no impact. They couldn't find people and primarily because it was clear that the policies were not really changing, it was just more lies. At the same time, more and more people were getting scared and demanding some level of protection. If you defended yourself, you were arrested so that was not even a reasonable talking point. That leaves the military. The military has been patrolling big city streets for a number of years now and by the government's own data it has not had an impact on crime. Of course they said that it was helping and that crime was down but anybody that looked knew otherwise. Nobody is punished so the deterrent of being caught and arrested has lost its value.

At the same time this was happening there were big government pushes to 'encourage' more and more people to move into the big cities. It became more and more unaffordable and unrealistic to acquire personal transportation and mass-transit was the only option for many. Not only were there changes in transportation, the programs that were available to fund living in the big cities seemed to be growing daily.

This directly ties to our objective in a couple of ways. I think that there are a couple people in this larger group that work in the big city that is our area, but I don't know if they live there. That city has more people than the entire rest of our area's population. That is by design. Setting up funding programs to one large city is far easier than doing it for hundreds of smaller cities. Also, if you draw dependent people via programs to the big city, you have increased the percentage of the population that is dependent rather than independent. This completely aligns with the government's push to eliminate the Electoral College. That has been a push for many years and it has come so close to passing and this could be the year. Without the Electoral College, not only will smaller cities be ignored, entire states (and most of them) can be ignored because the entire federal elections would be decided by a very few states, and very few cities in those states. All activity, campaigning, and social engineering funding would flow to those areas to buy more votes.

This clearly did not happen overnight, but it has happened and continues to get worse. If that is where decisions will be made, it seems unacceptable to not have good representation in the group from the big city. I want to get a better idea of who from the group works and lives in the big city because it seems that the big city should be a primary focus. It would be very inappropriate and ill-advised for us to sit in our small towns with insufficient big city representation and make decisions. I know that I stopped going to the city a number of years ago because it is not safe and I have not lived in a big city for over 30 years.

What do I know about the big cities other than the military that I can't trust will be on the streets and that crime is 100 times worse there than where I live? This big city move is one example of the need to understand our opponents' strategies in order to use them against them or at least counter them. Somehow, it does make me wonder how running for city council in my little town is at all relevant. I will add a related question to my list for the mayor but it will have to be in a way that is not related to our effort.

The big city concept seems like another thing that should be directed by a level above. There *must* be a strategy. There *must* be a plan. They couldn't have missed this could they? Are we not getting all of the direction that the national group is giving? Is it being received and ignored? I have to find out what is going on. If there is only one primary contact within the group, how do I find out what is going on if I don't know who that is? The method to submit recommendations is open to those that want it and apply the required technical solution. As far as I know it is a one-way communication. How do I know who receives it? Can other people in the group see what someone submits? Can the one contact see what is submitted? I have not logged into that system but I think it is time to check it out to see what I can see. Something about this feels wrong. How can an organization have so little organization? Well I guess I can answer part of that myself after consulting with many of the fortune 50 companies. Most of them are very unorganized (in my opinion), and yet they are fortune 50. Is it me that is off? I obviously don't think so.

It has to be obvious that the government's play is for the popular vote and that big cities have been the target for most of their initiatives. If that is the case, what are they doing messing with people like me in small towns? Maybe because they have such a tight grip on the big cities that they want a little insurance in case the big city plan doesn't complete as planned? Maybe they are just acting on a 'tip' from one of their faithful citizens that I am a risk. I still see that the big play is on big cities and the recommended solution from this small group needs to include, if not target, the big cities. Small town America would not like the concept that they are irrelevant, but then again most of the people in the big cities are irrelevant to our government as well. They are just numbers, and the big cities have lots of numbers. Big numbers equate to power.

Chapter 25
Evening Interlude
Evening Day 6

I am pretty relaxed sitting in my chair on the patio in the back yard on a beautiful night. The air is fresh, the stars are bright, and the world seems quiet until I hear a siren in the distance. It keeps getting closer until it seems as though it must be in front of the house. Now I can see the lights flashing between the houses and then they stop. I am not real clear on the different sounds of emergency vehicles like some people, so I have to go look. That might be a stupid idea, but if they were looking for me it wouldn't take too much investigation to walk behind the house. Reggie followed eagerly looking for some action. It is an ambulance parked in the driveway across the street and a couple houses down.

I don't know who lives there. It seems a shame that I don't know my neighbors, but it seems they didn't want to know me and I saw no reason to push it. I am genuinely concerned about what might be happening with a neighbor that I don't know, but I'm not going to do what other neighbors do to me. The crowd had gathered and I walked back around the house to sit. I could tell that Reggie was disappointed. He missed an opportunity to play and make new friends. Maybe *he* should run for city council.

I can wait to find out what is going on. I want to be respectful and not get in the way so we head inside and off to bed. I have a meeting in the morning and I have my list ready with one added question. My how my life has been different the past few days. At the same time, this event is a good reminder that life's individual challenges are still going on outside of the craziness that I have been focusing on.

Chapter 26
Big Fish, Little Pond

Morning Day 7

It seemed like I just laid down and the sunrise was already waking me up. I like that feeling of waking up to a sunrise in the morning. It is far different than many mornings of corporate life; I would be driving to work in the dark in the wintertime. The only time I set an alarm now is for something like an early flight, which is a rare thing. I am usually up between 5:30 and 6:00 without an alarm. It seems I get the most done before noon. After that the day seems to slow down, not that it has had too much time to slow down recently.

My meeting with Hank is scheduled for 8:30 so I need to leave about 7:45. That gives me plenty of time for breakfast, a shower, and a little wake-up time. I *must* have my wake-up time today. It is going to be another beautiful day (weather wise) and I have time for a cup of coffee outside before I leave.

I didn't hear any activity in the neighborhood after going inside last night, but I was pretty tired.

I get to Hank's real estate office a few minutes early but I can see people inside so I go on in. It is a small office with three desks in the main area and a couple more rooms in the back. Hank came out of one of those rooms and said, "Come on back" with a big smile. He is dressed like you might expect a mayor to be dressed. He is younger than me, but I'm not sure by how much because I am horrible at guessing someone's age. I think it is one of those things that I think is generally quite irrelevant.

I sit down across the desk from Hank and start with, "Thank you for taking the time to share your wisdom." He laughed and said, "I'm not sure how wise I am, but I am mayor." And with that he winked. I start right in with a little background stating that I am running for an open city council position in my hometown and I have never held a political office before. I was on a few Boards of Directors and the only one of those that was an elected position was and HOA, and I ran unopposed because apparently nobody wanted the position. I tell him what I have done so far regarding starting my campaign (if you can call it that) and then ask my first question, "What do you think it is that got you elected?"

When I heard the answer, it disrupted a number of the rest of my questions. "I have been in the real estate business for quite some time in this small town and I know a lot of people. I was asked to run and since my name is in the business name I have name recognition with for-sale signs all over town. There was nothing much that I had to do, which is very much not your situation." This somewhat deflated my hopes for this conversation, but I have to keep in mind that I really don't expect to win and I don't need to win in order to find some benefit.

I asked, "Knowing my situation, what do you believe would be my most effective way to spend time and very little money on a campaign?" Since he was in a different position he said that it would be hard for him to answer that. I am starting to wonder if this is a waste of my time and his.

I decided to try a different route. "Since you have been in office how do people most often communicate with you and how do you update them on issues." He was able to answer that, "Many people just stop by my office, or I run into them somewhere. There are monthly publications that go out to subscribers' emails and there is a website that is managed by the city that I occasionally get a question or comment from." I summarized, "So it seems like you get the most from people face to face and occasionally some electronic form?" He nodded.

I continued, "What would you say are the most common concerns of the people you talk to?" He said, "That's pretty easy, money and services and not necessarily in that order. When are we going to get a park on the east side of town? Why is my water bill so high? What are they building over there by the high school? That last one is more being nosey. They are concerned with what and who are coming into town because they like being a small town. They like the friendliness and the very low crime rate that we have." This is another reason why Hank's situation and mine are different. So I asked, "Do you know enough about my town to guess how it might differ from yours?" He did know a bit and offered, "Your town is a bit bigger and growing much faster, and that is by design. Your city council has been approving, if not pushing, significant growth. Your town has also seen an increase in crime along with the growth. The approach is quite different than here." That was actually quite helpful and I understood what he was talking about.

"Do you have any suggestions of things that I can or should do in my campaign? His answer was simple, "Be yourself." That sounds like good advice for life, but not for me in this situation. That would be a challenge, because I am a say-it-like-I-see-it kind of guy. And then I remembered the new question, but as I ran through the different ways that I thought to ask it in my head they all seemed inappropriate to the conversation and might imply something bigger than the scope of this town. I decided to abandon the question and just ask some fluff, "What are the most rewarding and frustrating aspects of being mayor?" That was intended to be a softball so I was expecting "fluffy" answers. He replied with, "I feel like I am helping my community. I feel that I give people a place to share and vent and give a little power to their voice where possible. That is very rewarding. The frustrating part is that some people seem to think that the government of this small town has money of its own and an almost unlimited budget. Some do not see it as spending their own money, if they did it might change the expectations. People don't do that intentionally, but there is this mentality among some that 'free' is an option. Fortunately this is still a small town mentality for the most part and people work hard, play hard, and help others when needed."

It was easy to see what this town meant to Hank. He was giving of himself to help his community. He also acknowledged the changes that are creeping in without stating his position and placing blame at the state and federal level for promoting their dependency agenda. I like Hank. He is a good down to earth caring man and sees how the agenda of centralized federal control and dependency is beginning to erode the pride, honor, and values of being a small town citizen.

This turned out to be better than it was looking to start with, but in a different way than I had initially hoped. I had to offer some response, "Mayor is a pretty big role for any town. Would you consider that you are a big fish in a small pond?" Hank almost looked offended and I wanted to instantly apologize for saying that even though I didn't understand what was wrong. He told me that, "I have never associated with that phrase. I am not a big fish. I am just another small fish with a different job. People sometimes assume that I have more power than I have and therefore expect that I can do more than I can. That is only propagated by the election process, when so many candidates make promises that they have no authority to make, people hear it and expect it." I asked, "I assume that you didn't do that did you?" "Of course not", was his reply. "That is part of what I meant by being yourself." There was the question again about how you win when your opponent is lying. Hank had already answered that question (for his situation) by sharing how he knew so many people and had name recognition. That was one answer but not an answer that applied to me. I'm not sure it applied to the bigger objective either, but I would have to think about that.

I stood and thanked him for taking the time to share his experience with me. He said, "I'm not sure that I was any help. If you think of something else, just give me a call. And remember, don't try to be a big fish in any size pond. That's not what it is about."

We shake hands; I thank him again and walk out the door. I see this town in a different light now. It has an appeal that wasn't present before talking with Hank.

Chapter 27
Organizational Structure
Mid-day Day 7

I almost hated to leave this pleasant small town, but I head out and drive past the "Now leaving Brayton – Come again" sign. It is another reminder of the nature of the town. Hank's words of "Don't try to be a big fish in any size pond" are stuck in my head and for good reason. I believe it was much more than a comment about me or my run for city council. Being a big fish or even wanting to be a big fish has characteristics that are anything but appealing, and I almost felt embarrassed for asking that question of Hank. The answer, however, is likely a very good ramble trigger for me.

This is not the first time this has come up for me but it has never been associated with the term 'big fish.' Big fish has all sorts of implications but to me it implies importance, some measurement of value recognition, power, authority, and possibly leadership. In that regard, the importance is not the small pond; it is about the big fish. If everything is relative, then it really is about the bigger or even biggest fish. It is about being at the top, or at least in the upper echelon. That is likely the reason that Hank was offended because he is not about power and recognition.

To those seeking power, the small pond portion of the phrase is insulting and demeaning. Those that thirst for power will never be satisfied with a small pond other than for a brief moment. The implication is that a big fish in a small pond is just another small fish in a big pond. That is not acceptable to those that seek power and control. The *scope* of control is critical.

Organizational structures require that the people at the top be identified and defined. The desire to be at the top drives behaviors that show the true nature of people. The path to the top is lined with bodies. Any action is simply the means to a desired end. I encountered organizational structures in my previous consulting work all of the time and it was almost laughable how transparent the behaviors were. They were not only transparent but they were almost identical across companies. One of the biggest organizational structures around is the government. The government is almost the poster child of organizational structures, and I don't mean that in a complimentary way. "Don't try to be a big fish in any size pond" made so much sense.

That does not mean to stop trying to achieve, or stop being a leader, or stop having ambition. It is about the purpose of the ambition. It's hard to find examples of leaders in corporations or government that are not solely in it for personal power and money. As the saying goes, they talk the talk but they don't walk the walk. The structure of an organization feeds that concept.

Leaders surround themselves with people that will agree with them and protect them. I was just getting going on this ramble when I noticed a very large caravan of military vehicles going the opposite direction on the highway. That is not a common site, but who knows what exercises they might be conducting. On the other hand, training areas would be more likely to be in rural areas or near their camps. There are no camps in the area or in that direction that I know of and that road leads to the big city. It certainly makes me wonder what is going on, enough to turn on the radio to see if I could hear anything.

Then I remind myself, even after all these years, that I can no longer turn on the radio for the real news. I would just get what the government wants me to get and if they are loading up military in big cities, they probably wouldn't broadcast it. Oh how I miss the 'old days' when journalists asked reasonable questions. What could be going on that would cause this extra military power over and above what is already there? Now *there* is an obvious question that I hadn't asked any of the groups; where does anybody get the real scoop about what is going on? You would think that if the group is focusing on the truth, they would at least share a way to get it with the group.

My thoughts about the military and where to get the scoop quickly melded back into the power-hungry leadership of organizations. This is not so much of a ramble about government but about human behavior and the lust for power that corrupts an organization from within. I believe the framers of the Constitution understood that aspect of human behavior and created the structure to try to protect against that almost inevitable result. That protection held and was respected (for a while) but it was also inevitable that those that seek the power would find a way to either circumvent or destroy those protections. They have been very successful at doing so. The structure of the three branches of government has effectively disappeared and only a facade remains.

The more typical organizational structure creates a tier of power that flows from the top, but the structure distorts on its way down because each layer contains those that seek and feign power within their scope and apply their own self-serving agenda. And so it goes until reaching the bottom. Along the way are clear inconsistencies that put each of the next layers in more of a position for potentially conflicting agendas. Even with those inconsistencies, objectives might be achieved but they will likely be filled with lies.

How many leaders in any layer within an organization would be willing to state the facts to the next layer up when they know that it would be detrimental to their own personal goals? It would likely be only the very few whose goals do not include advancement, or those whose personal integrity is more important. They would subsequently fail at climbing the ladder, but succeed at the more substantial goals of truth, honesty, and self-respect. Hank was right. Now add a twist in this ramble and remember the goal of the group; it is not about personal goals and climbing a ladder. The goal is about regaining rights as well as trying to preserve the Constitution and the country. That is a very important twist that changes the rules of the game, and when the rules change the strategy must change as well.

And now another convoy is going by in the same direction as the previous one. This one is even longer. Something is going on and I have to get home to see if I can find anything about it. I am almost there.

I turn the TV on as soon as I get in the house and am almost hoping that nothing would be there about it. If there is something about it, that would mean that they are in a position where they *have* to say something about it, and that would not be a good place to be. It won't be the truth but if they cannot just ignore it, *something* is happening. Maybe it's too local for national news and there won't be any local news until 5:00. How can I find out? I had a gut feeling that this was not just a simple military exercise. Was I being paranoid? I then remembered one thing omitted from my list, I had not called the number for the bank to close my accounts. If there is something more going down, I need to get my money before there is a run on the banks.

I looked up the number and called expecting a full barrage of questions and pushback on closing my accounts. I got none of that, they read their scripts of risks and about how much time it would take to fully close the accounts and that was that. They will send me most of my money from both accounts by check in 3 days and it will take 60 days to fully close the accounts. I don't care that much if they are closed. I just want my money. Fortunately I have almost everything converted to the credit union except for two auto-payments that I'll take care of right away. I will take the check to the credit union and deposit a thousand and get the rest in cash even if it has to happen over a couple days because they are a very small financial facility.

This structure and big fish ramble also took me in a new direction regarding not just our country, but also the entire world. It seems the scope of my ramble and my associated concerns were of an ever-growing scope. The world, in addition to the country, has become a volatile mess. Not only are they both a mess, they are intertwined. And not only are they intertwined, they are codependent. When we have a problem, our friends and enemies have problems and they react. The same is true in the other direction. The important factor, stating the obvious, is what the reactions are. It seems as though the world has been sitting on a bomb for the last few years, just waiting for someone to trip a wire that will blow the whole thing up.

It feels as though we are standing on the brink of a major change that will make the previous changes seem very small. This leads me to another safety measure that goes way beyond the FBI. I have thought for some time about investing in a generator. Many of my neighbors have solar panels, but I know they are not entirely operating on solar, and solar energy is weather dependent. I'm going to buy a generator and maybe one with auxiliary solar. I think that I can still find a gas-powered generator even though the government has banned the production of new ones. That's another obvious step that puts us at the mercy of those that would control us.

I need to slow down the ramble and step back into some action for today. I could look at my group lists again but I want to explore another avenue. I hadn't learned any campaigning techniques from Hank, but I had picked up some useful items. I'm going to go talk to some neighbors. This feels like a haphazard day without a list to fill my full day. Things are moving so fast, it really seems like I should have one, but I have a plan for now. Before I could get out the door, one of my phones rang and when I answered all I heard was "9:00 PM". That means I will be getting another communication within the day. With everything going on, I hope it's tonight. I also don't know if this is the small group or the larger one.

I was out the door and walking across the street while still trying to get a grip on what I might say. I didn't want to go back to where I had left off next to Cody's house, and I didn't want to go to the house that had the ambulance which was right across the street from Cody. I decide to hit the gossip group head-on and go straight across the street where the neighbors gather to observe me and my house.

I rang the doorbell and the door almost instantly opened as though someone was watching me cross the street. She was a rather large woman and she had a smile on her face which is a better start than previous doorbell rings. I knew her name to be Mary so I started with, "Hi Mary. I'm stopping over for a couple of reasons." She interjected, "Hi Carey. What can I do for you?" Okay, this was much better and quite unexpected. I continued, "I am wondering if you have security cameras that might have captured the activities in the street or at the front of my house a few nights ago?" I didn't see any visible signs of cameras on the outside of the house but somebody could put one inside pointing out a window and it was maybe a decent icebreaker. Mary did not seem at all fazed by the question, "We don't have any cameras." "But did you see activity even if it wasn't recorded?", I asked. "I sure did. It would have been hard to miss. We've had a lot of activity in the neighborhood lately."

My quick assessment of this situation was that she was likely a key to the neighborhood gossip and that she would likely gossip about anyone to anyone, but I would keep going to see how that played out. "What has all the activity been?" She said, "Well you know that the FBI came for you and just last night Mr. Jones was stabbed by his stepson." I started with Mr. Jones, "Is that what the ambulance was for last night? I didn't see any police cars." Oh she was eager to talk, "That was it. They took him out on a stretcher and the sheet was all bloody. They say he is going to be ok because it missed any major organs. They didn't know what happened until he was patched up and this morning the police came for the stepson. The stepson is in his early thirties and I think he has some mental issues." I wanted to say "you think?" but I didn't. I'm sure she would have talked more but I wanted to get to the FBI.

I am already trying to figure how this could be to my benefit or detriment and how much I should say. I had to comment on the Jones' situation, "That is so sad. I hope Mr. Jones recovers fast and that the kid gets some help." She gave a deeply concerned look and nodded. I continued after a pause, "I would like to share something with you about the FBI situation." Her gossip-driven ears perked up. "I haven't talked to anyone else about this in the neighborhood. The FBI came to my door and knocked it down." She said, "Yea, I saw." She was all lit up so I kept going, "They didn't show me a warrant, they took things from my house, and I had no idea what they took until the next morning. I have no idea why they came or what they were after." She looked suspicious of that statement. She wasn't really good at hiding her thoughts. That was fine with me. "I have no idea why and I went to the police and called the FBI the next day and they said they have no record of any warrants for me or any activity regarding me or my address."

She was obviously trying to process what she had just heard. Gossip is not a matter of facts, but a matter of juicy material and it usually doesn't matter who it is about. It does matter however that it comes from a 'friendly' source, so I was trying to be friendly. She was a friendly source to most for the neighborhood and probably beyond. I gave her a little more, "They were clearly at my house and they are denying it. That's why I asked if you had any security cameras that might have caught the activity. It wouldn't show everything they took or what they did to me, but it could at least show that they were there. I just really want to know *why*, but I can't even get the acknowledgement that it happened. People must think that I am a danger to the neighborhood if the FBI is coming to my house, but I have no idea what they want with me." I decided to stop. She was obviously processing still and I didn't want to create an overload.

She stood looking at me and then my house for a minute. Then she looked up and down the street. She pointed at a chair on her porch and said, "You want to sit down for minute?" I nodded and sat down. She started with, "I don't know you very well but I do know what I saw. If I had security cameras, there would be no harm in admitting it and letting the footage be used but I don't. I have a tendency to believe your story because I thought that it was odd that as the FBI was leaving your house they came to my house asking the same question that you did about security cameras." I just nodded so that I wouldn't interrupt her talking but *wow*. She continued, "When I told them that we didn't have cameras they asked about you and if I had any information about you that I would like to report. The idea that they used the word *report* and that they were fishing rather than asking specific questions seemed more like gossip rather than an investigation. I don't like gossip." I smiled and let her continue. "I know that they went to a few other neighbors' houses as well. Most didn't answer their door and at least one that didn't answer their door got a call the next day and they turned over the footage from their cameras. It seemed odd that they were not allowed to keep the footage from their own cameras. Some don't like that behavior and some just say it's the FBI so it's okay."

I didn't want to change the subject but I wanted to add a little more suspicion. "Did you notice the military vehicles going through the neighborhood?" She said, "I did but I didn't give it much thought. Do you know something?" I told her that I didn't know anything and, "I honestly didn't give it too much account, but after what happened to me I am looking at most things wondering if there is more to it. It will be better when I find out why, if I ever do." She was nodding through the whole thing and then offered, "I will check with some of the neighbors and see if they know anything and if they happen to have any camera footage of the other night. We are a neighborhood and we should stick together." If only I believed that I could trust her, but I did believe that she would stick her nose into things with far more success than I could.

This was my opportunity to change the subject. "I would really appreciate that and if you find anything please let me know. I don't want to drag anybody into anything with the FBI, I just want to find out why this happened to me. I have one more subject that is really not related and is at what could be considered an unfortunate time. I have decided to run for one of the open city council positions and I filed yesterday." I was glad again that she was so easy to read. I could tell that she could see it as a useful source of information and potential influence to have someone from the neighborhood on the city council. "Well, that's great." I couldn't really tell if she meant it this time so I added, "It was kind of a last-minute decision, but I am retired now and I want to try to help where I can. I don't really have any backing or any volunteers yet but I figured I would give it a shot. It seems like some decisions have been made that might not be in the best interest of our town, but I want to get out and hear what concerns people have about the town. So far the concern about increasing crime seems to be at the top of many people's list, that and road maintenance. " I wasn't lying even if the concerns were coming from me.

She then surprised me and said, "Let me know if I can do something to help. I think it would be great to have someone from the neighborhood on the council. If I find out something about the other night, I will call you and if you have something that you would like me to do for your campaign let me know." Wow, not what I expected walking across the street. I have to remember that she is still the prime gossip and will likely be standing outside the next time I burn toast, but right now she probably has an offering that I need. I said, "Thank you very much for the offer. Right now I would appreciate it if you could spread the word through the neighborhood." I tell her that I have a new phone number and the one listed on the HOA list no longer works, so I give her a few brochures that have my other contact information. I thank her again and tell her how nice it was talking to her and said, "I'll talk to you soon."

I walk across the street to home feeling her eyes the whole time and expecting that she will be on the phone to some of the neighborhood within a couple minutes. I just hope that I read her right. This also fit into the conversation with Hank. She is not in a formal organizational structure in the neighborhood, but she is potentially the primary gossip lead. Her word carries weight. She has the ability to influence what people think. She is to this neighborhood what I am not, a trusted known entity. Just like Hank knowing a lot of people, she is in that same position in the neighborhood. I'm not putting all of my eggs in that basket but it's a start.

Hank's view was neither about big fish nor small pond. It was not about structure and organization. It was about relationships and trust. His view of government is what is missing; government should be *part of the people* and serve the people rather than seeking the most power and control. I appreciate and respect that point of view. I would even say that I admire it. I believe that it should be, but is *not*, the mindset of our government. Hank is a good grounding position, but understanding the reality of the government is critical right now.

I sat down at my computer to check messages and saw "tonight". I still didn't know which group, but I am assuming this is the protocol for the larger group even though I don't think I was informed how the smaller group would be notified. I assume it would just be with a secure phone call, but I can find that out tonight regardless of which group this is. I start thinking of all of the questions that have come up for me in the last few days regarding the higher-level direction and communication.

As much as an organizational structure can in itself lead to corruption, it is still the power seekers that drive the corruption. The structure just increases the speed and strength of the corruption. While structure increases the ability for corruption, there can also be a significant problem when there is *no* structure. The efficiency and effectiveness toward a common goal requires some structure. I guess the key, as the framers of the Constitution knew, is to keep the evils of human nature at bay. I sure want to know more about this group's organizational structure.

Chapter 28
Worry and Fear
Evening Day 7

There's not enough time left to bother with a list for the rest of the day and my questions for the group tonight cannot go on a written list. If this meeting is the larger group, I believe that my major questions are around the higher-level direction and how that is coordinated. I also want to confirm that the real objective is to get the votes, and all of the remaining questions will logically follow from those two.

Since I don't know for sure that it is the larger group I should check my lists for the small group and update what I can. I got my computer, retrieved the flash drive, and pulled up the attribute list first. The list had just come up and the power went out. I was on my laptop so that didn't crash and it was still light out so it would have been almost unnoticeable except for the ceiling fan stopping and the digital appliance clocks in the kitchen going dark. There is also this 'calm' or stillness that seems to happen when the power goes out. It is not a common thing, but a power outage is usually during some sort of storm. This is not a storm but a rather nice day. I looked at the electric company's on-line map for outages and it is pretty lit up and each time I refresh the screen it is lit up even more. This is strange. I don't remember ever seeing such a widespread outage. It is pretty eerie.

I made sure I had flashlights and candles in case the electricity is not back on by dark and then realize it is suppertime and I haven't eaten since breakfast. I made a quick sandwich for me, fed Reggie, and took him outside. I thought I might as well work outside so I grab my laptop. I look through the citycouncilpolling file, as I had named it, and the only obvious item missing for me was *comments*. After talking with Mary, there are a few comments that would be worth capturing. I had thought that maybe her willingness to volunteer might be an additional one, but I think that will fit under one of the options in *support profile*. That will be able to hold a number of attributes like volunteer, committed voter, etc. There will be more that will be added as needs arise and as other sources provide data. We will hopefully utilize the companies so willing to sell or even give away people's information. That thought of getting data from data collecting companies brings my thoughts back to the next level up, or as many levels as there are, and the coordination of resources. There should be no need for this effort to collect the data more than once.

I am obviously concerned about the perceived lack of coordination. Is that undue worry? I do worry about things but this is not a concern that I would put in the worry category.

Worry is either a subset or an escalation of concern, depending on your point of view. Worry comes with a visualization that something bad can happen or something will not go as desired and can sometimes become consuming and even irrational. Worry usually causes one to consider possibilities, which is good, and yet worry can too often become an emotional state of mind that explains phrases like, "She worries all of the time" or "He is going to get an ulcer." That state is clearly not a healthy state.

It is true that it is possible to worry about things that are both in and out of your control and it can be helpful to recognize the difference. Worrying about things in your control can promote logical planning if held in check. Worrying about things out of your control is a whole different story. My kids are grown and I can't protect them or make decisions for them and sometimes I worry about them. There is nothing to do about that type of worry other than express your concern and move on. Concern, consideration of pitfalls, and the resulting planning are reasonable activities. Those things are not fear. Fear hits when your mind tells you that the looming bad is inevitable. There are no *absolute* lines, but these are good guidelines for me.

A life driven by fear is not only reactionary rather than planful, it is also likely illogical and just plain wrong. I have fears, but I try to recognize and remember that they are fears and illogical. That occasionally does not prevent them from ruling my decisions, but this is not one of those times. If the groups that I found following what happened to me with the FBI were on a strict and short timeline, my perspective might change. If I knew that the survival of the country was dependent upon these groups and that it would be too late to do anything at all if it was not done in the next 5 days, I would be worried. If I could see an inevitable horrifying picture of day six, it would likely be fear.

Fear is not the same as a sense of urgency and a plan that includes a great deal of caution is a better plan. There are too many bizarre things that happen and too many liars to not be cautious. The more people there are, the more liars there are. The more power people have, the more liars are created until it is nearly impossible to trust anyone that has *anything* to gain, even if the gain is perception rather than reality. Worry and fear are both real and so are liars and conspiracies. Being aware of when things are real versus perception, or real versus imagined is key to becoming a rational thinking being. Some might classify extreme caution in these circumstances as a 'healthy fear'. That seems quite an oxymoron to me. Fear is sometimes fear of real things and sometimes of imagined things, but the fear is real regardless and causes a change in behavior. I always *try* to be ahead of that disabling fear. Yes, fear disables rational and logical thinking.

One way to try to stay ahead of a disabling situation is to better understand what enables it and what triggers it. Some like motivational hype such as "courage is acting regardless of the fear" or "face your fears head on". That sounds like bravery is the answer, but the more realistic picture is far less heroic sounding. Facing fear is really understanding fear and understanding your priorities. A perfect plan would never create a situation where heroism would be relied upon, but perfection is not something that anyone can guarantee.

Plans B, C, and D are likely comprised of forethought with a great deal of caution. When all plans and backup plans fail, all that remains are priorities. Those concerned most with protecting themselves will likely run or hide, and those that have other priorities will execute toward those priorities with full understanding that self-preservation is lower in their priorities.

I walk through these considerations from time to time. It helps give me confidence in my planning process and is a good reminder of just how important priorities are. Priorities are why some people automatically help someone else and even put their life at risk to do so, and others stand and watch and take videos. Priorities say a lot about who people really are. I better get to my other list in case it's the small group tonight.

This list is short and the more I think about it, it *should be* short. There are two concepts of communication, but the actual implementation of both of them is dependent on the answer to not only the technical solutions but the answer to what is going on in the layer or layers about the group. The approach is only really effective if it is aligned with something bigger and if it is not, I might be wasting my time with this group.

It is about time to get going so I go through the computer, flash drive, and phone prep work for leaving. I at least got to spend a little more time with Reggie today than the previous few days. He laid right next to me as I was reviewing lists and rambling. I wonder if Reggie rambles. And I was out the door.

Mary is in front of her house when I pull out of the drive but this time she waves and smiles rather than that cold stare that I am more familiar with. I changed my route to the meeting place a little bit but still avoided the major highways with cameras. At this point I really don't think that someone is actively watching me, but data gets collected from cameras and they would be able to look if they wanted to in the future. I also could not be positive that nobody was watching. Protecting the group is still extremely important. I just need to know more about the group. The more I know, the more appropriate the placement will be in my priorities.

I'm in the alley 15 minutes early and this time I don't wait to be right on time. I knocked, stepped back, and John greeted me. I guess it is the bigger group. Good. John is manning the door and Tim is watching the cameras. There seems to be a higher level of intensity in the air. By 9:00 everyone is in and seated.

There was a lot of chatter prior to starting the meeting about why this meeting might have been called so soon after the last one. It is hard to know who is going to speak because of the lack of organizational structure. Sure, everybody had their roles and you might know who was responsible for facilitating the meeting and greeting people and researching and lots of various tasks, but who is in charge with enough authority to call a meeting so soon? I guess it could be that anybody could, but that might result in a meeting every other day. Somebody had to 'clear' the meeting.

Tim stood up and said, "I'm sure you all are wondering why we are having this meeting so soon after the last one." Of course heads are nodding all around. He continued, "We all are aware of some of the actions of the administration that have been eroding our rights. It has been identified that there has been an escalation in activities. People in this group may have noticed some things that have caused additional concern, but the general population still seems to be oblivious or even accepting of the escalations. We are here to discuss the escalations that have been observed and the potential resulting change in the structure of this group. These escalations that have been observed are not just local to our area and the subsequent changes to the group are not specific to just this group."

One thing seems obvious to me in these statements, so in my usual fashion there is no need to hide the question. "Does this mean that you are the single contact to the level or levels above?" He didn't seem all that surprised by the question and in a very business-like fashion simply said, "Yes it does. That is one of the changes to the structure and operations. There will still be safeguards in place to protect the group at all levels and between levels, but coordination is required that allows information to flow both upward and downward in a different fashion. There will still be a 'need to know' concept to protect people and the operations, but we need to act more uniformly because our opponent has become more aggressive."

I really wanted to say, "What the hell took so long to come to that conclusion?", but I decided to keep that for a more private conversation and I think Tim already knew that I thought that. This is not the group to ask the question of, it is the next level up. I decided to ask a question that I am not sure I would get an answer to. I wanted to ask how many layers there were and more about the entire structure but decided on, "Can you tell us if this coordination and direction is at a national level?" He simply stated, "At least." This is not such a simple answer. It is both comforting and concerning. It is good to know that it is a national effort and it is a concern, although not a surprise, that it goes beyond the country.

Tim started in again, "I will share what has been shared with me about observations and changes, but first I would like to hear if anybody in the group has noticed changes." There was at least 4 people starting to talk at the same time and within two seconds everybody realized it and there was silence with 5 people raising their hands like we were all in school again. That act told me a lot about this group. At a minimum it indicated group cooperation and respect. Both are essential for working effectively as a group.

My hand was one of the five. Sharon was the first to be called upon. She said, "I have noticed a lot more *we are here to protect you* and *you are safe* ads on social media." I have not touched social media since the FBI raid and I rarely did before that. Sam said, "I have been taking the same drug for the past 15 years and my drug store is out of it and has to call around to find it. That has never happened, but more strangely the same thing has happened to a couple of other people that I know and they are taking different drugs and are in different states."

I was kind of expecting everyone to have the same observations, but that was not the case. Carl was up next. "I drive around a lot to various towns and I have noticed a lot of military vehicles in a number of small towns that I have never seen before. I have also encountered dead spots for cell activity where they haven't been before." My turn, "I have seen the military activity in my town, but also a couple of quite large military caravans headed toward the big city. This is not a pattern of activity, but I also thought it was odd that the power outage tonight was so broad and ran from exactly 5:00 – 6:00."

Tim stepped in with, "That's a good sampling of observations. All this of course is on top of the slow erosion of the rights of people in this country and of the Constitution itself. The activity that has made the three branches of the government effectively one, along with the organizations of the FBI, DOJ, IRS, and NSA being political operatives, and the partnership with large corporations and the media has become more and more blatant.

"The military has been used to subsidize the local and state police to try to maintain order in the bigger cities, but it had been driven by the local authorities and at their request. That appears to be no longer the case. We believe that the move to military control in some big cities is based on crime that has now infiltrated their own ranks. Crime has been out of control and increasing ever since the move to demonize police and make the criminals the victims. Zero consequences have led to the lack of safety on the streets, which is why there has been armed military on the streets for years. Having them there provided the illusion of the 'authorities' doing something about crime. The crime had been contained for the most part to the areas that they really didn't care about and did not invade the area of their wealthy constituents or the government itself. That invisible barrier has been broken and the 'people that matter' are now insisting on protection of the highest order.

"The ads about safety and protecting the people clearly mean quite the opposite. People are not safe from the criminals *or* the military. Those in the government and their associates are identifiable with a scan from 50 feet away and will receive a pass from the military. If you are not identifiable, you are subject to any actions that they wish to take and they are free to take *any and all* actions in the name of *keeping people safe.*"

He wasn't done and continued after looking around the room for reaction, "This might seem like an opportune time to take advantage of their situation, when those that they have *enabled* are now turning against them. It might be, but as bad and obvious as it is so many people still believe that it is for everyone's benefit. I really don't understand that but it has been engrained over the years, which makes it hard to break such a deep-rooted belief. People can't imagine why their trusted government would lie to them. That may not last too much longer because there is something more at play.

"This government has used fear to their advantage in bringing people under their control. They made deals along the way to increase that power and control. The time to pay the piper is upon them. They created fear and hate based on lies and used it to bolster their position. There are real things that have been hidden that will hopefully soon be exposed. Of course they will continue to do their best to lie through the situation with blatant lies that deny reality. They will likely try to deflect people's interest. Deflection will likely be much more difficult because everyone will be directly impacted. Deflecting blame will inevitably be their only recourse and that is where we need to be prepared with the truth, but even that may not be enough. The situation has caused a shift in priorities from preserving the Constitution to one of preserving the existence of the country." It seems that *justified* worry and fear are about to set in.

Chapter 29
Keep Your Enemies Closer

Late Day 7

The questions were spinning in my head and I feel the need to write them down. I need to make a list, to get organized, and to collect more information. I know there is more to come and I did'nt want to interrupt Tim's flow so I bit my tongue, literally. I have an idea what he is referring to with everything that he has said so far and his previous answer of "At least". I have been concerned about this or something like it, if I am right, for many years. Others have previously raised concerns, but the concerns were always suppressed.

There was this slight pause and I am not the only one bursting with questions. Not everyone was able to bite their tongue. Sam burst out, "I have so many questions as I am sure everyone does, but first of all please get to what you believe is about to happen and why you believe that." I was halfway expecting the group to chant "Tell us, tell us", but it was a more reserved response than might be created by the *mobs* that we have become so accustomed to. Tim answered, "I am sure there are many questions and I have a lot of information to share. I will tell you where this started, what we believe is about to or is already happening, how we know this, and how our structure will change as a result."

Everybody, including myself, is anxiously waiting to find out more about what is going on. After a deep breath and a sigh Tim began, "As you are probably aware, the US government and large corporations have been doing business with China on an increasingly large scale for many years. An agreement was made by the government to allow China to have *all* intellectual property related to items not only produced in China but any items related to companies doing business in China. This has seemed totally absurd to me for decades but that is what was agreed to and that is only the beginning. Not only are we giving away all of the intellectual property to China, we knowingly allowed them to steal and create forgeries of products without consequences. Of course the government would occasionally state their phony outrage and the practices of China, but nothing changed and this is still just the beginning. Over this same time period China has been buying up our debt, buying into our major corporations, and buying up vast amounts of land some of which is next to nuclear facilities, missile sites, and military bases. Still more…they have created software and hardware chipsets that are part of our daily lives, including a significant portion of the country's government and infrastructure capabilities. It is not just that the government *allowed* such things to happen, they even *gave* China secret military technology. Was it stupidity or greed or something else?"

The question of asshole or stupid came to mind. Was he reading my mind? Tim continued, "It was clearly stupid but greed played a big role as well. Government officials and their corporate partners have been profiting from direct payouts from China and making deals that financially benefited the government elites for decades. There also seemed to be a very stupid expectation that they would be able to control China while using them to enhance their wealth as well as their power and control within our country. Regardless of their reason, you make a deal with the devil and the devil will always come for his due.

"The final straw in this, as if that was not enough, is that through their various 'we are taking care of you' programs, they managed to make our country more and more dependent on China. Our country, by design, would no longer be a manufacturing country (I guess it was too demeaning) so we had to rely on others to make things for us. That primary dependency was put on China. We played the game of eliminating our use of fossil fuel, while at the same time increasing the use of fossil fuel in China to produce our facade of no fossil fuel. We could not operate without the batteries, windmills, solar panels, and all of the devices that we are now dependent on China for. If those failed, we had no backup or ability to even survive, and yet the plan moved forward. All of the technology solutions that we designed and developed were now owned and controlled by China. All of our high-tech devices for our daily operations, which even include life-saving and life-sustaining medicine that so many are dependent on, are now controlled by China. We allowed the ramifications of a virus to kill millions with no consequences *at all*. This administration of ours as well as previous ones made the *deals* with China that gave our country away. They profited from it and probably thought that they were immune from any consequences because they were part of the *deal*. They thought that they would only become stronger, and richer. That plan was not sustainable. What do you give them to keep them at bay once they have everything they need?"

There is a 'tone' to the questions that I have because while those things are all horrible, they are nothing new to anybody paying attention. The country let it happen even when they were faced with evidence of corruption and told what the consequences could be. People are so enamored with lies and filled with hatred for anyone that disagrees or challenges the powers that are "looking out for them" that they refuse to see what is actually happening. These are prime examples of the results of years and years of hearing a single voice. Tim did a decent job of summarizing the international issues, but there were of course major internal issues that allowed that to happen. One question was burning. Why wasn't something done earlier? Why wait until we are in a state where the chance of turning it around seems nearly impossible? I am going to hear at least the next section of info before asking my questions. Maybe he will explain.

Everybody was pretty quiet and Tim was acting like he was waiting for some comments so I gave him one. "I don't know about everybody else, but none of this is much of a surprise and most of it was clearly out in the open and obvious that it was happening. Please continue with what you think or know is going to happen if everybody is okay with that."

Tim said, "I will and keep in mind this is obviously the condensed version. It is not just about what we *think* will happen. I will start with what has already happened. This group called out two of them in your observations. China is putting the squeeze on the administration. They warned 2 weeks ago that they would constrain a list of 12 specific drugs to show that they had the will and ability to do so. The brief shortage of these drugs is just a signal of power. What is left in stock will get spread out across the country over the next couple weeks, but it will still start showing up with people being very ill or dying very soon unless China opens the delivery again. They also told the administration that the power would go off in select areas in all 50 states. They provided the date, time, and duration and that is exactly what happened. This outage was just a warning and another show of power and control. The medication and electric outage are just a sample of the control that they hold."

Tim looked around at the intensity on the faces of the people in the room and then continued, "The administration is of course doing all that they can to suppress this information and the current and future threat that it presents. People have been misdirected to focus on so many other things that have nothing to do with the real threat. There are so many people, including some in the administration that think about warfare as conventional wars and invasions. They may think that the advancements allow for things like drones and satellite weaponry but the world has moved so far beyond that being the biggest threat of war. It is not even about borders anymore because with technology there are no physical borders. Can you imagine what would happen to the country if just the one single aspect of their control were fully executed – removal of access to electricity? You would have nothing functioning that uses electricity unless you have your own power source and once your power source is broken or depleted, there is no ability to replace it. Without power there would be no communication, no purchases with a credit card, no transportation because it either uses electricity or is dependent on it, no food preservation, no work or income, and no banking. Can you imagine the rush on banks, the general panic, and riots that would ensue?

"Electricity is of course just one of the strings that they can pull. We believe that they are playing with us like a cat plays with a mouse. These are just warnings or just fun flares of power for them. They want something more. We believe that they will likely start targeting certain people or groups of people. With all of the data, technology, and virus experimentation, we believe that they have developed DNA-specific biological weapons. Again, weapons are not what they used to be, they are as undetectable and as common as the wind, the air we breathe, and the water we drink. All this to what end?

"If you combine the agenda of this administration and previous ones that moved the country to a more socialist nature with less and less freedoms, we have to wonder whose plan it actually was. Sure the administration leaders and their friends got rich and gained more perceived power, but who was pulling the strings? If you put the country in total panic and despair and someone comes in offering a solution that will not only remove the areas of most recent panic but also restore order to the streets, many people would be extremely likely to accept it with open arms. It would seem less radical to many who have been conditioned over time to accept a communist form of living. There would be no speaking against the government (that's not new), so many regulations that you are not free to run a business in the way you want (that's not new), and the government provides for your needs as they see fit (also not new). People have been conditioned to look to the government for solutions so how many would not just accept calming the waters? Of course if you speak against the government or break their declared laws, you die; oh but what a small price to pay for being taken care of. I think you get the general idea."

I couldn't restrain my primary question anymore because this information made it even more pressing. "Tim, I know you are going to get to how you know this, but I believe you because it just logically makes sense. I also know you are going to talk about how our structure changes. My question is why did this take so long to react to what everyone has evidence of? You likely had more information than the rest of society and I was already concerned that the operational structure of this group and lack of national leadership seemed to be missing the point of the whole thing. Why not be more structured, organized, and purposeful before it got this far? It honestly makes me question whether the leadership of this organization (if there is such a thing) is part of the whole plan and we have been manipulated into ineffectiveness."

It seemed that most of the group was appalled by my outburst. I know what I said and I stand by the question. It is an honest concerned question and not an accusation and if someone has a problem differentiating the two, I probably can't work with them anyway. After giving others a chance to offer an outburst of their own Tim sat down and responded, "I would say that is a valid concern and prior to now, not much was shared with groups at this level. It might be true that this group, because of not having the full story, was manipulated but not for the purpose of enabling the government or our enemies. There were various tactics that were tried with various groups. Some tactics were aggressive and some were quite passive as this one has been. A lot has been learned from all tactics, including this one. It is also true that the more aggressive tactics were much more risky and people have died in the process. The information collected across all of the groups has been used to formulate a more holistic plan. Actually the previous plan was holistic, it was just not uniform in its approach across the network."

I wonder if people in the room glossed over the "people have died" part? It actually didn't shock me that people could die pushing back on the government. What it told me was that there was more to the holistic group than was visible. I also did take note that he used the word "network" for the first time since I have been involved with these groups. I simply said, "Thank you for that information."

Tim still had two sections left from his brief outline that he said he was going to share. The next should be how they knew what they knew and I thought that it was pretty obvious because the government seemed to be so arrogant and confident in its power that they didn't feel the need to hide much of anything.

Tim stood back up as if he was back to his teaching time rather than conversation time. "It is clear that much of what

I offered for background is public information and the things that you observed are obviously public for those that care to notice. What is not public is the operational information that is happening *now*. We do have insight into some high-level communication with China, the administration's plans for spinning this information, and the status of our vulnerabilities. Our network includes people in very unique positions that have access to top-secret information in the administration, some of the largest partner companies, news media, and a number of other carefully selected positions in many other areas. These people are obviously at significant risk if their affiliation with our group was to be discovered. That is one of the reasons that the protection of the identities and the communication process has been the way it was. We will still not divulge any of their identities or roles, but I can assure you that information coming from them as well as their positions of potential influence is extremely important to our purpose. We know from these sources that China has another show of power planned for two weeks out and that their ultimate purpose is to completely control the country. We believe the way that they would control it would be *through* the administration rather than a takeover of the administration. There are some of us that would say they have already been doing that, but there would no longer be a pretense with the administration that they are negotiating. The administration would simply agree to be controlled, take orders from China, and never tell the public the details of what is happening. It could be argued that even that is not that much different. They would just continue to lie but what they are covering up would be different. Without that arrangement, further action will be taken in two weeks or sooner. They conveyed two weeks but they also indicated that depending on how they see the agreement coming along, they might move the timeline up. They have not stated what the next event or events would be."

Now there were reactions to be seen around the room. This information was clearly beyond public knowledge. As much as it seemed inevitable that the country was allowing China to do all the things that would give them control and put the existence of the country at risk, it is disturbing to hear how far it has gone. I think that most people that gave any thought at all to the matter thought that it wouldn't really happen to our country. They believed or at least wanted to believe that our leaders were not trying to destroy the country. While I believe that some have been trying to destroy it, I also believe they thought that they would remain in power. I think that their stupidity and greed got in the way of being able to see that they were also rapidly moving down the path toward making their own involvement unnecessary."

I had anticipated an onslaught of questions and comments but the room was silent. I guess it was a lot to take in. Of course everybody would have questions, including me, but the information had to sink in a bit and the next part about the organization of our group and 'network' should prove to be very interesting.

Tim said, "I know that I have dumped a lot on you, but it is important that I get to the next part of this. It is not just how our structure will change, but our roles and purpose will as well. First off, let me say that some of these changes may cause some of you to rethink your participation in the group and that is fine, but I think that there will likely be an acceptable level of participation options based on your desire, relationship situation, and risk tolerance. Some positions will significantly increase an individual's personal risk. First off, our current structure includes our level of area groups that cover 2-12 counties, there are the more informal groups that you are aware of and some have had some participation in, and you are aware that there is something at a higher level above this group. There is actually a lot above this group. There are operations, intelligence, strategy, and finance groups. There is also one overarching leadership group above all of those. There are also international counterparts for operations, intelligence, and the leadership level.

"Our new structure will be quite similar with a few very important operational differences. The communication between the levels will be more open, while still protecting the network. I will share more details on that later with those that need to know. Activity level and engagement are going to push down a layer. This level of group (the area groups) will take a more active role that will require more time and will include a bit more risk. It is not full time but it will take more of a time commitment than it does now. Because of that, it is fully expected that this group will shrink a bit. It is also possible that a select few in the group will move up into one of the next layers. Those wanting to maintain about this level of activity and the more passive nature that this group has been will move to what are now the more unmanaged groups. Those groups will move up in their role to about where this group is now, but with more operational structure. People in those groups that do not wish that additional involvement and some form of structure will move into what we will refer to as interested parties. These are individuals that are of like mind and would like more information as it is available. They will not receive sensitive operational information, but they would like to understand more of the truth of what is happening and they would be likely to vote for a change if we can ever get back to that. Many people will want information, but would not want their name on a list for fear of being associated with something that the government would punish. That is okay; we will be trying to formulate more general public communications.

"It will be part of our overall purpose to get information to the people that are interested and build the 'membership', if you will, in the lower more informal layer. Support from people in that layer is needed for voting (if we make it that far), being a voice to others, or providing physical support for protests as the opportunities arise. The people in the groups at that level would not be committing to those actions, but would be provided the opportunity to participate. The groups such as this one and up will focus on a couple of key approaches. There are a few ways to put this and the easiest way might sound like submitting but it is not. We will be attempting to build temporary emergency infrastructure and supply chain mechanisms in order for a group of people and ideas to survive. That is survival, but it is a realistic view of the potential future and is a very aggressive objective. Another simultaneous approach is to try to undermine the communication and execution between China and the government leaders. We have some key roles that can assist with that. That approach is very dangerous and will need to have precise planning and execution. Timing is critical on those events and timing is very short on the survival approach. I know there will be a lot of questions regarding specifics but we have to move fast and people can always move to a different group after choosing. This is not a commitment forever, but I would like to get an idea of where you stand based on this information. The people that would like to stay around this level of participation, please gather over there. The people that want to stay in this group with added commitment and risk collect in the middle here and those interested in even more commitment and risk, move over there."

Tim was very animated with his hand movements for the places people were supposed to gather. This is going to be very interesting and could be a very small sampling of what it might be like elsewhere and across the country. It's not a big enough or diverse enough sampling to be predictive, but still very interesting. People started floating around and looking around. The looking around was quite interesting in itself. Is it really important for such a decision to try to determine what a friend or acquaintance would choose to do? I think people that are looking for that direction or reassurance want to or need to *follow* and will probably be better off moving down a group. At first it seemed like no groups were forming, just a lot of mingling and the volume of chatter got quite loud, but it is now starting to settle down. The volume decrease was proportional to the separation and forming of groups. And there we had it. Three groups.

I was expecting that about 80% of the group would not want more commitment and therefore move down. It ended up at about 50%. The group that would desire to stay in the same group with increased commitment is 30% and the group that I am standing in is 20%. Tim is in this group as it turns out because he is already in the intelligence upper-level group. I think that it is not a coincidence that this group is our small group minus Sam. I am pretty sure that Sam would have been in as well, but he has a family with four school-aged children. He has his priorities and I respect that. I know he will support what he can. He did stay in the same group with increased commitment and I am sure that is a stretch for him. The 50% probably includes some in similar situations that moved down rather than staying in the same group because of priorities in their life. There are also likely some in that group that just want to be purely passive throughout and would not consider any additional risk. It is still priorities that drove their decision.

The level of time commitment and communication started showing immediately as Tim announced to the group that the group moving down was dismissed and that they could expect that more would be communicated at their next meeting. That next meeting would take place in this place and would be communicated in the same fashion. After about ten minutes of slow goodbyes, we are here with half of the original group. It is already almost 11:00 and normally the group would be done by now, but I have a sense that it is just beginning and I am in for a long night.

Tim began again with, "Welcome to a new era of resistance." That word *resistance* had a feel about it that we have definitely engaged in something different. He continued, "I'm sure that you all realize that the activities that we are about to engage in would likely be considered criminal and treasonous by our government and of course by China. That is actually not new because they could have declared that at any time without proof, but this is a level up. We will actively resist what they are doing.

"For one brief moment I want to remind you how we got here. Out of both greed and stupidity our government engaged in a deal with China that has given them the power and leverage that they need to control our country. Was our government stupid enough to believe that they were following the saying to KEEP YOUR FRIENDS CLOSE BUT KEEP YOUR ENEMIES CLOSER? I don't think they could have possibly have been so stupid to think that. Keeping your enemies closer means to stay close enough to them to understand what they are doing so they don't take you by surprise. Our government did quite the opposite. It is also quite ironic that the saying about keeping your enemies closer came from a *Chinese* general many centuries ago, the same general that wrote the The Art of War. If our government had read that book, they maybe would have understood the tactics that would have prevented this situation. China has been open for centuries, and even more so in recent times, about their desire to rule the world. Did anybody think that they were just kidding? Yes, our government was that stupid. Instead of keeping our enemies close, they pretended they weren't enemies and thought they were making them partners because they were blinded by greed. Greed for power and money."

Chapter 30
You Reap What You Sow

Even Later Day 7

There are so many phrases that come to mind regarding this situation such as "You reap what you sow" and "You made your bed, now lie in it." There are apparently so many similar phrases because it is so common that this particular human behavior is repeated regardless of the warnings to the contrary. The impact that one's actions have is not always as obvious or devastating as these results, but they *are* going to happen. The ones most surprised by the results of their actions are those that failed to look beyond their short-term benefits and just applied their narcissistic views to the actions. They seem to believe that if it is good for them *now*, it must be a good decision.

That concept is giving the government an undeserved benefit of the doubt that they were not planning to turn the government over to China all along with the belief that they would be part of the Chinese elite. Good plan, if that's what it was. I am so eager to dig into more details of what has been done and start having some input into what can be done. I don't think I have been tuning Tim out while going on this brief ramble, but I should really focus. I am sure that there will be time for rambles later. There better be.

Tim was still talking, "… and we will have a very secure network of communication between the members of the groups and between the levels (still with a single contact), but the contact will be known within the groups. This approach and development of the technology was actually funded by the government. All devices are built in the US with no Chinese software or hardware and the communication uses a proprietary encrypted network. This reduces the impact that our government or China can have on our operations, but we *would* be impacted by an electrical outage. That is why we are also working on a small alternative electrical grid. That grid will take a bit longer but it has begun so it can be partially available in small areas. We will have locations as a fallback plan to house hundreds of people in many locations across the US if need be. Yes, we realize that *hundreds*, even times a hundred, is not many in the scheme of things but we have to start. These locations will not be divulged to anyone until they are needed other than to the people planning them. I could go on with the fallback plan but that is not the focus of this group."

Tim was clearly talking to the 30% group that was the current area group and he continued, "Your focus is going to be on trying to subvert the complete takeover. Keep in mind that there are about 500 groups like this across the US and your efforts will be supported by all of the groups above the area groups as well as the international groups. The subversion of the takeover will take place on a number of fronts and they do not all align with the previous set of operating guidelines. We would like to not use some of the tactics of our opponent such as hatred, mistrust, and manipulation but that may not always be possible. Part of the problem with this escalation is the engrained trust that the current administration has been able to create through lies, hatred, and programming. We cannot break that spell without breaking the administration and their partners along with it. The trust has to be broken and very fast. Each of you will be assigned tasks within your unique skills and positions to either take some action or collect information.

"Nobody is being forced to do anything and you can always change your mind, but we hope that you don't. This is more than enough information for one night so we will end here. The next meeting of this group will be in this place with the same method of communication for date and time. At that time more details will be provided and communication after that meeting will change. Sit tight for a day or two at the most and we will be in touch. This group is dismissed."

There was again the 10-minute slow discussion and shuffle toward the door and then there remains the four of us, Tim, Sharon, Carl, and myself. This is a small group and yet I suspect that we will not actually be a group for long. As we sit at a small table now facing each other there is somewhat of a group sigh and I said, "Well." It wasn't a question as in "what now?", but rather just a statement of "Here we are." The ball is clearly still in Tim's court and we are waiting, but this is also a more aggressive group, or at least made up of people that were willing to be. I'm thinking back to our small group meeting and how I had kind of taken over and realized that Tim was clearly holding back.

Tim spoke, "The problem that this group was put together to propose solutions for has, for the most part, been solved from a technology solution perspective by the government. We have the ability to use technology developed by the government through our members and contacts. This is a pattern that we will likely follow in most areas. We will use their words, technologies, and strategies against them. One could say that the plan is for them to defeat themselves and how appropriate that would be. We will no longer meet as the small group that we formed, but we will all be involved at a higher level. I want to let you know as well that everybody volunteering is not just a haphazard 'let everybody do what they want' approach. There were five people other than myself that were cleared for moving toward the upper ranks. Fortunately all three of you were part of those five. Your initial placement in those upper groups has also been defined. You can dispute that placement if you wish, but I think you will see it as making sense."

He was right. Our placements made sense and Carl and Sharon would be together in the operations team and I was on the strategy team. Since each of these teams would be unique in their focus and work to be done, a group meeting of this team was not really necessary. I suspect that we will all be busy enough with our respective roles. That did not mean that we would never see each other again, but we found ourselves wishing each other well. While we were doing that Tim had left and came back with three phones. These were satellite phones that would be completely off network and impervious to communication outages of any "normal" type.

It was odd to even think the word *normal* anymore. I am up for a challenge but this is definitely getting extreme. As I go back to thinking about the cause of this and how many years this has been in the works, I can't just blame the administration. Of course they made it happen; they planned, lied, committed crimes of untold nature, and manipulated people into doing their bidding. But many companies in this country stepped into this for their own greedy motives and the population of this country, regardless of how many lies were told, were in a position to stop this and they did nothing. They were either greedy in their own fashion of being bought out or too lazy to look at the reality in front of them and get involved. Oh, and there is the *A* or *S* again. It was too much work, their friends were all doing it, or any number of many childish and foolish reasons. Whatever their reason, they appear to be very near to reaping what they sowed.

Chapter 31

Read a Book

Just Turning Day 8

The night drew to a close just minutes before midnight and it was time once again for that very familiar drive home; another drive home when I am astonished by the events and discoveries of the day. Absorbing all of the information before getting home was not going to happen. This is going to be the trigger for rambles and more discoveries in perpetuity. These discoveries contain the type of information that is so engrained in human behavior that it will never end. All I can do is attempt to understand and use the information each and every day to try to make my life and everybody else's life better. That sounds a bit altruistic, but it is life as I see it, so maybe nothing has really changed other than the details. I always need to learn more, and the opportunity to learn has just had the doors flung wide open.

I am pulling in the driveway and I don't think there were any specific thoughts or rambles on the way home, which is unusual. I think I was just in a bit of a fog contemplating the massiveness of this thing that I find myself in. It is sad that our country is where it is and it is even more sad understanding how it got here. It is also exciting in a strange sort of way to be involved in an attempt to stop the lunacy. I walk in the house greeted by a very eager to get outside Reggie. I poured myself a drink and went outside to sit. Pouring a drink at this time of night (morning) is not typical, but this was not a typical evening.

It is now past midnight and I suspect that I am not going to get much sleep tonight. As I think about the way that the government has completely screwed this up and allowed the enemy to manipulate them into just what they wanted, the concept of "know your enemy" comes to mind again. Just who is the enemy at this point? China certainly is an enemy and the government has proven itself to be an enemy of the people. The people that support the government are, in a different sort of way, an enemy. That may seem disturbing to some but they are the enablers and it cannot change without them changing. We need to understand them. We need to understand all of them.

I thought about the phrase "Keep your friends close but keep your enemies closer" earlier and it was obvious that our government did not either understand or pay attention to the meaning. It is so ironic, not only that it came from a Chinese general but that it was created about 500 B.C. This is *not* a new concept. The Art of War is much more about winning without war than it is about war (as in physical fighting). The strategy outlined in that book was arguably created by one of our enemies and is a timeless strategy and recognition of human behavior. I happen to have a copy of that book and it makes sense for me to reread it, or at least scan it.

I know that one of the clear concepts in the book relates to knowing your enemy, but the concept is not understood by some or we would not be here in the way that we are. Knowing your enemy takes effort. A brief summary of that concept is that if you know both your enemy and yourself, you should have no fear in any battle. If you know yourself and not your enemy, you are likely to lose at least 50% of the battles. If you know neither yourself nor your enemy, you are destined to lose every battle. Battle does not mean a physical battle. We have been losing very close to all, if not all, of them on all fronts.

As I scan through the book I am reminded of more and more phrases and concepts that most people probably don't realize had their origin with Sun Tzu. There are so many, but another one that stands out to me in this situation is, "To secure ourselves against defeat lies in our own hands, but the opportunity of defeating our enemy is provided by the enemy himself." That sounds very much like the strategy that was discussed tonight. We need to use what the enemy provides against them. That is going to include not just knowledge of them but also technologies, strategies, and even people. Understanding who they are, what they offer, what they have done, and what they are likely to do will allow us the opportunity to defeat them.

I am going to continue to read this book and then start making a list of our enemies' actions at least at a high level that we might use it against them. It's cooling off and I better get inside and get to bed. I will attempt to read in bed, but not sure how far that will go at this time of the morning.

Chapter 32

Enemy Number One

Early Morning Day 8

As expected, I didn't read much more before falling asleep. Also as expected, I didn't sleep very long. The situation is quite critical and while I did get some much-needed rest, my mind is eager to get going in earnest again. Four hours of sleep under these circumstances is plenty. It often happens that thoughts and rambles continue into the next morning, but they continue with a different point of view that almost always seems to have a little more clarity. I was about to go down a path of the types of technologies, strategies, and actions that have been used by our enemies in order to use them against them, but it was clear this morning that was missing a step.

While my gut tells me that there are similarities in some aspects of our enemies, it seems quite likely that they are also going to have some significant differences. It is important to understand all of our enemies, but addressing them may require priorities. What is the sequence to address the enemies? What dependencies are there? What cause and effect is there between them in their creation as an enemy and in the solution? I may find through this consideration that this thought process is incorrect, but I have to follow it because addressing the enemies in the wrong order (if there is one) could be fatal. And I do mean literally fatal.

There seems to be a natural hierarchy to the three enemies with the people of the country that so misguidedly support, follow, or just allow the government to do what they are doing on the bottom. We cannot successfully change in the long-term without them, but they are *followers* so they are not in the lead position of the threat priority. Between our government and China, it might be more difficult to determine the priority. China outright ruling the country would be the most devastatingly obvious loss of the country, but it seems that is not their first plan of attack. The first plan is to get the government to submit, fully relinquish control, and take orders from China. I guess when I think about it, there is little difference between that and taking over the country other than the implementation. That would be another strategy straight from The Art of War, avoiding outright war and beating your enemies before the battle begins.

If I were to just look at the highest risk of irretrievable loss, I would be looking at China as the highest priority. If I did that and was successful (which I am not sure how that would work without the support of our government), the government will still be left to execute its greedy and stupid agenda on the country and their followers will likely continue to grow. They may even escalate their alliance with other enemy countries.

It seems like the government of our country needs to be the highest priority, but I always try to poke holes in my conclusions, especially ones that seem so obvious. Will the people rise up against the government if the government changes its position and direction? That answer is obvious. They have not objected to so many illogical direction shifts, contradictory statements, and bold-faced lies so far. It would be hard to believe that they would object to *any* content coming from the government even if it was the truth. Wait; there might be a fourth enemy that doesn't fit in the other three. What about the powerful companies that have both an alignment with our government and directly with China? They support the government and they not only make significant money directly from China, they are very outspoken in support of China and willing to provide them with technology related IP as well as vast amounts of data. The only way they are likely to stop is under direct order and supervision of the US government. They certainly wouldn't do it out of a patriotic or moral obligation. I am back to our government being the priority.

If we do succeed with the government alignment, what will China do when there is pushback? They hold the power to so many aspects of the country's operations. They apparently can control the power grid, the medical supplies, the majority of the supplies of products and components for all non fossil fuel sources, an untold amount of the software and hardware used by citizens as well as major companies and some of the government, and the list goes on. What impact would that have on people? It would be devastating.

It would seem at this point that focusing on our government is a priority, but we need to be simultaneously working a plan to 'dissuade' China from executing a full outright takeover through disruption and the creation of panic and chaos. Let's assume for a moment that the government can be transformed and will actually resist China. Let's also assume that we have a way to communicate with the masses of people in the country. Under those two assumptions (understanding that they are major assumptions), using the engrained pattern of hate might provide the opposite effect that it has been used for recently. Hate was a major factor in bringing the current administration to power, including hate for their political opponents and anyone that sided with them. They used hate as a divisive tactic in this nation, but hate can also be used as a unifying tactic. It brought their followers together but what if the enemy was no longer within the country? Would it unify? The tragedy of 9/11 had a unifying effect (with the right direction and support).

This conversation of hate is not one that they would have ever had in public, but it has clearly been a theme for decades. Hate creates division and they have been very persistent, repetitive, and ultimately successful at using hate to divide the country. Division brings weakness and chaos to the whole. Here is another opportunity to turn the tables on them with lessons from Sun Tzu. "With chaos comes opportunity" and "Appear weak when you are strong, and strong when you are weak."

They have been very good at creating chaos and crisis for their benefit, what they don't expect is that someone else could use the same chaos for their own opportunity. They are too arrogant to consider that they might be vulnerable. They are horrible at the second lesson. They do quite the opposite. They would make horrible poker players. I have come to this conclusion as an initial strategic operational opportunity, but I have yet to meet with an already formed strategy group at a national level. How is it that I am even allowed to know about such a group much less be part of it? It all seems so fast and too easy to just become part of such a critical initiative. That gives me concern and is raising some red flags regarding what exactly is going on. So far my concerns with the group have ended up being addressed. I hope the same is true for this. Simple math tells me something is not right. Even if there is only one person from each area group allowed into the strategic group, that means there would be hundreds of people in the group and that is just not even close to a realistic number for a functional group. It seems I might not have long to find out as my satellite phone is ringing.

Chapter 33

Process of Elimination (Part 1)

The Rest of Day 8

I answered the phone and I didn't know who it was. They instructed me to prepare to be gone for 3 days and that there would be a car to pick me up at 1:00. There was no room for discussion. There was no negotiation of time; just an expectation, but I guess that is what I signed up for. I was concerned before but it is escalating further. There is something about just being given orders to be ready and having a car pick me up that heightened my concern.

Prior to that it was a different kind of "why me?" I really cannot imagine why I would be able to make it to the national level of something as big as this. I work hard, I'm pretty smart, and I am aligned with what I believe their objectives to be, but I am what I consider to be a pretty ordinary guy. I have done pretty well, but I am not famous or rich by any means. I am not poor either so I just kind of sit in the middle as a generally unnoticed person. I have no need for notoriety or even what some might consider success. I care so much more about family than money and so much more about integrity than position. People with these values do not usually end up in a position that looks like where I seem to be headed. I feel honored in a way and yet I feel like there must be something that's just not as it seems. There must be more to the story. Why me? It can't be that easy to move from a retired guy with a dog in his living room to joining a national level strategy group to take on the government. This apparently even includes partnerships with other countries.

I am so far in at this point, I'm not pulling back now so I will move forward with a great deal of caution. I'm not paranoid; this is just some pretty crazy shit. Now I need to rapidly find accommodations for Reggie. I left him a couple times in kennels a number of years ago and that will be an absolute last resort. He didn't do very well. I'm going to give my daughter a call and see if she will watch him for those days. She has stopped in to feed him a few times but has never been able to take him home because they were renting, but now they have a house. I made the call and it was going to work out, but I had to pack up his stuff and get out the door fast. It was almost two hours round trip and that would only leave me a couple of hours to prep for being gone for three days.

The drive there was not hidden from anyone and Reggie loves going for rides, so it was just a good 'normal' adventure. If he could talk, he would be yelling "shotgun" as we headed toward the car. He likes sitting in the passenger seat and taking it all in. It was a nice break and it did feel *almost* normal. I hadn't seen my daughter for a few weeks so it was good to see her and catch-up briefly. I had to 'stretch the truth' (lie) when she asked where I was going. I told her that I had a consulting gig out of town. This was kind of true; it just wasn't *all* of the truth. I'm glad she didn't ask where because the truth of that is that I have no idea.

As I'm driving home I'm going over the enemy priorities and associated logic so that I could make the case to the group and then I started thinking about the complexity and potential next steps. How do we succeed against the government? Not only how do we succeed, but also how do we do it in a very short period of time. Voting them out is not an option in the short term. The election is too far away. And before I could get very far into that, I was home.

The first thing that I did was make sure that I had everything that needed to be secured in the house taken care of. I then realized that I wasn't sure if I could or should bring my laptop, but I assumed not. I was also pretty sure that I could not bring my phone(s), which made me wonder how my kids would get ahold of me if they needed to and what they would think if they couldn't. I turned my phones off and bagged them intending to bring them with; I was sure I would be told if I couldn't. I didn't have a lot of clothes to choose from and comfort is still the key. One small duffle bag took care of my clothes and toiletries. I'm not going to wherever I am going to impress someone with my clothes. I had never left a burner on or a coffee pot on when leaving the house, but something about this trip made me check things that I had never checked before. Yes, I was a bit nervous. I wasn't scared, it was more anticipation of what might be ahead.

Excitement might even be a better word, but that seems odd in such a dire situation.

It was 5 minutes to 1:00 and the house seemed so empty without Reggie; my bag was packed and the coffee pot was turned off. A car pulled in the driveway and holy crap; it looked just like the government black car that had been driving slow around the neighborhood the other day, dark windows and all. Someone got out and came to the door.

She was all business and without saying hello asked me to confirm my name and told me that from now on I would be referred to as Roger 5. Then she asked if I had any electronic devices and I showed her the phones in the Faraday bag and she said, "I need to take those. You will have access to them when the situation is secure and appropriate. Can we step inside for a minute?" We stepped in and she proceeded to scan me, and my duffle bag. I assume she didn't want the neighbors to see that. Her speech seemed to have no intonation at all and there was never even a smile, "We can go now if you are ready." I nodded, set the alarm, and locked the door. She took my bags and put them in the trunk and we were off.

I had remembered to take a closer look at the license plate before getting in the car and it was not a government plate, but I'm not sure that meant much at this point. I had no idea how long of a drive it would be, or if it would be a drive to the destination, or to another form of transportation. Maybe it would be a teleconference? These guesses could go on and on but it really didn't matter because I was not in control and I don't like not being in control of myself. She was not a conversationalist so it was pretty much silence in the car. It also didn't seem to take very long, but in actuality it was about an hour. The windows were dark and opaque from the outside and I could see through from the inside, but it was very dark and made it difficult to get a clear idea of my surroundings. It seems that we were pulling into a parking garage and when the car door opened that was confirmed.

There are no big signs that give away where we are and she quickly led me through a door and into an elevator. She pushed the button for 4 and as the door was closing with her on the other side she said, "I'll take care of your bags." The doors open and I am greeted by two men. One said, "Welcome. Please follow me." He leads me into a room and asks if I want something to drink. I pass and he tells me it will be just a minute. I thought, *what* would be just a minute?

It was just a minute before someone else walked in the room. She introduced herself as Naomi 2. To this point I don't think I had said one word since arriving and I saw no reason to start now to any significant degree so I just said, "Hi." She was dressed quite formally in business attire, almost looking like I would expect an FBI agent to look while in the office. Most of the people so far had been dressed far more formal than I was, but so what.

I long ago gave up on the importance of superficial items like clothes and even college degrees. Yes, I called college degrees superficial. They have become even more so in the past number of decades. I might even have a little chip on my shoulder over that one. People that are hired and rewarded purely on a piece of paper, or clothes, or skin color, or style of hair, or anything else are much more likely to be bad at their job. Slow down Roger 5.

Naomi 2 started with what seemed like was going to be a scripted speech, but I think I *might* see some expression on her face, "We appreciate you coming and volunteering for this assignment. I'm sure you have a lot of questions, but first we have some questions for you. As you can imagine, purely based on the number of area groups, we cannot operate a strategy group with hundreds of people. Our max capacity for members is 20 and we had 8 before all of the restructure happened. That means that we need to filter the 150 candidates down to 12. We have already eliminated about 40 from our background checks and now we are in the next stage. If you are still up for this, our screening process will take about 24 hours and will run from the time you were picked up until 1:00 tomorrow. Shall we continue?"

I think I was wrong about detecting some emotion on her face, but this has already answered a number of my questions about how they could possibly run a group with so many people. It also alleviated a number of concerns regarding the lack of structure as well as increasing my interest in the answer to why they waited so long. I suspect I will find out a lot more if I make it through the screening process. 150 down to 12 is a pretty heavy cut and I can think of all sorts of reasons why I would be cut, but I obviously didn't know what their criteria would be or the process that was facing me. I don't even know who these people are or for that matter, where I am. I am not a trusting person by any means and yet here I am, and here I go. "Let's get started."

The first test, if you will, seems to actually be an inkblot test. I did one of these many many years ago when I was much younger, and I don't recall even why I was given the test. I guess it's not really a test, but rather a method of evaluation that seems pretty subjective to me. They direct you to say the first thing that comes to your mind, but with my rambling and multitasking mind it is hard to say which of the three or four possibilities was the first. It is inevitable then, that I will use some rapid decision criteria to give what I might perceive as the most palatable response. This does not happen with all of them because some just seem to have one possible response. I complete that with no reaction at all to my responses. The next is more of a test of honesty and information gathering with a lie detector machine. That completed with what seemed like about 100 questions.

After playing 100 questions we took a brief bathroom and refreshment break and then we're back at it. It is another set of questions but these require much more creative thought than would have been appropriate for a lie detector. They were either strategy or puzzle type questions. This took us up to about 6:00 and she said that it is time for something to eat. I follow her down a hallway where she informs me that I am not to discuss anything that has happened since I was picked up or any potential strategies with anyone. We arrive at a large room set up like what reminded me of a school lunchroom. There must be about 30 people in here. Some are eating and some are in a line for their meal, again just like school lunch. I turn around and Naomi 2 is nowhere to be seen. I am hungry so I grab a tray and get in line.

Okay, so I am in a room full of strangers and I'm not supposed to talk about what is currently going on or what might go on. It is probably best to just not talk about anything other than the weather. I get my meal, which looks quite good and find a place to sit. I didn't scoot in between people, but I also didn't go hide in isolation either. I look at people that are nearby and receive and reciprocate with a couple of head nods. The guys seem to offer nod heads or a 'reverse head nod' (you know the kind where the head goes up rather than down) and the women seem to just smile or give a little wave. That's just a generalized observation, not a judgment. Some might say that was a sexist statement or even that I was profiling people based on their sex. So what. Hopefully nobody in this room would think that, not that I would care other than what it would say about them.

While everyone is eating there is some commotion going on in another part of the room where there are fewer tables. It appears as though games are being set up. What the hell? I'm not here to play games and I assume that they aren't either. This, like everything else, has to be part of the evaluation. I heard a couple of people talking about the games and what they might want to play. I also heard a couple people talking about the evaluation. I assume that everybody was told not to talk about it, but I don't know that for sure. Or maybe those people are 'plants'.

I watch as people finished eating and start migrating toward some of the games. There are games that were obviously strategic like chess and there are games that were more physical. All I want to do is watch what is going on with all of the people. Playing a game would be a distraction. I am more interested in what the assessors are assessing. We are obviously being observed. I started walking around the room and looking at posters and papers that were taped to the block walls. That is yet another thing in common with school. Are we in recess time? As I walk around I can hear some of the conversations and I assume that our observers can as well. It seems pretty clear to me that some of these people will not make it through. I am not the only one not playing games but most are. I think they see it as part of the challenge and maybe it is, but it isn't a challenge that I decide to accept.

I was looking for behaviors that might help me understand the people that were coordinating this. I need to know more. There are staff cleaning up the tables and banging around in the kitchen and I noticed that they were not all wearing the same uniforms, but they are all wearing either red, white, or blue. How patriotic of them. I looked around the room at the people playing the games, only this time not watching the games but the clothing. I saw no obvious patterns or colors in the clothing, but then I looked further down; there are some people that have a red, white, or blue stripe down the back of their shoes. I had to walk around the room to see them all and there is one person with one of those stripes at each of the game stations. Some games are only two person games and some have 4. I look again at the posters and papers on the wall and they are not *all* red, white, or blue, but there are *some*. If I ignore the content of the posters and stand back I see that there is a pattern to the red, white, and blue papers. There wouldn't be a 'test' that was so obvious would there? Maybe?

I continued down this path because if nothing else, it was interesting. It seems as though this area was set up to play games, but I believe that to be misdirection. All of the red, white, and blue items are not likely to be a coincidence, but to what end? Is there a message in the colors? A quick look around the room and I can see that all of the walls are block, the kitchen lines almost one entire wall, the other three walls each have a door, each door seemed to have one of those push-button locks on it (were we locked in?), there is a large American flag hanging on one wall, the ceiling is at least 16 feet high except for the kitchen, the floors are old tiled floors, and in all that I don't see too much of significance except maybe the flag. Maybe I need to take a closer look at the papers on the wall? As I was making my way over there without being too obvious I walked by the people cleaning up and noticed they had nametags. I haven't seen anybody with a nametag since I got here, but I'm really not sure I would have noticed. The first name I saw was Exit 2. That seems pretty clear that it is not a name, but then again Roger 5 is not a normal name. I then saw the other two and they were Exit 3 and Exit 1. They are wearing different colors and Exit 1 is blue, Exit 2 is red, and Exit 3 is white. I take that in and keep walking around the room to get a better look at the papers.

I start reading some of the papers and posters and notice that some words were bold and all caps on many of the papers. There were so many words that stood out in that form that it was hard to gather all the words. Some of them were a bit concerning like pain, evil, ghost, headless, and armor and others were pretty benign like pumpkin, sweet, one, swing, you, and quite a number of other words. There are just too many to make sense. There seems to be this obvious theme of red, white, and blue so what if I filtered the papers to only those colors? Doing this reveals that the same four words were repeated. They are *you*, *one*, *with*, and *take*. Now here I am in an unknown building, in an unknown city, with unknown people, engulfed in strange events, and I am having a blast. I love this. I have to consider whether I am getting played, but this would be a pretty elaborate play if that was the case and I am really just supposed to be playing checkers or dodge ball.

Through all of these activities there have been occasional announcements that seemed pretty irrelevant and benign so I was regrettably not paying too much attention. It seems as though they were just talking about game rules, prizes, and time remaining. Were they going to take us out of this room in some timeframe? I'm sure we would leave the room at some point, but I wanted to know how much time I had left. Another announcement came, as if on cue, and it stated that everybody had to change the game they were playing in 10 minutes. Okay, we are not leaving the room in 10 minutes but *something* is happening in 10 minutes.

Something told me that I might only have ten minutes to put all of this together. It's time to assess all of the pieces that I have acquired. Red, white, and blue are obviously a factor. I walked back to the dining area where people are still cleaning, which seems very odd. How long does it take to clean up? All of their nametags were Exit with a 1,2,3 (or maybe 3,2,1)? The words in bold had to make some sense and it was only four words so... *take one with you*? I can exit somewhere and take one with me. Exit where and take *one* what? What could I take with me wherever I was going? It has to be something that would be meaningful. Any object that could be taken of which there were multiples seems to make no sense. Take a game? Take a poster? Take a chair? Take an employee? Hmm, they would maybe know about this, and that would be too easy. Taking another one of the people being evaluated would be significant. I can't talk about the assessment or strategy or pretty much anything related to these events, but still take someone with me somewhere. I heard, "We will change games in 7 minutes."

I scanned the room very quickly trying to determine who it might be and where we might go, and the where slapped me in the face. The pattern that I suspected was there in the posters on the wall came into focus like one of those embedded images that you have to stare at to see. It was an arrow pointing in the direction of the flag. Of course there was a door under that flag, which would constitute an *exit*. I kept looking around the room and saw people still playing games and apparently trying to finish before time ran out. That is pretty much what I am doing as well. There are three people that are not playing games other than the people cleaning. One of those three people has a red stripe on the back of their shoes, so that leaves me with two. Of the two, one seems to have a hiding-type posture and wants to be left alone. The other seems to be just plain bored. He is looking around, but not in such a way that he is looking for clues. It looks more like he is wondering how much longer this is going to go on and what else he could be doing. He is my target.

I have picked a person and figure that I know the door, but it looks like it could be locked and how do I bring him with? I heard, "You now have three minutes to finish before you switch games." I walk over to the guy that is along the opposite wall of the door with the flag above it. I am running out of time so I just walked up to him and said, "Are you as bored as I am?" He nodded his head and rolled his eyes. I heard, "You have two minutes." I couldn't tell him what I had been doing, but I knew he was bored so I just said, "Would you like to get out of here and find something better to do?" He jumped on that even though he didn't know me, but then again I didn't know anybody either. He said, "I would love to but I think we are locked in. I tried one of the doors and it was locked." That answered that. The doors are probably all locked.

I turned a little and said, "Follow me." We start walking to the other end of the room and the person not playing with the red striped shoe is walking in the opposite direction on a collision course with us. I wonder if he knows something, but it doesn't matter because I couldn't say anything. He asked, "Are you guys going to pick a game this time?" I just kept walking past him and said, "We're working on it." This announcement seemed louder and slower for some reason, "You have one minute to complete your game and then you will have one minute to settle into another game." That was new and I could hear the moans from people that hadn't given their next game a thought and why would there be a time limit for picking a game. I took it to mean that I had one minute to get out the door once the time on the game ran out. If I was wrong, I didn't see any harm in trying. I had already missed the games if that was the actual point of this whole time. There are what appeared to be 'employees' at every game. Why would they do that if it wasn't part of the evaluation? There is usually more than one way to address a problem and I didn't have time for an extensive ramble right now.

We reach the door just as the announcement came, "Time is up. Please move to your next game selection." How were we going to unlock the door? The nametags were Exit 1, Exit 2, and Exit 3. It wouldn't be as simple as 1,2,3, would it? Everything was based on red, white, and blue. What color was Exit 1? I went through the colors of the clothes with nametags and glanced over to see if I could confirm but I couldn't read the nametags from here, but I could see the people and the colors. That is enough for me to go for it. I push the numbers on the keypad from the nametags in order of red, white, and blue, which was 2-3-1 and pushed on the door under the flag. It opens. I honestly don't know if it was even locked, but I am going to go with it was.

I walk through the door and it is a very dark hallway. I turn back and said, "Are you coming?" He looked stunned and said, "How did you do that?" I would be very suspicious if that had happened to me and I'm not sure if I would have chosen to follow a stranger through the door. I shrug my shoulders in response, he steps through the doorway, and the door closes behind him.

With that door closed it is now much darker. I don't have my phone to use as a light so I thought I would give my eyes a chance to adjust. Then my follower bumped into me and I asked him to give it a minute to see if our eyes would adjust. We didn't have to wait for that because there is now light in front of us and it seems quite bright. We are each asked to follow someone and they take us in different directions. I never even found out his name (even if it was not really his name).

I sat down in a room and I was kind of expecting Naomi 2 to walk in but she did not. A very large man walked in and introduced himself as Jasper 3 and then said, "What the hell do you think you were doing?" That wasn't what I was expecting. Maybe it was the objective to actually play the games. I don't care. I'm not about to suck up and apologize for something that was clearly there to be solved. He looked dead serious, but my answer still was, "Just being me. It seems there is too much important stuff going on to spend time playing games even though what I did was still apparently a game; just not an obvious one." I was actually fine if he told me that I could go home, but he smiled instead.

He asked me a number of things about what I had observed in the room. I went through all of the things that I used to open the door, but also shared what I observed about the people playing the games, the conversations, and my belief that they were able to not only watch what everybody was doing, but also hear and record everything. He then asked me what I would have done if the door hadn't opened or if it had set off an alarm. I told him that those were two different questions and that if the door hadn't opened I would have used the rest of my minute to try other combinations. If nothing worked, I would reassess and try again because nobody other than the assessment group and the person that came with me would even know that I had tried, and you apparently wanted someone to try or the clues wouldn't have been there. If an alarm had gone off I probably would have said, "Sorry, I was just looking for a bathroom."

Naomi 2 walked in as Jasper 3 walked out without saying a word. Naomi 2 sat down and asked what I would like to do now. I thought that was a pretty odd question since they were the ones that seemed to have the agenda planned. I thought for a moment, but only a moment, and said, "The list is pretty long. I would like to understand from your perspective what just happened. I would like to understand that if I am going to be in this thing, when the real work could start. I would like to know if there are any changes in what is happening in the real world, but I guess you asked what I would like to do, not what I would like to know. So all of that sums up into I would like to be briefed on what is going on and what the plans are. I would also like to be able to know if anyone has tried to call me or text me. And I am getting quite tired so sleep in a nice comfortable bed in the near future would be nice as well."

These were pretty cold people and I guess maybe they needed to be, but once in a while I would get a glimmer of humanity from someone and she just gave me what might have been a little smile with a slight hint of understanding. She said, "I can tell you that there has been no significant change in the real world as you call it, but things continue to escalate. Our formal assessments of you will be completed in the morning, which will begin at 6:00 AM. We will conduct more evaluations between then and 11:00 and then between 11:00 – 1:00 we will talk about where things stand.

"As for your calls and texts, we will bring a computer in this room that you can use to view the transcription of any calls and texts. If you need to respond to a text, you can do so on the computer. If you need to respond to a voicemail, you can record a message that will be delivered to their voicemail. If you have an emergency that requires interactive conversation, you will need to let us know so we can make the arrangements. Lastly, I cannot guarantee how comfortable the bed will be, but we do have a room for you that you are free to go to whenever you are ready."

I was impressed; not so much by the answers, but by the simple fact that there were answers. I had three requests and *all* were addressed. The world has become such that when asking for any type of service, the expectations are very low. If you ask one question, they answer a different question. If you ask two questions, you can be guaranteed that both will not be answered and maybe one will have a partial but confusing answer. If you ask three questions, you might get no response at all because it is just too much work to try to figure it out. They will likely be confused (if they care at all) and maybe go to someone for help that will only provide *one* wrong answer. It is very sad and very telling that so many people have just come to accept that as being the norm. People are conditioned to not only have low expectations, but will go so far as to defend them. So far this group of people seems both organized and competent. Another person walked in and put a laptop on the table and left.

Naomi 2 said, "Let us know when you are done and we will show you to your room." I almost asked how to let them know but I caught myself. They were watching and listening. There were no voicemails and only junk texts so I assume things are going well with Reggie. It took all of about three minutes and I was done so I closed the laptop and sat back. In about two minutes another person was there and said, "I'll show you to your room."

I followed him down a hallway that reminded me very much of my college dorm days. I was led to a room and the first thing that I noticed was that it had two beds, also like a dorm room. The second thing I noticed was that it had its own bathroom, much unlike my dorm room. I asked, "Am I going to have a roommate?" He said, "I don't know sir," as he handed me a folder. And then he was gone. That was the first time anyone had called me sir during this excursion.

There was a window in the room and even though it was dark outside, it appeared that the view was a brick wall about 2 feet away. The room was furnished very sparsely with only one picture on the wall, two beds with a nightstand between them, two chairs, one desk, a couple of floor lamps, and a clock on the nightstand. The bathroom had the necessary items and that was about it. The final object was my duffle bag sitting on a luggage stand against the wall at the foot of one of the beds. There was no bag by the other bed, but that really didn't mean anything conclusive.

I sat on the bed and opened the folder. It was about 8-10 pages of text with a heading of RECAP. I started reading and could tell right away that it was a repeat of what Tim had told the group. I thought that maybe Tim had left something out so I read and reread the whole document and there was no new information. It was good however to have it in hand as a refresher.

It was now only 9:00 and that would not be a typical bedtime for me, but it had been a very exhausting day and I was tired.

I wasn't going to try to wait up to see if I had a roommate; I couldn't really talk to them anyway. Naomi 2 had said that we start at 6:00 and I like to take a shower in the morning and wake up slowly so I set the alarm on the provided clock for 5:00. If I had a roommate, I guess they would wake up too. I got ready for bed thinking for a second that I need to let Reggie out. He is a damn good friend. I turned out the light hoping that I would get a good night's sleep.

Chapter 34

Process of Elimination (Part 2)

Morning Day 9

The alarm went off. I know that I set the alarm but I hate waking up to an alarm. On top of that there are those waking moments of "Where the hell am I?" that are only enhanced by actually being in a strange place. It didn't take me long to come about and there is nobody in the other bed and I see no sign of anyone else being here. I sit in the chair for about a half hour and then take a shower. I am ready by 10 to 6:00.

At 6:00 exactly the announcement comes that it is time to assemble for breakfast. I wonder if there will be more games? I really doubt that. I walk out into the hall and people are all moving in one direction like a school evacuation exercise. There are a couple of people standing in the hallway motioning everyone along and at the end we are back in the same dining room. It all appears to be about the same except that there aren't any games set up. I will give it a closer look once I get my breakfast.

Breakfast looks to be a standard eggs, meat, and potatoes meal with a glass of juice.

It appears that everybody is assembled and the group appears to be much smaller. Maybe it is just because all of the red, white, and blue shoes are not in the room? Where is my follower? I don't see him. I turned around and there he was behind me and said, "Mind if I sit here?" I waved him in. He sat, reached out his hand, and said, "Timothy 7." I replied "Roger 5." It seemed odd and I could tell that he thought so as well. I wanted to find out more about him like his real name, where he was from, what kind of work he did, and especially what group he was here for. I knew that I couldn't find out any of that, at least not now. I would have to settle for, "The food here is pretty decent." He nodded and it was obvious that we both knew that we were in for a quiet breakfast. So with a slight smile we went back to eating in silence.

We were less than 15 minutes in and people's names started being called. It seems like the group activities are done for now. There is no way to know without the previous striped shoes just how many are left in this process, but I assume that a fair amount have been eliminated before completing the evaluation. I was about the 5th one to be called. I walked over to the door opposite the flag, which I believe is the door that we came in yesterday evening. I think it is the door but we took a different path and I end up in a different room. It looks similar to the one yesterday, but the colors are different and the table is different as well. There is also a big clock on the wall that wasn't in the first room. Yet another person is in the room with me and she did not introduce herself. She asks me to sit down and then asks,

"Have you ever taken an IQ test?" I told her that I had but it had been some time. She explained, "This test has some of the same sections as one of the standard IQ tests but we have added a few variations of our own. This test is timed. I will see you in 150 minutes. Begin." And the door was closed. I assume that the abruptness of this was part of the test. No time to ramble on that or anything else; just dig in.

It was very much as I remembered the test to be to begin with. There were even some questions directly out of The Art of War. Then it took a turn and asked for essay answers. They still required answers to be selected, but the essay was explaining *why* that answer was the best choice. It was almost like 'show your work' except that it was not math. Actually most logic, if not all, can be stated in a formula like math and I did that a couple of times, but it can become confusing to some people that are not used to looking at logic as a formula. I'm not trying to impress; I'm just trying to convey my thoughts.

Many of the answers and the processes to get there were like many things, a process of elimination. If the answer can only be 1 out of 4 possibilities and you eliminate 3 of them, you know the answer simply by the process of elimination. It is not *always* that simple, but the problems that seem the most complex are often solved with a simple elimination process. Why doesn't my very large, complex, and multimillion-dollar computer work? You could start with calling a computer engineer and a whole host of very smart people or you could make sure it's plugged in. Eliminating the simple first is a process of elimination that can sometimes solve the problem.

All of us being evaluated were going through some form of a process of elimination. Can they keep their mouth shut and do they lie, are a couple of early indicators that were obviously used. I'm drifting a little and I have a test in front of me. Focus Roger 5! Some of the questions are not really IQ type questions. They are preference questions like "would you rather a, b, c, or d?" Why, in 5 words or less? I have 30 minutes left and I'm not sure how complex the rest of the questions are. I hope they are not essay and are more fact based rather than subjective solutions. I press hard and I am on the last section with 10 questions and 5 minutes left. 30 seconds per question. Fortunately they were not essay and they seemed to be factual. I just made it.

Naomi 2 walked in. I guess I wasn't expecting to see her again since I didn't see her earlier. She looks a little different but I'm not sure what it is that makes her seem different. It was now about 9:00 and she said that I could have 15 minutes in the 'break room' to stretch and grab a refreshment. I'm not sure why she referred to it as the break room now because it was the same room that we had dinner and games in last night. It's a pretty big room for a break room. There are a couple of vending machines in there that don't require money. I grabbed a soda and a pack of crackers and just paced around the room. I am tired of sitting. There are only 3 other people in here, which I thought was odd because we would have all likely finished at the same time. Maybe there are other rooms that were declared as 'break rooms' as well.

Jasper 3 walked in the room and announced that the break was over, but we would not be leaving the room just yet. "The next event is a team challenge and you must all complete the challenge. It is an *everyone-or-no-one* scenario. The problem is that there is a threat in the room. Your mission is to discover the threat and disable it. You have one hour. Everybody knows why they are here and everyone got the same RECAP folder, so all questions and answers are open except for personal information such as real name, address, etc. Time begins now." And with that he walked out of the room.

Multiple people started talking and one person started walking away. I tried to interrupt the group politely but rather loudly, "PLEASE. I would like to ask a couple questions because we obviously need a plan in order to work together and it is important that we understand what we have to work with. Please give me one minute and then you can decide if you want to continue down this path. Everybody is here because they volunteered or were assigned a group, correct?" Everyone either nodded or answered yes. "What group are you here for?" I heard "intelligence" and "operations" and "finance" and I said, "and I am strategy. Do you see that this is probably not a coincidence? We need to utilize our individual talents and interests, but still work together. One more question before planning; are any of you not being evaluated and work for the group doing the evaluating?" That caused a silence and everybody was looking at each other. Nobody really answered but everybody was shaking their head no and continuing to watch each other. "Okay, I would like to suggest that we pair up for 5 minutes and see what we can discover and then get back together. I will pair with operations, and intelligence and finance will pair. Is that ok with everybody if for 5 minutes we partner in twos and go look for threats or clues?" Everybody said okay and started walking away. I said, "Also for the time being how about if we refer to each other as *I*, *O*, *F*, and *S* representing our respective groups so we don't waist time learning assigned names *and* associated areas of focus?" There was another okay from everyone. As people were starting to move about, I saw a red stripe on the back of *F*'s shoes and went over to *I* and whispered in his ear discreetly. I had to wonder if they would be that obvious, but I have to remind myself that what seems obvious to me is not always seen that way by others. Others in the group had not experienced what I did.

I took off to the other side of the room with *O* and quickly explained what I had seen last night in this same room. I told him that I assumed that he might focus on technical or physical threats but anything was game. He agreed and we continued to walk around together. I looked over at *I* and *F* and was pleased to see that they are talking. *O* said, "I sure wish I had some equipment for scanning." We kept walking and got to the posters on the wall. I want to see if any details might have obviously changed or if there is more that I hadn't noticed. I hadn't noticed that some of the bold type on papers that were not red, white, or blue, were not actually words but rather symbols like &, %, $, and #. It seemed random and inconsequential at this point.

We continued walking and *O* stopped at the door, looked all around the doorframe, and then up to the ceiling and continued walking. He said, "Can we pick up the pace? I would like to finish looking for something before our time is up." I agreed and continued to scan myself. We only had three minutes left to cover the rest of the room and the kitchen as the kitchen seemed to be open and could possibly be considered as part of this 'room'. There was a lot of space yet to cover so we agreed to split because it seemed that *O* could scan faster for what he was looking for than I could. We connected two minutes later in the kitchen. I haven't been in here yet and there is so much to look at. It seems everything is in place, including all of the tools for cooking like knives. I did a quick scan looking for patterns in the kitchen and when we walked out of the kitchen I saw something on the papered wall that I had not noticed before and ran over to look closer and then back to the group for our 5 minute meet-up.

O started with, "There are at least 14 cameras in this room and the kitchen and I may have missed some because it was a pretty quick scan and I don't have any equipment. There is also some unexplained wiring and chips in places that don't make sense yet. I need more time and equipment." I asked, "Did you find, or do you think you could find a place that is not covered by cameras or audio?" He said, I haven't looked for that and it will be hard to be sure without equipment." Okay I get it, *O* needs equipment to feel comfortable but he has already seen more things than anyone else would have. I offered, "You are doing great without it but I understand there is far less certainty without equipment.

"*I*, would you go next and please be open about what I shared with you?" He shared what I had told him about yesterday and the fact that *F* is wearing a red striped shoe. *I* continued, "I asked *F* where the shoes came from and he said that they gave them to him to wear rather than his own shoes. Regardless of how I asked questions about him being part of our evaluators group, the answers were always stated in such a way to be a non-answer and direct questions were avoided. My gut tells me that something is up." I looked over at the wall of papers and pointed out all of the colors on the wall including the red, white, and blue that I used before. My discovery was one sheet of paper that was the only one of that color on the entire wall. It was a very subtle gray that kind of blended into the wall and on that sheet was a $ in bold. The gray doesn't fit with the rest of the papers and the $ along with it. Conclusion: Finance is not part of this group."

Everybody stared at *F* and he jumped to his feet and said, "Wait a minute. What is going on? How do you figure that is any evidence that I am part of those people?" I jumped in and said, "It is not evidence that holds up in court and this is not court. This is a one hour exercise where we need to prove that we can work together. If you are part of them, then you could be here to redirect or undermine our efforts and if you are not part of them what value does a finance person add to the overall efforts of this particular exercise?" *F* said, "Finance is about managing and accounting for money but can also be applied to resources, as in the most effective use of resources." "Okay", I said, "That is a reasonable answer, but providing direction on resources would also be a very good way of providing misdirection to undermine our efforts." We went back and forth about how any one of us, including me, could undermine our efforts, but in the end we had the indications provided as clues that pointed to him as an outsider. The risk of excluding him from some things seemed minimal compared to the risk of full inclusion. We all agreed to keep him around but exclude him from certain conversations.

I asked everyone if they were okay with me suggesting next steps and they were (except *F* of course). Since we didn't have a secure space to talk out of sight of observers this conversation would be seen and heard. That was okay for now. I suggested that for the next 5 minutes *O* focuses on trying to find us a dead spot for conversation and maybe determine more of what the unidentified wiring and chips were for. I suggested that *I* continue talking with *F* and look for anything that might be useful to *O*. The focus was really to see what he could get out of *F* and I think he understood that. I am going to continue to look for general clues and everybody in this group should try to come up with ideas of what or who might be at risk. Is the threat against us, this building, this city, country, or something else? Anything that might give a clue of what it is that we need to protect might help us narrow down what type of threat would endanger that type of target. We are now 15 minutes into this, and if 60 minutes didn't seem too short of time 15 minutes ago, it sure does now. We have 45 minutes to disarm an unknown threat to an unknown entity.

There must be something that would give a clue as to what the threat is. If the threat is to our mission, then simply identifying *F* as a plant might have solved that and sending him out the door would disable the threat. I'm not ready to go with that after how involved the puzzle was last night. I haven't spent much time in the kitchen so I headed there. It seems that everybody had some reason to believe or at least had a feeling that there is something to the kitchen, and I want to understand why if I can. It is full of 'stuff', that's for sure. I hadn't noticed before, but there is an office off from the kitchen and nobody is in there at the moment.

There is a lot of stuff in here as well. There is even more stuff than the kitchen and too many papers and folders to go through all of them, so I go for a scan. I open the file cabinet and I'll be damned if there aren't a few folders that stand out with a color other than manila. I didn't take them but instead went and asked *O* if he had checked the office and he had not yet. He said that he was just finishing the area that he was in and would head there now. I went elsewhere in the kitchen and started moving rolling shelves to see if anything was behind them. There were also drawers in the kitchen and I started going through them. One minute left and I step over to the walk-in freezers. I open the door to one and it is about half full and quite cold. The other freezer turned out to be empty and was not cold. Hmm?

We assembled back at the meeting place and the first thing I did was ask *F* to go to the other side of the room and wait. I guess he was done resisting this concept for now because he just walked away. I then asked everyone to get into a very tight football-type huddle and asked *O* if he had found a safe area. He said, "I have found a number of interesting things and I may have a safe area, but I can't guarantee it without equipment. That place is the unused freezer in the kitchen." I suggested, "On the chance that *O* is right, let's go to the freezer, okay?" We waved to *F* and the three of us walked to the freezer.

It was not a bad place. I wanted to hear more from both of them. "*O*, what else is it that you have found?" He went on, "There are more cameras, more wiring, and more devices than I had previously found. I believe that the doors in addition to having number locks on them have a bio-reader embedded in the top of the number pad. The tops of those readers are three different colors. They are red, white, and blue. I did find a camera in the office, but I could easily black it out or turn it to hide whatever part of the room you want."

It is *I*'s turn, "I had some good discussion with *F* and he hasn't admitted to it, but I believe that he knows what the threat is. I need some leverage or a plausible ploy to find out what it might be." I asked, "Do you think he would be more likely to cooperate if he thought he would be caught?" *I* clearly couldn't answer that but it was an approach that we might have to try so I told *I* to bring him in here if he thought it would help. I then asked, "Did anyone come across any clue as to what or who might be at risk?"

I said, "I think we are going to have an easier time finding the threat than we are finding the target. *O* can continue to search for the physical evidence but he really needs equipment. There are a lot of gadgets, including some electronics around the kitchen and office area. Maybe something could be made for him to use. Maybe if *O* and I work together we can come up with something."

I want to check out the folders that I had found in the file cabinet. "Can you give me one minute in the office before you go in there? And *O*, can you go black out the camera or turn it away from the file cabinet, whichever is faster before I go in?" They both agreed and we were off. I waited for *O* at the office door and it only took him a few seconds. I was scanning through the file cabinet and grabbed every colored folder. I then noticed that some of the alphabetical dividers had an * on them. I grabbed those as well, as there were only three. There was a thin attaché case on the floor next to the file cabinets and I put everything in there and cleared the room for *O* and *I*.

I have an idea that I want to explore in the large area where Jasper 3 had given us our mission. Recalling his words, he specifically said that the threat was in this room but he did not say that clues or the method to disable the threat had to be in this room. I think everybody assumed that the doors were locked but he specifically said the *threat* was in this room rather than saying our activities were limited to this room or any other possible ways to state it. We are now almost a half hour into this; what will we do if the doors are open? I went and tried each door and they are all locked. I also tried the code from last night on all of them as well as variations of 1,2, and 3. Nothing worked to open a door. I did see the top of the locks, where *O* indicated that there were bio-readers of different colors. The red, white, and blue theme still seems to have a presence; one color on each of the three doors.

Those 5 minutes went fast. *F* was just sitting at a table and looking quite irritated. He said, "Are you ready to let me help yet?" I just shook my head and he added, "I think you're going to need me." I kept walking to the freezer. We gathered again and as *I* and *O* were providing their updates I started examining the files while listening to them. I heard that they found some possible electronics to use and that they found what appeared to be a control panel behind a picture in the office. As they were describing the panel the folder dividers hit me. The letters on the dividers with an * were B, M, and O. On further examination the B divider had an * on both sides. I stated out loud, "We have a BOMB."

I handed them the dividers with the * on them and I started scanning the content of the colored folders. The contents seemed to be similar to the papers on the wall in that they had some words and symbols that were in bold. There were about 7 or 8 different colored folders. Sticking with the red, white, and blue pattern I grabbed those three to take a look inside. Inside the red folder the first paper was titled Financial. The white folder had a first paper titled Operations, and the third of course had Strategy. There was no red, white, or blue folder with intelligence on it. Maybe it was another color but I shared what I had found and asked the group, "Does anybody believe that F is not a plant". There is no confidence of that, but it is also not proven that he is. We need to find out.

I shared my theory with the group and got alignment to proceed. We needed to do something. There was a bomb; granted it was an exercise and I would say that it is pretty safe that the bomb would not actually explode, but we needed to proceed as though it is real. Everybody agreed to the plan. If it works, it will get us closer, but still not likely solve the problem and time was getting very short. We have 25 minutes left.

We walk back out into the big room and told F and I to go and stand in front of door 1 that had a red color on top of the door lock. O went to the one with white on top and I went to the last remaining door. I yelled, "On the count of three press your thumb down on top of the lock panel. I, make sure that F does that. One, two, three." Thumbs were placed and we held... Damn, nothing happened. I had one more thought and yelled again, "Same thing on three, only this time use your index finger instead of your thumb. One…Two…Three and hold." There was a dead silence and then clicks, hums, and cables moving. The red door opened and *I* and *F* scurried out the door after blocking it open. That was not the end of the movement. Cables were moving and a platform was lowering that had been hidden against the ceiling in the middle of the room. *O* and I watched as the platform came down. It stopped about 1 foot off the floor.

On the platform is what we might have expected if we had any idea that there was a platform. Our goal was to get *I* and *F* out of here and the discovery of the bomb was a big bonus. It had a classic look of an exaggerated large bomb made for a movie with lots of wires and a digital clock that was counting down. It was now at 22 minutes and 6 seconds, which coincided with our remaining time. I asked *O* to assess the bomb and anything that might be connected to it. He said, "Anything connected to it will likely be wireless, but I will look for possible ways to disarm it."

I am wondering how it is going with *I* and *F*. If they are gone the full 10 minutes or close to it, I will assume that they found the lie detector machine in the same place as when we were subjected to it. *I*'s intelligence experience will hopefully prove very beneficial. While *O* is looking over the bomb I am going through the rest of the folders that are not red, white, or blue. There was purple, yellow, green, and orange. There was nothing of significance that stood out anywhere. I asked *O* if he was getting anywhere, and he said, "I saw three buttons that are wired into this thing, but I have no idea what they do or what will happen if the wires leading to them are cut. Finding the right wire to cut or the right sequence of wires may never happen just by looking at it. There are so many interconnected wires that I am concerned that the wrong wire or sequence will trigger it."

I asked him if he had tools like a wire cutter and screwdrivers to work with in case *I* and *F* come back with something. He said that he had seen some things in the kitchen that should work. He came back in about 30 seconds with a kitchen scissors, a screwdriver, a corkscrew, a knife, tongs, and a mitt. I assumed that he had an idea of how those things might be useful. *I* and *F* came running through the door a few minutes early. *I* started talking before getting to us. I guess he figured at this point that it didn't matter if people heard us.

He led with, "*F* is definitely a plant. There is nothing that the people watching can or will do to interfere with the course of our mission. *F* was intended to misdirect what we were doing, but he will not physically interfere. He will likely continue to lie. The control panel in the office and something else in the office will help solve the mission. And the bomb is definitely the one and only threat." I can't believe what vital information he was able to attain during that short time. Of course we had to trust that *I* was also not a plant, but there was no indication of that.

We all headed for the office with just 11 minutes left. I was looking around the room for things that might have been missed, *O* was examining the control panel, and *I* was looking through the files to see if another set of eyes would find anything else. I yelled, "Anybody have anything?" *O* replied with, "The menu on this panel is quite odd." We all went to look (except *F*) and saw this:

1. Primary
2. Secondary
3. White
4. Clip

The secondary menu under option 1 and 2 said "Art Sequence", under 3 it said "Light", and there was nothing under 4. I think I had it. I asked *O*, "Were those three buttons that you found different colors?" He said they were, but he didn't remember what colors. He just knew that it was not red, white, and blue. We all ran to the bomb and the colors were close to red, white, and blue, except that white was replaced with yellow. That confirmed it for me. We have 7 minutes left and I once again asked the group if they would follow the directions and I would explain as we went along. They agreed and it felt like we were so close, but overconfidence can disrupt progress in a hurry.

I asked *O* to watch the bomb closely for any changes and everybody else to stand in front of one of the colored buttons. "We are going to go clockwise through the primary colors of an art pallet, starting with red. When I tell you, press and release your button." I told *I* to press and release red and everybody could hear an audible click, but *O* announced it. I told *F* to press and release yellow, and another click. I press and release blue and another click. *O* said, "Something moved under the middle of this thing, but I can't tell what it did. I can't tell if it's good or bad." I wanted to keep going and everybody agreed. We have a little more than 5 minutes left.

I explained that this time we would be pushing buttons in pairs to create the secondary colors. I would announce the pairs and then count 1,2,3, push. I told them it was important that they push and then release on the word push, not on 3. You will each be part of 2 pairs. "We are going to start with red and yellow. Ready?" Head nods. "Red and yellow, 1, 2, 3, push." There was another click. "Yellow and blue, 1, 2, 3, push". It's working, I think. "Last in this step, blue and red, 1, 2, 3, push." This time the click was followed by what sounded like a fast release of air and everybody stepped back except O. He was intently looking at the bomb and announced, "We have more movement." And with a big sigh, "and more buttons." I asked if they were red, blue, and green and he said, "How did you know that?" I didn't answer for the moment, but I am glad that I know, or my theory would have been blown with just a few minutes left.

I told O to be ready with something to cut a wire. "This time we are going to press and hold these new buttons until I tell you to release. Make sure you press your button all the way down." O said, "Something has moved on top of the bomb as well." I continued with 2:47 remaining on the clock, "Is everybody ready? On the same count of 1, 2, 3, push, everybody push and hold your new button." Everybody took a collective big breath. "1, 2, 3, push and hold."

There was a light the same color as each of the buttons that came from under the button toward the center and the reflected upward. The light going upward was white. The combination of these three colors of the light spectrum makes white when combined in equal amounts. The light went up the center and then reflected off something at the top and back down to a wire on the bomb with pinpoint accuracy. This was not a wide light;

it was more like a laser. The wire that it hit was a white wire. I told *O* to cut that wire and cut it now. He didn't even hesitate and that kitchen shears cut through the wire like cutting butter.

I looked around and it seemed like nobody was moving or even breathing. I broke the silence and said, "We did it! The clock stopped!" At that moment, all of the doors opened and someone walked in from each of the doors. I saw that Naomi 2 is coming in one of the doors, and *O* and *I* seem to recognize their contacts. Of course, *F* didn't have a contact. Everyone is sharing congratulations and this team seems to be getting split up, but I had to break away for a second to go shake their hands. "Good job everyone. It was a pleasure." And we walked out separate doors.

Chapter 35

Process of Elimination and More

Noon Day 9

It's difficult to accept that this last challenge was just one hour long. It's also hard to accept that it has been less than 24 hours since I left home and they said to plan to be gone for 3 days. From what I have been told, I think this phase is about over and we will just be talking about what has happened and what might be happening next. We stopped along the way at what looked more like a real break room and then I was led into a room that seemed like a city council meeting room with no people. It wasn't more than a minute and 3 people came and sat at the table on the dais. I am sitting at a table that feels like I am testifying before congress, but the room is too small to justify using microphones and I'm sure they have other ways of recording.

A fourth person than came in to add to the 3 on the panel and it was Naomi 2. They gave me no indication of where I stood.

There were no congratulations for solving a couple of puzzles or for anything. I assume that it was intentional to give me no indication of anything. Instead they asked me how I thought it was going. If you ask me an open-ended question, you better be prepared for either a very short answer like "fine", or a very long answer that is probably more than what you wanted or expected.

I decided to go the long route, "Since I don't know what your criteria is for evaluation rating, I have no basis for even guessing what your perspective might be on how it is going, but since I was not given any criteria or your perspective, all I have is mine. I suspect that there are multiple ways to solve the puzzles that were provided and that even the games last night might have had some criteria associated with them, but I found a less obvious game that provided what in my mind was a greater challenge. I am fairly certain that the IQ results were just fine and likely better than most. I believe that some people have been eliminated in this first 24-hour period and some of them simply for not being able to follow directions and keep their mouth shut. I'm not sure why anyone would believe that we were not being watched and monitored 100% of the time.

"I know that I am honest so the lie detector is a non-issue. I believe that you have likely been looking for personality traits as well as skills. Are people trustworthy, able to work with others without ego issues, listen closely, observe intently, and utilize their particular skills in a way that is beneficial to all? It is all a process of elimination. The ones that are not eliminated will win by default. Win is probably the wrong word when it is by default. I would hope that even after the process of elimination that there is further observation that sets a more precise direction for those remaining. Since you know the structure and needs and we do not, I would hope that those remaining would be directed to a useful position even if it were different than the initial intent.

"Finally, I questioned this organization when I was in previous groups, but your structure and process is commendable. However, I still do question why it had to come to such a dire need in the country before utilizing this structure in a more productive way. If there has been activity that I am not aware of, (which I assume is true), I am anxious to learn. I am eager to dig into the real problems rather than these testing problems that I understand and respect, but please let me start contributing."

Someone on the panel that had not been introduced said, "Well, we thought we might just get *fine*." And he smiled. "We do have a couple of questions and then we will share next steps. We will each ask one question. I will start. Please explain to us, in less than one minute, what you see as the challenge ahead." Hmm, I can say a lot of words in one minute. "I see the that the challenge is to get the country back to some form of a country that is reflective of the Constitution and secure its safety from outside aggressors, which would definitely include China at this point. There are many details to that, but that is the short version." I was done in less than 15 seconds and I saw no reason to expand at this point.

I got a thank you and the next person asked, "You seem to believe that the target is our country, but who is our opponent or enemy if you will?" I thought what an opportunity, but does this have a one-minute constraint as well? I had to ask, "Do you want this held to one minute as well?" I got a, "yes please."

Okay, I have to try, "I have thought about this and I believe there are four candidates; China, our government, the large powerful companies, and the people of the country. The people of the country because without their support the government would not have the unwieldy power that it currently exercises, the large companies because they manage information and contort it to support the government, China because it clearly wants to take over our country in any way possible and if it does we will never recover. While China is the most devastating unrecoverable enemy, the circumstances and timeline require that our government be the priority of our possible enemies, because it is only the government (with the support of others) that has any chance of stopping the road that we are on. I would explain more but my time is probably up."

The third person stated, "I would like you to explain your strategy to approach this task and in that answer explain if we can, should, or must use the same strategies of our enemies by using lies and manipulation. You do not have a one-minute constraint for this, but please try to keep it to under five minutes."

It didn't take me long to start. I felt like I was finally being asked worthwhile questions. "As for lying and manipulation, I would *like* to say that we should not, but I cannot say that. First, I would absolutely lie to China, but I'm pretty sure that's not what you were talking about. I believe that lying should be able to be avoided to the people of our country but manipulation cannot. The type of manipulation that I am referring to is nothing more than finding the right way to express the truth; expressed in the context of what appeals the most to the listener. This is simple but honest politics, of which there is very little today. There are a couple of key concepts that apply to this. For a very long time the government has not only been lying but also controlling all of the messaging. They are organized and we are not. I am not talking about your structure. I am referring to the party that believes in freedom, the Constitution, and limited government.

"These types of beliefs inherently have behaviors that support people thinking for themselves, being left alone to do what they want as long as they are not harming others, and supporting freedom of speech along with all of the other constitutional rights. When you have these types of beliefs and the limited government to go with it, it is counter to the beliefs to do what the other party does so well, manipulate and control people. It is difficult to speak with one voice when your belief is the freedom of all beliefs. They play hardball and we are playing with marshmallows. We are not united because we support real diversity of thought and action far more than their fake and superficial diversity."

I stopped for a moment to try to read the room but I wasn't getting much other than they seemed interested. That's good because I was just getting started. I continued, "In regard to strategy, a process of elimination works well for problem solving especially as it relates to inanimate objects, but it likely cannot be the whole story when people are involved. I believe that your evaluation here includes a process of elimination, but that is not all there is to it because you are using things like IQ testing and this interview to find out more about my capabilities, who I am, and how I think. Knowing your opponent is key. There cannot be only *one* strategy unless that strategy is to not have *one* strategy. A single strategy makes you predictable and will eventually not end well. I believe that our opponent has a single strategy or at least a very small set of strategies that are predictable and that should be able to be used against them.

"Another concept that applies is perspective over reality. What I mean is that a person's perspective regardless of its accuracy is more important than actual facts or even the truth. This makes people and our purpose extremely vulnerable to those things that influence perspective. Not having control of the media presents a challenge in influencing perspective but there are other ways.

"That brings me to understanding the motivation of the enemy. Presenting the enemy with temptation using their motivating triggers (more accurately presenting the perception of them) provides a manipulative opportunity. That does not mean lie, it means present the *right* information at the *right* time. The patterns of human behavior are a critical factor to rely upon. Patterns are discovered over time. Another strategy against an enemy with more resources, more power, more control, and more of almost everything is to use all that they have against them. They will not agree to that of course. They will not even know it until it is too late and maybe not even then." I paused.

I still saw some interest but also the look of wanting details so I tried to wrap up quickly. "If you expect that a strategy would come from me with details of an implementation plan, I cannot do that now and believe it would be foolish to try. I believe in the principles and strategic approaches that I have expressed, but details of an implementation plan requires detailed and accurate information. The information that I have is undoubtedly incomplete. I know my current perception of the enemy, but I believe that I have so much to learn from you about them as well as what you have done so far. The high-level principles will always apply, but the specific strategies and subsequent plans need to be agile and unpredictable. If I had to provide a little more direction *based on what I know*, I would likely suggest starting at the top of the enemy structure to find the weak points, because we don't have time to go bottom up."

"Did I make it in under five minutes?" I wouldn't have been surprised if had gone over but I heard a few quiet yeses and then Naomi 2 spoke, "The four of us have one collective question for you." There was a very long pause and I assumed it to be for dramatic effect or some form of intimidation, but I don't intimidate easily. She broke the silence and said, "What would you like for lunch?" All four smiled and it appears that this portion of the evaluation is done. I say 'this portion' because it was not 1:00 yet.

I didn't really expect that we would go out for lunch and we didn't. I also didn't expect that all of them would join me for lunch, but they did. We went to another more intimate room and lunch was brought in. We sat at the table together and this was more the feel of a conversation with friends rather than an interview panel or interrogation. We talked about general things including the weather, but then someone asked more about who I was. Not my name or history that they already have access to but who I am. The question was, "Where do your ideas, perspectives, and thoughts come from? You have a rapid and in-depth answer to some pretty complex questions and they include some interesting perspectives. Where does that come from?" The answer was easy, but I knew that they wouldn't understand. I said, "I ramble."

Of course I got very curious looks from that answer so I had to go into the whole explanation of what I meant by ramble. I told them how it offers opportunities to discover things that never would have been discovered with constrained thought or predetermined solutions, and how patterns become very evident through rambles. Patterns in thought, patterns in behaviors, and patterns of things that you never would have imagined had patterns. I went on in a non-rambling way about rambling and ended with, "I ramble." I take a bite of my sandwich and it is 1:00.

Chapter 36

In or Out

Afternoon Day 9

Okay, so it's 1:00 and this segment of the evaluation is over and I am sitting in a room with these people finishing lunch. Nobody has said anything about what is happening next. I had to ask, "So, what is my status and what is next?" Naomi 2 stood up and said, "Would you give us a minute please?" It really wasn't a question and they all stood and left the room. I wonder if this is really how they do business and if everyone else is being handled this way.

It was no more than one minute and they were back in the room. One of the people that had not shared their name started, "Thank you for sharing with us and now we would like to fill you in on your status. Fifty percent of the people that came in yesterday were eliminated yesterday. Another thirty percent were eliminated today. Half of the remaining twenty percent of the original numbers will be eliminated within the next two days. You will not be one of them." I had to think about the way that was put. Does that mean that I won't be eliminated or that I'm not part of the twenty percent and have already been eliminated?

He continued, "Instead of the planned next step, we would like you to meet with another group of people. I think you will find it very interesting. There will be no more testing, this will be real conversation about the current situation and the plans going forward. You will learn a lot and we hope to provide that group with an opportunity to learn more about you first-hand. They may have a few initial questions to get up to speed on you, but they will soon get down to business."

I heard that this is not what was planned. I heard that I am either not part of the twenty percent or the part of the twenty percent that will or won't make it. I need clarity. "I could guess what you mean by not following what was planned and the remaining twenty percent that will or won't make it, but I would rather not guess or assume. If there is no more testing am I through to the strategy group, am I being moved back to the area group, and who is this new group of people for me to meet with?"

Some other unidentified person answered, "I appreciate you being direct and asking for clarity. This is not our normal process. As you stated about a strategy and approach needing to be agile, we are being agile. You are not being moved to an area group. You are being moved forward and we would like you placed in the most beneficial location, which may or may not be the strategy team. The group of people that we want you to meet with to assist with that best placement is the leadership team that is over all of the groups. We normally handle all placements at this level but we have discussed this with them and they would like to meet with you."

The whirlwind of these recent days since the FBI raid just keeps getting more and more surreal. I know that I have skills, but it has been my experience that large corporations (even small businesses), and especially the government rely so much on credentials such as degrees and accreditations before looking at anything else. I know that people with a passion, including a passion to learn are far more prepared to benefit their employer than a person with a degree that is 'just working a job'. That is so unfortunate, but it is the reality that I have experienced my entire life. That combined with the willingness to suck-up gets people high-level positions, so this rapid movement through levels of this structure is strange enough that it continues to give me reason to be suspect.

I am suspect even though to this point my concerns have been mostly addressed within a short time of raising them. This group, however, is far more sophisticated than I gave them credit for and the potential for a sophisticated structure that can also recognize talents and passions outside of credentials certainly has its appeal. If I was going to try to lure someone like myself into something, that appeal is exactly what I would use.

Naomi 2 now said, "You will need to meet with them in a place that will require a flight, but we will still have you back within the 3 days that were agreed to. Is that okay with you?" I told her that it was fine but asked, "What about credentials for flying? I will need a traceable ID to fly, won't I? Mine is in the Faraday bag that you have." Naomi 2 said, "We will take care of all of that and you will need to leave this building in ½ hour. During that time, we can arrange for you to use a phone if you want to check on things at home. We will also provide you with a list of texts and voicemails as we did before. Are we good to go?" I confirmed. There was a round of thank-yous in both directions and Naomi 2 led me to a room with a computer and a phone.

I checked messages and there was nothing of importance and then called my daughter to check on her (and Reggie of course). There was no answer. I sat back to just take a breath. I closed my eyes for a minute and came close to that nodding off feeling where you suddenly pull your head up so you don't fall over. At some point I am going to crash. I had no idea how long the plane ride would be or what the accommodations would be like. I'm not sure if I did drop off, but Naomi came in the room telling me that it was time to leave. "Your bags are in the car and will be taken care of throughout your trip. It was a pleasure meeting you and best wishes to us all." She was the closest I had come to getting to know someone here, but I knew nothing about her at all. Maybe that would change some day, but I suspect not.

I followed someone back to the elevator and then to the parking garage. It appeared to be the same dark windowed car. It was about ½ hour to the plane and when I get out of the car I see that there is a small jet parked on the runway and we are parked next to it. There was no going through security or checking tickets and bags, just walking up the stairs and onto the plane.

It is quite nice inside and once the cabin door was shut there was only one other person who directed me to my choice of seats and asked me to buckle up for takeoff. We were in the air within about 10 minutes. She came by and asked if I wanted anything to drink or eat but I really just wanted to sleep. These are very comfortable seats and they recline to almost a full flat-out position. She brought me a pillow and a blanket. I heard a click of the intercom and then a female voice said, "This is your pilot. We appear to have clear skies ahead for our entire flight. Please sit back and relax. Our flight time is estimated at 3 hours and ten minutes. That puts our touchdown ETA at 6:05 Washington, D.C. time."

Chapter 37
Step Up
Evening Day 9

I must have slept because it seemed like just minutes and the pilot was stating that we would be landing in 10 minutes and please prepare. I couldn't really make out where we were, but I could soon see that the airport where we were landing was not a large airport. I sat back in the comfy chair attempting to wake up and mentally prepare for what might be ahead.

Some might see it as intimidating or at least as a challenge, but for me it is pure joy. It is an opportunity to be me. This is not a threat. There are so many threats in the world as we well know. Going on a stage, interviewing for a job, or going to talk to a group of people in Washington, D.C. are not threats. I really am not here to prove anything, I am here to try to help by being me and if they feel I cannot help, then I will find another way. That is what life is about. It seldom goes the way we plan it, but if we have our priorities and our integrity in place it is very difficult to be derailed.

I find myself repeatedly thinking about the incredible journey that I am on, and it has crossed my mind more than once that it might not even be real. Is this all a dream? Dreams can span a great deal of perceived time in a very short period of real time. Is it a long ramble? Maybe I went into a coma after being hit by the FBI and I have yet to wake up. Those thoughts are both rational and crazy. How would anybody know if it is a dream or a delusion until they wake up? I suspect that thinking people have these questioning thoughts on occasion when they are faced with particularly good or bad fortune. When someone gets bad health news, many turn to "It can't be real." They do this even though they have no indication that it is not real. They just don't want it to be. The same is true for some when good fortune hits. "This can't really be happening." That feeling may be out of self-protection because they think it may just go away and they will be left where they were before. Regardless of good or bad, the questioning of reality is one of the things that can actually keep us grounded and sane. It is a very legitimate thought process to question everything, including the things that might seem the most obvious.

When people find no reason to question reality, the alternative is usually not healthy. In the case of good things or great opportunities, they may take the path of arrogance and believe that they deserved it and it happened because they are better than anybody else that might have had this happen. They could also take the low road and assume that it will end soon, so why put any effort into it because they will only be hurt by the letdown. Someone experiencing bad things may choose a denial route and miss the opportunity to address what is really important or they completely accept it and give up, and in that instant their life is over. I will occasionally question reality to keep me grounded. If my conclusion is wrong, I have the knowledge that I did the best that I could with what I knew at the time and I will always try to know more. Nobody can do more than that, but so many do far less. We are in this situation because so many did far less. Regardless of reality, something still needs to be done because what if it is true and I did nothing or less than I could have?

I'm no Superman. I'm nobody extraordinary. Ordinary people occasionally do extraordinary things when they don't talk themselves out of it and just do it. I know that I have my priorities, a sense of what is right and wrong, and the integrity to defend my beliefs. Beyond that, what else can I do? Why would I care what these people think, because what they think has nothing to do with my priorities, my beliefs, and my personal integrity? If I discuss these concepts with others, which I rarely do, they think that I am being altruistic, completely unrealistic, and way over-simplifying life. That is why I rarely discuss it. It only furthers their belief that I am promoting how good I think I am. They are seemingly unable to see the point. I don't care how good they think I am. I just need to try to do what I believe. I personally feel better when I do, regardless of what others may think. I know that I don't always succeed in doing that and fail to do what I know is right at times. My failures are in not following what I know to be right, not in a failure to provide a better impression of me to someone else.

How do I reconcile all of that with the understanding that, operationally, perception is more important than reality? It's really not a stretch to do that. My perception is what I defend and act on, just as others act on their perceptions and priorities. It may be that many of them have not given thought to their perceptions and their priorities; nonetheless they do make decisions based on them. If someone were trying to change me, it would not be the most productive path to try to get me to stop defending my perspective (perceptions, beliefs, priorities, and integrity). They would have a better possibility of success if they were able to change my perception. They might even be more successful if they were to understand and utilize my perception. If I tried to change their actions that get them money and power, it would be a very hard sell. I would have a better shot at either changing their priority of money and power or showing them another way to achieve their perception of money and power. Changing the source of their perceived money and power has a much better probability of success. Their drive for power is likely so engrained in their very being that changing it would likely trigger a blind reaction of self-protection, whereas the source of their money and power is likely irrelevant to them.

I stepped off the plane and it really is not a big airport. It is the same situation as getting on the plane, down the stairs and onto the runway. There is a car waiting and I got in like I had done this a thousand times before. I have never done it before but when faced with an opportunity, the right thing to do is step up. I have a feeling I will be doing a bit more of that.

The ride was quiet and relatively short in distance I think, but the traffic was quite bad so it took a little over an hour. We are now into the evening hours and I wonder if I will actually be meeting with anybody today. I think it even less likely when the car pulls up to a hotel. I am about to get out when the driver says, "Please wait here sir. I will go check you in." That feels a bit odd, but then I remembered that I have no identification on me and they might not want me checking in with my name to be tracked by who knows who. I guess the people and hotels of D.C. are probably used to secrecy.

It didn't take long and the driver was back out with a room key and escorted me into the hotel. He was walking close to me as we walked through the hotel door and the city is quite noisy with sirens seeming to come from multiple directions. It made me feel like he is not only a driver but a bodyguard as well. The hotel lobby is quite elegant and old looking as I might have pictured a D.C. hotel to be. We go straight to the elevator and to my room. As I enter the room the driver said, "Your bag will be brought up shortly and someone will be in touch within the hour. In the meantime, if you need anything use this to contact me. Just push redial. This phone will only call me." He is obviously more than just a driver. Before closing the door he said, "You can order room service if you like, but I would do it soon. Is there anything else?" I had no idea what it would be so I just said, "I'm fine. Thank you."

I guess I'm fine. I sure am wondering what is next and who I will hear from, but I am hungry so I call room service and turn on the TV. I usually avoid the so-called news stations that are readily available through the major cable networks, but now it feels like a good way to see what the other side is up to. These news broadcasts that are primarily propaganda actually have news to offer if you understand what you are watching. In the more recent years you didn't even really need to have any insight into what was going on, you only had to really watch. Many will show a video, but then they will consistently lie over the top of the video that completely contradicts what they were saying. This is one of those times. They are showing the military 'protecting the people'. What I knew of the threat from China, that others didn't know, didn't seem to matter. At best they were protecting the people from themselves and from the runaway crime that was all over the city, but even more likely is that they are protecting themselves from the people.

I wondered why I hadn't encountered that when I pulled up to the hotel, but all I had to do was look outside and I could see from this height that about 5 blocks away was a very different story. I can see people in the street, military blockades, and fires in a number of places. I can hear sirens that I had originally written off to big city noises. The rate at which crime has increased is astronomical and is up over 500% in most big cities. I suspect those numbers are suppressed and it is actually even higher. They have chosen to allow the 500% number to make the reporting because they use it as another trigger for hatred and dependency. Their story is that there is so much crime because people are poor, and they are poor because the other party didn't give them enough money when they were in power. The answer is to give people more money and continue to eliminate the punishment of people that are committing crimes because they are poor and they need the government's help. They say that people are out in the streets right now supporting the government bringing in the military to protect them.

All you had to do was watch the video in the background to see that the people in the street are resisting the military. They were throwing Molotov cocktails at them. People that got too close to the barricade were being shot by the military. The perimeter that has been set up by the military has nothing to do with protecting the people; they are protecting the government. Just look what is behind the barricade. Outside of the perimeter, stores are being burned and looted, people are being killed and robbed and it is total chaos with no movement or indication from the military to stop it. Again, all of this video evidence is being displayed with the narration of the government stepping in to help the people. How do you fight that? How brainwashed or stupid do people have to be to not see what is right in front of them? And how arrogant is the media to show all of this with the lies on top of it? The conditioning of the news media and the people watching is actually quite frightening.

There is a knock on the door and my food is wheeled in on a cart. I go to grab for my wallet to tip the person and they say, "It's all taken care of." That is a good thing because I realized at the same time that they said that, I don't have my wallet so all I can do is say, "Thank you." They leave and I set up my plate at the desk. I thought I was hungry and the food looked okay, but I have lost a bit of my appetite. Maybe it was the news, or maybe it is what is outside my window.

I remember the sharing that Tim had done about the military and China, but from looking at the TV it would appear that China has nothing directly to do with the threat that the military is guarding against. I'm not sure if anything other than total chaos and anarchy is behind the current volume of people in the streets. Maybe it is purely an uprising against the military, maybe news has spread about other things, or maybe people are sick of this government. I don't think it's the latter because the people that are sick of this government and their lies would likely respond in different ways. That does make me wonder what would happen if China took some additional action and it became evident enough to cause panic. What is going on now is mild compared to what that would create.

Imagine if China cut power for days or weeks, cut off cell service, shut down banks, or cut off medical supplies, just to name a few. The country would be in ruin because of the outburst of panic. People would be killing in the name of survival. Some would look for the government to help them and the government, just like today, would be protecting themselves and trying to find a way for them to survive regardless of the impact to the people. I suspect they would soon find that the deals that they thought they had would be absolutely meaningless. I could keep going with these potential scenarios and how it would flow, but that is of little benefit at this point. The conditions created by someone causing that type of chaos through those means would be, in my mind, declaring war. Survival is important, but it is far more important to avoid getting to that point. Another quote from The Art of War comes to mind; "The supreme art of war is to subdue the enemy without fighting."

I have eaten very little from my room service delivery and I am expecting the phone to ring at any moment, but there was a knock at the door. I have to admit, it was not only unexpected, it made me a bit nervous. I used the peephole in the door and it is the driver. I open the door and he explained that nobody would be calling and that there is a slight change of plans. He would like me to follow him and we would walk to a location. I get my shoes on, grab the room key, and off we go. We walk to the elevator and he slides a card in a slot that I hadn't noticed and pushes a button that is not marked. It was to the right of B, which I figured was basement, and the blank button was maybe below the basement? We exit the elevator and then enter a room with a semicircle table, chairs around the table, and a large screen inside the circle. He flips a few switches and adjusts a camera so that I am clearly in view. Individual images of four people come up on the screen. It feels kind of like the cheap on-line videoconference concept except the images are crystal clear, life size, and completes a virtual circle from the semicircle table in the room.

One person started with, "We appreciate you making this change on such short notice and we will keep this quite short for this evening. There are obviously four of us on this conference and there are two more that are not here. We were asked to look over your file as well as the recap and recordings of your evaluation. We have done that and feel that it is worth our time and yours to discuss the state of our situation in detail. A very extensive background check has been done on you in addition to what you are aware of. You could possibly recognize some people that are in this group, which is all the more reason for its secrecy. We are the leadership group over all of the activities that you have been involved with. All operations, intelligence, strategy, and finance come under our direction. We have been in existence in the background for many years, but the current circumstances require that we take a more active role. For that reason, we are considering adding two more people to our group to add new perspectives as well as resources to the process. It has been recommended that we consider you for one of those positions."

It seems like once or twice a day I have to wonder what the hell is going on. I'm just a guy from a small town in the middle of America. I believe in doing what I can and stepping up, but I also don't want to get in over my head and do harm rather than good. I had to say something; there was dead air that felt as uncomfortable as dead air on the radio. Knock, knock, is anybody there? "I am honored to be considered and I am honestly a bit stunned. I had no idea what the purpose of the trip was. I am certainly willing to do what I can, but I also want to be realistic about who I am and what I can do and not enter under any false pretenses. I absolutely want to dig in and yet I feel that I am missing information that would allow me to make the best informed contribution that I can."

A different person answered. "We believe that we know you quite well and there is very little false about you. You see things in a way that many people have forgotten, especially in this place. The corruption on top of corruption is so deep that untangling it becomes what seems like an insurmountable task. We heard your perspective about priorities and our enemies and it is in alignment with our way of thinking, but as you said there are a lot of things that you do not know. Those things make the identification of the enemy and subsequent actions exponentially more complex. It is late and we are not going to start in on that now, but we will share a great deal with you in person tomorrow. What you will hear and even this conversation should be considered *extremely confidential and top secret*. It is expected that you will talk to no one about the information shared in this group or even your participation in this group. Nobody! That includes previous contacts with other related groups, your family, friends, or anyone outside of these walls. Are you okay with that? If you are not, please say so now."

I answered immediately with, "It seems that it is a little late for that question after I am already here and have virtually met with you." I got a quick response, "We have no question of your desire to participate and your integrity regarding the secrecy; it was simply an offer as a courtesy." I continued, "Of course I will honor the confidentiality and secrecy. I want to do what I can and I very much want to hear more of what is really going on. I know that I will be imagining all sorts of possibilities tonight, but I understand the benefit of starting fresh tomorrow. I am sad for the current state of affairs and have been for many years, but I am grateful for an opportunity to potentially do more than watch with frustration and write blogs that are never published."

Yet another person spoke this time., "We are looking forward to getting your perspective on the situation once we fill you in. We will meet in person tomorrow in a different location. I understand that you would be apprehensive about your selection in this effort. It is clearly not because of your degrees, certifications, or awards. It is about your ability to be open to the unexpected pieces of information, process them logically and rationally, and do that in a way that considers the past, present, and future. You do not stand out, you stand *with*, and we need that."

The last person in the group took her turn, "We know that this a lot to process and it will be even more so tomorrow. We also know that you have a lot of questions, but unless there is something that you feel needs to be asked tonight I suggest that we break here and continue tomorrow. We will then do formal introductions and begin in earnest."

There is no way that I could find anything that had to be asked tonight. I just needed to hear what they are going to tell me tomorrow. Asking anything before that would likely be a waste of time and there is no time to waste. Goodbyes and goodnights were shared and the screen shut down. I followed the driver back to my room. In some way it felt like I was an important person being escorted by a bodyguard and in other ways it felt like I was a puppy dog following someone around that knew so much more than I did and would just tell me what to do. Maybe it was both but if he is going to be around I need some way to refer to him other than driver. "Thanks for showing me the way back and looking out for me. What can I call you?" He said, "You can call me Mike. Is there anything else I can do for you this evening?" I said, "No thank you Mike. Will I see you tomorrow?" He replied, "You will, bright and early. I will be here at 6:30 to pick you up. Please lock your door and it would be in your best interest not to leave your room. Call room service for anything that you want. Goodnight sir." "Goodnight Mike and thank you again."

Chapter 38

Can't Judge a Book by Its Cover

Day 10

I'm not sure that I even remember crawling into bed, but apparently I had set my alarm for 5:30. I do miss the days of waking up without an alarm, but I miss the days of freedom more, so here I am. I'm really not complaining, it just impacts my day. As far as impacts, it would seem that mine have been very minor to this point in regard to what is happening in the country considering what is happening. Right now I am simply wondering if they will have anything to eat at the meeting, so I order a bowl of cereal from room service and get in the shower.

I get out of the shower and there is a knock on the door with an announcement of, "Room service." I wrap a towel around me, peek out the peephole, and let room service in. I obviously was not going to reach for my wallet so I just said, "Thank you." I got dressed, ate my cereal, and sat in the chair at the desk with my head back trying to imagine the day. I know it's a waste of time, but I can't help it. Who are these people? A couple of them did look familiar, but I can't place their names or how I might know them. Is this going to be a long debriefing or a short recap? I suspect that if these players are of quite a high level, they will not waste their collective time trying to bring me up to speed. Where is this meeting going to be and why are we meeting in Washington, D.C.? I would have to assume that some if not all of them are based here, which again points out that it is crazy that I am here. I was just starting to get on a real unproductive roll and a knock on the door saved me. I check and it is Mike. I am more than ready to go.

I open the door, step out, and say, "Good morning Mike." He smiled and said, "Ready to go?" I was walking down the hall and almost taking the lead, "I am more than ready. Let's get to it." I know where the elevator is and figured we won't be meeting on this floor and likely not even in this building. We stop at the lobby and proceed out to the car that is parked in a no parking zone. Something tells me he isn't concerned about a ticket.

We drive only about three blocks and into a parking garage. The sound of sirens and the mist of smoke still fills the air. We go down two or three levels in the garage and park in a reserved parking spot. Before we get out he hands me a lanyard and tells me to put it on. "Your name is John for now, but don't talk to anyone until we get to our destination. We shouldn't run into anyone that wants to talk, but if we do I will do the talking." I nod and follow Mike. We go into the small area where the elevators are and a few people are waiting. We stood behind them and when they got on the elevator, they held the door for us and Mike said, "We'll take the next one." The elevator door closes and Mike headed off through a door to the right of the elevators after swiping his badge on the wall. It is one of those doors that have a push bar that says, "For Emergency Exit Only. Alarm Will Sound." There is no alarm and I follow through the door. The door closes behind us and we are in a dimly lit hallway. From the fact that we went a couple of levels down in the garage, I am assuming it is actually a tunnel.

There is a cart sitting just inside the door. I mean it is like a golf cart or a motorized airport carrier. John got in and motioned me to get in. Of course he had a key to turn it on and off we go. We are going rather fast through these dim and somewhat narrow tunnels. There are occasionally intersections in the tunnel and at one of those intersections I thought I saw someone down another tunnel. It is either too early for activity in the tunnels or not many use or have access to them.

I have no idea what direction we are going, but after about 5 minutes of ripping through this tunnel Mike pulls over into what looks like a designated parking spot. I had to get out on Mike's side because my side was up against the wall. We walk a little further to another elevator lobby and get in the elevator. I am quite curious what building we will be in when we rise up and get off the elevator. I am hoping for a view. Mike pushed a down button after again swiping his card, so I guess no view.

When I think about my initial perception of Mike, it was so wrong. I like to think that I am not judgmental or superficial and yet everyone draws conclusions about people and situations all of the time. It is human behavior that is unavoidable regardless of what we may want to be the case. I am not talking about racial judgments. That is a whole other ramble to not get caught up in right now.

So many phrases relate to this concept and when there are so many, it likely means that there is very a longstanding and worthy merit to the concept. Some of those include:

- You can't judge a book by its cover
- Things aren't always what they seem
- Appearances are often misleading
- All that glitters is not gold
- First impressions matter
- Looks are deceiving
- Anything essential is invisible to the eye
- And many more…

It is obviously a well-observed phenomenon that will likely always continue. There are probably many, like myself, that make an effort not to do this and we might be much more successful if it were only about superficial aspects of a person like skin color, hair style, weight, age, and others but it is not just about those things. There are so many roles, mannerisms, language, and underlying behaviors. When someone wishes to control and manipulate people, what better method than to prey upon what are inherently human behaviors.

Some people lock into superficial things and will use them as their only criteria for decisions. Money is one of those superficial things and the use of superficial criteria for decisions in their lives makes people vulnerable. People wishing to manipulate and control, will exploit those vulnerabilities. It is far more complicated than the obvious physical traits; it is about rapid conclusions drawn from all inputs, including the situation and a person's actions. Self-preservation can kick in, sometimes at a very low level and sometimes at a very heightened level. Keep in mind that the self-preservation mode is based on *perception* rather than reality and the terms such as *first impression* become much more impactful.

Sometimes it is very innocuous and it is just a rational observation (that still could be very wrong). This applies to my observation of Mike. It was not a derogatory assumption or a judgment that I gave any thought, it was a reasonable assumption that Mike was a driver because he was driving me places. It gave me a basis for how to interact with him. If I had locked-in to that initial assumption and had not been open to accepting more information, I would have continued to see Mike as a driver rather than what he likely is. He is protecting me, but he also knows the operational ins and outs of how to maneuver through not only the locations but the people as well.

Mike is a good example, but it is so much broader. Take the things in life that seem the most obvious and understand that they may not be what they seem. That could be disabling if obvious evidence was rejected and the original perception was just believed. The key is to understand the possibilities and be open to them. What would happen if people were actually open to new information? Being willing to change a previously formed conclusion is critical. People generally do not take the time to investigate deeper, and who can blame them? There is no time to do that with everything in your life. Unfortunately people also, for some reason, go so far as to *protect* their first impressions or acquired impressions as though they are sacred.

Circumstances change, new information can be presented, but so many times it is not given a second thought because it is already so deeply engrained that it has become an *emotional* part of the person. People will defend those emotional perspectives with passion (as well as a lack of rationality). That is another human behavior that can be and has been exploited.

I realize that some of my rambles take on a feel of already knowing the answer and talking to myself as though I am talking to someone else. I may do that occasionally as a way for me to vet my thoughts and play both the instructor and student. I believe that the situations that I apply this method to are probably starting to get close to a high-probability conclusion, if not a rant.

I have been rambling on this while blindly following Mike. It is pretty crazy how so many thoughts can flash through my head in a matter of seconds. Some may think that rambling is a waste of time and I must just sit for hours contemplating random thoughts but that is not how it works (at least not most of the time). We arrive at a room with a heavy door that Mike opens and I walk in. Mike said, "I will be outside the door." I think Mike has clearly been assigned to me and I am very glad for that.

The room is a conference type room with whiteboards on three walls and a circle of tables that looked similar to the virtual table. There are nice leather chairs surrounding the table and I just walk about the room. I am the only one here. A door opens on the opposite wall of the door that I came through, and one of the people from the videoconference last night comes through the door. He walks over to me, shakes my hand, and introduces himself as William.

He said, "Let's sit down. It's just going to be you and me for a while. As you might imagine, not everybody in the group can allocate time to bringing you up to speed. You will meet with everybody later to discuss potential next steps, but right now there are things that you need to know. I will try to hit the highlights and some things that may have a big impact on our strategy and operations. If you become part of this group, you will have access to volumes of information in great detail. Are you ready to get started?"

I am more than ready and feel so privileged to be able to be in this position to hear whatever it is that I am about to hear. I nodded and said, "Let's go." William took a deep breath and began. "It feels as though this story should start with *Long ago and far away* because it so incredibly close to a fairytale of a nightmarish nature, but this is very real and the knowledge of some of this would likely disrupt not only the country but the entire world order. That in fact is the plan, but in a very different way. As you have probably gathered by the information shared with you about China as well as your own observations, the things that our government has done to destroy the Constitution and the freedom of people in this country is not new. We do not know the absolute date of origin but we have evidence of it being at least one hundred years and we have absolute proof of its escalation and change in methods over a number of decades.

"Our sources of this information are from very reliable people. These sources are former and even current participants in the process. These are very brave people. I cannot stress that enough. I am aware of your premise that, for many things, people are either assholes or stupid, or both. There is one factor that is missing and it is extremely relevant to our situation. That is *fear*. Our enemy uses emotions like hate so well, it should be no surprise that they use fear just as well. Fear can be far more poignant and controlling than hate. Fear comes in many forms, but using it as a controlling mechanism takes on the shape of a threat. They may be implied threats or explicit threats, but in order for them to hold tight control the threat must have basis and evidence of its validity. The things that people fear in this case are very real. They fear exposure, they fear loss of property, and most of all they fear for their lives and their family's lives. That fear has been proven to be very real. It doesn't take very many destroyed or taken lives for people to believe that the risk and threats are real. These people also know how easy it is for the people holding the control and power to get away with it.

"You would think that with all of the things going on that somebody would have exposed the plan. They have. They are no longer with us and you have not heard anything about it other than occasional dismissal of lunacy conspiracy theories. I say these things for two reasons. The first is so that you respect the great risk that some of our members take and secondly for you to better understand our enemy and the risks involved in this effort."

He paused as if he had asked a question and was waiting for an answer. This was crazy stuff that I was hearing and yet it felt nothing more than an acknowledgement of things that I had already imagined possible. I didn't want to sound like I was minimizing what he was saying so I just said, "I'm still here. Keep going please."

He continued, "This does not mean that everybody involved is being threatened. There are many, in fact the majority, for which greed or pure stupidity is plenty. The threatening tactics are typically reserved only for those that threaten the operation. Most do not threaten the operation, again because they personally gain from it or they are blind followers. It may be obvious, but the higher level the position, the more likely it is to be driven by greed. These are also the positions that are more influential."

He shared real examples of large company CEOs, heads of federal organizations, news media moguls, union leaders, and certain members of Congress. "These are people that are fully aligned with their agenda because they personally get richer and more powerful. They can shape the results of elections and hold people's futures in their hands. They believe they have no vulnerability because of their perceived power. I can tell that you noticed that I used the word *perceived*. With this type of power and the control of massive wealth, it is reasonable to ask how they can be defeated.

"I want to take a moment to once again refer to the history and various methods that have been used. The manipulation of the country has been decades in the making. The control and manipulation of the education system, the obvious control of communications and the so called news, the squelching of free speech, the use of racism to create division and hatred, the removal of equality and equal opportunity by only measuring equity, the destruction of small business and control of big business, the weakening of our international status, the weakening of the dollar, the forced dependency on the government at the expense of those that can least afford it, the dependency on other countries for critical military and survival components and supplies, and the list goes on and on. There is a significant amount of proof and details that you will be given access to. Background can help, but we are where we are and the bigger story is yet to be shared. Questions so far?"

I have so many questions and I want to hear more of the story, but I have to ask just one thing. "You seem to have a lot of information and what you refer to as proof and very credible sources; can you give me an idea of the sources or types of sources?" He had no hesitation, "You will meet some of them later, but we have people in the CIA, the FBI, Congress, Unions, major news networks, the CDC, the FDA, Governors' offices, the DOJ, many of the fortune 50 companies, and the White House itself to name a few. These are people in high-level positions that have direct access to information. I have to imagine that sounds like a pretty impressive and powerful list, but remember the power of our adversary and the fear factor. You might think that if they are such high-level positions that they would be able to influence change, but changing a couple things or even slowing change is doomed to fail because of how pervasive the government is throughout all aspects of life. But what if we go to the top; will everything and everybody not be forced to follow? That is a question that has been asked for some time and the concept of voting comes into play to change the people at the top. That would be a rational belief, but it is not what it appears to be. You might think that an approach would be to use the weaknesses of the people at the top to *change their minds*, but the country is no longer what it appears to be. You can't judge a book by its cover."

I have a feeling that he is getting to the big stuff now. Why was he stopping? Maybe to just catch his breath, he has been talking a long time. Maybe he was considering whether he should tell me or not, but it seems like it might be too late for that. How much worse could it get? Oh, I could really get caught up in imagining so many things that could be worse if I let myself go. I need to resist that because he is right here and he obviously has something more to say. This pause is longer than previous ones and he did not announce this pause, he just stopped talking. He finally made eye contact with me and said, "I'm sorry. How about if we take a short break?" I said, "Sure", but I was thinking, "You've got to be kidding me!"

It is late morning now and I am hoping this isn't going to be a break for lunch. He took me out of the door that he came in and showed me where the restrooms were and then back into the room. I grabbed a cold bottle of juice from the cart and just wandered around the room. I didn't realize how much I really needed this stretch break and how intently I must have been listening to him. I can feel the tightness in my neck and shoulders and my eyes seem like they haven't blinked in more than an hour. It's interesting how little time it takes for a complex ramble and yet so much time passes when listening to others. That may just be because it is so much faster to think than to talk and listen. Maybe that's why so many people don't really listen anymore and communication is made up of short sound bites and memes that convey zero depth.

The break had been about 15 minutes now and more people started coming in the room. It appeared to be the group from last night. I noticed something that hadn't hit me before; they are all wearing suits and I am just this casual guy from Middle America. It didn't matter to me and apparently it didn't matter to them, but it felt a bit unusual based on my conditioning. If I were entering a room for an interview that I was fairly certain would be with people in suits, I would be wearing one. The reason that I would wear one would be that first impression thing again and the judgment that happens before I even open my mouth. This group seemed different than the rest of world. That is both refreshing and concerning. How different can they actually be? Maybe they have seen enough of reality to have a better grip on the deception and failures of superficial judgments?

One of the new additions to the room asked William if we are on track for the next segment and he confirmed that 'we' are. The yet to be identified speaker said, "Let's start with some introductions. You will likely notice that all of us in the room right now are of ex-positions. The reason for that is that this group takes more time and secrecy than current high-level positions would allow. We are designed such that no one person is a single point of failure, but we all add value in our own way, primarily with our past experience and current contacts. Those current contacts are committed to our cause, but cannot commit the time required to be fulltime in this group. They are considered not only sources of information, but consultants."

"I am Harrison, and I am ex-head of Homeland Security." The next person introduced himself, "I am Lance and I am ex-Chief Of Staff for the President." He was one that I recognized seeing before. The next stood and said, "I am Natalie and I am ex-director of the Department of Health." I have been introduced to everybody in the room, but I did not know William's role or ex-role. I looked at William and without me saying a word he stood up and said, "You know I am William and am the former Ambassador to China."

It just kept getting more and more unrealistic that I could be in the room with these people. I am either very lucky or I am on one hell of a ramble (or dream). Harrison spoke up with, "I know that you have been on quite a ride for the last week and what you have heard today is another level of information, and it is information that very few people have. We have more to share and that information is known by even fewer people. Before we get to that, I would like to ask you for your impression so far. Are you okay with being put on the spot like this?"

I was quick to answer; "I don't consider you asking me for my impression as being put on the spot. My impression is my perspective based on what I know, what I have been told, and the limited time that I have had to process it. I am more impressed and humbled rather than put on the spot, knowing that you are interested in my impression. Much of what has been shared by William is not a shock. The events, purpose, and processes over the years are nothing more than I have thought possible. What is a surprise is that you have the sources and proof that you do. I started off just a couple of days ago thinking I was joining a somewhat unstructured and unorganized group of like-minded people and now I sit here in this place with high-level former government officials and am being told that there are members that are active at high levels in the government and other influential places. That is the biggest surprise and with surprise comes both appreciation and apprehension. Through my journey of the last few days I have found myself with concerns a number of times and as I have raised them I have received very adequate explanations; I suspect the same will be true here."

Harrison replied, "Thank you for sharing that and I suspect that you might be wondering if we have such information and connections why it is that we haven't been able to stop this. In addition to what we have shared about the pervasive power and control, there are also the tactics that they will use that instill fear and the more you know the more reason you have to fear. People do disappear and people have accidents that are never attributed to the actual cause, and in most cases they are brushed under the rug so there is little visibility to stir even so much as a raised eyebrow. We have people who are willing to step up, but it must not be in vain. You might think that with such influence and access we might be able to turn the President using our own form of either fear or his biggest weakness of greed. I will get to that but I am going to take a breath in case there is anything you need to ask."

I couldn't wait to hear the rationale behind the complication of "turning" the President. I said, "Please continue." Harrison looked down and said, "I am not trying to hold back this information or delay sharing, but there is another piece of background that you should hear first to put it in context."

Our opponent has made all aspects of the government one, which destroys the purpose and intent of the Constitution. Separation of powers was created to prevent just such things from happening, so they destroyed the separation of powers because it was in their way of claiming total control. They are on the verge of eliminating the Electoral College because it is in their way and gives too many people across the country a voice. They have all but eliminated the concept of a republic, where states control their own laws and enforcement and made it a single federal state. All of these things are devastating to the country, but it is hard for people to accept that it has happened because we did have elections, so it *must* be the will of the people. That is how it is supposed to work and so many assume that it still does."

I interrupted and said, "Excuse me, but anybody that is paying attention knows that is happening. I know they manipulate elections by promoting lies and withholding the truth but how does this change what is happening and a potential plan to impact the direction of the government by impacting the leaders?"

Harrison stood up and said, "I see that you are ready for me to get directly to the point." I thought (but didn't say), "I have been ready for that for a long time so yes, get on with it." He answered my question. "We cannot address the situation by impacting or influencing the leaders because *we don't know who they are*. You heard that right. Things are not as they seem. Before the second party was made completely ineffective you would think that the administration's plan would have had some opportunity to be derailed. Even within their own party there were variances between elected officials that could have swayed the direction. There was even talk of term limits to try to hold down the corruption. There was no altering the course because the elected officials are no longer the ones running the government and have not been for quite some time. Let that sink in a minute."

Okay, they got me with this one. I have to admit that some of the stupid people that have been elected led me to believe that they were not capable of the responsibilities of their office and somebody must be telling them what to do and say. Spanning the entire government for potentially decades is definitely a surprise. Wow! "Okay, so you know that someone else is running the country, but you don't know who? You probably have some information that points in a direction but don't have proof; is that right?"

Harrison answered again, "Yes, we have plenty of indicators and we believe that we know some of the people involved at the highest level but not all. We also believe that it is set up similar to our structure in that not one person or even small group of people will disable the entire group. We do not know the group's operational structure but we do know that the group contains previous government officials, current officials (just not the ones you would expect), and very rich people that have never worked directly for the government. There is more information that we can provide as deep background, but that is the gist of the problem that we face. Your assessment of the priority enemy made sense before you knew this, but does it still? We don't expect a full answer or recommendation of plan, but we would like your reaction."

This one is not going to be as easy to answer, but I know myself well enough to know that I will answer with something. This does explain a number of things that have been a bit puzzling like how this could happen with seemingly such morons running the country. I started without a full grip on what I was going to say, but they might as well hear my thought process. "It certainly changes my perspective of the primary target because it would seem that the government is not actually the government. It is still the function of the government but the person or persons to be targeted are not as imagined. It is difficult to wage an attack on an enemy that is unknown. It would seem that an immediate primary initiative would be to identify that enemy and learn as much about them as possible in the next few days. That may be a ridiculous and obvious statement, but you will find that I am not afraid to state the obvious because too often the obvious is either overlooked or assumed that someone else is addressing it because it is *so* obvious."

I took a breath to slow myself down. It was probably clear that my passion was coming through which is good, but I want to put enough checks on myself to make sure that my thoughts don't just runaway, after all there is so much that I still don't know. I continued, "Maybe the behavior could be attacked rather than the person, but that doesn't seem too likely since so much of the 'buy-in' is based on who is saying it. It still seems that the right people need to communicate a change, but then those actually running the show will shut it down. We need to find the weakness in their ability to shut it down presuming that we could get the supposed leaders to comply. They will use fear and greed as they always have and somehow both have to be at least partially disabled. This is just a gut reaction, but it is clear that there is a lot I don't know and my impression could change dramatically with more information and a little time to process. My only conclusive reaction is that I need to know a lot more.

I also recognize that this information not only complicates the approach, but it is clear that they have already changed our form of government to a perpetual totalitarian dictatorship."

I went on to rattle off an incomplete list of things that I felt that I needed to know. Even though I'm sure the list isn't complete, I started with things that included:

- What is it that you know about the potential or probable actors that are really running the show?
- What do you know about their operations and processes?
- I assume that they are aware of the issues and threats from China. Do you have any idea what they plan regarding China, or are they part of it and would be happy with the US falling to China?
- What have you considered and what do you have in place as a defense or survival plan if China takes action?
- Who are the highest-level people in government and in the private sector that are not part of the group running the government? That list is probably too long so I will ask, do you think we can get the President to cooperate with us?

It was probably clear to them that I wanted to know as much as they could feed me and I was just giving them examples, but Harrison did respond. "Let me answer a few of the items on your list, but it is clear that you will not get all you are looking for in this meeting. You will have access to these things and more once we are done with this meeting."

He was looking up, maybe trying to recall all of the examples, maybe trying to decide where to start, or maybe contemplating the type of information he was sharing with this new person. I was new but I was well vetted. He began, "The people that we believe are part of the highest level within their group include a former President, a former senator, and a *very* rich financial backer. There are also many involved at all levels of government that execute the orders from the upper level. What we do not have a good grip on are all of the people that are under their thumb, but we believe the network of those willingly participating or participating out of fear spreads fairly wide. It is also likely that the majority of them do not understand the extent of the takeover that has already taken place. Most, if not all, started willingly and began operating out of fear when they tried to leave. You do *not* leave that organization.

"We believe that this hidden organization has been closely working with China under the belief that they would be immune to the negative impacts from a takeover, much like the officials not in their group. People in the government and the ones running the government are working different paths (with similar intended outcomes) but they are not coordinated. Because of that it is fair to assume that China knows more about the situation than we do. It would be difficult to believe that both have not started to see that they are not the partners they thought them to be and their payout might be in jeopardy. That is only a guess at this point. They were stupid enough to enter into any collaboration with China so who knows how stupid they are being now. We know of no viable plans that they have to mitigate the risk."

He told me about some of the survival plans and indicated that there were many approaches being considered and worked on, but there are none that prevent chaos or cover more than 15% of the people in the country. The bottom line of this message was that something will be in place, but it will be way too little and the consequences will be extreme. The only viable option for the country is to prevent the catastrophe, but they plan to continue working on what they can for survival.

"The highest-level people that we strongly believe will be willing to step up (for a significant price) includes some of the cabinet and the President of the United States. The Chief of Staff is on board and is our liaison to the President. I do not want to oversell that; it will take a lot of money and a lot of assurances for success because they all fear for their lives and their wealth. It will be extremely difficult to coordinate if it is possible at all. You may have noticed that it seems that the people elected in the most powerful positions are there because of many factors, but intelligence or even competency is not one of them."

I had to ask one more question, "I know that I could go on forever with questions, but I will respect your decision to let me catch up on details on my own if that is what you feel is best. I would like to ask one more question about who we might be able to get aligned. Do you have anybody in the news media that can impact control of the communication for any amount of time?"

Lance answered this one, "We do but there are similar constraints plus one more big one. If they do let something go through, it will likely be walked back in a matter of minutes and would likely negate any value." I thanked him and just sat waiting for them to direct what was next. They were talking amongst themselves and I realized that they did say *if* I continued in this group. It was probably better that I didn't think of it in that way. I am just being who I am and giving what I considered to be some very obvious and generic responses to their asking for my impressions. What could they tell from that other than I didn't run away? I hope their criterion is more than the fact that I didn't run away. I have to admit that I would be disappointed if they sent me home and back to an area group because I would like to be able to impact as much as possible and this is clearly a high-level issue. I can't imagine that all of the area groups out there would be able to do much more than help prepare for survival and maybe spread the word if a mechanism was provided. Maybe I should have told them that but they really didn't ask.

This pause seemed like ten minutes, even though it probably wasn't and it was starting to feel uncomfortable. I needed to break the silence. "I don't know if you would like to hear more from me. I have plenty of ideas of how various roles and levels might help, but I have to say that based on the information that you have provided me, I feel that my ideas would likely change with more detailed information and providing you with my thoughts based on limited information would be a waste of all of our time. I am eager to dig in, learn more, and be able to contribute to this group. I am not scared away by the severity of the situation and its risks. In fact, it emphasizes the need to get a viable plan together and take action before it is too late."

Again there was silence. Okay, this was just getting weird. They went back to talking amongst themselves. I have worked in careers where patience was essential, but that was some time ago and may have used it all up. These people are not children, and now is no time for games. I was about to say something again when Natalie said, "Excuse us for our sidebar here. We were just informed that the President is meeting with China one week from today. We were discussing whether we thought there was any immediate action needed." I guess that explains the silence, but they still could have said, "Give us a minute." It is a good reminder that the reason I questioned why I am here amongst these high-level people is not because they are so much better than me, it is because people at their level seldom recognize the potential value in others. It is more of my surprise with them than with myself. I believe they have a need for someone like me. They are just people and so are the enemies. Everyone, and maybe especially ones at high levels, because of how they got there, has flaws and weaknesses.

Rather than them asking for my thoughts or me asking if they wanted them I asked, "Who set up the meeting?" They almost simultaneously said, "We did." Then the obvious question was, "Who is we? The visible government or the hidden government." Harrison said, "We believe the hidden government." And they continued debating any immediate action. "It would seem to me then that your immediate action is to verify who was behind setting up the meeting. Whoever did, has a purpose. The other trigger for me would be that regardless of who set this up, it presents an opportunity for us. A significant amount of resources should be applied to defining a plan around that meeting. All eyes will be on that meeting and it presents what may be a very fortunate opportunity if we are able to maximize our impact to the situation. I would not let anyone outside of your most trusted consultant know of the plan to look at this as an opportunity, especially the President. There is no value, only risk in that. I know you didn't ask for my opinion and I know that I still need a lot more information, but I can't resist trying to help."

William spoke up for the first time in a while and said, "Thank you for your input. We have a lot to discuss so we are going to cut this process short and send you home. We believe this is best under the circumstances. You will hear something from us in the next day. Your driver will take you to the plane and someone will collect your things to go with you."

There was so much that I could read into that. There was the obvious wonder if they were put back by my blurting out my comments and had enough so they sent me home with an implied, "Don't call us…" What hit me as well was the comment about my driver. Did they not know Mike's name or that he was more than a driver? Of course they knew. They maybe just assumed then that I didn't know either his name or his role. They don't give me much credit if that's the case. Oh well, maybe they just assume the lowest common denominator with people, which I have to admit is what I do if I don't know them. But they have enough detailed information about me to know me pretty well or I wouldn't be here. I don't need to know the answer, but it is just further evidence that I might have abilities that they don't. Again, it is just surprising when someone recognizes that others, regardless of position or credentials, may have something to offer. I walked out the door and Mike was right there.

We took the cart ride back and it was just as deserted as it was coming this way. I had lost all track of time and am just now realizing that I am hungry because it is *way* past lunchtime. I mention this to Mike and he said that there will be food available on the plane or we could make a stop at a fast-food joint. I opted for the fast food. I'm a fast-food kind of guy. I never really understood spending a lot of money at fancy restaurants when some cheap food tastes so good.

We didn't stop long, but it was a nice break from being rushed around and I had a nice talk with Mike. It seemed okay in this situation to be sharing personal information in both directions. We were told not to during the evaluation, but that is over and I believe I find myself in a position where my life is in Mike's hands. The more I find out about him and spend time with him, the more I am good with that. It is seldom that I am around someone so dedicated to a cause and he is a very sharp guy. He is clearly not a person to judge by his cover.

We arrive at the airport in a similar fashion with the car driving up to the plane. This is a little different because now I am with someone that I know. I shake Mike's hand and say, "Thank you Mike. I hope to see you soon. Be careful." He smiles and just says, "You too." I turn and get on the plane. I can see Mike still on the runway as we taxi away.

I don't think that I slept on the way home and the trip didn't seem to take long. My mind is full of rambles, questions, and wild stories of what the future could hold. Similar to departing, there is a car waiting for me on the runway to take me home. It is good to be home.

Chapter 39

Home Again
Morning Day 11

The comfort of my own bed likely contributed to my hard sleep. I wake with that uncomfortable feeling that usually happens with an unplanned sleep. I can tell that I am in my own bed, but I'm not really sure if it is day or night or if I am supposed to be somewhere. That somewhat panicked feeling set in and then I remembered some of the events of the last couple of days, I think. My progression through the various groups, taking a private jet to D.C., and conferring with Washington big-wigs about our government, China, and what seems like almost inevitable doom of the country. Those seem like the events of a nightmare, a long dream, or a drug-induced trip.

Then I remember that all of that started when the FBI broke into my house and that I didn't remember going to bed that night. Is everything that has happened after the night with the FBI just a dream? Did they knock me out and I'm just waking up now? Did the dream maybe even include the FBI breaking in? Was any of it real? I remember stating how surreal it was throughout the events as they just became more and more fantastic. It *seemed* real, and yet I constantly questioned how it could be real. I had to get up and try to get some clarity because this is very uncomfortable to say the least, and my next steps depend on my conclusion. I either have a lot to do or I need to see a doctor.

I sit up and start wiping my eyes clear and I can see that the bedroom closet is empty. Okay, I am pretty sure the break-in happened. I remember that they took all of my clothes and even now, that is weird. I looked around and where is Reggie? Is it the morning after the break-in? Where's my dog? I was just starting to get out of bed and the doorbell rang. I grab my phone to look at who is at the door. Wait, I have a phone. Did they not take my phone or is this the new one? The last I remember the new one was in a Faraday bag being held by the people that I was with for evaluation. This one is next to my bed. That does *not* add to the clarity.

Looking at the front door camera, I see a man standing there. He is holding something, but I can't see who it is or what he is holding. I used the speaker and said, "Can I help you?" He turns, holds a badge up to the camera, and says, "FBI."